The
Calypso
Directive

The Calypso Directive

A MEDICAL THRILLER

Brian Andrews

Arcade Publishing • New York

Arcade Publishing books may be purchased in bulk at special discounts for sales promotion, corporate gifts, fund-raising, or educational purposes. Special editions can also be created to specifications. For details, contact the Special Sales Department, Arcade Publishing, 307 West 36th Street, 11th Floor, New York, NY 10018 or arcade@skyhorsepublishing.com.

Arcade Publishing® is a registered trademark of Skyhorse Publishing, Inc.®, a Delaware corporation.

Visit our website at www.arcadepub.com

10 9 8 7 6 5 4 3 2 1

Library of Congress Cataloging-in-Publication Data is available on file.

ISBN: 978-1-62872-665-7
Ebook ISBN: 978-1-61145-767-4

Printed in the United States of America

For Karen

Association for Molecular Pathology
v.
United States Patent and Trademark Office & Myriad Genetics
(Federal Circuit Court of Appeals, July 2011)

"While the process of (gene) extraction is no doubt difficult, and may itself be patentable, the isolated genes are not materially different from the native genes. . . . Merely isolating the products of nature by extracting them from their natural location and making those alterations attendant to their extraction does not give the extractor the right to patent the products themselves.

In that respect, extracting a gene is akin to snapping a leaf from a tree. . . . Plucking the leaf would not turn it into a human-made invention."

Excerpts from the dissenting opinion of Circuit Judge William Bryson, after being overruled two to one in favor of permitting companies to continue patenting genes.

Chapter One

THE HOSPITAL GOWN he wore was faded and weightless. After hundreds of washings, it was more tissue paper than cloth. Yellow bruises from daily blood draws blotted his forearms like dried coffee stains on paper. Beneath his bare feet, the cold gray linoleum greedily sipped the warmth from his body. Goose flesh stood up on his skin. He ignored all of this. Concerns of the body were not his priority at the moment. He had a job to do, and they would be coming for him soon.

He had sensed a progression of late. A subtle shift in the daily rounds, an unfamiliar urgency in the air. He knew his window of opportunity was closing. They were getting close now, and it was imperative he act before it was too late.

After five months in quarantine, he had not lost focus. Patience was the only compass that could navigate him out of these most impossible of circumstances. Even with his body at its weakest, his spirit had won the hearts of those who tended to him. One of the nurses had even taken to routinely loosening the bindings meant to confine him to his bed each night.

Alone in the darkened laboratory room, he stood in front of a stainless steel refrigerator. He took a deep breath and pulled open the door. A pale fluorescent light flickered on, accompanied by a rush of cold air that made him shiver. His six-foot frame cast a distorted, hulking shadow on the wall behind him. Accompanying it was a motley cast of eerie characters—chrome and steel monsters—that paraded as innocuous laboratory equipment during the day.

He squinted, his eyes adjusting to the light, and began to survey the contents of the refrigerator. On the middle shelf were dozens of glass vials, some filled with blood, some filled with exotic microbial cocktails, and others filled with experimental biopharmaceuticals, all neatly arranged in plastic trays. With mechanical precision, he searched the inventory, lifting vial after vial, scanning each label and then returning the container to its place.

P-10, P-12, P-36, P-47 . . . P-65. Jackpot.

The row contained ten P-65 vials filled with blood. He paused; it was twice the quantity he had anticipated. The flimsy hospital pants he wore did not have pockets, and it would be impossible to carry such a load. Still, he couldn't afford to leave anything behind.

He cringed. The other way would be safer. Disgusting, but safer. After removing the rubber stopper, he raised the first vial of purple-red liquid to his lips.

Bottoms up!

He gagged as the cold, viscous fluid coated his tongue and throat. The taste was metallic, primal, terrible. Robotically, he repeated the drill. After the sixth vial, his stomach protested and sent a repugnant belch rolling up his esophagus. For an instant, he was afraid he would not be able to finish, but then he reminded himself of the price of failure and pressed on.

After gulping down sample number ten, he returned his attention to the fridge. He needed information. Proof. First, he located a vial of cloudy liquid labeled *Yersinia pestis*. Whatever it was, he recognized it as the substance they had injected him with five days ago. Carefully, he removed this vial from the tray. He resumed scanning the shelves, until a vial labeled *AAV-564: P-65 Transgene Trial 12* caught his eye. It sounded important, and it had his patient number on it. He smiled and removed it from the rack. The rest he would destroy.

The overhead lights flickered on.

"PATIENT-65—PUT DOWN THE SAMPLE," a voice blasted over a loudspeaker. "REMAIN WHERE YOU ARE."

Wild-eyed, he turned to the door. No one was there. Then he saw the tiny camera mounted in the far upper corner of the room. It was pointed directly at him.

He cursed and grabbed a roll of gauze tape off a nearby metal tray. Working quickly, he strapped the two glass vials to the inside of his pant leg with two wraps of tape around his thigh. Then, staring defiantly at the camera lens, he smashed all the remaining vials of the refined product on the floor.

The megaphone voice exploded behind him, ahead of him, everywhere.

"PATIENT-65, STOP. REMAIN WHERE YOU ARE."

He ignored the command. All that mattered now was executing the escape sequence. He bolted out the door. He was in Corridor B, sprinting to reach the stairwell at the end of Corridor C. He had conducted dry runs several times during the last two weeks, always in the dark, and always in less than the fourteen minutes that the night-watch rotation afforded him. Forty-five minutes earlier, he had prepped the stairwell without detection. Everything was in place.

"WARNING—CONTAINMENT BREACH ON LEVEL FOUR. LOCK DOWN LEVEL FOUR. ALL PERSONNEL DON BIO-HAZARD SUITS," the megaphone voice commanded over loud-speakers throughout the building. "IMMOBILIZE PATIENT-65."

The combination of the freshly waxed corridor and his bare feet afforded him superb traction for running—every footstep connecting with a smack. As he fled, the building began to close in on him. Like falling dominoes, magnetic door locks engaged down the length of the corridor, lagging his position by a mere half second. Without breaking stride, he plowed into the double doors at the end of Corridor B. The right door gave way easily, smashing loudly into its doorstop. But the left door traveled only a few inches before abruptly springing back with a thud. On the other side, a red-haired man in a white lab coat collapsed into a heap, cupped his hands over his bloody nose, and howled in pain. Patient-65 leapt over him and charged toward the stairwell at the end of Corridor C.

Ahead of him, a lone orderly appeared. Crouched like a wrestler at the ready, the young man took up a position in the middle of the hall, blocking his way. He heard the swinging doors crash open behind him, followed by another yelp from the red-haired man. Multiple pairs of footsteps now echoed in the corridor. He glanced over his shoulder, sacrificing a stride. Two men wearing yellow biohazard suits with ventilators were in pursuit.

Teeth clenched, he ran straight toward the crouching orderly. The instant before the collision, he dropped his right shoulder and drove it squarely into the man's chest. His momentum sent them both to the ground. He almost managed to somersault free, but the orderly grabbed a fistful of his hair with one hand, a fold of his gown with the other, and pulled him back.

He straddled the orderly's chest and grabbed the hand clutching his gown. He peeled the fingers free and bent back the wrist. The orderly groaned and responded by yanking down on his hair. Hard. Fury erupted in him, and he forced the other man's arm backward past the shoulder. The orderly shrieked in agony as his wrist and elbow gave way. Ligaments popped. Bones cracked.

He jumped to his feet. The quicker of the two pursuing yellow-suits was already upon him, lunging for his waist. He felt his hospital gown pull taut against his chest, rip, and then give way completely. The diving yellow-suit tumbled to the ground, tripping his partner in the process. Without a backward glance, he raced toward the stairwell, his shredded hospital gown falling to the floor behind him.

A horde of footsteps echoed in Corridor C. It sounded as though every employee in the building was converging on his position. He smiled. Escaping from a place like this was a game of one versus many—success would depend on timing, confusion, and crowd control.

Despite their uniforms and short haircuts, the security staff was decidedly nonmilitary. They were unpolished, like hired hands, and Patient-65 had come to question their proficiency and gumption. He predicted that a real crisis would send everyone flying blindly toward the action, like moths to a flame. He wanted them to converge—as many guards as possible—right here, right now, to the third floor.

Because he was going to leave them all behind.

He burst through the door into the stairwell and breathed a sigh of relief. They were still there: eight flat bedsheets, taken from the laundry bin outside his room each night between 23:04 and 23:09, while the beds were being stripped in the two rooms adjacent to his own. The makeshift thirty-foot rope of knotted, folded cotton was exactly where he had left it, coiled neatly on the landing with one end tied to the metal railing.

He wrapped the free end of the sheet-rope around his right arm, about his chest, under his armpit, and then around the same arm yet again. He snugged it tight and took a deep breath. Then, he jumped.

The door slammed open behind him. The leader of the swarm of yellow-suits lunged for his legs, but Patient-65 was already airborne, catapulting over the handrail. One by one they rushed to the edge and peered down at the pale, half-naked form plummeting into the dark. Starched white bedsheets ruffled and flapped as he made the otherwise silent three-story plunge.

The fall was terrifying, idiotic. As flights of stairs rushed past, thoughts of impending injury flooded his mind: His shoulder would be dislocated, ripped from the socket most likely. His neck would probably snap. He had not imagined it happening this way. With half a second to spare, he reached up and grabbed the sheet above him, as if trying to climb away from the fall. He drew his arms together, slightly bent at the elbows, in preparation.

The force of the deceleration hit him like a Freightliner. The section of sheet that was wrapped around his chest absorbed most of the energy, compressing his ribs and driving the air out of his lungs. His abdominal muscles tore. The tendons in his shoulders burned like individual strands of fire. He could taste fresh blood in his mouth. Still, the fitted sheets had held, and the eight slipknot shock absorbers had performed exactly as intended, popping like firecrackers and averting multiple fractures and dislocations from the one g-force fall.

Suspended in midair, dangling four feet above the concrete floor, he gasped for air. He unraveled himself from the sheet-rope and dropped to the ground in a heap. Footsteps echoed in the stairwell as his pursuers renewed their chase from three flights above. He smiled despite the pain. The jump had won him a substantial lead, and in a chase where seconds would determine success or failure, he needed each and every one.

He looked up at the sign on the door in front of him. GROUND LEVEL—CORRIDOR E. His injured stomach muscles screamed in protest as he pushed open the heavy metal door. Before it slammed shut, he could hear the footsteps growing louder.

Corridor E was silent and empty. Thirty yards away, freedom beckoned. He could just make out the words EMERGENCY EXIT—ALARM WILL SOUND stenciled in large white letters across the red fire escape door at the end of the corridor. His legs responded grudgingly to yet another call for action, and he managed to move toward the exit in a gait feebly resembling a run. He spied a jacket draped over an open door, in a row of employee lockers along the wall of the corridor. He snagged it midstride, gambling it might fit.

As he closed the gap, panic began to well up inside him. The emergency exit was the only element of his plan he had been unable to test. The truth was that he didn't know what would happen when he tried to go through that door. It might be locked; that wouldn't surprise him in this place. It could lead to another corridor or to a lobby full of security personnel. It could even be bricked over on the other side.

In any case, he had no choice. There was no turning back now.

He barreled into the red door.

It opened so easily that he lost his balance and went tumbling to the concrete. After two awkward somersaults, he came to an abrupt stop on his hands and knees, staring down into a puddle of cold, muddy water. Behind him, the emergency exit alarm shrieked, announcing his arrival like a royal trumpeter, and then fell abruptly silent as the door slammed shut. He struggled to his feet. He was standing in the middle of a deserted sidewalk along an unfamiliar city street. His pupils were still adjusting to the darkness of night, and he could not make out the street signs or recognize which avenue he was on. A stiff, cold breeze sent a crumpled paper advert, with strange Cyrillic words, tumbling over his foot. Bewildered, he surveyed his surroundings as he shrugged on the jacket, covering his bare torso.

In all the months of planning, he had never considered what he would do after he was out. His escape fantasies had always ended at the red door.

His heart pounded; they would be on top of him in seconds.

He started running.

Any direction would do.

As he pushed his battered body onward, the illuminated roof lamp of a taxicab caught his attention. It was bright, yellow, and beautiful. The taxi was stopped at a red traffic light at the nearest intersection, some twenty meters away.

Panic erupted inside him. If the light changed to green before he could close the gap . . .

The emergency exit alarm shrieked anew behind him. They were coming.

He hurtled himself toward the cab.

Ten meters to go. Still red.

A car, traveling on the cross street, braked to a stop. The light would change any second.

Three meters.

It flashed to green.

"Wait," he yelled.

In a final adrenaline-charged burst, he flung himself against the side of the taxi, just as it started to pull away. The cab jerked to a stop, and he fell onto the street next to the curb. From his knees, he opened the rear door, and hauled himself into the passenger compartment of the beat-up sedan.

The cab driver turned to greet his new fare. The jovial smile he wore melted immediately to a frown at the sight of the beggarly-looking man huffing in his back seat.

"Drive. Anywhere. Please, just go!" Patient-65 said as he slammed the car door closed.

He looked frantically over his shoulder. Yellow-suits were pouring out of the emergency exit like angry bees from a rattled hive, and still the cab was not moving.

"Please. Help me. They're coming."

The cab driver looked into the other man's pleading eyes and saw fear. But that was not what moved his foot to the accelerator. In Patient-65's eyes he saw decency; he saw goodness. It didn't matter that he would sacrifice a fare. It didn't matter that he would probably lose his driving permit—again. All that mattered was a kindred spirit needed saving, and he was the only one in the world who could do it.

"We go! I save you," the cabbie exclaimed as the turbo diesel engine launched the sedan into motion.

With only one hand on the wheel, the cab driver whipped the taxi through a squealing right turn onto the cross street. After slamming the shifter into third gear, he turned up the radio—almost as if to add a soundtrack to their getaway. He shouted unintelligible expletives as he swerved around a slower-moving car. As they sped away, Patient-65 turned for a final glance out the rear window. He watched the angry yellow-suits until they had completely faded from view.

For ten minutes, the cab driver piloted his sedan at a lunatic pace, racing down avenues, squealing around corners, and narrowly avoiding collisions with oncoming traffic. When they eventually reached the outskirts of the city, Patient-65 came to a startling realization. The skyline before him was not one he recognized. Nor could he recall passing any of the landmarks he knew so well.

It couldn't be. It wasn't possible.

He was not in New York.

In between lurches, he reached forward and patted the driver on the shoulder.

"You can slow down now."

Without a word, the cabbie swerved to the right and brought the sedan to a screeching halt alongside the curb. He gave the parking brake a yank, put the manual transmission in neutral, and turned around. After a moment's study, he noticed his passenger was battered, his lips crusted with dried blood.

"You are hurt! I take you to doctor, yes?"

Patient-65 looked away and out the window.

"No, no. I'm okay," he said. "No hospitals, please."

The cabbie was silent, lost in speculation about the curious American sitting in the backseat of his cab.

Patient-65 looked back at him. "Where are we?" he said, gesturing to the world outside.

The cabbie laughed loudly and then threw his chest out like a prizefighter. "Praha, of course. The greatest city in all of Europe."

Speechless, Patient-65 stared at the smiling middle-aged Czech.

Feeling the need to say something, the cabbie added, "You are safe now, yes? Then you tell me now—where you want to go?"

Raising his eyebrows, the cabbie waited for direction from the most unusual tourist he had ever serviced. But Patient-65, Will Foster, had no instructions.

Only questions.

What the hell am I doing in Prague?

Chapter Two

New Brunswick, New Jersey

THE PRODUCT WAS gone.

Meredith Morley pressed the "End Call" icon on her iPhone and set it gently on the nightstand next to her bed. She took a deep breath and exhaled slowly. Then, she congratulated herself for showing such remarkable restraint. She had not screamed. She had not thrown her phone. She had not ordered anyone drawn and quartered.

Yet.

The report from Xavier Pope—her lead scientist and project director in Prague—was so absurd that it bordered on comic book fantasy. According to eyewitness accounts, Patient-65 escaped from his locked room, accessed the secure sample room, smashed the full complement of their most promising Adeno-associated virus vector serum, and stole a vial of weapons-grade *Yersinia pestis*. He then outmaneuvered a trained security staff of twelve by jumping down a four-story stairwell, breached containment by running out the fire escape door onto a city street, hailed a taxicab, and drove away. Meredith closed her eyes and rubbed her temples. What had been the most promising opportunity of her young and highly decorated career at Vyrogen Pharmaceuticals was now on the verge of becoming her own personal Chernobyl.

What vexed her most, however, was that Pope's report had taken exactly eight hours and fourteen minutes too long to reach her. According to Pope, the security supervisor on duty had neglected to notify him of the episode until morning, foolishly believing he could "rectify the situation" on his own before shift turnover at eight o'clock in the morning. *A weak mind begets a weak character.* That was what her father had said to her when she was sixteen and tried to cover up a speeding ticket from an unsanctioned joyride in his Porsche. She had carried those words with her ever since; one could even argue the phrase had become her personal mantra. Pope assured her that he had fired the dolt on the spot, but that was little consolation. The damage was already done. Patient-65 had an eight-hour head start, and with every passing hour the cone of uncertainty surrounding his position was growing exponentially. Immediate action was imperative. She swung her legs off the side of the bed, slipped her nightshirt off, and walked naked into her bathroom. She turned on the cold water tap in the shower and stepped into the icy stream.

•   •   •

IT WAS ONLY five short months ago when a strange notice from one of the H1N1 vaccine trial administrators floated across her desk. As the Director of Research & Development for Vyrogen, Meredith was required to review and sign all anomaly reports. Since the H1N1 vaccine trial was technically classified as an R&D activity, she found herself regularly barraged with H1N1 administrative minutiae. Late one evening, while leafing through a stack of such reports, she came across a blood panel anomaly that made her gasp. A previously undocumented genetic aberration with groundbreaking implications had been detected in a study participant and tagged for further review. She moved swiftly; no one was going to snatch an opportunity like this away from her.

She directed three of her most loyal scientists to perform a preliminary assessment of the anomaly and ascertain what resources would be needed to go to the next level. The report was discouraging. The team advised her that outside expertise was needed, and only one man was on their list—Xavier Pope. Recruiting Pope away from the Centers for Disease Control and Prevention had been more difficult than she could have imagined. First, he demanded a copy of the lab data, a violation of Vyrogen policy. After much consternation, she reluctantly acquiesced. This was followed by a week of radio silence. Then, late on a Friday afternoon, he phoned her with additional demands: complete autonomy as project director, a 20 percent salary bump, and a new Audi company car. It chafed her to do it, but she agreed to his demands.

With Pope aboard, the project had wings, and initially things progressed steadily. However, Meredith wasn't satisfied with a "normal" development cycle. Unlike Alexander Fleming, who discovered penicillin in 1928 but was not able to mass-produce therapeutic antibiotics until seventeen years later in 1945, she had a more aggressive timetable in mind for achieving scientific immortality. She had given her team a target of nine months to decode the mutation, synthesize a gene therapy based on it, develop a delivery mechanism, perform preclinical toxicity analysis, and complete all essential bioanalytical testing. If they succeeded, she would be ready to start phase one clinical development trials within a year. To cement her personal commitment to the cause, she wire transferred ten thousand dollars directly from her personal bank account into the private accounts of each of her top five scientists, and promised a matching payment in nine months if the milestone was achieved.

Scientific accomplishment and monetary incentives alone proved to be insufficient levers to keep the team on pace with the schedule. Extraordinary measures were necessary. Moving the project offshore to the Czech Republic—away from prying corporate eyes and stifling procedural protocols—had been her first mandate. Patient-65's compulsory participation was her second.

Nicknamed "The Calypso Directive" by Pope, the project mushroomed into a tremendous professional risk for everyone involved. The provenance of the nickname was not lost on her; she had googled it. Calypso was the nymph who kidnapped Odysseus and held him prisoner on her secret island. Calypso needed Odysseus. She loved him, and in exchange for his love, she offered him the godly gift of immortality. Patient-65 was Meredith's Odysseus. The laboratory in Prague, her secret island. While the babbling Hippocratic demurral from her staff tested her resolve daily, she was resolute in her conviction that the ends would justify the means. In true Homeric fashion, she would bestow on her patient-hero Calypso's gift. Together, they would be gods—Morley and Foster—immortal in the annals of medical history.

With Patient-65 sequestered safely within the BSL-4 confines of her Chiarek Norse facility in Prague, Pope and the research team methodically dissected the assignment. The first step, decoding Patient-65's genome, was purely a matter of computational power. This hurdle she could overcome with money and supercomputer-sourced processing time. The second step, however, synthesizing the mutation into an efficacious biopharmaceutical, was a nightmare. The crux of the problem was figuring out how to take the naturally occurring mutation in Patient-65's immune system and program it safely into another human being's DNA.

Meredith understood that gene therapy was a field of medical research rife with risk, complication, and uncertainty. Reprogramming a human's genetic code, while perfectly logical in theory, had proven to be disastrously difficult in real life. Human gene therapy products were still not approved by the Food and Drug Administration for sale in the United States, making all gene therapy a purely experimental endeavor. Furthermore, patients who chose to undergo gene therapy faced daunting risks: toxic shock from severe immune response to the viral vector or transgene; inappropriate DNA insertion by the transgene causing mutation or cancer; and the potential for the vector virus to mutate, propagate, or exchange DNA with other viruses, thereby infecting the host. There was no silver bullet when it came to gene therapy, Pope had complained to her once over a neat glass of Dewar's. Trial and error was the modus operandi of biopharmaceutical development. Their luck changed, however, when she learned of a groundbreaking gene therapy experiment at Boston University that used a bioengineered Adeno-associated virus as the vector.

Hijacking the research had been simple. The editor of the renowned science journal *Immunology* owed her a favor; she called it in. The term of her repayment was a copy of the pre-publication paper outlining the BU experiment. The work was the brainchild of an unknown researcher, a graduate student named August Jameson Archer. After Xavier Pope confirmed that Archer's research was germane to their endeavor, Meredith obtained the raw data and project files from Archer's lab. A thousand dollars cash, a willing BU coed infiltrator, and a USB "air card" modem was all it took to obtain everything she needed. The payoff was epic. Archer's research pointed Pope and the project team in a direction they hadn't considered, saving her millions in cash and months of precious pretrial development time. She was so confident that a production-ready formula was imminent that she had even begun drafting her presentation slides for the annual board of directors meeting.

But when Patient-65 went running half-naked into the streets of Prague, her crystal ball exploded into a million tiny pieces.

•   •   •

SHE WRAPPED A towel around her head, shrugged on her favorite bathrobe and padded into her study. The cold shower had shocked her body awake and readied her for battle. She pressed the power button on her aluminum-encased MacBook Pro and felt a surge of adrenaline. Had she pursued a career practicing medicine, she would have been an ER doctor. In medicine, the word triage describes the process of systematically prioritizing actions to redress injuries as a function of both their severity and urgency. Successful triage requires equal parts judgment and action.

This was triage.

She had two bleeders demanding her attention: retrieval and damage control. The former was a matter of urgency, the latter a matter of severity.

With Patient-65 on the run, retrieval was going to be a problem. The longer her wayward genetic prodigy was missing, the harder it would become to find him. Swift, local intervention was the key. While Meredith preferred to clean up little messes like this on her own, desperate times . . . desperate measures. She sighed. Outside help was going to be necessary. Over the years she had come to realize that some jobs, especially the distasteful ones, were sometimes better to outsource. Every thorn has its rose, she mused. There would be no paperwork, no signatures or contracts that could be traced back to Vyrogen or to her. She would use an intermediary to make the necessary arrangements. Arm's length separation. Plausible deniability. It was better that way. Safer. While she had never used the Zurn brothers before, as far as bounty hunters go, they came highly recommended and had a reputation for pertinacity.

She made the call.

Damage control she would handle herself. She began typing a list. Records would be moved, shredded, or scrubbed as necessary. Archival data would be copied, transferred, and then deleted from the Chiarek Norse servers. Equipment, materials, and staff would be relocated to an alternate facility outside the Czech Republic. This needed to happen fast. Within forty-eight hours, she decided. Loose lips had to be sealed. Payments would be made to ensure stories matched and memories were foggy. A cover story needed to be formulated and supporting press releases drafted. Her fingers danced on the keyboard at breakneck pace for over an hour. When her damage control plan was complete, she clicked "Save" and leaned back in her task chair.

She looked wistfully at the framed picture on her desk, the one depicting her father jokingly handing her the keys to his Porsche. Maybe someday she would be able to look back on this crisis and laugh, just as she and her father had done about the speeding ticket, twenty-three years ago. Probably not. One can only prepare for so many contingencies before something catches you off guard. There was no way she could have seen *this* coming, she told herself.

She did not want to do it, but this was triage. If the Zurns failed to capture Patient-65 within twenty-four hours, she would be forced to hedge her bets. She pressed the "Contacts" icon on her iPhone, touched the letter "N" on the sidebar, and scrolled through the list of surnames until she found *his* name. It had been two years since they had spoken. She was certain he would answer her call. The question was . . . would he help her?

Chapter Three

Boston, Massachusetts

AUGUST JAMESON ARCHER rubbed his eyes with the back of his wrists, not his fingers, just in case his fingertips were contaminated with the chemical dye he was presently applying to a new batch of samples. Phosphorescent green sclera could be a cool Halloween trick, as long as someone else was the test subject. To observers, his eye-rubbing technique was an oddity, but for AJ Archer the behavior had become so rote—because of his incessantly itchy eyes—that he adhered to the practice even when outside the laboratory. The samples he was preparing today were not related to the core focus of his dissertation, but he had a hunch he wanted to follow. This hunch, like most of his hunches, had come to him while eating. This was a ramen noodle mixed with canned tuna hunch, which if past experience held true, most likely would be a miserable dead end. Yet, he was of the strong opinion that any hunch pertaining to science, no matter how ludicrous, must be investigated.

Technically, his dissertation was complete. It was only April, but his PhD was in the bag. The next two months were what his faculty advisor called the tail end of the roller coaster ride. The hills, the loops, the corkscrews were now just nauseating memories; the train was coasting into the station. This was not the case for all his peers, however, especially those whose research had not yielded publishable results. For the unlucky ones, the graduate student express was in a free fall, plummeting into the abyss below with no sign of pulling up. He shuddered. Thank God it hadn't happened to him, for it easily could have. Such is the way with scientific research. His advisor, Tim McNamara, had warned him at the beginning of the program five years ago: *Nature does not yield her secrets easily. Don't be surprised if you hit more than one roadblock in your quest for answers.*

But he hadn't hit any roadblocks. Quite the opposite in fact. AJ had tenaciously dug his way into a pharaoh's tomb of microbiological findings, and for the past eighteen months he had been cataloguing the treasure. His rookie success had made him somewhat of a pariah on campus—celebrated by some, loathed by others, and envied by all. Even the tenured faculty could not help but take notice of his groundbreaking success. The stars had aligned for August Jameson Archer, and he knew it.

"Hey AJ," called a grad student, standing in the doorway to his lab. "There's some guy here to see you."

He swiveled around on his stool. "Who is it?"

"I don't know," she said. "Some old guy. He's in Tim's office, and I get the impression Tim knows him."

•   •   •

AJ PAUSED AT the threshold of his faculty advisor's office door. He peered through the narrow gap between the mostly closed door and door frame at a man in a dark blue suit talking with his mentor of the past five years. The stranger was facing away from the door, so only the back of his jacket and a neatly trimmed head of pepper-grey hair were visible. Whoever he was, he wasn't from academia; his clothes screamed Wall Street, not college campus.

The professor caught a glance of AJ loitering in the hallway and motioned with his hand, *come in.*

"AJ, I have someone here who would like to meet you," said Tim, gesturing toward the other man.

"Jack Briggs," said the man in the blue suit, extending his hand. "It's a pleasure to meet you, August."

"Call me AJ or Archer. Nobody calls me August except for my grandfather, and he has to, because it's his name and he can't bring himself to admit he hates it too," AJ said, shaking Jack Briggs' hand.

"Fair enough. You can call me Briggs," said Briggs, taking a seat. "Tim tells me you've recently finished your dissertation, and that you've accepted a postdoc position at Stanford in the fall. Congratulations."

"Thank you. It'll be a big change from my life here in Boston, but I'm looking forward to the challenge." AJ paused, and an awkward silence filled the room. "What do you do for a living, Mr. Briggs?"

Briggs made eye contact with AJ. "I match talent with problems."

AJ shot him a quizzical look. "You mean like a headhunter?"

"Not exactly. Think of me as a recruiter."

AJ looked to Tim. "Tim, how do you know Mr. Briggs?"

"Oh, Jack and I go way back. I do consulting work for his firm, from time to time," Tim replied with an unusual nostalgic tone to his voice.

"Are you here to recruit me, Mr. Briggs?"

"Yes," Briggs said plainly.

"But I've already accepted the position at Stanford. I'm not interested in the private sector."

"Why do you assume this pertains to the private sector?"

"Your expensive suit. Your Piaget wristwatch."

"I trained him to be observant," Tim interjected with a chuckle.

"I'd expect nothing less," Briggs said, and then turned his attention back to AJ. His gaze intensified. "I should probably clarify. I'm not asking you to give up your job at Stanford. I'm looking to fill a temporary position. It's an exigency, so to speak, in need of prompt analytical attention from an individual with your specific skill set. When the assignment is complete, you would be free to return to your old life."

AJ lowered an eyebrow. *Old life?* The conversation was unorthodox, but Jack Briggs had piqued his interest. "What kind of work would I be doing?"

"The same type of work you've been doing here. Investigating immunological response."

"Where?"

"At a lab here in Boston, mostly. There may be some travel and field work involved though."

"When would I start?"

"Tomorrow."

AJ ran his fingers through his sandy brown hair. "Tomorrow? Ahhhh, I can't just drop everything I'm in the middle of . . ." He then began to ramble. "I'm running a new sample batch, there's the class I'm teaching, I still have to plan my move, I'm—"

Briggs held up his hand. *Stop.* The gesture was so abrupt, so deliberate that AJ didn't realize he'd stopped speaking in mid-sentence. Like a general in the military silencing a subordinate, Briggs had commanded his complete surrender. Briggs reached into his suit jacket pocket and retrieved a business card and ink pen. He scribbled *$50,000* on the back of the card and handed it to AJ.

AJ flipped the card over, and he stared at it.

"What is this?"

"That's my offer."

"Are you kidding me?"

"Do I look like someone who kids?" said Briggs and then added, "Half now, half when the work is done."

"But you said I would only be working for you temporarily, until I go to Stanford."

"That's right."

"This is . . ." AJ stammered.

"A lot of money?" Briggs interjected.

"Yeah."

"Obviously, my firm thinks your talent warrants this measure of compensation. And that's net, by the way. We'll gross it up to cover the income taxes."

AJ looked at his advisor and friend for validation.

Tim raised his eyebrows, as if to say: *You're on your own, kid.*

AJ flipped the card over in his fingers. He found himself reflecting on the quality of last night's dinner of ramen noodles mixed with canned tuna. Without warning, the image morphed. Suddenly he was at a five-star restaurant, dining on seared sushi-grade ahi, served on a bed of rice noodles, and topped with a pineapple ginger sauce. He was dressed in Jack Briggs' suit and wearing Jack Briggs' Swiss watch. He smiled. He was handing the valet a paper ticket to pull his new BMW . . .

"I'm afraid I need your decision, AJ. The project kickoff meeting is tomorrow," Briggs pressed. "If your answer is no, then this is good-bye. I have another candidate to interview at Harvard Medical School this afternoon."

AJ blinked twice. "What if the project runs over, and I have to leave for Stanford before the work is finished? What if I don't find you the answers in time?"

"Then you keep the upfront money and we depart amicably. That sometimes happens when life and business intersect. We don't hold grudges," Briggs said.

AJ rubbed his eyes with the back of his wrists and made a noise that was half sigh, half grunt. "Okay, I'm in."

"Very good. Meet me at the park bench by the *Make Way for Duck-lings* sculpture in the Boston Public Garden tomorrow morning at eight o'clock sharp. We'll walk to the office together."

"Okay, I know the spot."

The two men shook hands, and then AJ looked at Tim.

"I'll catch up with you later, AJ. Jack and I have some other matters to discuss before he goes," Tim said.

"Oh, and Archer, don't be late," Briggs said.

"Okay. Thank you. I won't. I mean, I'll see you at eight," AJ stammered.

He fought to suppress a giddy grin as he left the room. Fifty-thousand dollars for two months' work! He couldn't wait to see the look on his girlfriend's face when he told her. Her jaw would drop to the floor. A celebration dinner was in order tonight. Five-star, of course.

As he strutted down the hall, he flipped the business card over to look at the front side.

JACKSON BRIGGS

RECRUITER

It was a strange business card. No company name. No address. No contact details whatsoever . . . just a name, title, and an image of a bee.

"Recruiter," he muttered. "Recruiter for what?"

Chapter Four

Prague, Czech Republic

R AUCOUS LAUGHTER WOKE him.
In his dream, he was reliving the escape sequence from quarantine, but in the disturbing stop-motion detail that only exists in dreams. He drank the chilled, purple blood from the glass vials. Then, the megaphone voice boomed, each syllable a hammer blow against his skull. He fled and evil yellow-suits gave chase through never-ending corridors. Magically, the Level Four stairwell appeared in front of him, and the door opened politely without a touch. He laughed. He was going to make it. He jumped, sailing over the railing into the abyss. But this time, as he made the four-story plunge in the stairwell, he realized something was different. He had forgotten the bedsheets. He was free falling without a safety line. Yellow-suits and orderlies lined up along the stairs and balconies, peering over the railings at him. They were laughing. Laughing at stupid Will Foster as he plummeted toward his death.

He sat up in the narrow bed, hyperventilating and clutching the bedsheet in his fists.

"Whoa, dude!" a shaggy haired boy in a Rutgers T-shirt said. "That must have been one wicked nightmare."

Will was completely disoriented. He could not remember where he was or how long he had been asleep. His surroundings were strange and unfamiliar. A chocolate brown mural with a cartoon depiction of the Brevnov Monastery and a white tour bus adorned the wall facing him. Then he noticed two other people in the dimly lit room, staring at him.

"Where am I?"

"You're at Miss Sophie's, dude."

"Miss Sophie's?"

"Yeah, you know, the youth hostel. Miss Sophie said that you've been out cold since late last night. You must have been smoking some really good shit, man," said a jock sporting a New York Mets baseball cap. "I wanna know where you party."

"What time is it?"

"It's like, almost ten at night. We just came back from the pub and you were twitching and moaning like crazy. I thought you might be, like, an epileptic or something, but Frankie said you were just having a nightmare," Rutgers said.

"Yeah, we were dying with laughter. Sorry we woke you up, man," Frankie said, eyeing Will from under the brim of his Mets cap.

The cobwebs in Will's mind were beginning to clear and the details of the previous twenty-four hours were coming back to him. The cabbie had driven him to what he had called "a good, safe place." Will had thought Miss Sophie's was a budget-priced inn, but now he surmised it was a hostel—the kind of place frequented by backpackers, young adventure seekers, and the university party crowd. A two-minute conversation had taken place between the cabbie and a Czech woman with a kindly face and it ended with a hug. No money had changed hands, so Will suspected the cabbie and Miss Sophie were more than mere acquaintances. The woman had led him to a dorm-style room, sparsely furnished with steel framed beds. After sizing him up, she returned several minutes later with a pair of blue jeans, a T-shirt, and a pair of filthy athletic shoes from what he deduced must be the establishment's equivalent of the lost-and-found bin. He vaguely remembered unwrapping the gauze tape that held the vials to his leg and stuffing them into his jacket pocket, before collapsing from exhaustion onto the bed. If the time was indeed ten o'clock, then he had slept for twenty hours straight.

The vials!

He jumped out of bed, frantic. He needed to confirm that the vials were safe. He scanned the room for the olive-green army jacket, but saw only two large North Face backpacks propped up against the wall. Perhaps Miss Sophie had placed it under his bed with his newly gifted garb. Will knelt on the checkered parquet floor, dragged a white rectangular clothes locker out from under the bed frame, and flipped open the metal-hinged top. Inside were the folded blue jeans, grey T-shirt, and dirty athletic shoes neatly arranged, but no jacket.

Rutgers burst into laughter. "Dude, check out his pajama pants."

Frankie chortled. "Those are classic. They look like what I wore in the hospital when I was six and had my tonsils out."

"Yeah, totally."

"Have you guys seen my jacket? I had it right here under my bed. Now it's gone."

"Maybe it's in that closet," Rutgers said, pointing to an IKEA birchwood wardrobe. He walked over to the wardrobe, opened the doors, and tugged Will's green army jacket off a hanger. "Is this it?"

"Yes. Give it to me."

"Dude, this is sweet. I've been looking for one of these vintage army coats for-eva. Do you mind if I try it on?"

"Actually, I . . ."

It was too late. Rutgers was already shrugging the coat onto his muscular shoulders. "It fits. Tell ya what. I'll give you thirty euros for it."

Will shook his head. "Nah. I need that coat. It's the only one I've got."

Rutgers looked at himself in the mirror and flipped the collar up. He winked at himself and pretended to fire a finger pistol at the guy in the mirror. "Okay, fifty euros and I'll throw in my old J. Crew barn jacket. But that's my final offer."

Will considered. He needed the money. With fifty euros, he could buy food, an international calling card, and maybe even a Eurorail pass. The army jacket *was* the only thing of value that he had to barter. Certainly, Rutgers had no interest in his blue, polka-dot hospital pants.

"All right, you have a deal."

Rutgers trotted over to his backpack, unzipped a pocket, and retrieved fifty euros in small bills and the barn jacket from the main compartment. He zipped the bag closed, threw the canvas jacket on Will's cot, and slapped the cash into Will's outstretched hand.

"Thanks. I just need to get my things from the pockets," Will said, taking a step toward Rutgers.

On hearing this, the kid immediately shoved both his hands into the coat pockets; Will heard the glass vials clink together.

"Careful!"

"Dude, what do you have in here?" Rutgers asked as he jerked his hand out of the pocket. The vials were longer than the narrow splayed opening of the pocket, and one of the rubber stoppers snagged on the fabric.

Will watched helplessly, jaw agape, as one of the glass vials slid from the kid's grip and rotated end over end toward the ground. The vial struck the hardwood floor on the bottom glass curvature and exploded. Glass fragments and liquid rained over everything and everybody.

"Shit, dude. What was that?"

"Don't touch it!" Will yelled, but it was already too late. Rutgers had stepped away from the point of impact and was wiping his lower legs with his free hand. At the same time, Frankie was on his hands and knees collecting glass shards with his fingers and tossing them into a nearby waste bin.

"Both of you—STOP." Will ordered. "Don't touch the glass. I'll clean it up. Now, please, carefully hand me the other vial. Then go wash yourselves with soap and hot water."

Rutgers and Frankie gave Will a strange look, but did as instructed. Will inspected the remaining glass tube, checking that the stopper was firmly in place. Next, he read the label: *AAV-564: P-65 Transgene Trial 12.* That answered that question. The shattered vial was the one containing the cloudy liquid, with the Latin name he could not remember.

•   •   •

BY EIGHT O'CLOCK the next morning, Rutgers was coughing and sneezing, and Will was frantic. By eleven o'clock, the kid was moaning, spewing phlegm, and splayed out on his cot. Frankie was red-faced and vomiting. Both of their foreheads were hot to the touch. Miss Sophie generously tended to them, bringing the boys cold drinks and wet towels, oblivious to the deadly truth. The vial of *Yersinia pestis* Will had stolen from Chiarek Norse contained a highly virulent strain of the bacteria. Both boys were infected with full-blown pneumonic plague, and their bodies were rapidly losing the war raging inside them. Will kept vigil in the room. What he was witnessing was familiar but made no sense to him. Two strong and healthy college students were suffering more in twelve hours after exposure than Will had suffered during his entire quarantine.

At a quarter past twelve, Miss Sophie hurried into the room with a terrified look on her face. She grabbed Will firmly by the upper arm and whispered to him in heavily accented English. "The taxi driver, Mikiel, warn me this could happen. Right now, men are at the door; they are looking for *you*. They show me your picture. They say they are police. This is lie. I know how police look. I tell them they can't come in and I shut the door. But they will come in anyway. It will be bad for me and bad for you if they find you here. You must go now! Follow me."

Without a word of protest, Will grabbed his new coat and followed her down a flight of stairs to a back door that opened into an alley. She unlocked the door and peeked outside, scanning first left and then right.

"It safe. Go now!"

Loud repetitive pounding from the entry door echoed down the first floor hallway.

He took a step across the threshold, then stopped. He looked her in the eyes, and she read his thoughts immediately.

"I take care of the American boys. You go now."

He bowed his head to her. "Thank you, for everything," he said and then sprinted off into the darkness.

Chapter Five

Boston, Massachusetts

Briggs crossed his legs and shifted his weight in a fruitless effort to get comfortable. The chairs in Robért Nicolora's office were nice enough to look at, but despite their solid walnut construction and crimson leather upholstery, they were abysmally uncomfortable. Nicolora liked it that way. He preferred to keep his office guests distracted while they were in conference with him. *"As goes the body, so goes the mind,"* he had once told Briggs.

Nicolora's own chair, while similar in style, was contoured, soft, and supportive.

Though he was five years Briggs' senior, Nicolora looked at least ten years younger than his longtime friend. His lean frame, olive complexion, and full head of hair belied his fifty-nine years. A naturalized US citizen of twelve years, he had been born in a small town outside of Budapest, Hungary. His linguistic capabilities had always left friends and colleagues awestruck. At the age of thirty, he was fluent in seven languages: Hungarian, Czech, Russian, German, French, Spanish, and English. His current project was Mandarin. He spoke English with a perceptible and yet charming accent that came from a subtle mix of his Eastern European roots and Western European schooling. He could shed the accent when necessary for negotiation purposes, but he preferred the sound of his English to that of native British or American speakers. Most of the women he courted seemed to prefer it as well.

When he was a small child, Nicolora's parents moved his sister and him to Madrid. On his eighteenth birthday, he left home to attend university in Barcelona. In his twenties, Nicolora lived and worked throughout Europe, spending time in Paris, Munich, Amsterdam, and London. It was during his time in London that he met an American named Bradley Wells. Over several months, the two men became close friends, and it was Wells who recruited Nicolora to join an elite think tank that served the US government during the Cold War. Neither a government bureau nor a corporation, the brain trust did not officially exist on any government org charts. Within the innermost circles of the State Department, however, the group was known as The Think Tank.

To its members, it was simply and affectionately referred to as The Tank.

In 1997, Nicolora was appointed Director. In December 2000, one month before President George W. Bush took office, the Think Tank Project was quietly disbanded and its members scattered to the wind.

In theory, The Tank had ceased to exist.

•   •   •

"DID HE ACCEPT?" Nicolora asked, knowing the answer already.

"Yes."

"Did he make a counteroffer?"

"No."

"Hmm." Nicolora rubbed his chin. "Do you think he can handle our type of fieldwork?"

Briggs shrugged. "Fifty-fifty. But McNamara assures me this kid is the real deal. A 'tenacious technical mind' were his exact words. Besides, you said it yourself, Archer's dissertation practically is the case."

"What do you have planned for him today?"

"I'm meeting him at eight in the Public Garden. Paperwork, followed by the standard tour."

Nicolora smiled, expectantly. "Did you give him any location ciphers to figure out where to meet you?"

"No. We don't have time for that bullshit. I can't afford to waste a day picking him up somewhere ridiculous like Iceland."

Nicolora laughed. "Don't tell me you're still sore about Reykjavik. That was ten years ago." Briggs grunted.

"I seem to remember your first day being a little rough." Nicolora winked.

"Not my fault. I was merely following your instructions," Briggs said. "Your ciphers have always sucked."

"Not true. You've just never been able to figure them out." Nicolora reached for a pen on his desk. "Do you want me to write it down? I still remember it."

"Bastard." Briggs swiped the pen away and pretended to be angry. He squirmed again in his chair. "And have I mentioned that I hate these goddamn chairs?"

"Not since yesterday."

The two men stared at each other for a moment like street toughs in rival gangs, then burst into laughter.

After he had caught his breath Briggs asked, "What did our contact in the Czech Ministry of Health have to say? Does the Czech government know anything yet?"

"Nothing. Meredith is keeping it very quiet. She's in lockdown mode, holding *everything* back . . . even from me. But whatever went down, it was big."

"Containment loss?"

"Not likely, or it would be all over CNN by now. Industrial espionage is my guess."

"Or it could be a cover-up for a major league screw-up."

"Always one of my personal favorites," Nicolora chuckled.

"Has she decided what she wants to do?"

"Not yet."

Briggs grunted again, this time with real disdain.

"I know you don't like her Jack, and I don't care," Nicolora said. "If Meredith decides she needs our help, then we're going to help her, damn it."

"Even if it means taking down the Foundation in the process?"

Nicolora tensed, but quickly regained his composure. "Now you're just being melodramatic." He stood, walked around the corner of his desk, and stopped in front of the still-seated Briggs. Looking down at him, he added, "If our people do what they're supposed to do—what they're paid to do—then that will never happen. Regardless of the assignment."

Briggs stood and put his hand on Nicolora's shoulder.

"Be careful, old friend. If I recall correctly, it was you yourself who once said: *That woman's lips are hemlock.*"

Chapter Six

Prague, Czech Republic

WILL SAT ALONE on a cold stone curb, in a narrow deserted alley, his face buried in his hands. Visions of the two American college students from the youth hostel, writhing with fever and pain, flashed through his mind like snapshots in a grotesque photo album he could not bring himself to close. It was his fault they were dying. Did that make him a murderer?

He did not know whether it was exposure to the contents of the broken vial or contact with him that had infected them. They were exposed to two potential vectors. As far as Miss Sophie was concerned, when Will last saw her, she was not exhibiting signs of infection. That leant credence to the broken vial argument. Of course, that was hours ago. By now, she could be as sick as they were.

When he was a boy, his father told him a bizarre piece of trivia. If you place a frog in a pot of cold water, and slowly heat the water inside to a boil, the frog will linger, incognizant of the danger until it perishes in the heat. But if you drop a frog into a pot of boiling water, the frog will jump out immediately—scalded, but alive. During his third month of confinement, it occurred to him that he was the frog, and quarantine the pot of water. His captors were turning up the heat gradually, and he had been oblivious to the change. At that moment of epiphany, he began planning his escape:

He started by shifting his sleeping pattern—forcing himself to nap at every opportunity during the day—so he could be alert at night when the staff was at one-quarter strength. He learned the assignments on the watch bill and memorized the times and routes for the roving personnel. He studied the guards and orderlies, noted their idiosyncrasies, and became familiar with their habits. Eventually, he built up the courage to sneak around Level 4 during the break between the hourly security tours after midnight. Systematically, he scoped out the entire floor including: the laundry room, the server room, the sample room, Laboratory 1, Laboratory 2, the hospital rooms housing other patients, and a room with a label in another language, which he could not read. This room, along with the server room, was always locked. Until one night, he found the door shut, but not latched.

The room was cold, dimly lit, and the back wall was lined with rectangular stainless steel refrigeration modules that bore the nameplate MOPEC. Two identical modules sat side by side, each housing nine chambers, arranged three rows high by three columns wide. An empty gurney was parked up against the left wall. A chill ran down his spine. He knew what this place was. He turned to leave, but then stopped. He couldn't help himself; he had to look. To his surprise, the handles were not locked. He took a deep breath and opened one of the rectangular doors in the middle row. The door hissed as he broke the seal and 39° F chilled air tickled the hair on his forearm. He grabbed the lip on the telescoping stainless steel tray inside and pulled. The tray extended smoothly, despite holding the weight of a full-size adult body inside a black zippered body bag. Two yellow BIOLOGICAL HAZARD stickers were affixed to the bag, one at the head and one at the foot. He took the zipper in between his thumb and forefinger, held his breath, and pulled. A wave of rank, putrid air that stank of excrement hit him like a punch in the face. He gagged and reflexively took a step back. Then, he saw it—the face of a monster. The cadaver inside looked like he had been bludgeoned to death, but Will knew otherwise. The tip of the nose and fingertips were blackened and gangrenous. A grotesque, purple bubo bulged on the side of the dead man's neck, and blue-black plague spots covered his trunk and cheeks. The body was fresh and Will was sickened to see that it had yet to be cleaned. Dried blood and pus stained the skin beneath the dead man's nostrils and trailed from the corner of his left eye. Fighting the urge to vomit, he covered his nose and mouth and reluctantly stepped closer. He recognized this man. He had seen him the week before, languishing in a hospital room five doors down from his own, hacking and spewing phlegm. Like a bug trapped in a spider's web, the man was hooked up to a tangled mess of tubes and wires, waiting to die. Will zipped the body bag closed and shoved the corpse back inside its refrigerated tomb. He opened the adjacent door and repeated the process. This time the zipper opened to reveal the cadaver's feet. He noted the toe tag: P-62. He looked down at his wristband and his heart skipped a beat. P-65. Frantically he checked the other cadaver coolers. P-59, P-47, P-61, P-43 . . . P-64. Fear gripped him as the gravity of his situation took hold. In this hospital, regardless of the treatment, the patients died. All of them.

His mind drifted from that fateful night two weeks ago, back to the present. To his surprise, he suddenly found himself contemplating going back. What if he belonged in quarantine? Maybe he really was infected with a deadly disease, just as they claimed. The last thing he wanted was to hurt people. Better to live in a bubble, than to be responsible for filling Mopec chillers with the bodies of innocent men, women, and children. He was certain he could find his way back to the building from which he had escaped. Within seconds of walking into the lobby, the guards would surround him. Angry yellow-suits would converge from every direction and thrust him back into the familiar nightmare of needles and isolation. It would be horrible, but at least he would avoid hurting more innocent people.

Yet despite the mental anguish he was suffering, *physically* he was feeling better by the hour. Sure, the fire escape plunge had taken a toll on his body; his joints ached and his muscles throbbed. But the symptoms from the last injection were completely gone. His breathing was strong and steady; his head and sinuses were clear. As much as he wanted to be sick, deserved to be sick—sick like Rutgers and Frankie—his body was on the mend.

He hugged himself against the cold while working to clear his mind and tried not to shiver. He felt like he had a pile of jigsaw puzzle pieces that looked like matches on first inspection, but didn't quite fit when he tried to snap them together.

Puzzle piece number one: The doctors told him he was infected with a deadly virus. This he could not prove or disprove. Months ago, when he was first placed into quarantine he did not feel sick. He did not feel sick now. The only time he ever felt sick was while he was in quarantine. Still, he knew that empirical observations of his health did not rule out the possibility that he was a *carrier* of a disease. What if he, like Typhoid Mary in the early 1900s, was spreading a disease for which he exhibited no symptoms?

Puzzle piece number two: The doctors told him they were using experimental treatments to eradicate a virus lurking in his system, but every *treatment* only made him feel worse. The scenario had always been the same: injection, followed by flu symptoms, then rapid recovery. This was why he stole the sample with the cloudy liquid. His intellect told him the injections were not treatments. Far from it. The vial of cloudy liquid had been the key to understanding this puzzle piece, but now that key was lost.

A hint of a smile crept across his face. Even though the vial of cloudy liquid was destroyed, remnants of the substance were coursing through his veins. What if someone could identify the foreign compound using a sample of his blood? He also still had the vial of the clear liquid, another puzzle piece in need of deciphering. To gain access to such analyses, he would need help from the one person in the world with whom he was not on speaking terms. Julie Ponte was an American molecular biologist working in Vienna and his only hope. The trick would be convincing her to listen. It had been ages since they last communicated, and it was he who had ended the romance between them.

He stood abruptly. His legs itched and tingled from sitting for so long. He rubbed the back of his thighs, trying to get the blood flowing. Then, he started to pace. From his front pants pocket, he retrieved a wad of crumpled bills: thirty-one euros. He had spent seven euros on a hot sandwich and a liter of bottled water at a café, his first real meal since breaking out of quarantine. He had spent another twelve on an inexpensive maroon scarf and grey wool cap from a second-hand store—not just for warmth, but also to conceal his face. If they were already casing youth hostels, then it was safe to assume they were looking for him in all obvious places where a half-naked man with no money might try to hide. Homeless shelters, park benches, under bridges—anywhere a vagabond might go. He needed to get out of Prague, away from the dragon's lair, but without a passport, booking a flight or a train ticket was out of the question. Complicating matters, he still had no idea who "they" were. The most logical assumption was that the people looking for him were the security personnel from the lab. The very guards he had outmaneuvered were now the ones trying to bring him in. Other operatives could also be on his trail. Bounty hunters? Government agents? What about the Czech police? Were they looking for him too? He had no idea how deep this conspiracy ran. Paranoia was the only reason he had not marched right up to the US embassy in Prague, knocked on the door, and said, "Please take me home."

He had been quarantined, drugged, and smuggled out of the United States, without any intervention or investigation by the various agencies of the Department of Homeland Security. This told him that either the smuggling was sanctioned by DHS, or that the information surrounding his case never reached DHS. Either way, the conclusion was the same. Whoever did this to him had some very powerful people on their payroll.

To avoid capture, he needed to fly under the radar; to solve the puzzle, he needed help. These two goals were not mutually exclusive, but the latter did risk the former. His mind raced. How could he contact Julie covertly? Certainly not from the sanctuary of this alley, he thought. Fuck it. He stepped into the daylight onto a crowded intersection in Old Town Prague and scanned both sides of the street for an Internet kiosk, a well-heeled café, or even a modern hotel where he could sneak some computer time. Thirty-one euros would buy him plenty of time online, even if it took hours to reach Julie.

He walked south, past Hlavní nádraží, the largest and busiest railway station in Prague. He crossed Jeruzalemska and Růžová, but neither street had what he needed. When he reached Politickych veznu, he turned northwest on a whim and soon found himself in Wenceslas Square. At 700 meters long and sixty meters wide, Wenceslas was a Square in name only, and he found himself stopping for a moment to take it all in. He felt a charge of energy from the vibrant boulevard; its shops and sidewalks were bustling with life. The abundance of automobiles, asphalt, tourist shops, and window advertisements overwhelmed the Old World charm that flowed from the roofline architecture. He suspected that if one could magically wipe away all the commercialism, Wenceslas might be beautiful. But Wenceslas Square was no more or less beautiful at that moment than it had been more than six hundred years before, when King Charles IV founded the *Konskytrh,* or "Horse Market," in a brainstorm of urban planning. It was never a panorama of grand buildings and cathedrals like the Old Town or Prague Castle. The Square was— and always had been—Prague's central market. It was not the showpiece. It was the *hub.*

Will looked toward the end of the Square, past the modest gardens dividing the wide tree-lined boulevard, all the way to the imposing National Museum, with its majestic cupola and brightly illuminated Neo-Renaissance facade. Positioned fifty meters in front, stood a statue of a knight atop a horse. Wenceslas immortalized.

His nervous stomach reminded him that he had work to do, and he strode off. Ten minutes later, he spied a small Internet café. A bilingual sign in the window read Three Euros Per Hour in Czech and English. It was a better price than he had dared to hope for. After waiting forty-five minutes for a computer terminal in the back with a view of the entrance, Will took a seat. The room was amply heated, and he wanted desperately to strip off his winter garb. But he left the wool cap untouched upon his head and the maroon scarf wrapped snugly around his nose and mouth to hide his face.

As he logged into his email account, he was taken aback. The date stamp on his last sent message was over five months old. Five months! He felt the color rising in his cheeks as he thought about his imprisonment. No phone calls, no email, no letters, no walks outside, no contact with anyone.

He took a deep breath, calming himself so he could concentrate on the task at hand.

He sorted the email in his inbox by sender. Hundreds of messages flooded the screen, but not a single one was from Julie. With the way they had left things, she probably didn't even know he was missing. Maybe no one did. He hadn't exchanged emails with Julie for over a year. To make matters worse, he couldn't remember where she worked. He knew she ran her own lab, but the details of her employment had never been a heated topic of conversation between them. Still, he had a starting point; he knew her instant messaging account name. If she had changed *that*, then he was in serious trouble.

He opened MSN Instant Messenger.

"C'mon Julie," he said quietly. "Be there." A blue task window popped up on the screen with a friendly chime:

Hello Will, 0 of your contacts are online.

Shit.

He clicked back over to his email account to compose a message, addressing it to Julie's personal email address:

To: juliepontephd@gmail.com
From: willfoster724@hotmail.com
Subject: Urgent! Need help.

Julie - I'm in trouble and need your help. I'll be logged onto IM for the next 24 hours. - W

He hit "send" and sank into his chair. In the past, Julie had checked her personal email periodically throughout the workday, but there was no telling how long he would have to wait today. For the next ninety minutes, he reacquainted himself with the world, scanning news sites for current events and checking his favorite blogs. It was a sobering experience. So much had happened while he had been locked away, and the more he read, the more alone he felt.

As he clicked from site to site, he kept one eye on the front desk and the people around him. It was a diverse crowd, but not a *dangerous* crowd.

Bing.

The sound seemed unnaturally loud, and Will was momentarily afraid that the computer had somehow betrayed him. He glanced around wildly, but no one seemed to be paying any attention to him. In fact, he could hear other people's computers making similar sounds.

It was an instant message alert.

☺ Julie:
will? is this a joke?

His breath quickened, and his hands started to shake. He could barely type.

☻ Will:
no joke. i'm in trouble and need your help.

☺ Julie:
why me? what about your girlfriend?

☻ Will:
we broke up

He waited . . . his stomach tied in knots. After what seemed like an eternity, the message window refreshed with new text.

☺ Julie:
I'm pissed at you. you break up with her and don't bother to tell me? you're a jerk.

☻ Will:

I am. But something really bad happened to me . . . I couldn't contact you til now

☺ Julie:

tell me

☻ Will:

I was kidnapped, but I escaped. now, i'm in Prague.

☺ Julie:

kidnapped? WTF are you talking about?

☻ Will:

I was put in quarantine, drugged, smuggled to Prague, and held against my will in some kind of hospital. but not a real hospital, more like research lab. they locked me in a room, did tests on me, injected me with things. the past five months of my life have been a nightmare, but last night I escaped.

☺ Julie:

i don't have time for this crap

She didn't *believe* him! Desperation flooded his mind, and he assaulted the keyboard with a barrage of keystrokes.

☻ Will:

EVERYTHING I'M TELLING YOU IS TRUE! I'm in Prague, with no fucking money, wearing somebody else's clothes, and the two kids who shared a room with me at a youth hostel last night are infected and are probably dying right now. I'm running out of time. I know this sounds crazy, but I need help and you're the only person in the world I can trust. PLEASE JULIE . . .

Another pregnant pause tormented him until at last she replied.

☺ Julie:

okay, you've got my attention.

☺ Julie:

do you have money for a train pass?

☻ Will:

the train is not an option. they're looking for me and I don't have a passport

☺ Julie:

ok. vienna is less than 300km from prague. i'll drive there and pick you up later tonight.

☻ Will:

you are a goddess! when and where should i meet you?

☺ Julie:

2AM at the astronomical clock in the center of town. it's a famous landmark. ask any local about the "Orloj" and they'll point you in the right direction.

☻ Will:

okay. I'll find it. but I need to tell you something else. when I was in quarantine the doctors told me i was infected. i think they were lying, but i don't know for sure. i might be contagious. i might be a walking biohazard!

☺ Julie:

what are you talking about?

☻ Will:

i've been in quarantine for the past five months. u know the kind with men in yellow bubble suits who talk with Darth Vader voices.

☺ Julie:
sounds to me like you have the flu and a very high fever which is making you delusional.

☻ Will:
i'm a basket case, not a mental case. . . . i'm serious about this. i have no idea what they've done to me. what if i infect you?

☺ Julie:
how can I help u if I can't get near u. do you want my help or not?

☻ Will:
yes, but i wanted to warn u first.

☺ Julie:
i'll try to round up a N95 surgical mask for you to wear. Just try not to bleed on anyone in the meantime. now tell me about your symptoms so i can do a little research before I come.

He rubbed his temples. The itchy maroon scarf was still wrapped around his face, and the stench of his own breath was beginning to make him sick. He hadn't showered or brushed his teeth in days. If Julie did actually come to get him, he could clean himself up. Eat real food. Drink a beer. Thinking about this made his mouth begin to water.

☻ Will:
right now, my symptoms are gone—i'll explain that later, but the frat boys had stomach pain, fever, tons of mucus, and then it seemed to be spreading to their lungs. in quarantine, some of the other patients i caught glimpses of were actually coughing up blood. also, some of them had gross purple bumps on their necks and

He stopped typing. Something had changed. He could feel the weight of another person's gaze on him. He glanced at the front desk. The attendant, a young Czech girl, was pointing at him and talking to a man dressed in a collared shirt, black pants, and gray trench coat. The man's lips curled into a thin, malevolent smile—a wolf's grin that made Will blanch.

    ☻ Will:
LOG OFF RIGHT NOW!

    ☺ Julie:
What's going on?

    ☺ Julie:
Will?
Will!

Chapter Seven

Boston, Massachusetts

AJ ARCHER GLANCED up at Thomas Ball's statue of General George Washington, seated majestically atop a prancing steed. It was a grand equestrian statue, twenty feet tall and oriented to make an impressionable greeting to all visitors of the Boston Public Garden entering through the Arlington gate. For a late April morning, the temperature was unusually temperate. The morning sun had already knocked the previous night's chill from the air, and some of the park's joggers were even wearing shorts. He skirted around the left side of the statue and selected a path toward the *Make Way for Ducklings* sculpture where he was supposed to meet Briggs. A striking woman wearing a black pantsuit and a white silk blouse caught his attention. As she strode toward him, she flashed him a smile and then shyly averted her eyes. His gaze drifted from her eyes downward. Her liberally unbuttoned blouse flicked open in the breeze, offering him a fleeting glimpse of her ample cleavage.

The force of the collision spun him halfway around. Unable to catch his balance, he tumbled to the ground and felt another body come down on top of him. When he opened his eyes a large embroidered "B" filled his field of vision. A man sporting a navy blue Red Sox cap and wearing a backpack was splayed out on top of him, flailing about like an overturned beetle trying to right itself.

"I'm *so* sorry, bro," the man said as he untangled himself from AJ. "I totally wasn't looking where I was going."

"Don't worry about it," he said through clenched teeth. His left side ached where he had fallen; he was surprised he hadn't cracked a rib. Before getting up, he glanced down the sidewalk in an attempt to catch one more glimpse of the raven-haired beauty in the white blouse. He spotted her just as she rounded a bend and was sure he glimpsed a smile. She had seen it all. No doubt this kind of thing happened to her all the time.

"Did you see the pair on that chick?" the guy in the Red Sox cap said, looking in the same direction as AJ.

AJ grunted as he got up. "See them? How could I miss them? They're the reason I ran into you."

"They don't call them knockers for nothing, I guess," laughed the man in the Red Sox cap.

AJ gathered himself and looked at his watch, 8:04 AM.

"Shit! I'm late."

He took off running north along the lagoon, ignoring the curious glances as he dodged left and right between morning commuters. As he approached the *Make Way for Ducklings* sculpture, he scanned the area for Briggs, but he didn't recognize anyone resembling the recruiter he'd met the day before. He sighed in relief and shuffled over to the bronze casting of a mother duck with her ducklings in trail—frozen forever in mid-waddle.

"You're late," a voice called from behind him.

He spun around. Jack Briggs was sitting on a park bench directly behind him. Briggs had a *Boston Globe* newspaper folded neatly in his lap and a cup of Dunkin Donuts coffee in his hand. AJ was taken aback; he didn't recall seeing anyone sitting on the park bench a minute ago.

"You're right, I am. I'm sorry about that, Mr. Briggs."

Briggs snorted as he reached inside his coat and pulled out a folded stack of documents. "Take a quick look at this CA. Throw your John Hancock on the dotted line when you're done."

"A confidentiality agreement? For what?"

Briggs stared at him. "For confidentiality."

He stared back. The man standing in front of him looked like the same Briggs he had met in Tim's office, but his persona had hardened. AJ grabbed the papers, and leafed through the legalese. Halfway through the stack of pages, he sighed, flipped to the last page, and dutifully signed his name.

"Mr. Briggs, I have some questions about—"

Briggs raised his hand, stopping AJ mid-sentence, just as he had done the day before in Tim's office. He took the signed papers, stuffed them back inside the flap of his coat, and then shifted his gaze to the bronze ducks.

"Appropriate, wouldn't you say, Archer?" Briggs said. Then, with a smile only in his eyes, he added, "There will be time for questions later. Follow me, son."

•　　•　　•

AFTER A TEN-MINUTE walk, they arrived at the steps of a renovated seven-story brownstone on the east side of Commonwealth Avenue. Embossed on the glass-paned entry door was a logo:

"This is where you work: The Nicolora Foundation?" AJ asked, remembering the enigmatic bee on Briggs' business card.

Briggs regarded him, but didn't answer.

"What is the significance of the bee?"

"Metaphor, Archer, metaphor."

"So I'm to be the newest drone in your collective hive?"

"A clumsy, shallow interpretation," Briggs said, shaking his head. "Certainly not what Mr. Nicolora had in mind when he chose the bee as the symbol of this organization. The ancients revered bees, not only because of their industriousness and loyal diligence, but also because bees are agents of fertility, renewing the cycle of life in the flora community around them."

AJ nodded, making a connection in his mind. "Information is our pollen?"

The corners of Briggs mouth turned up ever so slightly. "And the wisdom distilled from our efforts is our honey."

Briggs pressed a small black button next to the door. A bell rang, and AJ heard the heavy click of a magnetic lock disengaging. They walked into an elegant foyer that smelled of fresh-cut flowers and furniture polish. A brass plaque next to a grand wooden staircase read: RECEPTION — 2ND FLOOR.

He headed toward the stairs.

"Not so fast," Briggs called after him. "That's where the tour *ends*."

AJ nodded, trying to hide his confusion.

Briggs walked to the back of the tiny foyer and disappeared behind a corner. AJ chased after him. He found the recruiter standing inside a polished stainless steel elevator, holding the door open, and tapping his foot.

He stepped in without a word, and the door slid shut. He spied something flat and silver in Briggs' hand, but it was back in the recruiter's pocket before he could identify what it was. The elevator began to move, accelerating downward with the smoothness of a well-tuned German automobile.

"Some elevator," AJ said.

"It's German."

The doors slid open just as he was beginning to notice what a *strange* elevator it was. No railing. No keypad. No floor indicator. No emergency call button.

"First stop, Level Zero," Briggs said.

They stepped out of the elevator into a sea of office cubicles. Briggs kept a half-pace ahead of AJ as they walked, steering his duckling among the cramped walkways. AJ took in the scene, trying not to gawk. He had seemingly stepped out of the lobby of a nineteenth-century vintage brownstone and into the middle of a humming research facility.

Technicians greeted Briggs and nodded at AJ as they passed. They soon arrived at a corner office. The nameplate next to the open door said: A. ST. JEAN. Briggs knocked on the door frame, and a woman looked up from the computer where she was typing. She smiled.

"Jack!"

"Abbey."

"Nice to see you still find time to visit The Pit."

Briggs turned to AJ.

"AJ Archer, meet Abbey St. Jean, our Chief Engineer."

Her mousy brown hair was pulled back in a short ponytail, and two perfect dimples framed her easy smile. AJ was hypnotized at once by her huge brown eyes, and although he offered his hand to her, the words of salutation in his mind never manifested from his lips.

"Nice to meet you too," she said, chuckling. "Everyone down here calls me Jeanie; they know I *hate* it, of course. You can call me Eng, or Gadget Girl, or GG, or Queen of the Nerds, or Abbey, or even St. Jean. I have so many handles that it's hard to keep up with the flavor of the day."

"I think I'll go with Gadget Girl," he said.

Briggs rolled his eyes.

"So, what do you do down here?"

She smiled. "What we *do* down here is kick the collective butts of Apple, IBM, and DARPA eight days a week. You know the IT race you hear about in the media all the time? We're winning it." She shrugged, and then added, "Not that anyone will ever know."

AJ raised an eyebrow.

"Is his welcome kit ready?" Briggs interjected.

"I have it right here."

"And his phone?"

"Of course. What kind of ship do you think I run down here?"

"A tight one."

"That's right, and don't you forget it, Briggs." She winked at AJ. "Alrighty, then. First stop: the dentist. Follow me."

He followed her to a small room outfitted like a typical dentist's office. In the middle of the room was a single reclining dentist chair with blue vinyl upholstery.

"Root canal?" he joked, nervously.

"Why? Do you need one?" she asked.

"No."

"Are you sure?"

"Positive."

"Okay then, no root canal. Have a scat and opcn up," she said, gesturing to the chair. "This will only take a sec."

"What are you going to do?" he asked as she shoved him into the seat.

"My technician, Jessica, is going to glue this on the back of your left upper incisor," Abbey said, showing him a tiny white disc, the diameter of a pencil eraser and the thickness of a dime.

"Wait a minute—what is that?"

Jessica the technician said, "Open up . . . just a little cleaning to prep the surface . . . a little air to dry the enamel . . . okay, now we place the device. You're doing great . . . blue light to cure the adhesive . . . and you're done. Easy as pie."

"Say something," Abbey said to him.

"What did you just do to my tooth?" he asked in between exploratory swipes with his tongue.

Abbey looked down at the tablet computer in her palm. "Good signal strength. Good clarity. Voice ID set. Perfect."

"Did you just install a microphone in my mouth?"

"No. I just installed a transceiver on your tooth."

"You mean you're going to listen to everything I say?"

"No, no. Don't be silly. We're going to transmit everything you say."

"*Everything?*"

"When you're on the job, yeah, pretty much everything. This device enables you to have hands-free communication with any company resource at any time. It transmits voice data to your phone. The phone either archives the data, or retransmits the signal if you are making a call. The phone has its own built-in microphone for redundancy and to record ambient sound that the tooth transceiver misses. This feature enables you to make digital recordings of all your meetings, calls, and field operations."

"And what about my private life? Is that on candid camera too?"

Abbey laughed. "Don't worry, AJ, your personal life is not of any interest to us. If it bothers you, then when you're off work, turn off your phone. We'll give you a pager, and you'll be on call . . . like a doctor," Abbey said. "But I think that after a couple of weeks, you'll wonder how you ever got along without our T3 system."

"What's next, James Bond camera glasses?" he quipped, trying to defuse his nerves.

"The boy's quick, Jack," Abbey said, turning to Briggs.

As they walked through Level Zero, AJ scrutinized the work around him. A myriad of projects were underway in disciplines as diverse as chemistry, material science, electronics, and robotics. He paused, mouth agape at a clear glass cylinder measuring ten feet tall and four feet in diameter. Inside were bees, except they were not like any bees he had ever seen before.

"They're my newest prototype. Do you like them?" Abbey placed a hand on the enclosure. "Go ahead, step closer. Get a better look."

"How do you prototype . . ." He stopped mid-sentence. The bees inside the glass were not actual bees, but rather robotic impersonations of bees. "Those aren't bees!"

"They're not *real* bees, but they don't know that. They fly like bees, navigate like bees, work collectively like bees. They even sting like bees."

"What is it with you people and bees? Why are you making robot bees?"

"The applications are practically infinite. They're perfect little infiltrators. I can use them to collect reconnaissance—put eyes and ears in places where people can't go. Or, I can program them to deliver drug injections to uncooperative targets. And with twelve of these little guys working together, I have a small, infinitely configurable, mobile antennae."

"Unbelievable. Tim would love this! Tim wouldn't believe this," he mumbled. "Any other robot bugs on the loose around here I should know about?"

"Yeah, spiders. They've been in the field for twelve months. Maybe you'll get to see them in action," Abbey said.

Briggs spoke up. "Okay, show-and-tell time is over. Time to get moving. Say good-bye to the Queen of the Nerds. We've got work to do. Let's go see your lab."

"Nice to meet you, Abbey," AJ said as he turned to follow Briggs to the elevator.

"Likewise," Abbey replied with a grin. "Gadget Girl, out."

•　　•　　•

"HERE WE ARE," Briggs said, motioning to a dark room with a partially closed door. A shining new nameplate was attached to the wall next to the door frame and etched into its surface were the words: AJ ARCHER — RS:BIO.

AJ shot Briggs a quizzical look. "I was expecting to be working in a lab."

"That's right. You will be. *This* is your lab," Briggs said. "Go on. Take a look inside."

AJ hesitantly pushed the door open and stepped across the threshold. The lights in the room brightened automatically upon entry. The windowless workspace was semicircular, with an expansive brushed stainless steel desk that graced the full curvature of the facing wall. Three black leather task chairs were parked underneath the overhang of the desk. Rich, brightly colored computer images suddenly illuminated on the wall panels in front of him. The images appeared as if they were projected, but he saw no projector in the room. Upon closer inspection, he found no LCD monitors, no plasma screens, no seams or bezels—the light simply emanated from the wall, in tidy 16:9 aspect ratio windows.

"OLED fabric wall covering. Infinitely configurable. Multitactile, pressure sensitive. Pretty cool, huh?" Briggs remarked.

AJ dragged his fingertips along one of the images, lightly caressing the surface. The window shifted, repositioning with his touch.

"Cool," he mumbled and then turned his attention to the desk. Neatly positioned before two of the task chairs were wireless keyboards and wireless trackball mice. In front of the third chair rested a sleek notebook computer, screen open. "Do these control the screens on the wall?"

"Yes. And the notebook computer is yours to keep. It's linked to our cloud servers so you can always access all of your files, whether you're in or out of the office."

"Nice." Then his giddy schoolboy grin slowly morphed into a bewildered stare. "This is a cool command center, but it's not a lab. There's no stuff here. No microscopy, no analyzers, no batch bioreactors, no centrifuges or microbial storage . . . nothing, but a very shiny desk."

Briggs laughed loudly. "Archer, you're in the big leagues now. We're not hiring you to stain microscope slides; we're hiring you to direct, analyze, and interpret lab work performed by others." Briggs pressed the "0" button on his mobile phone.

"C. Remy. How may I help you, Mr. Briggs?" a woman's voice resonated from hidden speakers in the ceiling. Her tone was placid and calming.

"Coordinator, I'm here with our new hire, Mr. Archer, in Bio Lab One. Can you please bring Bethesda online so Archer can see his laboratory," Briggs instructed.

"Yes, Mr. Briggs. Bethesda biolab coming online now," C. Remy said.

As fluidly as the nightly news transitions from the anchor desk to a remote camera on location, the screens on the wall switched to camera views inside a bustling microbiology laboratory. A young, handsome Asian man entered the camera frame labeled "Bethesda" and took a seat in front of what AJ surmised was a webcam.

"Bethesda, online."

"Dr. Kim, say hello to AJ Archer, our new RS:Bio. Archer has been doing some intriguing work at BU under McNamara. We expect he'll be subcontracting a sizable chunk of your laboratory capacity in the coming months. We expect great things from him."

"Excellent to have you aboard, Mr. Archer. I read your thesis last night after I heard the news you'd been hired. Intriguing work you've been doing. When you're ready, we'll make the resources available for whatever you need," Kim replied.

"How did you," AJ started to ask Kim, but then turned to Briggs instead. "How did he get my thesis? It hasn't been released for publication."

Briggs ignored him. "Very good, very good."

"I can support an STO this morning if you like," Kim said.

"Thank you, but we don't have time for that today. Besides, Archer is a quick study . . . and I know you'll set him straight when he screws up."

Kim chuckled politely and signed off.

"Will that be all, Mr. Briggs?" the voice from the ceiling asked.

"Question: Have Archer's phone and ID card been activated?"

"Yes, sir."

"Very well. Then that is all, Coordinator," Briggs stated. His hand disappeared into his pocket and then reappeared holding a mobile phone. He tossed it to AJ. "Here you go, the only phone you'll ever need again."

AJ turned the sleek mobile phone over in his hands. "Is this Abbey's handiwork too?"

"Of course."

"Want to give me the rundown?"

"Sure. Think of that phone as your own personal command center. GPS, video camera, wireless ready—on all bands and protocols. Multitactile touch interface. For hands-free operation, there's a wireless earbud. It pops out of the left side, here at the bottom. It fits down in the ear canal, completely hidden so you don't look like some government spook with a curly wire hanging down your neck. It is a little tough to fish out at the end of the day, so use the magnet on the tip of your stylus. You already saw the dentist for your mike, which is voice activated, so you don't have to mess with that. The unit is designed so that you can leave it in your pocket, or in your bag. Just jiggle the phone and the voice command software will sound a tone in your earbud indicating the phone is ready. If you need a Coordinator, just press the '0' button. Coordinators are always available to assist you, twenty-four seven, but don't abuse it. The first Resource I hear tasking a Coordinator to order him pizza is going to have his butt kicked by me personally. Got it?"

AJ smiled and nodded, then looked at the floor.

"What? Is there a problem, Archer?"

AJ raised his head. He took a moment to look around, taking in the scenery of the command center that Briggs called his lab. He then threw his hands up. "The *problem*," he said, trying to sound calm, "is that I still don't have the first clue what is going on here." He jerked his thumb back at the curved multimedia wall. "What's with all this? And recording my every word? Why is everything here so strange? You still haven't told me what this company actually does, nor have you told me what my assignment is."

Briggs nodded. "All perfectly fair questions," he said, as if trying to calm an upset child. "You'll have your answers, trust me." He glanced at his watch. "But right now, we have a meeting to go to. There is someone waiting who would like to meet you."

Chapter Eight

Prague, Czech Republic

"WILLIAM FOSTER?"

Will flinched, but did not acknowledge the call from the man in the gray trench coat approaching him. He casually logged off the computer, stood up from his chair, and began to walk away. He hoped that logging off would be enough to conceal Julie's identity, but when it came to anonymity and computers, he had his doubts.

A hand came down on his left shoulder from behind, stopping his progress toward the exit.

"Thank God we found you. You've had us all very worried. You're quite ill, Mr. Foster. Come with me sir, we need to get you back to the hospital . . . for treatment."

Using his best college German, Will feigned incomprehension. *"Ich heiße Hendrick Wrobel. Entschuldigen Sie mich, bitte."*

"Ach, sehe ich. Moment mal. Erzählen Sie mich dann, Herr Wrobel, von welchem Staat sind Sie," the man in the gray trench coat replied.

Will turned. So much for that idea, he thought. "Fuck off, I'm not going anywhere with you."

The smirk on the German man's face transformed into a scowl. His sinewy fingers tightened, crumpling Will's barn jacket inside his clenched fist.

Will's thighs began to tremble.

"Mr. Foster, please don't make this difficult, after all, you're not well and we wouldn't want to have to call an ambulance for you," said the man, giving Will a shake.

Will looked down and checked the other man's stance. A voice inside his head reminded him that there's no such thing as fighting dirty when you're fighting for your life. He steeled himself and then drove his knee squarely into the other man's groin. The bounty hunter's eyes bulged, and he barked a hoarse, unintelligible expletive. Then, like a condemned building collapsing after the crash of the wrecking ball, Raimond Zurn fell to his knees.

Will stepped out onto the street, trying to breathe. Trying to think. He turned left instinctively, back toward the direction of Wenceslas Square, and he ran. He kept his eyes forward, scanning faces in the crowd. It was unlikely the man in the gray trench coat was working alone. He tried to resist the urge to check for a trail, but fear overpowered. He looked over his shoulder and traded glances with a hulk of a man in a black motorcycle jacket moving toward the entrance of the cybercafé.

Commotion erupted behind him, as the brute in the motorcycle jacket launched into pursuit. Will kicked up his speed into a full sprint. The street was a sea of pedestrians, forcing him to dodge and swivel as he ran, impeding his forward progress. He glanced over his shoulder; his lead was dwindling. He was not surprised. Foster men were like draft horses, built for power, not for speed. It was inevitable. He would have to turn and fight.

As he entered Wenceslas Square, he heard heavy, pounding footsteps behind him. Allowing himself to be tackled would be a disastrous mistake. It was time to make the switch from defense to offense. He took two braking strides, spun one hundred and eighty degrees, and assumed a wrestler's ready pose—knees bent, feet wide, arms up and poised for grappling.

The look of surprise on his pursuer's face affirmed his tactical instincts. Instead of making the takedown, his foe was forced to dodge right, narrowly skirting Will's grasp. Unlike the guy he had faced in the Internet café, this assailant was a monster. With a tree trunk neck, shaved head, and massive shoulders, he looked like a cage warrior from the Ultimate Fighting Championship. Will frowned as the other man slowed his forward momentum by running a tight arc around him and then, with surprising agility, whirled to face him.

UDO ZURN LOOKED into the American's eyes and saw exactly what he wanted. Fear. He did not need a weapon to win this fight. He could pound the American into a useless, bloody pulp and toss him into a garbage Dumpster without breaking a sweat. Unfortunately, his brother Raimond had been firm and explicit—their employer's orders were to deliver the American alive and unharmed. Where was the sport in that? He grimaced in annoyance and reached inside the flap of his unzipped motorcycle jacket. His fingers found the contoured plastic grip and closed around it.

The spectators, who had already begun to aggregate, uttered a collective gasp as he pulled out his weapon of obligation. Since he was not above showmanship, he squeezed the trigger and let the crackling, purple arc of current announce to the crowd that he clutched not a pistol, but a stun gun. One zap and the fight would be over. One million volts of electricity would transform the American into a limp, helpless pile of flesh and bone on the pavement.

Udo smirked and in heavily accented English said, "When you think of this day, remember that Udo, not God, gave you this pain."

As the word "pain" rolled off his tongue, he lunged at Will Foster's chest.

IF NOT FOR the eight years of high school and college wrestling practice, Will would have been down for the count. Instead, his reflexes took over, twisting his body clear of the crackling electrodes. The smell of charred fibers on his coat sleeve wafted through the air, lingering evidence of the near miss.

He circled, trying to maintain six feet of separation from his long-armed foe. In a position of weakness, the key was to keep moving. Dart and feint. Keep your opponent off-balance and guessing. To gain the upper hand, he would need to grapple, but a traditional takedown would be risky. Even if he were successful at grabbing the German's legs and upending him, his own back would be exposed and vulnerable during the takedown. His only chance was to wait for his adversary to make a mistake. Then, and only then, could he grapple.

An unbroken chain of onlookers now encircled them, hesitantly enjoying the unusual spectacle. After a minute of circling, Udo made a second lunge at him, followed by a third, then a fourth, and then a fifth—each time shocking nothing but air as Will darted about like a hummingbird. Udo's face twisted in frustration, and with a throaty growl, he charged. Will rotated his torso parallel to the vector of attack. As the German sailed past, he pounced, like a lion clawing the flank of a stampeding cape buffalo. The two bodies crashed to the ground as one, with Udo absorbing the brunt of the impact. Will wrapped his left arm around the big man's neck from behind, fashioning a headlock. In his peripheral vision, he noted that Udo was still clutching the stun gun in his outstretched right hand, so he grabbed Udo's wrist. Udo tried to roll over and free his left arm, which was now pinned beneath his chest, but Will's legs were extended outward in a wide inverted "V," giving him just enough leverage to exert control. The stun gun arced and sparked as Will dragged Udo's hand across the pavement. Rough as sandpaper, the textured concrete tore the skin from the big German's knuckles. As soon as he felt the tendons in Udo's wrist slack, he smashed the hand on the pavement. The tactic worked, and the taser popped loose and skidded across the ground. Udo jerked violently to reach it, dragging Will with him. Still maintaining his headlock, Will crabbed his lower body to the right, giving him a better angle to reach the stun gun with his right hand. Both men's fingers pawed at the plastic handle, but Will found a grip first. He tightened his headlock and then arched his back to lift his foe's chest off the ground, exposing a target. Then, he slammed the shiny protruding silver electrodes into the brute's sternum and squeezed the trigger.

Udo's body seized violently, went rigid, and then fell limp.

Will released his headlock, lifted himself off the big man, and rose up onto one knee. Udo blinked and shook his head, trying to snap himself out of the fog of pain and disorientation. After a second's pause, Udo cursed and tried to stand, desperately wanting to get back into the fight.

Will zapped him in the back of the neck, this time depressing the trigger for a full five seconds. Gasps, cheers, and even laughter erupted from the crowd around them, as a dark, wet stain spread across the groin of the bounty hunter's blue jeans. Will ignored the commotion. He had to stay focused. He studied his fallen foe for a moment just to be sure. Udo was out; it was over. He stuffed the stun gun in his coat pocket, turned, and then plowed through the wall of spectators caging him in.

He had no idea where he was running, but it didn't matter. He needed to put distance and bodies between himself and Wenceslas Square. Law enforcement officers were no doubt already en route to the site of the scuffle; surely cell phone calls had been made. Dodging tourists and window-shoppers right and left, he barreled through the streets of Old Town Prague. He yanked the wool cap from his head, pulled the maroon scarf off of his neck, and shoved them into his bulky jacket pockets as he ran. Running was necessary, but it also attracted attention. He needed somewhere safe to bide time until two o'clock when he would meet Julie at the Orloj. His first thought was to hide in an alley, but that was too obvious. He needed somewhere public but private, if there was such a thing. His mind raced, generating options and then quickly rejecting them. He came to an intersection and turned right on instinct. After rounding in the corner, he slowed to a walk.

He needed to change his appearance. His barn jacket had a weathered tan canvas exterior and a plaid flannel inner liner. Technically, it was not reversible, but he was improvising. He shrugged the coat off, pulled both coat sleeves inside out, and then slipped it back on. When he was in college and needed a quiet place to study where nobody could find him, he would hole up in the campus library. A library. That was the perfect place to hide. He could get lost in rows and rows of books. Besides, thugs and books have a natural aversion to each other.

It took him only two attempts—stopping and soliciting helpful-looking pedestrians—to obtain directions to the "big library." Ten minutes later, he was standing outside the grand Klementinum complex, which appeared to span two full city blocks. The ornate Baroque facade was crafted using decorative columns and alternating panels of contrasting beige and brown plaster. As he approached the entrance, he noticed an armed security guard walking a leisurely perimeter patrol. Inside his pocket, he fingered the stun gun nervously. In a post-9/11 world, metal detectors at museums and national landmarks were commonplace. He couldn't risk it. He waited until the guard was facing the opposite direction and dropped the stun gun into a trash receptacle.

Once inside, he approached a directory and considered three landmark attractions: the Mirror Chapel, the Astronomical Tower, and the Baroque Library Hall, which housed the National Library of the Czech Republic. He turned toward the National Library and followed the signs to the Baroque Hall.

After purchasing a single day pass for access to all the library reading rooms, he walked through the Baroque Library Hall. He marveled at the opulent marble works, dramatic frescoes painted by Jan Hiebl, and tiers and tiers of leather bound books. After exploring, he settled into a routine, splitting his time between the Reference Centre, the Main Hall, and comfortable chairs in the various reading rooms. He stayed in the library until closing time at ten o'clock. With his hands in his pockets, he smiled at the front desk attendant and strolled back out into the world.

It had rained while he was in the library and the wet cobblestones of the street glistened in the moonlight. He surveyed the immediate landscape, trying to decide which way to walk, when he spied a bald man wearing a leather coat. Panic erupted inside him. The man's back was turned, and he was standing alone, in the middle of the tiny parking lot at the entrance to the Klementinum. The fact that he had not seen Will's exit was a miracle. Will resisted the urge to sprint; instead, he turned and walked briskly away in the opposite direction. The sound of tires driving on cobblestones sent a shot of adrenaline into his bloodstream. Shit. Will glanced back over his shoulder expecting to see the two thugs in pursuit, but instead he saw the bald man embrace a blonde woman and get into the passenger seat of her BMW 135i. As the couple sped away, Will took several deep breaths, collected himself, and then set off walking.

He decided he would spend the remaining time hiding in a local pub. He wanted somewhere lively, crowded, and packed with tourists. Somewhere he could get lost in the herd and maybe even talk a happy drunk into swapping jackets. After ducking his head in several pubs, he finally found the perfect spot. Were he not running for his life, he would have happily capped off every night in Prague at a place like this. He milled about the bar until he saw a corner table open up. He slid into the booth from the right side at the same time a woman slid in from the left. They bumped hips, locked eyes, and burst into laughter. She was at least fifteen years his senior, hailed from Dublin, and was on vacation with her husband who was standing in line at the bar. He chatted happily with the couple, sharing the booth for the better part of two hours. While they entertained him with stories of their travels, he sipped on a glass of dark ale. It had been over five months since he'd had a beer, and every swallow was a sumptuous kiss to his palate. However, his body was so unaccustomed to alcohol that halfway through his first pint, Will was already buzzing. He resisted the temptation to order another; it was imperative he keep his wits about him. Eventually, the Irish couple excused themselves, and he was left alone.

His thoughts drifted to Julie. He imagined how the reunion might happen. Would she recognize him? Had the years been kind to her; was she still beautiful? What would it feel like to hug her? Would she let him embrace her? What would she think of him—drawn and unkempt as he was. Unexpectedly, he felt nervous as a wealth of memories and feelings he had suppressed for years came rushing over him.

The rowdy crowd in the tavern mellowed and thinned as the night wore on. During his time at the library, Will had printed Google maps depicting the streets between the Klementinum and the Astronomical Clock. The tavern was conveniently located only a few blocks from the Orloj, so he decided to stay put until the hands on the clock above the bar showed ten minutes until two o'clock. When it was finally time to go, Will paid his tab, stuffed his hands in his pockets, and set off to meet Julie. Within minutes, he was standing in front of Old Town Prague's most famous landmark.

The Astronomical Clock of Prague, or Orloj, features two vertically stacked and richly appointed dials—each colored predominantly in shades of blue with intricate gold detailing. It was crafted and installed in 1410 by the combined talents of a clockmaker and mathematician. Even to the untrained eye, it is obvious that the Orloj is much more than a traditional clock. The upper dial, in addition to keeping the local time, also displays the times for sunrise and sunset, ancient Czech time, and the celestial movements of the sun, moon, and zodiac constellations. The lower dial is a calendar with elaborate inset paintings representing each of the twelve months.

A cast of colorful wooden puppets comes alive every hour animating the clock's exterior: Vanity—forever admiring himself in a mirror; The Miser—shaking his bag of gold; Death—with his signaling bell; and the Turk—with his flute. Even more renowned than the four animated figures is the Walk of the Apostles. Each hand-carved wooden apostle is as large as a man, dons a halo, and carries a unique symbol in hand. Every hour, on the hour, the twelve apostles parade in succession through two wooden doors that open above the upper clock dial—six apostles walking from the right, six from the left.

It took Will a moment of study before he could decipher the complicated clock dial. Eventually he ascertained the time: 1:57 AM. He looked from side to side, scanning the area for a five-foot-five, hardly inconspicuous blonde. Not finding her, he wandered over toward a darkened restaurant, Café Milena, which was directly opposite the Orloj. He took a seat at one of the many empty chairs left outside by the evening manager.

It was amazing. Even at the late hour, people still congregated, waiting to watch the Walk of the Apostles. So he sat, watching them watch the clock. After a few minutes of sitting, legs extended and comfortably crossed at the ankle, he began to relax.

It wouldn't be long now, he mused.

His eyelids suddenly felt heavy.

She should arrive any second.

His head began to bob.

He couldn't wait to see her.

And as the Orloj struck two, and the apostles began to march, he fell asleep.

Chapter Nine

New Brunswick, New Jersey

"YES, MS. MORLEY, I did exactly as you instructed, but Mr. Zurn says that terminating his services is not an option. He says he wants to speak with you directly," Meredith's executive assistant Cynthia reported nervously.

"First of all, there is no 'me' to speak to. He is just trying to manipulate you. Second, the terms of Mr. Zurn's employment are not his decision to make. He and his brother failed miserably and now they're fired. It's that simple. Thank him for his efforts, tell him he may keep the first installment as severance, and reiterate that we no longer require his assistance. After you've hung up, terminate the VoIP account so he can longer contact us. And just to be safe, reformat the hard drive on the notebook computer you've been using," Meredith said.

"Umm, Ms. Morley, he didn't call the VoIP number. He called the office directly. Mr. Zurn is holding on line one and he asked to speak to you by name."

Meredith shifted her gaze to the Polycom phone on her desk. Her heartbeat quickened, falling into cadence with the rapidly blinking red LED light next to the line one button. Were she not battle-hardened, she would have gasped. Instead, she flashed Cynthia a glib smile and picked up the handset.

"Mr. Zurn, it seems your dossier needs to be updated. I had no idea you possessed such IT prowess."

Brian Andrews

"No, no. I can't take credit for this. Hacking is a form of art, and an artist I'm not. But the true measure of a man's utility is not *what* he knows, but *who* he knows," Raimond Zurn bantered.

"If you have such a vast talent pool to recruit from, then please explain to me how a man who is practically on his death bed, with no clothes, no money, and no resources not only outwits you, but also out-muscles you?"

"The intelligence you provided me with was wrong. He has clothes, and money. And he is far from on his deathbed. Foster is not a man to be underestimated. Your misrepresentation of the target's capabilities is to blame for the failure in our first encounter."

"Excuses are for amateurs. I hired you because of your reputation for discretion and efficiency. A wrestling match in the middle of Old Town Prague is hardly what I had in mind. Let's cut through the bullshit, shall we? You had your chance, and you blew it. Your services are no longer required, Mr. Zurn."

"Be careful not to confuse your world, with its lawyers and paper contracts, with mine. Our agreement was made in the underworld— think of it as a blood pact. You hired me, but you can't fire me. I never agreed to any time limit. Bounty hunting is not child's play; it is not paint by numbers. You *will* get your prize back, and you *will* pay the negotiated fee . . . in its entirety."

Meredith swallowed, trying to maintain her composure. Zurn was willful, motivated, and nefarious. By circumventing her firewalls and piercing her veil of anonymity, he also demonstrated more prowess than she had given him credit for. She suspected that her personal safety would be at risk if she crossed him. Best to keep the viper's fangs pointed at somebody else. She cleared her throat.

"Everybody deserves a second chance, I suppose. What do you intend to do now?"

"I need to broaden the search radius. Europe is not like it used to be. Foster will be able to travel easily between countries if he stays inside the European Union. Once he is on the move, I may have to hire additional resources, and that means more money."

"Under no circumstance can he leave the Czech Republic. With every passing hour, with each mile of ground he covers, the probability of locating him plummets. Your failure left me no choice but to make the Czech government aware of certain details of the situation. Official efforts are underway to locate and quarantine Foster. The Czech national police and INTERPOL are now involved. Border checkpoints are being set up on all the major roads. If he tries to board a train or airplane out of the country, he'll be detained," she said.

"This complicates things considerably," the bounty hunter said. "What if the Czechs apprehend Foster before I do?"

"Then you'll need to orchestrate a kidnapping and take him back."

"If he is placed in military quarantine, that will be impossible."

"You're the one who refuses to quit. So I suppose that makes it your problem."

"No, Ms. Morley, it's yours. We tried playing by your rules and things didn't work out. From this point forward, we do business my way, using my methods."

She felt a knot form in her stomach. Who the hell did Zurn think he was, dictating terms to her? He was working for her, not the other way around. "You listen to me—I want Foster alive and unharmed. That is nonnegotiable."

"Maybe you didn't hear me. The arrangement has changed. You'll take Foster in whatever condition we deliver him. He'll be alive, but that's the only promise I'll make," Zurn snarled. "By the way, if you get any ideas about withholding payments or trying to cross me, well, let's just say your dirty little secret will no longer be a secret. When the journalists at the BBC and CNN hear about this, they'll jump at the chance to help. Just think, with the power of broadcast media, and an army of concerned European citizens helping, your precious Foster will be located in no time. Maybe you'll even be interviewed on television."

Her blood boiled. She loathed negotiating from a position of weakness; it was like jousting with a broken lance. Desperation begets weakness, and she had grown desperate.

"You are a persuasive man when you want to be, Zurn. When you find Foster, maybe you can try putting your persuasive powers to the test before clubbing him over the head. I think the end result would be better for all parties."

"*Nicht.* Clubbing is much easier. Plus, none of the annoying American empty threats to listen to. Oh, and one more thing, from now on I deal directly with you. No more intermediaries."

She resisted the urge to slam the phone down on the receiver. In hindsight, hiring the Zurn brothers was a terrible mistake. Partnering with unsavory actors of the underworld was a tricky business. In the devil's bargain, the negotiated price is never the final price, and the final price is always more than you're willing to pay. To level the playing field she needed divine intervention.

She checked her watch: 1:07 PM. A little early for scotch, but damn it, she needed a drink.

She walked over to the maple wood credenza opposite her desk, picked up a Baccarat rocks glass, and filled it one quarter full. Neat. Nicolora was a connoisseur of fine scotch, and it was he who she credited, and blamed, for indoctrinating her into this very expensive habit. She took a mouthful of the amber liquid; she let it linger on her tongue and wash over her palette before swallowing. The initial astringent bite of alcohol quickly subsided, giving way to fragrant waves of smoke, earth, and oak. She closed her eyes and exhaled.

She set the glass down and turned to leave.

It was time to pull the trigger.

Chapter Ten

Boston, Massachusetts

AJ FOLLOWED BRIGGS from his new lab, up a flight of stairs, and through a hallway until they reached a pair of floor-to-ceiling double doors. The doors were crafted from solid mahogany, and fitted with polished brass handles and hinges. Briggs placed his thumb on a steel plate next to one of the hinges; a green light flashed, and he pulled the rightmost door open.

Seated at the end of a long mahogany table was a man AJ knew could be none other than Robért Nicolora himself. The man was dressed in a dark, perfectly tailored suit. His hair was onyx, brushed with silver at the temples, and meticulously trimmed. His hands were folded, resting comfortably on the edge of the table. Like fictional characters brought to life, to his left sat the oaf in the Red Sox cap from the Public Garden. To his right, the siren in the flowing silk blouse. AJ blinked twice, doubting himself.

"Welcome, AJ, to the Founder's Forum," Nicolora said. "More importantly, welcome to The Think Tank."

AJ wanted to answer; he should have answered. Instead he stood, stupefied by the scene in front of him. First, the bizarre recruitment by Briggs at BU. Now, a charade in the Public Garden revealed to him. Who were these people?

Briggs coughed politely. "AJ, this is Robért Nicolora," Briggs said, nodding in the direction of the man seated at the head of the table.

"He is one of the founders of this organization, and he is also the Principal Director."

AJ took a breath and this time forced words from his mouth.

"Nice to meet you, Mr. Nicolora," he managed.

Nicolora smiled, amused. He then gestured to the man in the baseball hat, who produced AJ's wallet from the pocket of his jacket and set it on the polished table. Nicolora picked up the leather billfold, and studied it a moment. "This belongs to you, I believe," he said and then slid the wallet across the table to AJ.

AJ caught the wallet, tipped it in the air toward Nicolora in acknowledgment, and then sheepishly slipped it into his back pants pocket. It had been over an hour since he had been pick-pocketed in the Public Garden, and he hadn't even noticed his wallet missing. He glanced at Briggs with both hope and doubt in his eyes, but Briggs' face offered no safe harbor. He turned again to Nicolora. "Does this mean that I failed some sort of test?"

Stifled laughter filled the room. AJ's face flamed red.

"No, certainly not. That was just Kalen's way of saying hello." Nicolora's voice was soft, reassuring. "Kalen is an RS:Physical. And to my right is Albane Mesnil. Albane is an RS:Social. She will take over orientation duties for Briggs, now that the recruitment process is complete."

"Nice to meet both of you, officially," AJ said, and then added, "since I suppose the Public Garden doesn't really count."

His response earned him a grin from Kalen, but only a mute stare from Albane.

He looked back at Nicolora. "Can I ask you a question?"

"Of course, but first, take a seat. This is not an oral exam, AJ."

He slid into an open chair next to Briggs. "What do those titles mean? RS:Physical and RS:Social?"

"RS:Physical is our shorthand for a Physical Resource. Think of Kalen as a Navy SEAL, an illusionist, and a professional stuntman all rolled into one. RS:Social means Social Resource. What RS:Physicals do with their bodies, RS:Socials do with their minds. Albane is equal parts psychologist, linguist, actress, and human polygraph machine. In addition to Socials and Physicals, we have many other resources in the Tank: Coordinators, Legals, Medicals, Technicals, Chemicals, and the list goes on."

"Oh, then if that's the case, what am I? I mean, what Resource am I?"

Nicolora turned to Briggs.

"Jack, you've kept our young hire in the dark, I see. Like a mushroom," he admonished playfully, and then turned back to AJ. "You are our newest RS:Bio, or Microbiology Resource. Of course, our expectations for you go way beyond the confines of microbiology."

"What do you mean?"

"You think of yourself as a graduate student in a lab coat. Maybe even as a budding scientist. We don't. Your achievements, your interests, and your natural skills are all elements of a picture you've painted in your mind—a mental self-portrait that your psyche has become quite comfortable with. The frame of that picture is a boundary. Subconsciously, it limits you. You don't look outside the frame, because that's just wall space, and the picture inside the frame is what is interesting to you. We don't have these constraints. We're going to extract the canvas from the frame, and we're going to stretch it. We're going to expose the edges, and start painting there too. If you let that happen, you may surprise yourself. Your self-portrait will change, become more vibrant, and more interesting. The boundaries you've set for yourself in your mind will suddenly be visible; they will become lines that you desire to cross."

"What if I don't change, or can't change like you want me to?"

"Change is inevitable, AJ. To fight it is like carrying buckets of water back up a waterfall."

"What, then, do you expect from me?"

"Nothing more than what you should expect from yourself. Nothing more than what we expect from every person employed in this organization. The Tank is a meritocracy. Put another way, we offer no tenure here. It is not academia. The more capable you prove yourself to be, the more responsibility and opportunity you will be given. The more meaningful your contribution to the team, the more meaningful your compensation will become. The day you stop making a meaningful contribution is the day you will find this facility closed to you."

AJ nodded and tried to take it all in stride. Nicolora's speech sounded more like a threat than a "welcome to the team" pep talk.

"Since you mention the facility," AJ said, glancing behind him, "the front door of this building says The Nicolora Foundation, but you referred to this place as The Think Tank." He looked around the room, inviting anyone to answer. "I had the impression from the local media that the Nicolora Foundation was a nonprofit trying to solve world hunger and stuff like that. From what I've seen today, it seems more like a covert office of the CIA. Am I being recruited by the CIA?"

"No. This is not the CIA. The intricacies of our organization will be made clear to you later," Briggs said.

AJ did not want to look the fool again, but he was equally afraid this might be his only opportunity for straight talk with the Principal Director for a very long time.

"To be frank, sir, today has not been anything like what I expected. I assumed that I was being recruited for a biotech firm involved in hush-hush government contracts, but that does not appear to be the case. If you could humor me for a moment and tell me exactly what this company does, it would go a long way in calming my nerves."

Nicolora laughed. "It's very simple—we solve problems that others cannot. Every Think Tank employee is a specialized, highly trained expert in his or her field. Unlike most companies, where experts are tasked to work with like-minded individuals on a single project for months or even years, we operate differently. We have adopted a model where the 'best-of-the-best' are combined into cross-functional teams that exist only until the assignment is complete. When a job is done, the experts are reshuffled into new teams and assigned to different problems. Resources are maximized. Great minds are kept fresh."

"I thought the Nicolora Foundation was a not-for-profit organization full of PhDs and social scientists working to solve the world's social and environmental problems?"

"It is, and we are," said Nicolora. "You are free to take a tour of the Foundation at anytime. The people working on Level 2 do commendable work. I would stack my Foundation up against the RAND Corporation or the Cato Institute any day of the week. But you weren't recruited to work for the Foundation."

"Okay, then who do I work for?"

"You work for me."

AJ was tempted to speak, but held his tongue. The whole cloak-and-dagger routine was clearly a charade that everyone he'd met thus far seemed hell bent on playing. He felt like a kindergartner in a game of keep-away on the playground, except he was the poor oaf chasing a ball he would never be permitted to catch. It was pointless.

"I didn't answer your question, did I?"

"With all due respect, no sir, you didn't," AJ replied. "Why all the secrecy? Why the James Bond gadget lab in the basement? Why run a business that you conceal from the world? This place seems more like a covert branch of the government than a think tank."

Nicolora clasped his hands together. He inhaled and stared at AJ with narrowed eyes. Then, he began.

"Throughout recorded history there have been many great leaders. Kings and queens, prophets and saints, chiefs and generals, presidents and prime ministers. Some leaders are benevolent, others not. Some are motivated by power, some by greed, some by doctrine, and others by righteousness. Some are celebrated, and many are despised. Regardless of the unique mark they leave on history, all leaders have one thing in common. They do not lead alone. Behind every leader stands a cast of advisors and confidants whose influence and counsel quietly shapes the world. These men and women are the unsung heroes of legend and lore, and these men and women are we."

AJ pondered the power of Nicolora's words.

"You see AJ, the notion of a think tank is nothing new. Think tanks have existed as long as governance itself. Oh, maybe not in name, but certainly in practice. What chief had not a council, what king no court, what president no cabinet? Through the millennia, we have been called mystics, wise men, advisors, mentors, counselors, and even apostles—whatever the name, our charter has remained unchanged: to provide information, options, and guidance to those who make the decisions that shape the lives of men. It is a daunting task. It is a duty that should fall only on the most worthy and capable of minds."

"Still, why operate in secrecy?"

"Many reasons, but I'll give you the top three. Because our services are primarily solicited by entities who demand secrecy. Because our embedded resources' effectiveness is directly proportional to their anonymity. And most importantly, because our operation would be viewed as a terrible threat by some who maintain positions of power in government and industry."

"And the field agents?"

"AJ. Don't disappoint me by asking questions you should already know the answer to," Nicolora chastised. "Why do you think we have resources trained to operate in the field?"

Nicolora was right; he knew the answer to his question. He had known it his entire life.

"Because if you want something done right, then you'd best do it yourself?"

"Exactly. In the beginning, we naively believed our charter was to provide a place where our clients could come for answers—solutions which they would go on to implement independently. We learned quickly that our clients not only have trouble problem solving, but they are equally dreadful at executing. Hence, our field resources were born."

"Is The Think Tank tied to the US government?"

"Around here, AJ, we just call it The Tank," Nicolora corrected.

A chime sounded from the ceiling, interrupting the conversation. Nicolora looked up.

"Yes?"

A smooth, ethereal voice answered. "Mr. Nicolora, you have a priority call waiting."

"Who is it, Coordinator? I'm in a meeting."

"It's Ms. Morley from Vyrogen Pharmaceuticals, Sir."

Nicolora's face hardened. "If you all would please excuse your-selves. I need to take this call. AJ, I'm sorry but I need to cut our Q & A short. Albane can handle any other questions during your orientation today."

"Yes, Sir, thank you," AJ replied.

"One more thing . . ."

"Sir?"

"Welcome to The Tank." Nicolora smiled and then shot Briggs a knowing glance.

AJ nodded respectfully, stood up from his chair, and followed the others out of the room. Nicolora waited until the doors had shut and then pressed the flashing green Line 1 button on the confer-ence room table phone.

"Hello, Meredith. What time should I send the plane?"

Chapter Eleven

Boston, Massachusetts

H ER BEAUTY WAS gravity. Raven hair, milky smooth skin, full lips and a diva's curves. Pulling his gaze from her took a physical effort. More than once she had admonished him with her eyes for his adolescent impropriety, but AJ could not help himself. He had never encountered a woman like Albane Mesnil before.

She was an enigma. He had spent the entire day with her and still knew nothing about her. Unlike most people, Albane's favorite subject was *not* herself. In fact, she'd shrewdly coaxed him into talking volumes about "AJ" while defusing his attempts to learn reciprocal information about her. Still, it hadn't stopped him from trying.

From outward appearance alone, it was impossible to guess her age, and he dare not ask. He imagined Albane could pass for a college girl of twenty-one just as easily as she could a business woman of thirty-five. She simply had one of those remarkable faces. Her demeanor betrayed what her skin belied. Poise and confidence like hers came only from years of experience. Albane was seasoned, of that much AJ was certain.

AJ was not alone in the category of those left to wonder about Albane and her shrouded past. Her private life was a carefully guarded secret she kept locked away. In the entire organization, only Nicolora knew something of her life before the Tank. He had taken a chance on Albane, and since her hire, she had yet to disappoint him. Occasionally she would say or do something to pique his curiosity, tempting him to lift a stone he knew better than to look under, but he always resisted.

The irony of it all was that Albane had nothing—at least as measured by modern tabloid standards—worthy of hiding. She was born in Paris, the only child of a doctor and a pastry chef. She attended an all girls' school during her early years, which she loathed, and then later was accepted into the Sorbonne where she concentrated her study in language. When she was twenty-six, she moved to New York City and attended Columbia University to earn her MA in psychology.

As a child, Albane exhibited an unnatural proclivity for language, excelling in English at a level three years ahead of her peers, and learning Latin from her father and his collection of medical texts. She loved her father, and he returned her love unconditionally. Nine days after Albane's fourteenth birthday, François Mesnil was mugged on the way home from the hospital and bled to death in the middle of the street, alone. For the next five years, Albane retreated into herself.

The impact on her mother was catastrophic. An intense woman, whose self-destructive tendencies were kept in check by the rock-solid presence of Dr. Mesnil, Albane's mother fell into a dark depression after her husband's death. One morning, Albane awoke to a silent and empty apartment. On the second day, she notified the police of her mother's absence. On the third day, she was informed by a solemn man with a gray face and gray overcoat that her mother had committed suicide. The police had found her mother's body floating face down in the Seine, bloated and waterlogged. At sixteen years old, she had to face the Parisian media alone, arrange the funeral, sell her mother's patisserie, and take control of the family finances. All of these things she did, and did alone.

During the happy years, her parents loved to entertain, and threw lavish parties at their flat in the city. Already famous in Paris for her desserts, Noëlle Mesnil's parties drew the crème de la crème of the Parisian elite. But by the end of the night, it was always young Albane, and not Noëlle, who had enchanted the room of intellectuals, socialites, and local politicians. The Mesnils would joke that

Albane was the world's only eight-year-old sophisticate, displaying the grace and wit of a seasoned hostess. When it was her bedtime, Dr. Mesnil would escort Albane up the stairs to her room, where his young daughter would tell him what she thought of every monsieur and madame she had met during the evening, all in exacting and vivid detail. "Her intuition and perceptiveness are uncanny," he would tell his wife as they undressed for bed, "I think she is the best judge of character I've ever met."

During primary school, her teachers observed that young Albane was fearless, cowing to neither challenge nor bully. Even so, she was shy around her classmates and preferred the company of her teachers and adults. Albane had a way of reaching inside adults to find the substance and purpose beneath the facade. From a ten minute interaction, sometimes less, she would know everything she needed to know about a person. Not in a historical sense, but rather in an intuitive way. She could read motives, sense emotional cues, detect intellectual profundity, parse through words and find purpose beneath, all without effort. Moreover, her moral compass was finally tuned, and in a blink of an eye she could accurately sense the character of any adult she met. But when it came to children, her gift failed her. So as a child, she kept to herself.

As a teenager, life hurled more challenges at her. At age fourteen, she experienced an aggressive pubescent growth spurt, her body lengthening six inches in one year. With the arrival of her new, longer arms and legs, came an embarrassing clumsiness that she did not grow out of until she reached university. At a time when blonde bombshells were plastered across the silver screen, Albane became acutely self-conscious of her dense, long black hair and rail thin physique. Even though she had gained twenty pounds with her growth spurt, her hips were still narrow and her bosom flat. While the other girls were dancing with boys, Albane was dancing alone with her self-loathing.

At seventeen, the swan inside her began to emerge. Her body blossomed, and suddenly her height and her raven black hair, qualities that had been a liability at fifteen, now gained her favor with maturing male peers. She quickly recognized the power that her physique gave her over men. Men of all ages stood up and took notice of her wherever she went. At first, it was disconcerting for her, but gradually the bold and captivating confidence she'd once possessed as a young child reemerged. During her university years, she became conscious of her gift for reading people. She was a good listener, a rarity that made people flock to her. Despite pressures to pursue graduate schooling in psychology, Albane yearned to see the world. For all the languages she had learned, she had never left France. She had been prudent and miserly with her parents' small fortune, and she decided that the time had come for her to go on her first adventure. She would explore the world, meet its peoples, and embrace them in their native tongues. And so on her twenty-third birthday, she left Paris, never to return.

• • •

"THIS IS FOR you," Albane said, handing AJ a white business card.

AJ looked at it.

August Jameson Archer
Laboratory Director

Motion Genetics, LLC
"Therapeutic Genetic Solutions for the 21st Century"
ajarcher@motiongenetics.com

"What is this?"

"Your business card . . . in case anybody asks," she replied, and then added, "Remember the CA you signed this morning? We don't talk with anyone outside the firm about the work we do in The Tank. Especially girlfriends."

"It's not a serious relationship; I'd describe it more like friends with benefits."

"No matter," she said, cutting him off. "You get my point."

He recoiled at her curt response, but he didn't argue. "Motion Genetics?" he said, his eyes flicking to the card. "What do we do at Motion Genetics?"

"At Motion Genetics, we develop therapeutic genetic solutions for the twenty-first century," Albane said with the tone and inflection of a television spokeswoman.

"Anything else I should know about the *company*?"

"Motion Genetics is a start-up biotech firm that recently secured second-round venture capital funding. You have been hired as the lab director in charge of early-stage animal testing of a viral delivery mechanism for a promising gene therapy aimed at suppressing debilitating auto-immune diseases."

"How do you do that?"

"Do what?"

"Expound complete bullshit so eloquently off the cuff like that?"

"I'm an RS:Social. That's what we do."

He smirked. "Point taken. Is orientation finished for today?"

"Orientation, yes. Work, no," she said. "We have a three-thirty briefing in the Founder's Forum. And after that, I have a feeling it is going to be a long night."

•   •   •

AJ GLANCED AT his watch, 3:53 PM, and the meeting still had not started.

"What is this briefing about?" AJ asked Albane, swiveling his chair to face her.

"I don't know."

"You have no idea?" he tried again, certain she knew more than she was letting on.

"No, AJ, I don't."

To his left, he heard the man who had tersely introduced himself only as "VanCleave, RS:Technical" snicker under his breath.

To his right sat Kalen Immel, the guy who had pickpocketed him in the Public Garden. After a quick exchange of pleasantries, Kalen quickly became lost in his handheld—furiously thumb-typing emails. Likewise, VanCleave was hard at work coding a simulation on his notebook computer for a client he chose not to divulge. This left only Albane to talk to, and AJ sensed she was beginning to grow weary of his company. He decided to stop trying to make small talk and just wait for something interesting to happen.

Ten minutes passed with only VanCleave's keyboard strokes punctuating the silence. Then AJ heard the magnetic lock click on one of the large double doors at the opposite end of the Founders' Forum. Nicolora walked in first, followed by a striking middle-aged woman with auburn hair.

VanCleave abruptly closed his laptop screen with a slap, drawing stares, while Kalen imperceptibly slid his handheld into his pocket. They all sat up straight in their chairs, except for Albane, who was already sitting tall. Nicolora gestured to an empty seat for his guest and then assumed his usual position at the head of the table, his fingertips touching in a steepled position.

"We'll begin tonight's meeting with introductions. Team, this is Ms. Meredith Morley of Vyrogen Pharmaceuticals. Ms. Morley is Director of Research & Development, and she just flew in from Vyrogen's New Jersey campus," Nicolora began.

"Hello, everyone." Meredith said, nodding.

"On our side we have Mr. Kalen Immel, Mr. AJ Archer, Ms. Albane Mesnil, and Dr. VanCleave," Nicolora said. He turned his body toward Meredith and added, "As is our custom in the Founder's Forum—and since there is no better expert in your problem than you—I will turn the floor over to you, Meredith."

Nicolora handed Meredith a remote control and pressed several buttons on the table—dimming the lights and revealing a massive OLED wall screen hidden behind mahogany paneling. On this cue, she got up from her chair and took station next to the illuminated screen.

"Thank you, Robért. I imagine my standing in front of you is the loudest statement of all, but I am here because I desperately need your help." She pressed a button on the remote, turned toward the screen, and continued. "This is a list of the most virulent and deadly diseases known to man. The top five include smallpox, anthrax, plague, tularemia, and a class of pathogens known as viral hemorrhagic fevers. The viruses and bacteria on this list are naturally occurring pathogens, organisms that have been evolving alongside us, and within us, for millennia. Like all nature's creatures, it is through the process of natural selection that these particular pathogens have risen to the top of the human disease hierarchy. But even within a single disease family, variability exists. For example, if I could somehow magically round up all of the anthrax bacteria in the world and analyze them, I would find some strains which are more virulent than others. Some strains which are more contagious than others. Some strains which are more resistant to antibiotics than others. Some strains which multiply faster than others. Etcetera, etcetera. Combine the genetic advantages of all these strains, and you create an über-strain."

She paused for moment to let the power of her words sink in before continuing.

"What is so frightening about a biological weapon is not that it is made from anthrax bacteria per se, but rather that it is made from über-strains of anthrax refined in a laboratory to be a hundred times more virulent than any naturally occurring strain. Once the process is complete, these über-strains are then cultivated into a stockpile, and paired with an optimized delivery method—like aerosolization—to achieve weaponized status. All together, the process of weaponization ensures that anyone who is exposed to the pathogen becomes mortally infected. You can see the problem here—we've taken natural selection and traded in its walking shoes for a Ferrari. When pathogens are released in such a manner, a person's immune system is quickly and completely overwhelmed. By the time the body has recognized something is wrong, it's already too late; the disease has proliferated inside the body to a population too immense for the immune system to cope with.

"For the past ten years, Vyrogen and its subsidiaries have been working on developing vaccines and treatments for the diseases that can be used to create biological weapons. We are also searching for treatments for other global killers such as malaria, AIDS, ALS, etcetera. You name it, we want to find a way to treat it."

Meredith paused and then changed the slide to a picture of Will Foster. "This man's name is William Foster. A little over forty-eight hours ago, he managed to steal one of the most important products in Vyrogen's drug pipeline—a breakthrough product so earth-shattering that we believe it will change the way medicine approaches disease treatment forever."

"When you say product, are you referring to a therapeutic or a vaccine?" Dr. VanCleave asked.

Meredith's nose crinkled with displeasure, as if someone had just squirted pickle juice in her mouth.

"I'm afraid I'm not at liberty to say. The details of this product are highly confidential. We do not feel that divulging specific details of our product is necessary for you to successfully complete your task. The objective of this case is to find Will Foster and retrieve the Vyrogen property he has stolen before it falls into the hands of unscrupulous entities who will profit at our great expense."

Meredith turned back to face the group at large. "To put it bluntly, Vyrogen is out of our league here. We are scientists, trained to unravel the mysteries of the human body; we are not equipped to deal with industrial espionage."

"Have you consulted with the FBI?" Kalen asked.

"Federal law enforcement participation in this exercise would be problematic for several reasons. Number one, discretion is paramount. The last thing I need is a bunch of bureaucrats leaking the story to the media creating bad press for the company. Number two, time is of the essence. We believe Foster will attempt to turn over the formula to a buyer within the next twenty-four hours. The FBI can't tie its shoes in twenty-four hours. And finally, number three, this entire exercise requires a sophisticated level of damage control. Last time I checked, that was not part of the Bureau's mission statement."

"Fine. Point taken," Kalen replied. "Do you think that Foster was contracted by one of your competitors specifically to steal this breakthrough product?"

"We don't know, but we suspect he has the backing of a highly capable financier—either an entity wanting to obtain our product or an intermediary who will sell it to the highest bidder."

Meredith suddenly felt uneasy. She scanned the faces at the table, locking eyes with Albane. Albane's blank expressionless stare was unnerving. Invasive. She was trying to catch a glimpse inside; Meredith would not permit that to happen. She could already tell that this woman was going to be a problem.

"Meredith, what other information can you share with the team about Foster, the events leading up to the theft, and his possible motives and whereabouts?" asked Nicolora.

"Mr. Foster came to us through one of our subsidiary companies. We believe this was intentional. Think of Foster as a human Trojan Horse. He followed the script right out of Homer's *Iliad* and we never saw it coming."

"I'm not sure I follow you," VanCleave said.

"I'm sorry. I'm getting ahead of myself. Five months ago, Foster signed up as a test subject for our fast-track H1N1—a.k.a swine flu—vaccine trial. Vyrogen was contracted by the US government to fast-track a vaccine for a new H1N1 variant that has been cropping up in the Baltic countries and is associated with severe respiratory symptoms. The normal vaccine development timeline needed to be dramatically reduced. We started our first round of clinical trials about six months ago at one of our subsidiary companies, Leighton-Harris Pharmaceuticals. Foster applied to be a compensated test subject in the Leighton-Harris H1N1 attenuated live virus vaccine trial. This was his first step in infiltrating our organization.

During the trial, we monitored the test subjects' general health and immunological response to the vaccine itself. To our surprise, Foster became ill during the trial period. Testing revealed that he was infected with a mutated strain of H1N1—but a different strain from the one we were targeting with the vaccine. This warranted placing him in quarantine and contacting the Centers for Disease Control and Prevention."

AJ raised his hand, like a schoolboy, turned red and quickly lowered it. Meredith smiled and gestured for him to speak.

"It seems highly improbable to contract a mutated strain from a vaccine. Are you suggesting this was the result of an antigenic shift?"

"An excellent question. Your thinking is in line with our own at the time. Mr. Foster's case took the staff by surprise, because an antigenic shift in an attenuated virus is highly improbable. However, improbable and impossible are not the same thing, and since we weren't sure what we were dealing with, we placed Foster in quarantine and contacted the CDC. As a precaution, of course. We took additional blood samples from Foster to try to ascertain exactly what was happening. It was upon further investigation that we became convinced that the mutant strain of H1N1 that Foster was infected with originated outside of the Leighton-Harris vaccine trial."

"Excuse me, Ms. Morley," Albane interrupted, "but when you began this briefing you named William Foster, in no uncertain terms, as the primary suspect in a case of industrial espionage against Vyrogen. You went on to say—your words now—'think of William Foster as a human Trojan Horse.' It sounds to me that you are suggesting Foster purposely infected himself with a mutated strain of H1N1 so he could infiltrate Vyrogen and steal your research? Why would a man subject himself to such risk?"

Meredith crossed her arms and tucked both her hands under her armpits. "If you would permit me to finish, you can draw your own conclusion." She then unfolded her arms and smiled.

Albane stared at Meredith, but offered no rebuttal.

"As I was saying, we contacted the CDC and they sent a top director-level scientist in infectious diseases, Dr. Xavier Pope, to New Jersey to assist with the case. By the time Pope arrived, Foster's condition had deteriorated. As the CDC is one of our key government clients, Pope had knowledge of a promising and experimental immune-boosting product in our pipeline. He asked me if Foster was a candidate for treatment with this experimental product. At that time, the product had only been tested on non-human primates, so Pope's request caught us off guard. Besides ethical concerns, we faced legal complications. Ultimately, Foster was given the choice. He elected to undergo the experimental treatment. He was transferred to our Chiarek Norse research hospital in Prague to undergo the treatment regime. Unfortunately, Foster developed pneumonia as a complication of his H1N1 infection before we could start the trial. Foster's condition deteriorated so quickly, the decision was made to place him on a ventilator and into a medically induced coma. Obviously, this prompted new concerns about administering an experimental treatment while he was in a drug-induced coma. As we argued internally about what to do, Foster's condition continued to worsen. When all hope was lost for his recovery via conventional means, I made the decision to start the trial. It was a clinical trial of one that ended with resounding success. Our experimental product eradicated both the pneumonia and mutated H1N1 virus from his system. For the past six weeks, he's been recovering and gaining his strength back. We were just about to clear him for discharge when he made his move. He broke into our main storage bank, stole a sample of the product, and then destroyed all of our remaining inventory. Then poof! He vanished into the night." Meredith shook her head, defeated.

"I'm still not clear on how Foster became infected with a mutated H1N1 virus if not from your vaccine trial. Where would he gain access to such a virus?" Albane asked.

"I've told you everything we know. Many questions remain unanswered. Which is why we have come to your organization for help, Ms. Mesnil." Meredith frowned. "Oh, and there is one more thing you should know. There is a possibility that Foster has in his possession a glass vial containing a particularly virulent strain of bubonic plague bacterium—also stolen from our Chiarek Norse facility. If he did steal a plague sample, then Mr. Foster is a deadly liability."

"Excuse me! You're saying Foster is on the loose, wandering around a city of nearly two million people in the middle of Europe, with a biological weapon in his possession?" VanCleave exclaimed, his voice pitched with agitation.

Meredith nodded. "That's the worst case scenario, yes. At this time, we are not able to account for all numbered *Yersinia pestis* samples in our inventory."

"Why would Foster do something so dangerous?" AJ asked.

"I think his message is pretty clear . . . pursue me at your own peril," Nicolora said.

AJ looked at Albane. She gave him a subtle nod of understanding, but the blank expression on her face did not change. She returned her gaze to Meredith. AJ sensed a palpable tension between the two women.

"Ms. Morley, do you have any idea where Foster is now, or an educated guess about where he might try to go?" Albane inquired.

"He was last spotted in an Internet café in downtown Prague. I had some of our people out scouring the city for him. He got spooked and managed to slip away. I notified the Czech Government that he is on the loose and that he possesses a biohazard. Hopefully by now, they have circulated his picture among law enforcement personnel and the border patrol," Meredith said. "As for his rendezvous location with the buyer, I haven't a clue. After he turns over our formula, I imagine he'll go into hiding a very rich man, and we'll never see or hear from William Foster again."

The room was silent. Meredith looked around the table, beckoning more questions and trading glances with everyone, everyone except Albane.

AJ raised his hand.

"Mr. Archer."

"Can you tell us anything more about the experimental product that Foster was treated with? What makes it so unique that he would gamble with his own life to steal it?"

"As I said before, the product is highly confidential. I'm not at liberty to disclose anything more than what I've told you already. Instead, I'll leave you with this question to ponder: If Foster knew the product would save him, was he really gambling with his life? By making himself appear the victim, one could argue that Foster is the world's most convincing and sympathetic thief."

"Any other questions for Ms. Morley?" Nicolora said, but his intonation signaled the contrary. The Q&A session was officially over.

After ten seconds of silence Meredith added, "I cannot emphasize enough how dire this situation is. Foster must be found. We desperately need your help. My entire staff will be at your disposal twenty-four hours a day, for as long as you need us. Tell me what you need, and I'll get it for you. Good luck, and God help us."

Nicolora stood up, and on this cue, so did all the other members of The Tank. "Thank you, everyone. That will be all." He turned to Albane. "Albane, you're team leader for this assignment. The clock starts now. I want Foster located within twenty-four hours."

Albane nodded and stared with unblinking eyes as he escorted Meredith out of the Founders' Forum. She checked her watch. "All right team, you know the drill. Pack quickly. I want to be airborne and en route to Prague in ninety minutes." Then, with narrowed eyes she added. "We have a man on the loose carrying around in his pocket the same disease that wiped out over a third of the population of Europe in the Middle Ages."

AJ turned and looked at the picture of Will Foster still glowing on the screen; he smirked. He was certain that his experience over the past day was only the tip of the iceberg when it came to The Tank's capabilities. Whoever Foster really was, one thing was certain . . . he didn't stand a chance.

Chapter Twelve

Prague, Czech Republic

JULIE PONTE SMACKED her lips together. She had just finished applying a fresh coat of lipstick, and was using the tiny lighted mirror of her car's sun visor to make sure the job had been done properly. Adequate coverage with no smears. No red on her teeth. Good. She ran her fingers through her blonde hair, trying to fluff in some body. The shampooed luster and bounce from the previous morning's shower was gone. She sighed and let her arms fall into her lap. She felt foolish.

"Why am I nervous? There is absolutely no reason to be nervous," she muttered.

It had been over five years since she had last seen Will.

He shouldn't have trouble recognizing her, she thought. Her hair was shorter, but only by three or four inches. Nothing a guy would notice. Her eyeglasses were new; her staff had commented that they made her "look serious." She didn't know about that. Realizing she was still wearing them, she quickly took the thin brown frames off and threw them in her purse. With one final peek in the mirror, she was ready. Five minutes was already too much time to have wasted primping in a parked car. She was late, and it was time to rescue Will.

She had visited Prague a number of times since moving to Europe, and she knew her way around the city center. From where she had parked, even at a brisk pace, it would take her ten minutes to reach the Astronomical Clock in the center of the Old Town. The walk would give her a few more minutes to stew.

There was much to be worried about. The abrupt way Will had ended their online IM conversation had scared her. Maybe the police had arrested him. Then, there was the babble about being kidnapped and put in quarantine. She had trouble swallowing that one. Finally, there was the issue of his health. Although she wanted to believe his claims, she had prepared herself for the possibility that Will was suffering from paranoid delusions.

She checked her watch: 2:11 AM. One more block to go.

As she rounded the corner, the pointed Gothic spires of the Church of Our Lady before Týn rose into the skyline. Like twin sentinels standing watch over the Old Town, they towered over every other structure in view. In keeping with gothic architectural coda of their era, the spires were built asymmetrically—with the broader right spire and the thin left spire representing the masculine and feminine elements of society. Her gaze shifted from the spires to the courtyard in front of the Astronomical Clock.

She scanned the faces of the sparse crowd for Will. A handful of people were loitering around the clock, even at this late hour, but Will was nowhere in sight. Her heart sank. He had logged off the computer before she could give him her mobile number. She had no choice but to wait. She would stay all night and through the next day if necessary. She spotted some chairs left out in front of one of the nearby cafés and decided to sit and wait for Will there.

As she approached the chairs, she noticed a man sleeping in one of them. The pose was unmistakable—classic Will Foster. Legs extended, crossed at the ankle. Chin against his chest with one fist jammed uncomfortably under his left cheek. Many a college night she had found him asleep in the library, in this position, with a textbook sprawled across his lap.

She smiled.

Up close, she was taken aback. He looked terrible. The dark circles under his eyes reminded her of how football players look with their grease paint before a game. The three days of stubble on his face was not enough to camouflage his sunken cheeks and un-natural pallor of his skin. Most disturbing of all, however, was that she had never seen him so thin. Her heart melted; she wanted to stroke his chestnut brown hair and tell him the nightmare was over. She was here to rescue him; she would take care of him now. But she resisted.

She stood over him, bent slightly at the waist, and tried to wake him. "Will, wake up. It's Julie."

Nothing.

She tried squeezing his shoulder. "Will, wake up. It's me."

Without warning, his left hand shot out and clamped onto her throat. His eyelids popped open, revealing fully dilated pupils. His right hand balled into a fist, which he recoiled into the "cocked and ready" position beside his temple.

She yelped. His hand was a vice on her throat. The carotid artery in her neck throbbed, and it was becoming difficult to breathe.

Will did not remember falling asleep. One minute he was sit-ting waiting for Julie—admiring the twin spires of a church whose name he did not know—and the next minute they'd found him. Like thieves in the night, they had snuck up on him, and grabbed him on the shoulder. His heart was in his throat. One thing was cer-tain, he would not go quietly.

"Will! Stop. It's me," she managed in a raspy whisper.

Like a lighthouse beacon guiding a ship into safe harbor, her voice drew him out of his fog. The scowling orderly in a white lab coat morphed into an angel.

He released her throat.

"Julie?"

She rubbed her neck with her fingers, and took a step backward, trembling. "Christ, Will. If you could've seen the look in your eyes . . . For a moment there, I thought you were going to kill me."

Standing up, he opened his arms wide to her. "I'm so sorry, Julie. I thought you were . . ." At first, her mouth crinkled with doubt, but then the corners of her lips curled into a grin. She stepped in and they hugged each other for a long moment, and for the first time in months Will felt the touch of human warmth against his cheek.

Like an alarm siren in his mind, an image of Rutgers and Frankie, writhing in misery, popped into his conscious. Abruptly, he pulled away from her.

"Julie, we need to keep a buffer between us. I don't know if I'm contagious. If you became infected like the others I've been in contact with, I don't know what I'd do."

"For you, it's a risk I'm willing to take. Besides, if you were infected with something that virulent, then you'd probably already be . . ."

"Dead?"

She grabbed him firmly on both his arms. "It's obvious you're not well. I mean Jesus, Will, I've never seen you so thin. But, don't worry about me. Would it make you feel any better to know I have Ciprofloxacin, Streptomycin, and Doxycycline in my purse?"

"What are those?"

"They're three of the most powerful antibiotics on the market. So if you have a dangerous infection—an infection worthy of being quarantined, like tuberculosis—then you'll start popping pills, and I'll start popping pills, and we'll find a way to get through this. On the other hand, if you have a virus, then even the best antibiotics won't help you. Either way, we need to get you checked into the research hospital in Vienna."

"No hospitals. Absolutely not."

Julie considered arguing the point, but they didn't have time.

"Okay. No hospitals." She grabbed his hand, and with a tug, she began leading him back to the car. "Let's go."

Her confidence bolstered his spirit.

"God, you're a sight for sore eyes," he said.

She smiled. It had been a long time since anybody had told her that.

"Thanks. You too."

•　　•　　•

"*nice*," WILL EXCLAIMED as she unlocked the driver's side door of her 2005 navy blue Opel Astra.

"What? This is Europe, Will. Not everyone drives an SUV here. Europeans are very practical, you know. Besides, this car has more personality than some of the technicians in my lab."

Within ten minutes they had reached motorway D1 heading south out of Prague. At two thirty in the morning, traffic was light.

"God, this is so surreal . . . you being here," Julie said.

"Surreal for you. The end of a nightmare for me." He looked over his shoulder and out the rear window for the third time in as many minutes.

"Why do you keep doing that?"

"To see if we're being followed."

"We're not being followed."

"The only way to know if we're being followed is to watch and see if we're being followed. Those same headlights have been behind us for a while now."

Julie sighed. "That car was already on the motorway when we got on. I merged in front of him. Relax. No one is following us."

"Easy for you to say. You don't know what they're capable of," he grumbled.

Julie was silent for a moment. It was as good of an opportunity as she was going to get. Enough small talk, it was time to learn what she was dealing with.

"Will, tell me what happened to you."

He nodded but didn't answer. He wanted to talk to her; he wanted to tell her everything. He also desperately wanted to sleep. His aching body reminded him that he still had not fully recovered from his four-story plummet in the stairwell. He rubbed his eyes, trying to organize his thoughts.

"Start at the beginning. I'm here to help, not to judge," she pressed.

He exhaled a deeply. "It started with Natalie. No, actually it started when I lost my job."

"You were fired?"

"Yeah. The recession hit my firm pretty hard. I made it through the first round of cuts, but not the second. Then, not even a month after I was axed, Natalie dumped me. Things sort of spiraled out of control from there."

"That sounds like Natalie. What did you ever see in her anyway?" Julie said, with a hint of wry satisfaction.

He sighed. "You never even met Natalie."

"I'm sorry, go on."

"Anyway, things got rough for me. Try living in Manhattan without a job—that equation doesn't factor very well. Plus, Natalie spent money like a fiend, so my cash situation was shit."

"Did you get severance?"

"Three months, but I used it to pay the rent, the bills, and to eat. I was freaking out. I needed a job desperately, but there was nothing. *Nuh - thing.* Nobody was hiring. I couldn't even land an interview."

"What happened?"

"A buddy told me about this gig he did in college to earn extra cash. He signed up for a clinical trial to test a drug that stimulates melatonin, or something like that. He said all he had to do was take these pills and show up twice a week for blood draws. He said they paid him three thousand bucks for it. He must have been in the placebo group, he said, because nothing ever happened to him. Er, nothing he knows about anyway."

"Tell me you didn't," she groaned.

"I did. I signed up for a fast-track swine flu vaccine trial. Five hundred bucks to be a guinea pig for the vaccine. I figured it was something the doctors would probably recommend I get anyway, so why not get paid for it?"

"Whose vaccine were you testing?"

"What do you mean whose vaccine? It was an H1N1 vaccine."

"No, I mean who was the manufacturer running the trial? Glaxo, Baxter, Novartis?

"None of those. It was a company called Leighton-Harris Pharmaceuticals."

"Never heard of them."

"Apparently the vaccine I was a test subject for was a live virus variant."

"Okay, so what happened?"

He fiddled with his hands. "At first, nothing. They gave me two shots, a couple weeks apart. They also took some blood samples and cheek swabs. Then, out of the blue, they called me back. I met with a new guy, a doctor, not just the regular admin weenies. The doctor told me I was infected with a mutated strain of the H1N1 virus."

"That's virtually impossible. Did you tell him that's impossible, Will?"

He raised an eyebrow. "You *do* know what my previous job was, right? I was the account manager for those annoying singing chicken ads. Cluckers Fried Chicken was my biggest client."

She shot him a quizzical look.

"Oh, come on. You know the jingle:

> *Don't be a sucker,*
> *Ya gotta eat at Cluckers.*
> *When you're pickin' chicken,*
> *Follow me!"*

She rolled her eyes. "Oh, that's terrible. Did you write that?"

"Of course not, I was the ad program manager. I'm the guy who puts it on TV to torment everyone in the country during primetime. Anyway, my point is: Do you really expect *me* to banter with a virologist about the minutiae of the H1N1 virus?"

She made a conciliatory grunting sound. "They told you you were infected?"

"Yes, and that I needed to be quarantined for public safety."

"What! Quarantined? Were you symptomatic?"

"Keep your eyes on the road," Will said clutching the armrest as the car drifted dangerously onto the shoulder. Julie jerked the wheel, piloting the sedan back into its lane. After a deep, calming breath, he continued. "Anyway, what was so strange is that I felt completely fine."

"Did you tell the doctor that?"

"Of course, that was the first thing I told him. He said that was part of the reason I needed to be quarantined. The mutated version of the virus was something they had never seen before, and it had unprecedented concentration levels in my blood. He said that he had no idea what the virus was going to do to me and how contagious or virulent the strain was."

"Will, this doesn't make any sense at all to me. It's completely unorthodox. Do you remember the name of the doctor who told you this nonsense?" Julie said, her ire rising.

"Xavier Pope. Shit, how could anyone forget a name like Xavier Pope."

"Xavier Pope was the doctor who quarantined you?"

"Have you heard of him?"

"Of course. He's famous, well, in the medical community he is. But Xavier Pope is not a doctor. He's a research scientist, like me."

"Wait a minute, are you telling me this guy Pope lied about being a doctor?"

"No, he's a doctor, but not an MD. He's a PhD. Pope is a microbiologist who specializes in infectious diseases."

Will's mind began to race. The events of the past five months had never made sense to him, but he had grown comfortable with certain basic assumptions, like the fact that Dr. Xavier Pope was a *real* doctor. Now everything he saw, heard, and believed had to be called into question. The deception was growing more complex at every turn.

"Julie, what exactly does Xavier Pope do?"

"He does the same kind of work I do, except while I specialize in finding cures for cancer, he focuses on finding cures for pandemic viruses and bacteria. Of course he's much more famous, and published, and brilliant than I am, but in theory we're colleagues."

"Why would he be working on my case?" he asked.

"H1N1 is a hot bug right now. The CDC is worried about a resurgent pandemic. It makes sense that he would have been called in," she said, drumming her fingers on the steering wheel rhythmically. "What happened next?"

"After my meeting with Pope, things happened very quickly. They told me they were placing me in quarantine. I was kept in virtual isolation, completely cut off from the outside world. I call those days the 'bubble boy days' because they kept me in a glass room, and everyone I interacted with wore protective masks and gloves. A lot of poking and prodding, but not much two-way communication. That lasted about three weeks or so, then their lawyer came to see me."

She stiffened. "Please tell me you didn't sign anything, Will."

He was silent.

"Did you read the documents before you signed?" she asked, her hands gripping the wheel.

"I tried, but there were hundreds of pages of legal mumbo jumbo. A man would go blind, or mad, trying to decipher all that legalese. Besides, who knows what drugs they were pumping into me. I can honestly say that I wasn't thinking straight at that point. Regardless, the lawyer's arguments were very persuasive."

"Did they threaten you?"

"In a manner of speaking. Pope was there too. He told me that I had to sign the papers before they would treat me. If I didn't sign, he said he couldn't say how long I would be in quarantine. Six months? A year? If I signed, they could use some different experimental protocols to try to eradicate the virus, so I could get my life back."

She pressed the brake pedal and the car began to slow. Red lights dotted the road ahead of them. "That's strange," she said.

"What's strange?

"There's a line of traffic ahead. We're almost at the border where we cross into Austria. I've made this trip half a dozen times, and I've never seen anything like this before."

"Pull the car over, Julie."

"What?"

"Pull the car over NOW."

She piloted the Opel off onto the shoulder, a kilometer behind the last car in the line. She put the automatic transmission in park, and looked over at him.

"They're looking for me. We need to find another way across."

"Will, don't be crazy. They're not looking for you. This is Europe. Both these countries are in the EU. Traveling between Austria and the Czech Republic requires only a cursory glance at our passports and we're through."

"Julie—I don't have a passport."

"I know that. I borrowed my roommate's boyfriend's passport. He looks vaguely similar to you except he wears a beard. It's perfect. If they give you any grief, just say you shaved your beard. Can you still speak German?"

"I'm rusty," he replied, rubbing his temples.

"We'll be fine."

"No. It's too risky. They're looking for me. I'm sure the border patrol has a photograph of me. We need to think of a different way to get me across."

They sat in silence.

"The trunk," she announced decisively.

"What?"

"You can hide in the trunk. They don't search vehicles at border crossings in the EU. It's unheard of. I have never had a car searched in all my travels throughout Europe. Not once, Will."

"Are you crazy? Absolutely not. I'd rather take my chances crossing the border on foot. Do you have a map?"

"Yes, but Will," she pleaded as she reached across his body and into the glove box to retrieve a map. "I don't think it's a good idea for us to be separated."

She unfolded the map and handed it to him. He held the paper at an angle so the faint light emanating from the glovebox lit the page. "We're heading south on 422. We just passed through the town of Nemocnice Valtice. If I get out here and walk a couple kilometers east and then a few kilometers south I can meet you here in Schrattenberg on the other side of the border. You drive through border control by yourself and wait for me on the other side. I'll look for you parked along the L22 in town. It'll probably take me an hour or more, so drive thirty minutes out of town and then turn around and come back. That way you minimize the time you're loitering. Park the car along the curb and wait for me, with the doors locked. I'll find you."

"I don't know, Will. It sounds pretty risky to me. If someone sees you trying to cross the border then you're guilty by default. They would apprehend you, arrest you, and probably hold you for weeks. I would be powerless to help you."

"And what would happen if they find me in the trunk?"

"Touché, touché. But they won't look in the trunk. I promise."

He didn't answer.

"They won't, Will. Trust me. I've gotten us this far, haven't I? We're in my backyard now, experience says they don't look in the trunk."

He nodded.

He was tired of making decisions. Maybe, she was right.

Chapter Thirteen

Prague, Czech Republic

"YOU WANT ME to do what?" the young woman behind the reception desk exclaimed.

"I want you to close the Internet café for thirty minutes. I have a very important email to write, and I cannot be disturbed," Raimond Zurn repeated. His brother Udo stood towering behind him, scowling at the young woman.

"But, Sir, we are full of customers."

Raimond surveyed the Internet café. "Full of customers? I see only two. Besides, it's very late. These people should be at home asleep. You'll be doing them a favor."

"We are the only twenty-four hour Internet café in Prague and we never close. That's the owner's policy. Besides, you're not my boss. We don't close the store because a customer wants to work on a computer alone," she said with nervous conviction.

Raimond smiled. He could snap the girl's neck so fast that her brain would not even register that she had died, but killing this young woman was entirely unnecessary for him to obtain what he wanted. It was the power to decide the fate of others that intoxicated him. He immersed himself in moments such as these and wished he could slow down time to revel in her uncertainty for hours instead of seconds. The girl's courage was as real as it was foolish, and he admired her for it.

The smile faded from his face as he reached into his pocket and pulled out a wad of rolled bills.

"Maybe we should start again. In my hand is five hundred euros. I would like to buy thirty minutes of time on all the computers in the café right now."

"You're offering me a bribe?"

"No. I'm offering to buy thirty minutes of time on ALL the computers. How you account for the time and payment is up to you."

The clerk looked down for a moment, considering. Then she nodded and said, "Okay. Thirty minutes for five hundred euros, you have a deal."

His lips curled into a tight smile. "See, I knew you would make the right decision."

The young woman turned to her computer and began typing on the keyboard. Groans and expletives filled the air of the café as she systematically performed an administrator logoff of all the computers. She stood up and made an announcement in Czech followed by the same announcement in English.

"I apologize for the inconvenience, but a virus has been detected on our network. To prevent infection of all the computers, this gentleman must perform a virus scan on all workstations. I will give a refund to all customers for your remaining time or a voucher for a free hour to be used at another time. Once again, I apologize, and please don't forget to take your personal items with you when you leave."

Once the Internet café had emptied, the girl turned to Raimond and asked, "Which computer would you like to use?"

Raimond pointed to a terminal in the back corner against the wall where he had confronted Will Foster.

"That one," he said.

The woman typed a flurry of keystrokes on the master computer and wrote down a username and password on a slip of paper and handed it to the bounty hunter. "Okay, it's ready. Just type in this login and password and you will have thirty minutes."

Raimond snatched the paper from her hand. Then, to his brother he said, "Go and wait by the door. No one enters until I'm finished."

Udo nodded and took station at the entrance.

Raimond walked to the computer and sat down. He retrieved a portable hard drive from inside his overcoat pocket and then connected a USB cable to one of the open ports on the back of the computer tower. He inserted a CD-ROM into the disc tray and loaded a program designed to copy the entire contents of the computer's hard drive onto his portable hard drive. In fifteen minutes, the computer's hard drive was mirrored onto his drive. He disconnected the cable, ejected the CD, and tucked the hardware back inside his gray overcoat.

He walked to the reception desk. The coed eyed him suspiciously.

"Were you able to send your *email?*"

"Yes."

"You still have fifteen minutes left, you know."

"I finished early," he replied.

"You still have to pay me the full amount. A deal is a deal."

Raimond reached out and grabbed the young woman's hand, turned it palm up, and placed five one-hundred euro bills inside her curled fingers.

"Thank you," she said as he turned to leave.

Raimond looked back and winked at her, but said nothing as he walked away, leading his hulk of a brother.

"Did you get it?" Udo asked.

"Ja."

"Now what?"

"We send it to Stefan and he works his magic."

Udo nodded. His brother's words could not have rung more true. Computers were magic boxes beyond comprehension. He had listened to the debate between Raimond and Stefan about whether they could retrieve any useful data from the cybercafé computer, but their discussion of browser caches, temporary files, and key-logging spyware was beyond him. Even if he had spent the rest of his life in study, he would never be able to perform even the simplest of hacks. Each of the Zurn brothers had been born with a gift. Raimond was cunning. Even as a young child, he had exhibited an uncanny ability to manipulate people and circumstances to his favor. Stefan, the quiet one, possessed an intuitive understanding of machines.

Raimond once said that Stefan's mind was the perfect marriage of inventor and engineer—a place where insatiable curiosity lived in harmony with methodical precision. As for Udo, his aptitudes had always resided below the neck. In primary school, he had been a star player of both rugby and soccer. His strength and speed were one-and-a-half times that of normal men. And he had never lost a brawl—that is, until Will Foster had humiliated him in public.

Udo could not stop seething over the American. He yearned for their next encounter. He felt anxious and invigorated, the same feeling he used to get the night before a championship rugby match. Of late, Raimond's jobs had been boring. Udo couldn't remember the last bone he had been permitted to break, the last jaw he had been directed to smash. He clenched his fists. Breaking Foster into little pieces would be very, very pleasurable. Raimond had promised Meredith Morley that they would deliver Foster alive, but that was all he had promised. After the embarrassment Raimond had suffered in the cybercafé when Foster kneed him in the balls, Udo was certain his brother would not intervene during the pummeling session he planned to unleash.

"Where do you think the American is hiding?" Udo asked.

"Difficult to know. Without a passport and money, he cannot leave the Czech Republic without help from the outside. I'm certain he came to the Internet café to arrange his extradition. I need to see what information Stefan extracts from the hard disc before I plan our next move."

"If we do catch him, then what?"

"Don't you mean *when* we catch him, then what?"

"Ja, of course."

"I think I'll turn my back for twenty minutes and let you teach Mr. Foster what it feels like to be a rugby ball. Would you like that, Udo?"

Udo smiled. "I was hoping you would say that."

Chapter Fourteen

The Czech–Austrian Border

JULIE FIDGETED IN the driver's seat. The border guards were talking to the driver of the car in front of her, and it had been a lengthy interrogation. She told herself to relax. Looking nervous would only create suspicion. Trained law enforcement officers would see right through her if she didn't bring her A-game. She inhaled deeply and then exhaled with her lips pursed. She ran her fingers through her hair, tilted her head and smiled. The act of smiling seemed to take a little of the edge off. She looked down at her chest and undid the second button on her blouse. Not quite enough. She undid the next button. She folded her arms and squeezed to create some cleavage.

"Ridiculous," she said aloud, feeling foolish. She refastened the third button, shaking her head.

The brake lights dimmed on the car in front of her, and it began to pull away. Her palms began to sweat.

"Oh, what the hell," she mumbled and quickly unbuttoned the third button of her blouse again before putting the car into gear.

She idled the car forward to the checkpoint and then put the transmission into park.

Two young uniformed men approached her vehicle, one on the driver's side and the other on the passenger side. The officer on the driver side rapped with gloved knuckles on the window and shined his flashlight on her face. She squinted hard and rolled down the window. The other officer used his flashlight to survey inside the passenger compartment.

"Reisepass."

She handed her passport to him, but accidently released it before his fingers found a grip.

The passport fell onto the pavement beneath the driver side door. The young officer's mouth twisted with annoyance as he bent down to pick up the folded booklet.

She flushed.

"I'm sorry," she said.

The officer stood up, passport in hand, and shined his flashlight on her laminated picture. He stared at it for a moment and then shined his flashlight back in her face again. This time it seemed he the let the beam linger in her eyes for several extra seconds. Retribution for dropping the passport, she surmised.

"I am an Austrian resident. I live in Vienna," she said.

"I see. What were you doing in the Czech Republic, Ms. Ponte?"

"Visiting my boyfriend."

"How long have you been away?"

"Just one day."

"I see. Why are you out at this late hour?"

"If you must know, we had a fight, so I left."

"I seeeee."

"Sie ist allein," the other officer said from the other side of the car.

The officer on the driver side nodded, and then turned his attention back to Julie. This time, when he aimed his flashlight at her face, she shielded her eyes with her hand. She sighed with irritation and made sure it was loud enough for him to hear. He reached into his pocket, retrieved a folded piece of paper, and unfurled it by shaking the paper violently in the air with one hand.

"Do you know this man? He is an American like you."

She looked at the paper with its black-and-white scanned photograph of Will. She felt the blood rush to her face and a strong and sudden need to use the bathroom.

"I said . . . Do you know this man?" the patrolman repeated.

She shook her head. Then she looked up at the officer's face and added, "No, I don't."

"I see. Open the rear luggage compartment, bitte?"

Her heart pounded . . . he didn't believe her.

She leaned toward the officer and squeezed her upper arms together—her breasts bulged in the open "V" of her blouse. "Officer, is it really necessary to search my vehicle? I promise you that I'm traveling alone."

The patrolman directed his flashlight beam to her cleavage, let it linger a moment, and then let it drop to the ground. He locked eyes with her; his face morphed into his trademark sneer. "Open the rear luggage compartment, Ms. Ponte. Now."

Chapter Fifteen

Boston, Massachusetts

NIATROSS.

That was the name painted in silver script letters on the tail of Robért Nicolora's private jet. A means of conveyance that probably should not have existed, but did nonetheless, the Cessna Citation X was a magnificent and ludicrous product of capitalism and human ingenuity. Not only was it capable of whisking its occupants across the blue at a speed of .92 Mach, but also pampering them with every conceivable luxury in the process. AJ could think of no better way to travel. Before boarding, he walked 360 degrees around the aircraft on the tarmac. He imagined its exterior lines were born first from an artist's brush stroke, and then later honed to aerodynamic perfection by the mouse clicks of an engineer. With its backward sweeping wings, and rising throat-like fuselage, the Citation X reminded him of a bird of prey. Even the cockpit was angled, so in flight it looked like the cocked head of a falcon surveying the sky.

Inside, AJ was surprised to find the cabin was outfitted like NORAD. Next to every seat was a flat panel computer screen, fixed to the interior wall on an adjustable arm. At the front of the cabin were additional flat panel monitors capable of displaying television, webcasts, satellite imagery, and even live video feed from the custom-built fuselage mounted camera system. Special antennae had been incorporated into the skeleton of the plane and snaked just below its thin aluminum skin, making **NIATROSS** a mobile communications platform rivaling Air Force One. AJ's favorite feature was something he did not notice until take off—silence. It had taken Abbey St. Jean's Level Zero resources two months to develop, but she eventually devised an inter-cabin high fidelity sound system with active noise cancellation that made Nicolora's aircraft as quiet as a Lexus driving on freshly paved asphalt.

He had chosen the leather bucket seat directly opposite and facing Albane. She sat angled in her seat, with her knees together, ankles crossed and tucked underneath. Kalen slept, reclined in the seat to AJ's left, with a black silk handkerchief draped across his eyes. VanCleave typed on his computer—lost in a world of mathematical formulas and spreadsheets—while perched on a bench seat at the rear of the aircraft.

"What, no champagne?" AJ joked as Albane handed him a cold bottle of water.

"You haven't accomplished anything worthy of celebration yet. Maybe on the ride back," she said, with a hint of a smile.

"How long is the flight?"

"A little over seven hours, nonstop. This Citation is modified with winglets and an extra fuel reserve, so Prague is barely inside our four thousand mile range."

"Is it always like this?"

"Like what?"

"Fast and furious. One minute we're in Boston, the next we're jetting off to Prague to chase down a guy with a biological weapon."

"Actually, yes. What you've seen is only the tip of the iceberg."

AJ pondered her words. "Tough job for a relationship. Are you married?"

"No."

"Otherwise committed?"

"Definitely committed otherwise," she said, tapping her Think Tank–issued mobile phone.

He smiled and looked out the porthole window into the night sky. After the awkwardness settled, he turned back to her. "Albane, Meredith Morley said something that I've been thinking about."

"Go on."

"Her theory is that Foster participated in the H1N1 study so he could become a mole inside Vyrogen. To pull that off, however, would mean that he had to become infected with the mutated H1N1 strain *after* he was administered Vyrogen's trial vaccine; otherwise Vyrogen would have detected H1N1 antibodies in his prescreening blood samples."

"What's your point?"

"Foster's exposure to the mutated H1N1 virus could only have occurred during a very narrow window of time. In other words, after the trial started, but before he was put in quarantine. Whoever he is working with, had to make contact, and inject Foster during that window. Also, the list of organizations with the capability to engineer a mutated H1N1 virus is a very select one. With a little digging, I think we could narrow this list down to a half dozen companies or so. Take these two pieces of information together, and we have the *when* and the *who* to start investigating."

"One day on the job, and you're already starting to think like one of us. Good work. However, we need to consider another scenario equally plausible to the one Meredith is promoting," Albane said. "What if someone inside Vyrogen—someone with access to confidential company information—solicited Foster after he joined the vaccine trial? Let's assume the insider orchestrated everything, and Foster was just a mule. In this scenario, the insider would be the one delivering the product to a competitor, not Foster. Accordingly, we would need to broaden our search to include investigating Vyrogen personnel, not just Foster."

AJ's eyes widened. "How do we determine which scenario is the truth?"

"We investigate both simultaneously, of course. We start with a background assessment of Foster. At the same time, we go digging inside Vyrogen and look for people who fit the profile."

"How do we do that?"

Albane raised an eyebrow. "Why don't you get a Coordinator online and pull our team together for a roundtable session."

AJ felt befuddled; he was still unfamiliar with The Tank's protocols and code words. He hated sounding stupid. Most of all, he hated being a rookie. He wondered if he should just speak aloud like he had seen Briggs do in the lab earlier that day. Would the Coordinator just appear on the screen like a genie summoned from his lamp?

"Request Coordinator, C. Remy," AJ announced boldly.

Albane giggled.

Instead of feeling embarrassed, he was enthralled. It was the first time he had seen a glimpse of the real Albane sneak past her polished facade.

"In a scheduled session, such protocol would be correct, but in cases such as this, just dial zero."

"Got it." AJ pulled out his phone and pressed "0". Within three seconds, the screen displayed a live video feed.

"Coordinator R. Parish."

"Yes, I'd like to hold a roundtable session on the NIATROSS. Profile subject: William Foster for the Vyrogen case. Full background investigation," AJ said.

"Very well. One moment," R. Parish said. The large flat panel screen at the front of the cabin energized and began to fill with information.

AJ smiled and looked at Albane for recognition.

She almost acquiesced a smile but instead said, "I'll wake up Kalen. You see if you can reel in VanCleave from the depths of whatever mathematical ocean he's trawling. It's time to go to work."

•   •   •

VYROGEN CASE—ROUND TABLE SESSION—NIATROSS

R. Parish—*RS:Coordinator.* "William Foster, thirty-four years old, born in Springfield, Illinois, to George H. Foster and Elisabeth Meyer. Graduated from Tulane University with a degree in economics. Currently resides in New York City. Employer of record: McEwen & Rogers, an advertising firm in Manhattan. Marital status: single."

A. Archer—*RS:Bio.* "He's in advertising?"

R. Parish—*RS:Coordinator.* "Yes. Is there a problem?"

A. Archer—*RS:Bio*: "No, I just assumed Foster worked in pharmaceuticals or biotech. I'm just surprised he's in advertising, that's all."

K. Immel—*RS:Physical*: "I think we should start with casing his friends and family. The first person Foster will try to contact is someone he trusts. Identify this person and bingo, we have a road map to Foster."

A. Mesnil—*RS:Social*: "I'm not so sure about that. The minute he broke out of Vyrogen's Chiarek Norse facility, Foster went from being a research subject to a fugitive. It would be very unusual behavior for him to contact a friend or loved one in this scenario. In fact, the natural inclination for him would be to hide everything from his friends and family. Shield them. Foster wants to keep this little endeavor a secret. He will eventually want to go back to his old life—back to being good ol' Will—except of course for the seven-figure bank account in the Caymans he sets up after his payoff."

R. Parish—*RS:Coordinator*: "Excellent points, but Foster does not have family left to turn to. Both his parents are deceased. His mother died in an automobile accident in 1994, and his father passed away from a heart attack last year. Foster is an only child, has never been married, and has no children out of wedlock. By all accounts, he is alone and on his own."

K. Immel—*RS:Physical*: "Then who's been taking care of his personal affairs while he's been a human guinea pig all these months?"

R. Parish—*RS:Coordinator*: "Foster assigned temporary power of attorney to a corporate trustee after he was placed in quarantine. This document was included in the packet of documents turned over to us by Ms. Morley. Also included was a confidentiality agreement, Vyrogen test program enrollment paperwork, a hold harmless waiver, an acceptance of experimental risks statement, as well as a generous compensation schedule to be paid by Vyrogen in exchange for Foster's submission to experimental treatment in quarantine. All these documents are signed by Foster and appear to be legitimate."

K. Immel—*RS:Physical*: "What about his apartment?"

R. Parish—*RS:Coordinator*: "His apartment rent, plus utilities and parking, were paid in advance for six months by Vyrogen. Part of the terms of the agreement."

K. Immel—*RS:Physical*: "His job at his advertising firm?"

R. Parish—*RS:Coordinator*: "He was laid off four months before enrolling in the H1N1 vaccine study."

A. Mesnil—*RS:Social*: "I want interviews with his supervisor and coworkers at McEwen and Rogers. Send a female RS:Social. In fact, send Rebecca Knight. I want confirmatory evidence for all of this. Also, find out who is his closest male colleague at the firm. I want two interviews with him: one at the office and one after working hours, somewhere private. Find out everything he knows. Was Foster in debt? If so, how much did he owe? What kind of guy is he? What accounts did he handle for his firm? Does he have ties to or contacts in the pharmaceutical, biotech, or government realms? What was he working on right before getting mixed up with Vyrogen? Did you get all of that, Coordinator?"

R. Parish—*RS:Coordinator*: "Yes. I'll make it happen. What else?"

A. Archer—*RS:Bio*: "I think we should try to validate Meredith Morley's story about the mutated H1N1 strain. I've never heard any mention of this in popular news or in scientific journals."

R. Parish—*RS:Coordinator*: "Okay. I'll add that to the list."

A. Mesnil—*RS:Social*: "Next topic?"

K. Immel—*RS:Physical*: "The events of the theft and Foster's next steps. Meredith seemed convinced that Foster was working with a powerful individual or corporation to steal the formula. If that's true, Foster will be trying to contact that entity, turn over the product, and get paid."

E. VanCleave—*RS:Technical*: "It's all so inelegant. It doesn't make sense."

A. Mesnil—*RS:Social*: "What do you mean?"

E. VanCleave—*RS:Technical*: "Let's assume Foster was hired by someone to steal the formula. Let's further assume this someone is powerful and has resources at his or her disposal. Then why steal the formula like this? If I were the mastermind behind a plot to steal Vyrogen's secret drug, then I would have deployed other agents and technology so, that at the end of the research trial, my mole could walk out of quarantine with the formula secretly in hand. Why make a public spectacle of it? It's too clumsy to have gone down like this on purpose."

K. Immel—*RS:Physical*: "Good point. Why would Foster have ever signed onto this gig if he thought *he* was going to be the fall guy?"

A. Archer—*RS:Bio*: "Maybe his hand was forced. Maybe Vyrogen learned about the plot, and he had to act immediately or he would lose his window of opportunity."

A. Mesnil—*RS:Social*: "And if we follow that line of reasoning, then Foster taking the plague sample was probably an impromptu decision. Think insurance policy—it may be the only leverage he has. If the authorities corner him, he can threaten to release the agent. If the buyer tries to screw him, he can threaten to release the agent. It's what I'd do."

E. VanCleave—*RS:Technical*: "That's good, Social, I hadn't thought of that."

K. Immel—*RS:Physical*: "Regardless of his motive, one thing is certain, Foster is a man on the run, and he needs help. I think we should focus on identifying his accomplice. If I were in his shoes, the first thing I would do is contact my Daddy Warbucks, tell him to 'show me the money,' and then get my ass on a plane out of the country. We should brainstorm the most likely candidates for Daddy Warbucks. Who has the most to gain from stealing Vyrogen's miracle drug?"

A. Mesnil—*RS:Social*: "According to Archer, we should be looking at a list of biotech companies capable of creating the mutated strain of H1N1 that Foster was reportedly infected with."

E. VanCleave—*RS:Technical*: "I can shorten that list considerably based on the probability matrix I constructed. We should begin our search by focusing on pharmaceutical companies in direct competition with Vyrogen for BioShield funding."

K. Immel—*RS:Physical*: "What is BioShield?"

E. VanCleave—*RS:Technical*: "Mr. Parish, can you please brief the team on Project BioShield?"

R. Parish—*RS:Coordinator*: "On July 21, 2004, President George W. Bush signed into law Project BioShield. The Project's stated purpose is to provide funding for new medical countermeasures against chemical, biological, radiological and nuclear threats. The stakes: five and a half billion dollars of appropriated funds for the purchase of countermeasures against the most deadly biological agents, including smallpox, anthrax, plague, and others." Project funding is managed by the Biomedical Advanced Research and Development Authority, or BARDA.'"

A. Archer—*RS:Bio*: "I remember hearing something about this. Didn't Congress just reallocate a portion of the BioShield funding?"

R. Parish—*RS:Coordinator*: "Yes, approximately one and a half billion has been reallocated. To date, two and half billion dollars has been contracted, and of that amount nearly one billion has gone exclusively to the manufacture of anthrax vaccines. Which leaves roughly one and half billion remaining."

A. Archer—*RS:Bio*: "The article I read stated that one of the criticisms of the program is that no broad-spectrum countermeasures have emerged from the efforts to date."

R. Parish—*RS:Coordinator*: "That is correct. Our research shows that since its inception, all BioShield contracts have been allocated to specific threat agents. In the industry, this is commonly referred to as the 'One Bug, One Drug' approach."

K. Immel—*RS:Physical*: "No wonder Morley is so hot and bothered."

A. Mesnil—*RS:Social*: "Kalen, be serious."

K. Immel—*RS:Physical*: "I am serious. She's mad at work on a supposed cure-all drug, and before she can swoop in and claim *all* of what's left of BioShield for Vyrogen, Congress starts stealing from the honey pot."

A. Archer—*RS:Bio*: "He's right. If Vyrogen really has discovered something that combats a range of viruses *and* bacteria, then the federal government has no reason to spread the wealth. Why continue to follow the One Bug, One Drug approach, when you could invest all the remaining funds in one silver bullet? Just like Parish said, BioShield hasn't awarded a single contract to a broad-spectrum countermeasure. If what Meredith Morley told us is true, then Vyrogen's product would be the first."

E. VanCleave—*RS:Technical*: "If I were Vyrogen, I'd negotiate to use BioShield money to fund the remaining clinical testing for my miracle drug. Then, in addition to my government contract, I'd have an FDA-approved product I could turn around and sell in the private sector for tens of billions of dollars."

A. Mesnil—*RS:Social*: "This product is like Excalibur. Whoever possesses it holds the power to rule Camelot. In this case, Camelot is the global market share for therapeutics associated with infectious disease."

A. Archer—*RS:Bio*: "I think we have a working theory."

E. VanCleave—*RS:Technical*: "Coordinator, we need a list of names, Director Level and above, in every company that competes with Vyrogen in the infectious disease and vaccine sector."

R. Parish—*RS:Coordinator*: "Understood. Any other instructions?"

A. Mesnil—*RS:Social*: "Give us everything you have on Meredith Morley. I'm not ready to rule out her involvement."

R. Parish—*RS:Coordinator*: "I'm sorry Ms. Mesnil, but Meredith Morley's personal file is restricted access. Founder Level only."

A. Mesnil—*RS:Social*: "What? On whose authority?"

R. Parish—*RS:Coordinator*: "Founder One. I'm sorry but you'll have to take this matter up directly with Founder One."

A. Mesnil—*RS:Social*: "Understood. While we're waiting on the data to come back to us, we should focus on locating Foster before his trail goes cold. The first step is to—"

R. Parish—*RS:Coordinator*: "Excuse my interruption, but I just received a report from one of our assets in Prague that three individuals have checked into a hospital in Prague exhibiting plaguelike symptoms. They were immediately placed into quarantine and are undergoing further testing."

K. Immel—*RS:Physical*: "Looks like Foster's trail has just heated up."

A. Mesnil—*RS:Social*: "Mr. Parish, please make the necessary transportation arrangements upon our landing. Interviewing the infected witnesses is our number one priority . . . that is, if they're still alive by the time we get there."

Chapter Sixteen

Czech–Austrian Border

J ULIE STOOD AT the back of the sedan fumbling with her keys. The border patrol officer stood next to her, impatiently tapping the toe of his boot on the pavement. She tried to steady her hand as she reached to unlock the trunk, but the keys rattled noticeably. The lock mechanism clicked when she turned the key, and the trunk popped up. She lifted the lid the rest of the way, and the young officer eagerly shined his flashlight inside.

After a quick survey, he turned to her. The look on his face was a mixture of both disappointment and suspicion. He stared at her a long moment, but said nothing. Except for an old gray blanket and the spare tire, the trunk was empty. The fugitive whom the officer was hoping to find was presently one kilometer to the west, hoofing it across the border.

"You can close the lid," the officer said.

Julie exhaled and walked toward the driver's side door.

"Ms. Ponte, are you certain you do not know this American, William Foster?" he said following her.

She paused. It was critical to sound convincing, but not too convincing. She told herself to imagine he was talking about someone else, a different William Foster. The man he was referring to probably called himself Bill or Billy. She had never met Billy Foster before.

"I'm sorry, but no, I do not know the man you are looking for."

He fixed his icy stare on her. She surmised he was looking for nonverbal cues to indicate she was lying—rapid blinking, averting of the eyes, or maybe a tensing of the facial muscles. She knew trained interrogators used facial expressions as litmus tests for truth telling, but she was not an expert in such matters. In trying to manipulate her expression, she might inadvertently tip off to the very secret she was working so hard to conceal.

Then, like Apollo in his sun chariot chasing away the stygian night, the headlights of an approaching semi-truck illuminated the space around them. Someone brazenly honked. The traffic queue, now four vehicles deep, created psychological pressure for progression. An expectation of advancement. It was time for Julie Ponte to be on her way. With purpose, she reached for the door handle.

"Ms. Ponte?"

Her heart skipped a beat. "Yes, officer?"

"Don't you want to close the lid?" he questioned, gesturing back to the open trunk.

"Oh, yes. Thank you for reminding me."

A bead of sweat trickled down her forehead and fell to the ground, glistening in the yellow glow from the headlights of the car now idling ten feet behind her Opel.

She jogged back and shut the trunk lid.

"Is there anything else, or am I free to go home?"

The young border patrolman's brow furrowed. His mouth twisted into the frustrated expression she had become so intimately familiar with over the past ten minutes. He clicked off the flashlight and slid it into a holster ring fastened to his belt.

"No more questions. Welcome back to Austria, Ms. Ponte."

"Thank you. Gute Nacht."

Chapter Seventeen

Schrattenberg, Austria

"CHRIST, WILL, YOU scared me to death," Julie said with one hand on her chest.

"You were asleep inside a locked car. How else was I supposed to get your attention besides by knocking on the window?"

"I mean back at the border. I watched you get into the trunk of the car. How did you pull off that Houdini act?"

"I started to get in, but at the last minute I panicked and ran for cover. I ducked into the field before the car behind us got close enough to see me in their headlights."

She gave him a hard look. "At the border, they were looking for *you*, Will."

"I told you."

"Let's get the hell out of here." She started the engine and piloted the car onto the motorway in the direction of Vienna.

"How are you feeling?" he asked, tentatively.

"Panicked, now that I know you aren't delusional," she said. She was gripping the steering wheel so tightly that the skin on her knuckles was pulled taut and shown like eight tiny snowcapped peaks in the glow of breaking dawn.

"I knew I shouldn't have involved you. It's too dangerous."

"Knock it off, Will. I just need time to think."

After an awkward silence he said, "You're not feeling sick, are you?"

"No."

"Have you been sneezing, or coughing, or having chills?"

"No, I feel fine. Don't worry about me." She put her hand on her purse and jiggled it. "Remember, I've got a whole pharmacy in here." Then, she added, "Hey, why don't you finish your saga."

He took a deep breath. She was making an effort to keep calm; he appreciated that. "Where did I leave off?"

"Quarantine and Xavier Pope."

"Ah yes, quarantine. It was strange because even though I exhibited no symptoms, they kept me locked up anyway. At first I thought it was just a precaution, a way to safeguard everyone else in case I was contagious, but by the end of the second week, the hospital had transformed into the Twilight Zone. I asked to be discharged and my request was refused. I asked to be transferred out of quarantine, and instead they posted a security guard outside the door to my room. I asked for phone and Internet access, and they told me I was not authorized to communicate with anyone until I was cleared from quarantine."

"They wouldn't let you make a phone call?"

"No."

"Will, this is highly unusual. I don't understand," she said. "The CDC has rules and protocols to follow. They can't deny you your basic human rights."

"Maybe on paper they can't, but they did. They stalled for two weeks. Every time I asked for a status report, they told me in twenty-four to forty-eight hours I could expect the necessary paperwork to be issued by the CDC for my release from quarantine. That was just a line to keep me placated. Eventually, I got fed up and demanded to be released. I shouted and pounded on the door, but they were like robots. Everyone, except for Xavier Pope. He put on a pressurized biohazard suit and came into the room to talk to me."

"What did he say?"

"He told me that they could not release me because the level of virus in my bloodstream had not decreased. He said that they did not understand why I was asymptomatic, but that I was a carrier and that the virus was dangerous. He said I would be a Typhoid Mary and that the lab technician who had taken my blood had contracted the mutated virus and died within forty-eight hours. He asked me if I wanted my legacy to be remembered as Swine Flu Foster. I said no, of course not, but that I refused to spend the rest of my life in quarantine. He said he would personally guarantee that would not happen and assured me that they would check my blood every twenty-four hours. Once the live virus was not detectable, then the government would authorize my release. Until that day, he said, I would be living like a rat in cage. He apologized repeatedly and asked what he could do to make my stay more comfortable. I told him that I wanted a TV and a mobile phone. They brought me a TV."

"If it was anyone other than you telling me this, I wouldn't believe it. This is all so unorthodox. They were holding you prisoner."

"Pretty much."

"What happened next?"

"Next, I was drugged and woke up in Prague. Of course, I didn't know it was Prague at the time, because nobody told me anything. What they did tell me was that I had been transferred to a secure military hospital. And, they changed their story about the virus, now claiming that it was not a naturally occurring H1N1 mutation, but by a biologically engineered variant of unknown origin. I was told that my case fell under government jurisdiction, and I was going to remain in quarantine for additional testing. That's when it began."

"What began?"

"The injections," he said.

"What kind of injections?"

"I'm not sure. That's something I was hoping you could help me figure out. Do you think that traces would still be in my bloodstream?"

"It depends on what the substances were," she said.

"If we can solve the mystery of the injections, then we can solve the mystery of why I was put in quarantine."

"Then we better start looking. When we get to my apartment, I'll draw a blood sample and take it to my lab for testing. If you were injected with something unusual or dangerous, antigens will show up in a blood panel. If you're infected with mutated H1N1, or anything else for that matter, then we'll know. We need answers, and you need peace of mind."

"Okay, I'm in. But you need to understand, that the people we're up against are powerful, dangerous people. I don't think we're dealing with the CDC anymore. Everything I was told in quarantine was subterfuge. This is a conspiracy that crosses continents. If they can put me in quarantine and smuggle me out of the United States without anybody knowing a thing about it, then God only knows what else they're capable of. If we're not careful, you'll end up like me . . . a fugitive."

Her face softened and she seemed close to tears.

"What?" he asked.

"Nothing."

"No, tell me."

She swallowed. "It's just that you're not alone in this. I'm with you."

Dormant feelings he thought lost and forgotten washed over him. His emotions were a raging river, dragging his mind toward a dangerous cascade. To stay one step ahead of his enemies, he needed to stay focused, free his mind from distraction. Emotion was a liability, passion a luxury, neither of which he could afford. If he somehow managed to survive unscathed, then and only then, would he think about rekindling a relationship with Julie. His first priority was evading capture long enough to unravel the mystery behind his quarantine.

He exhaled. Trust was a splinter digging in his mind. Could he trust Julie unconditionally as he once had? Could he trust her with his secret? His hand instinctively went to the one remaining vial in his pocket. He had not told her everything. It was prudent to be cautious, he told himself, even with Julie. He would dole out information as he deemed necessary. What was the military expression? On a need-to-know basis. Was Julie being equally cautious? Was she hiding secrets too? If so, he wondered, what was she was not telling him?

Chapter Eighteen

Prague, Czech Republic

"**B**MW SEVEN SERIES. I should've guessed." AJ mumbled as he stepped out of the NIATROSS and onto the airport tarmac in Prague, squinting in the early morning sun.

"760Li to be precise, equipped with special order security and comms packages," Kalen said, standing beside him. "I spec'd it out myself. Do you like?"

"Does a baby like milk? The black on black with privacy glass tint is a nice touch too. It says I'm dangerous *and* pretentious."

"Actually, I was going for '*Outta my way, asshole.*" Kalen grinned. "But these wheels aren't for me. I prefer to ride alone."

The whir of a high revving Diavel Testastretta 11° engine pierced the night. A helmeted rider on a black Ducati Diavel Carbon rocketed onto the tarmac and then abruptly came to a stop next to the parked BMW.

"This job is not about the money," Kalen said as he walked toward the motorcycle. "It's about the toys."

AJ shook his head. He turned to Albane who had walked up to stand next to him. "Is he always like that?"

"No. He's usually much more excitable," she said.

From inside the BMW they heard VanCleave yell, "Every minute we delay increases the cone of uncertainty for Foster's position."

AJ looked at Albane and raised an eyebrow. "Is *he* always like *that?*"

"Unfortunately, yes." Albane began walking toward the black BMW. "Let's go. We have plague victims to interview, and I fear our window of opportunity may be closing."

•   •   •

A TALL BLONDE woman with a Russian accent and horned rimmed eyeglasses greeted the team as they stepped out of the BMW. "My name is Veronika Viskaya. I work inside the Ministry of Health. I contacted your Coordinator, Mr. Parish, a few hours ago when your team was en route. I am assuming that he has fully briefed you on the situation here, but if you have any questions for me before we go in, now is the time to ask."

"Is access for interviewing going to be a problem?" Albane asked Veronika.

"I do not think so. I filed the necessary clearances myself this morning, but if the military has arrived in the interim, things could get . . . complicated."

"Aliases?"

Veronika nodded. "Mr. Archer and Dr. VanCleave, you are both doctors from the CDC in Atlanta, and Ms. Mesnil, you are from the World Health Organization in Geneva. Here are your papers. Any other questions?"

"Are the patients lucid enough to interview?" AJ asked.

"The situation is grim. One of the two American college students died this morning, and the other is in critical condition with full-blown pneumonic plague. The Czech woman's infection was not as advanced as the others. Her body is responding to the antibiotics, and the infection has not spread to her lungs. The only problem is that she is not talking. She's in shock, I suppose. We've had three different people try to get through to her, including a psychologist, but she just stares off into space," Veronika explained.

"Don't worry, she'll talk to me," Albane said quietly.

"Will you need a translator?"

"No, that won't be necessary. I'm fluent in Czech."

"Okay, very good," Veronika said, then added, "There is something else I did not report to Mr. Parish, but given the facts of this case I am beginning to suspect it may be relevant."

Albane nodded, "Go on."

"One of my duties in the Ministry of Health is to monitor and track all mysterious, contested, or unexplained deaths reported by hospitals, prisons, elderly care facilities, and law enforcement agencies in the Czech Republic. These records are aggregated, reviewed, categorized, and then entered into a database so that they may be readily requisitioned by Interpol, the Czech Central Intelligence, forensic investigators, legal counsel, and even family members in cases associated with civilian deaths. Military records are exempt and maintained by the military. I mention this because I flagged an anomaly in the database last month which I am presently investigating."

VanCleave fidgeted excitedly and then pounced. "Anomaly? What kind of anomaly? Regressional, correlational or outlier?"

Veronika cracked a smile at VanCleave's statistical bravado. "Actually a skewing of the mean in an annual distribution of reported deaths of homeless persons in Prague over the past four months. We've seen a spike in the number of homeless deaths from January to April of this year. One hundred and forty-eight percent higher than last year."

"Have you run correlations with mean winter temperature?" asked VanCleave.

"Yes. No correlation. This winter we have recorded historically average temperatures in Prague."

"What about inflation of food prices or food shortages?"

"We've looked at that. No correlation. I've also investigated into the possibilities of increased closures of homeless shelters, increased city drug proliferation, a change in police policy toward the homeless, and so on and so on. The one and only thing I've found a positive correlation with is an increased number of coroners reporting organ failure due to acute toxicity as the cause of death. I just assumed this meant the homeless were drinking homemade vodka or isopropyl alcohol from the pharmacy this winter, but now I'm not so sure."

Albane looked to AJ. "Does this mean anything to you?"

"In my line of work, acute toxicity can result from a hyper-immune response to gene therapy. It is a well-documented phenomenon in primate-based gene therapy studies where adeno-virus vectors are used to deliver the transgene, especially when targeting the liver. Alternatively, toxic shock syndrome is not unusual in cases of severe bacterial infection, such as those caused by antibiotic-resistant *Streptococcus pyogenes* or *Staphylococcus aureus.* Did you happen to have a bad influenza season in Prague this year?"

"I'm not sure, why?"

"Toxic shock syndrome is most prevalent in persons with weakened immune systems, and there is a documented correlation of TSS occurring after physically stressful events such as childbirth, influenza, and the chicken pox," AJ explained.

"Actually, I remember hearing that this was supposed to be a bad influenza season, and we had panic in Prague over the new H1N1 virus spreading from the Baltic states. In fact, free inoculation clinics were held this year in the city, until the stockpile of vaccines were depleted," Veronika said.

AJ eyed VanCleave, his head cocked. VanCleave nodded. They were on the same page.

"What is it?" Veronika pressed.

"Ms. Viskaya, could you please pull whatever information you have on these free inoculation clinics? Specifically, we would like to know where the clinics were held and who was the supplier of the vaccines," AJ said.

Veronika nodded curtly.

"Also, we'd like copies of any coroner's reports that list toxic shock as the cause of death for all persons who died in Prague in the past five months," VanCleave added.

"Of course. I will have the digital scans transmitted to the Coordinator as soon as possible. Anything else?"

AJ shook his head.

"We should probably tend to the issue at hand, interviewing our plague victims. Ms. Mesnil, are you ready?"

Albane nodded and began to walk away with Veronika, when AJ grabbed her upper arm. "Shouldn't we wait for Kalen?"

"No. Kalen has other matters to attend to." She reached into her handbag, pulled out a thin leather case, and opened it. Inside was a pair of horned-rimmed glasses, similar to the ones worn by Veronika. Albane unfolded and donned the eyeglasses. She turned to AJ, tapped the frame of her glasses, and winked. "Superman has X-ray vision. We have Gucci with HD video capture."

"What? No contact lens camera?"

"Abbey's working on it, I'm told."

"I'm not surprised . . . Albane?"

"Yes, AJ."

"Do you really think this is such a good idea? Can't you interview the woman from behind the glass? You know, where it's sterile, safe, and free from aerosolized plague bacteria."

Albane reached up and put her hand on AJ's cheek. She looked deeply and tenderly into his eyes, and as she did he felt his pulse quicken.

"AJ, it's not the questions we ask, it's how we ask the questions. I cannot show this woman compassion and tenderness from behind the glass. These people are dying. They need human interaction. They need human touch, even if that touch is separated by a yellow plastic biosafety suit."

He nodded, speechless.

Albane withdrew her touch.

"See, it works," she said with a coy smile. As she walked away with Veronika, she looked over her shoulder at him and added, "But I appreciate your concern."

• • •

"THE SUSPENSE IS killing me. What did you find out?" AJ asked.

"I was only able to interview the woman; the one living American boy is in pretty bad shape, delirious with fever."

"Would she talk to you?"

"Yes, but only after we had a good cry together," Albane replied. "She is terrified that she is going to die. From what I could gather, her name is Sophie, and she is the proprietor of a youth hostel in Prague. She met Foster less than two days ago. A cab driver, who she is friendly with, brought Foster to the hostel in the middle of the night. She said that Foster was battered. The cab driver said that Foster told him he had been robbed and had his wallet and clothing stolen. The cab driver also warned her that the men who had attacked Foster could come looking for him. She took pity on Foster and gave him some old clothes and a bed in one of the dormitory rooms. When two other Americans, college students, checked in, she put them in the same room with Foster. Then the story gets a little fuzzy, but from what I could glean there was some sort of accident involving a glass tube shattering and spilling liquid in the room. She said Foster made her disinfect the room with bleach, but it didn't matter. By that night, the two boys were exhibiting plague symptoms, and she and Foster tended to them. Of course she didn't realize it was plague; she thought they had the flu."

"The broken glass tube must have been the plague sample Foster stole," VanCleave said.

"My conclusion as well."

"What else did she say?"

"Two men showed up at the hostel with a picture of Foster asking if she'd seen him. Sophie lied to the men and said no. Then, she warned Foster and helped him escape out the back door."

"Were they the Czech police?" Veronika asked.

"No. She said they looked like the mafia."

"Any more info about the stolen vials?" VanCleave asked.

"She was light on the details. She said Foster was very upset because the tube had broken and the boys had touched it. Apparently, Foster had insisted that they all check into the hospital, which is why, when Miss Sophie started to feel symptoms, she called an ambulance."

"You know what this means, don't you?" AJ asked rhetorically. "Unless Foster has another sample, he's lost his leverage."

"That's nothing to cheer about, AJ. God help us if this becomes an outbreak," VanCleave said.

"The Czechs are taking appropriate measures. The hostel has been cordoned off. Our two surviving victims are in quarantine, and according to Sophie, there were no other guests checked in at the time. It's out of our hands," Albane said.

"What's our next move?" AJ asked, feeling again like the rookie without a clue. He looked to VanCleave, who sniffed, but said nothing. He turned back to Albane.

"It depends . . ."

"On what?"

"On whether we believe that our client has been telling us the truth."

Chapter Nineteen

Vienna, Austria

"HERE WE ARE," said Julie, as she opened the door and turned on the lights to her apartment. "Home sweet home."

"Cool place."

"Thanks. I love it. And it's in a great location. We're in the embassy district of Vienna, near the Karlskirche."

"Two bedroom?"

"Yep. I have a roommate. Helps with the rent."

"Is she, or he, here?"

Julie laughed. "No, *she* is on holiday in Greece. She's not supposed to be back until tomorrow night."

"Oh. That's good," he replied awkwardly. "I mean it's good that we don't have to try to explain anything."

"You mean like the time my mom walked in on us over Christmas break our sophomore year in college."

He laughed. "Exactly."

She motioned to a vacant wooden chair next to her tiny kitchen table. "Sit."

"Okay," he said. "Are you cooking breakfast? I'm starving."

"Help yourself to anything in the fridge. I'll be back in a sec."

She went into her roommate's bedroom and returned with a tiny syringe to find him gobbling down a leftover half of a sandwich.

His eyes went wide at the sight of the needle. He shuffled in his chair, almost toppling over onto the floor.

During his time in quarantine, he had grown to despise the hypodermic needle. Regular blood draws and injections, which in the beginning he viewed as a nuisance, morphed into something sinister. The hypodermic needle was designed for a single purpose: *to violate.* Pull the plunger to extract life essence. Push the plunger to impregnate with foreign material. For five months, he had been raped—again and again—by a twenty-gauge stainless steel hypodermic needle.

"What are you doing with that? No way you're going to inject me!"

"Relax. I'm not going to inject you. My roommate is diabetic. This is an insulin syringe. Tiny needle. See?" she said holding it up in front of him. "It's not designed for blood draws, but we'll have to make do."

He eyed her warily, but said nothing.

She sat down next to him. "Remember what we talked about in the car? With your permission, I'd like to take that blood sample now."

He sighed and pulled up his sleeve exposing the white bare flesh of the inside of his elbow. This surrender was the ultimate act of trust. He would let her violate him—take a piece of him—but only because he *did* trust her. And because she had asked his permission.

She smiled, a sweet innocent smile, and scooted her chair next to his.

He turned his head to the side, averting his eyes from the needle.

She positioned his forearm across her lap. "Make a fist."

He did as she instructed. She ran her finger gently over the yellowed bruises and needle marks dotting his arm.

"Remember the time you serenaded me in front of my entire sorority house in your underwear until I agreed to go out with you," she said, distracting him, while she tapped her fingers on a swollen blue vein.

"I can't take all the credit for that. Jack Daniels was involved."

"Yeah," she chuckled as she slipped the needle under his skin with practiced efficiency. "And thirty of your fraternity pledge brothers egging you on."

He did not wince, but despondence washed over his face as he watched the syringe fill crimson. "What a rowdy bunch of hooligans we were."

"No argument here."

"Speaking of old memories, remember when we took our first road trip to Asheville, North Carolina?"

She flashed him a knowing smile. "Are you kidding . . . that's not the kind of thing a woman forgets."

•   •   •

JULIE STOOD MOTIONLESS and watched the rhythmic rise and fall of Will's chest as he slept in her bed.

In her bed. She felt flushed. She had fantasized about this moment plenty of times since their break-up. Of course, in the fantasy, he was not asleep—at least, not until after the deed was done. A flood of old emotions she had tried to suppress had been reawakened in her. Her mind would run away from her, making plans, hopeful plans, about all things they would do together, until she reined her thoughts back in under the cool pragmatism of her scientific intellect. Yet no matter how hard she tried to deny it, a part of her could not help but trust to hope.

Like a bucket of cold water dousing a fire, the exigencies of the present shook her from her daydream. She was getting ahead of herself. She needed be cautious with him, emotionally distant. It had been years since they had been together. Why was she letting herself be so vulnerable? Before entertaining anything other than friendship, she had to deal with the strange and preposterous mystery he had embroiled her in. Suddenly, she felt like Little Red Riding Hood standing at the threshold of a dark and portentous forest. Every instinct telling her not to tread forward, but knowing that the dangerous journey was necessary if she wanted to reach the Happily Ever After.

She bent to kiss him on the forehead, but stopped short. A kiss, even the slightest caress of her lips, would probably wake him. He was in such a fragile state at the moment; he needed rest. She blew him a kiss instead and tiptoed out of her bedroom.

129

Julie's roommate, Isabella, was on holiday with her boyfriend and was not scheduled to return for another day. Hopefully, that would give her enough time to run the necessary tests, develop a plan, and depart with Isabella none the wiser. She went to the kitchen and picked up the Ziploc plastic bag holding the syringe full of Will's blood. She pulled out a second Ziploc and decided to double-bag it just to be safe. She wrapped the bagged syringe in a dish towel and placed it gently in her purse. She made sure to lock the apartment door deadbolt when she left.

She had only slept for two hours—hopefully it would be enough to carry her through the day.

It was nine fifteen in the morning. She would arrive at the lab by a quarter to ten, at the latest. That would give her an hour to prep microscope slides before the lab emptied for lunch. But making blood smears was a colossal breach of biosafety protocol. If Will's blood contained an unknown virus or other deadly microbes, then working with his blood would require Biosafety Level Four controls. The campus was only permitted as a BSL-3 facility. To complicate matters further, she was an oncology research scientist, not a virologist. Although her work involving the STAT protein overlapped with immune system function, she did not have the requisite experience to make proper diagnoses of bacterial or viral infections. Just as a circus acrobat has no business standing in for a lion tamer, she had no business delving into the realm of infectious diseases.

A bead of cold sweat dripped from her underarm and ran, trickling over her ribs. She had never contemplated actions like those she was about to carry out, let alone violated company safety protocols before. Best-case scenario, she would be fired and professionally discredited. Worst-case scenario, she would unleash biocontamination that would result in the infection of thousands of people and then be prosecuted as a terrorist. She took a deep breath and tightened her grip on the steering wheel. She needed to find another angle.

She tried to pay attention to the traffic instead of worrying. An idea would come to her; it always did. But as she drove, her mind drifted back to Will. She wanted so much to protect him. To shield him from the world and from the awful men who had done this to him. What could she do? How could she ever hope to stand up against the powerful and faceless foe that Will described as their enemy? The more she thought about it, the heavier the dread lodged in her abdomen became. What if Leighton-Harris Pharmaceuticals and the CDC were co-conspirators? Was Xavier Pope really a Dr. Frankenstein? The Julie Ponte of twenty-four hours ago would have thought the idea of illegal quarantines and illicit human experimentation preposterous. She had worked in the pharmaceutical industry for six years and had only known noble and dedicated scientists and staff. Was she naive? Was Will changing her into a conspiracy theorist kook?

She was convinced that she did not possess the particular subject matter expertise to analyze his blood and generate a working hypothesis about what was happening to him. It had been unrealistic to think she could tackle a mystery like this without help. Whom could she trust? She startled rattling off names in her head. Heindrick Fabian. No, too nosey. Elizabeth Raynor. Maybe? No, too publication hungry . . .

A name interrupted her internal monologue.

Bart Bennett.

She smiled.

Bart Bennett was a hopeless genius who worked in virology. As one of only a handful of Americans working in her lab, it was inevitable that she and Bart would meet and become friends. Bart was from Seattle and was a proud and vocal coffee snob. Periodically, Julie and Bart would eat lunch together, swapping anecdotal tales about life as an American expat in Vienna. Once, she had even reluctantly agreed to meet him at a Viennese coffeehouse he frequented. A big mistake. By the end of the thirty-minute date, she feared he might drop down on one knee and propose to her—pulling forth a ring hidden beneath a layer of creamy froth atop his cappuccino. From that day forward, she had regularly affirmed their "only friends" status by limiting their interactions to cafeteria lunches and harmless hallway chitchat. Today, though, she might have to take advantage of poor Bart's affections.

She turned onto the laboratory campus driveway and drove past the marble sign at the entrance:

Wien Bioscience
a Vyrogen Pharmaceuticals Company

She entered the parking garage and parked in her reserved slip. She placed the automatic transmission into "Park," turned off the engine, and took a deep breath.

"You can do this," she mumbled to herself.

•   •   •

INSIDE THE LAB, Julie carefully drew a small volume of blood from Will's test tube with a syringe. Next, she transferred it to another vial she had prepared with a dummy label. This was the sample she would give to Bart. Five minutes later, she knocked on the door to his office.

"Hey, Julie," Bart exclaimed. "You must have smelled the espresso. Check out the new machine I just got. It's small enough to fit on the corner of my desk. Now I can have espressos whenever the urge strikes."

"Wow. It's a cute little guy, but are you sure that's legal? If you drink four or five espressos a day, your blood-caffeine level will be above the legal limit and you'll be SUI," Julie teased.

"SUI?"

"Scientist Under the Influence."

Bart smiled and forced a polite laugh. "I've already had two espressos this morning and I'm still yawning. That must be a good sign, right?"

"I guess so. Hey, um, do you have a second? I was hoping you could run some tests on a blood sample from one of my subjects in the STAT protein study I'm working on."

"What kind of tests?" Bart asked.

"I noticed an elevated white blood cell count, and I'm worried this subject might have an infection. I spend my time looking at tumor markers, not viral or bacterial ones, so I'm way outta my league here. I was hoping you could run ELISA on the sample to see what antibodies are present."

"Sure, just drop the sample off in my lab with Jon, and we'll get to it when things slow down a bit."

Julie grimaced. "I was hoping that you could maybe run it now. I'm really worried about this subject and feel it's my responsibility to notify this person of their condition."

"You want me to drop everything and do it now? We've got a busy day planned," Bart resisted.

"Please," she said, with puppy dog eyes. "As a favor to me?"

He rubbed his beardless chin. "Since you haven't given me any direction as to what virus or bacteria I am supposed to be looking for, I'll need to check a fairly extensive list of possible diseases. And since this is such a small sample volume, I'll need to amplify using real-time PCR and then run multiple assays. It's not as easy as you think, Julie."

"I know, but if you were this patient, wouldn't you hope that a brilliant guy at Wien Bioscience named Bart Bennett was willing to do the right thing to save your life?" she asked.

"Okay fine. But I want you to know, your Jedi mind tricks don't work on me."

"Is that so?" she said, smiling as she grabbed him by the arm and dragged him out of his chair. "You will take me to Jabba now."

•   •   •

"WHAT DID YOU find?" Julie asked.

Bart and his Austrian lab technician Jon Henning were standing together talking when Julie approached them.

Barely able to contain his excitement, Jon spoke first. "I don't know where you found this sample, but it's either from a laboratory primate or a special forces soldier who's been inoculated against biological warfare."

"I don't understand. What do you mean?"

"This blood is packed with antibodies. Exotic bugs, too. I ran a broad serological workup and found smallpox, anthrax, even

Yersinia pestis antibodies. Check out this list I compiled," Jon said. "But that's not even the most exciting thing we found."

She took the printed page from Jon, and scanned the list. It took all her willpower not to gasp at the report. She looked at Bart who seemed uncharacteristically melancholy, especially when contrasted to Jon's bravado. Bart would not look at her and instead was staring off at some imaginary point in space. "What's the exciting part?" she said.

"I have several scanning electron microscope images to show you. I false colored the image so you can tell the different cells apart. The flattened donut-shaped cells are of course red bloods, and these little cream-colored blobs are platelets. This green cell is a monocyte. All normal," he said and advanced the screen to a new image. "In this image, over here you can see two more lymphocytes, again normal. But this cell, colored blue, I don't know what it is. It appears to be a lymphocyte, but it is too big. Lymphocytes are seven to eight micrometers, this cell appears to be twelve or thirteen."

Julie bent over and rested her palms on the desk, bringing her face closer to the monitor for a better look. "Is it neutrophil?"

"No. It's not a neutrophil, basophil, or eosinophil. Granulocytes have multi-lobed nuclei; this cell is mononuclear."

"Maybe it's a monocyte then?"

Jon advanced to another image with higher magnification. "I don't believe so. Because if you look closely at the microvilli on the surface of the cell they resemble those of a lymphocyte. Monocyte microvilli are longer, more densely packed, and . . ." He gestured with his hand in the air in a motion like a car traveling over a hilly stretch of road. "What's the word in English?"

"Wavy?"

"Yes, wavy," he said.

"Are you sure about the size?"

"Yes, I'm sure," Jon said. "Since your are the cancer expert here, I was hoping you could tell me if you think it could be a cancerous lymphocyte?"

"It's hard to identify cancer cells when viewed in isolation, but the shape of this cell is uniform. From outward appearance, I'd say it looks like a healthy cell."

"That's what I thought too," Jon said, with schoolboy excitement. "So I decided to run more tests, and I found something else."

Julie nodded.

"There are five major categories of antibodies: IgA, IgG, IgM, IgE, and IgD. The IgG anti-bodies are the most common type, found in all bodily fluids and tissues, and comprise about seventy-five percent of the antibodies in circulation at a given time. IgA antibodies make up about ten percent and are found predominantly in the entry and exit orifices of the body—nose, ears, eyes, etcetera. IgM antibodies are . . ."

"I'm up to speed on my antibodies, Jon. You can skip to the something else part," she interrupted.

"Ya, okay. I ran a quantitative immunoglobulin screening, and I found an immunoglobulin that doesn't fit into any of the existing classes or subclasses. I don't know what it is or what it does." He minimized the SEM images and pulled up a data table.

Julie looked at the screening results. "If you had to guess, what do think it is?"

"Maybe it's new subclass of IgG, but I have no way to test this right now. So, I was thinking about running an IgY test just for the hell of it?" Jon replied.

"IgY? Isn't that an avian antibody?"

"Yes, bird and reptile. I don't think this is IgY, but I have the EIA to test for it. It could be a starting point. After that, I was thinking about performing a TCR diversity assessment on the lymphocytes in the blood sample."

"What's a TCR diversity assessment?'

"TCR stands for T cell Receptor. Analyzing the receptors on a lymphocyte is one way to identify what kind of lymphocyte it is. T cells and B cells are so morphologically similar that scanning electron microscope images don't provide a reliable means of distinguishing them. So, I need to analyze them chemically. Maybe the mystery lymphocyte in the SEM image is responsible for generating this new antibody . . . we could be looking at a breakthrough discovery."

"Bart, what do you make of all this?" Julie asked.

"It's definitely an anomaly, but at this point it's nothing to get too excited about. Where did you say you got this sample from?"

"From a clinical subject in the STAT protein study I'm working on. Why?"

"Oh, just curious."

This was not the response she had expected from Bart. He was usually excitable and talkative, especially when it came to questions in his specialty. The more she thought about it, the more Bart's behavior made her nervous. First, she would have expected him to be downright euphoric over the discovery of this strange new lymphocyte. Second, she had expected him to panic about her violating BSL safety protocols given the antibodies found in the sample. The one response she had not expected from him was indifference.

"Jon, can you print copies of the SEM images and the other test results for me?" she asked.

"Not a problem," Jon said. "Hey, maybe we can get this subject in for some tests. Is this a local subject pool, or are these samples being shipped in from somewhere else?"

Julie hesitated and then replied, "The samples are from our UK office, but I'll call over there this morning, report what we've found, and lobby for this subject to fly here for tests."

"Great! I'll go grab the pages off the printer for you."

"Julie?" Bart put his hand on her shoulder. "I'd like you to turn over the rest of the blood samples you have from this patient to me this morning. With the antibodies we found in the blood, this subject's blood needs to be controlled with Biosafety Level Three protocols."

"If I recall, you said this was nothing to get too excited about."

"I did, and it's not. But safety is paramount, and with the type of antibodies present in this sample it would be prudent to treat it as an infectious agent."

Julie paused, trying to formulate her response. "The vial I gave you this morning was all I have left from this week's delivery, after running all my usual tests. I'll contact the UK branch this morning, however, and instruct them that biosafety hazard protocols need to be implemented regarding this subject."

Bart looked if he was about to speak when Jon returned from the printer holding the pages she had requested.

"Here you go, Julie. If you're not busy, you are welcome to help us. Bart and I have plenty of other tests we can run this morning. This is very, very exciting."

"I need to discuss this with the folks in my department and call the UK office, but I'll pop back in later. This could be huge if we've discovered a new lymphocyte," she said. She folded the printed pages in half, tucked them inside her purse, and headed for the door. On her way out, she called back over her shoulder, "Thanks, guys. I really appreciate you jumping on this for me."

Bart stood in silence and watched her leave with a scowl. Then he turned to his assistant. "I'm going need the rest of that sample, to run some more tests. Oh and Jon, until we know what we're dealing with here, I think it would be best if you not discuss this with anyone. Okay?"

"Ya, okay," Jon replied with a raised eyebrow. "You're the boss."

•　　•　　•

JULIE WALKED AS swiftly as she could, without running, through the corridors toward the west exit. Something was wrong; her intuition was burning like a five-alarm fire. This was not the first time Bart had seen antibodies like the ones in Will's blood. He was hiding something from her . . . and she was certain that something had to do with Will.

Chapter Twenty

Prague, Czech Republic

ALBANE TWIRLED AN ink pen around her forefinger like a tiny propeller with rhythmic flicks of her right thumb. With her left, she pressed icons on a touch screen tablet computer that she had propped on a small table in the hotel suite in Prague. For the third time, she cued up the recording of the brief with Meredith Morley from the Founder's Forum. The software even allowed her to insert "chapters" like a DVD movie, for ease of navigation and playback.

The first time through, she just listened.

During the second playback, she edited out all other speakers except for Meredith and made time-annotated notes.

She was the team's RS:Social—deciphering human behavior was her specialty—and she wanted as many data points as possible. So, for the third playback, she fetched AJ and asked him to listen. She wanted to watch his expressions, compare his untrained visceral reactions to her own conclusions, without having his judgments influenced by hers.

"Are you ready?"

"Yes," he said.

She pressed "play" and watched AJ in silence. She had not told him why she wanted him to wear headphones, and he had not asked. As he listened, she took notes on a clean sheet of paper. If he twitched, nodded, sighed, changed his facial expression, or even blinked, she would jot down the time from the playback counter. When the recording finished, she retrieved the notes from her previous listening session and laid them next to the notes she had just taken. She scanned the time stamps for matches. She had made nineteen entries on her sheet, and seven on his. Between the two sheets, she identified two times that matched to the second.

"Interesting," he commented as he watched her work.

She nodded and cued up the first matching time.

"Shall we listen to the two matching sections together?"

"Absolutely."

"Okay, here is the first one we both reacted to."

"For the past ten years, Vyrogen and its subsidiaries have been working on developing vaccines and treatments for the diseases that can be used as biological weapons. We are also searching for treatments for other global killers such as malaria, AIDS, ALS, etcetera. You name it; we want to find a way to treat it."

"When you were listening to this, you scratched your neck repeatedly with your index finger below your right ear," she said, looking at her notes. "What bothered you about this segment?"

"I'm not really sure. Why does it matter that I scratched my neck?"

"Neck scratching is a common reaction by a listener indicating anxiety or disagreement to what a speaker is saying."

"I didn't know that."

She lifted her notes for him to see. "When I listened to this segment, the following thought came to mind."

TREATMENT ≠ CURE

"Interesting," he mumbled.

"I thought so, too. Why would Meredith say 'you name it, we want to find a way to *treat* it' and not 'you name it, we want to find a way to *cure* it'?"

He nodded. "If we take her words literally, then she doesn't want to find cures. She wants to find treatments."

She smiled. "Exactly. Now replace the word 'find' with the word 'supply'. She doesn't want to *supply* cures; she wants to *supply* treatments. It seems like nuance, but it's actually paradigmatic."

"Go on."

"We should ask ourselves the following question: Is Big Pharma, like Vyrogen, in the business of selling cures or selling treatments? Consider this: if you cure a patient of disease, you make a sale, but ultimately you lose your customer. But when you treat a patient, you have an ongoing revenue stream. Keeping their customers for life, that's the strategic business model that benefits Vyrogen most. Why do you think drug companies like to label every ailment a disease or syndrome? Is acid reflux really a disease? What about obesity? Drug companies want us to think so. That way they can sell us a little purple pill that we have to take every day for the rest of our lives."

"That's cynical."

She sighed. "That's reality."

"What about BioShield? How does that fit into this equation?"

"I'm not sure yet, but the web is growing more and more tangled, isn't it?"

"I'd say so. I guess it's our job to untangle it."

"We wouldn't be paid like sultans if it were otherwise," she replied. "Let's move on to the next match."

She entered the time of the second match and pressed PLAY to hear the clip.

"To our surprise, Foster became ill during the trial period. Testing revealed that he was infected with a mutated strain of H1N1—but a different strain from the one we were targeting with the vaccine. This warranted placing him in quarantine and contacting the Centers for Disease Control and Prevention."

"What did she say here that's suspicious?" AJ asked.

"It's not what she said, but what she did when she was saying it. Let me play the clip back again on mute."

AJ watched intently as Albane played the video. "I don't notice anything unusual."

"Watch again in two times fast forward."

"Oh! It looks like she's swatting at her nose. She did it twice, in rapid succession."

"You didn't notice it before at normal time lapse because our mind is accustomed to screening out familiar gestures as mundane. Changing the speed of the video opens the mind to a new perception."

"What does it mean? The gesture, that is?"

"Nose touching is one of the most informative tells for lying."

"Maybe she just has a cold or allergies. I have allergies and my nose and eyes bother me all the time," AJ said. "I'm always rubbing my eyes and wiping my nose."

"It's a question of context, of course. The cornerstone of reading body language is first understanding the context in which the subject is interacting. In this case, Meredith is speaking publicly, and she is the center of attention. I can say with confidence that the tell is legitimate, not allergy related."

"Why is nose touching a tell for lying?"

"It's a well-documented and -studied phenomenon. Research has found that when a person is lying, a chemical called catecholamine is released in the body, causing tissue inside the nose to swell. The increased blood pressure inflates the nose. This in turn causes the nerve endings in the end of nose to tingle, resulting in an unmistakable itch. Without professional training to suppress the behavior, a liar will invariably rub his or her nose to alleviate the sensation."

"You're kidding. Sounds like Pinocchio."

"It's actually referred to as the Pinocchio Effect."

"What is she lying about?"

"The tell isn't that specific. It only tells me Meredith is lying, but not what piece of information she's lying about."

"We know for certain that Foster was infected with a mutated version of H1N1, or they wouldn't have put him in quarantine," AJ said.

"Not necessarily. You are falling into the trap of assuming that everything the client tells us is true. In my experience, we should question all assumptions. Nothing is fact until we corroborate the information ourselves."

"How can we ever move forward if we have to fact-check every aspect of the case?"

"Sometimes it's better to jog in place, than to sprint down the wrong path and be forced to double back."

AJ hesitated. "Chiarek Norse? We're not seriously going to . . ."

"What you are alluding to is something we refer to in the Tank as *sampling the client*," she said.

AJ nodded, no further explanation was necessary. "Isn't that a bit, uh,—"

"Risky."

"I was going to say illegal, but yeah, I guess risky sums it up."

"Sampling the client is sometimes a necessary part of our job. Once you're in this business long enough, you come to realize that our clients are not always entirely forthcoming with us," she explained. "Sometimes we need to take a peek inside the purse of the lady of the house, while she's in the other room. The decision to sample the client is not a decision that you or I have the authority to make."

"Nicolora?"

"Yes. It's Nicolora's call, and his alone."

AJ was about to ask the obvious question when they heard the door lock disengage, signaling that Kalen was back from his reconnaissance outing. Albane sent AJ to fetch VanCleave and Veronika, who were working in the adjoining suite.

"So?" Albane said once the team was gathered.

"The facility is located inside the city, housed in a four-story stone building, built around the turn of the twentieth century. Access is through a main lobby and controlled by an attendant at a security desk and an armed uniformed guard. Elevator banks have RFID security tag readers. Standard external and internal ceiling mounted security camera system. A fire escape stairwell exit is located on the west side—blocked by a hollow steel door, wired, with no external handle or lock. The facility is a research hospital and laboratory owned and operated by a Czech company called Chiarek Norse, which according to our research is a wholly-owned subsidiary of Vyrogen Pharmaceuticals," Kalen explained, crossing his legs casually.

"What is your accessibility rating of the facility?" Albane asked.

"On a scale of one to ten, where the Pentagon is a ten and and your grandma's house is a one, I'd rank it a solid six. How serious are we?"

"It's Nicolora's call, but I have reason to believe a sampling op is warranted," she said.

AJ's stomach was in knots. Albane was convinced Meredith was hiding something, but breaking into the Vyrogen facility seemed extreme. What if they were wrong? Even worse, what if they were wrong and they got caught? They would probably end up in jail.

The phones of all the Tank team members in the room began to chime in unison. It was Parish signaling that new information was available for discussion.

VYROGEN CASE—ROUND TABLE SESSION—PRAGUE

R. Parish—*RS:Coordinator.* "The purpose of this conference is to report the findings of the tasking I was assigned during our last Round Table. Continued background investigation on Foster reveals that his life before Vyrogen was quite unremarkable. He has no criminal record, no legal action pending against him, and no discernible enemies."

A. Mesnil—*RS:Social.* "What about insight into Foster's professional life and personal life? What did Ms. Knight learn from her interviews with Foster's work colleagues?"

R. Parish—*RS:Coordinator.* "Ms. Knight identified and interviewed one of Foster's closest friends. She learned that he was laid off from his job nine months ago. His girlfriend at the time did not adjust well to his strained financial state and also let him go. From what Ms. Knight uncovered, we can conclude Foster was struggling, both financially and emotionally, around the time he became involved with Vyrogen."

A. Mesnil—*RS:Social.* "How dire was his financial status?"

R. Parish—*RS:Coordinator.* "Foster had been living paycheck to paycheck. He carried a credit card balance and was still paying off his college tuition loan. His corporate 401(k) showed an early withdrawal, with penalty, a few weeks before he signed on as a test subject in the Leighton-Harris vaccine trial. He had also enrolled in another paid drug trial with Pfizer, but he did not participate because of the quarantine."

K. Immel—*RS:Physical*: "Looks like we can add money to the list of possible motives."

A. Mesnil—*RS:Social*: "Did you uncover any connections or relationships Foster may have had with other pharmaceutical companies?"

R. Parish—*RS:Coordinator*: "None, but we're still looking."

K. Immel—*RS:Physical*: "What about government contacts?"

R. Parish—*RS:Coordinator*: "Nothing."

A. Archer—*RS:Bio*: "What accounts did Foster manage for his firm?"

R. Parish—*RS:Coordinator*: "Primarily, the Cluckers Fried Chicken account."

A. Archer—*RS:Bio*: "Does Foster's firm handle any pharmaceutical accounts at all?"

R. Parish—*RS:Coordinator*: "Yes. They manage the cholesterol-busting drug Plaxzer's ad campaign, and were behind Synthgen's infamous Stimulex erectile dysfunction drug ads."

A. Archer—*RS:Bio*: "So, we can't rule out contacts at Synthgen."

R. Parish—*RS:Coordinator*: "No. I have a resource looking into it."

K. Immel—*RS:Physical*: "Another detail has been nagging me. Why do you suppose Foster was transferred to Vyrogen's Chiarek Norse facility in Prague instead of staying at the New Jersey campus? What's so special about the Chiarek Norse facility that Vyrogen wanted Foster out of the country? In my opinion, Chiarek Norse is the white elephant in the room. If Meredith Morley is keeping something from us, we'll find it in Chiarek Norse."

E. VanCleave—*RS:Technical*: "What makes you so you sure that the information we need is inside Chiarek Norse?"

K. Immel—*RS:Physical*: "It's obvious to me, but if you need a reason, then call it instinct."

E. VanCleave—*RS:Technical*: "Instinct is not sufficient. Without an explanation of your decision-making processes, I am forced to conclude it is your testosterone talking, and not your intellect."

K. Immel—*RS:Physical*: "You sound exactly like Briggs."

E. VanCleave—*RS:Technical*: "I'll take that as a compliment."

A. Mesnil—*RS:Social*: "Enough with the schoolyard banter. I realize that everyone is tired and stressed, but we all need to take a deep breath and focus on the task at hand. Let's shift gears. I reviewed the entire recording of Meredith Morley's briefing in the Founder's Forum, and I have ascertained that on at least three occasions Ms. Morley either withheld or misrepresented information about the case. Couple this with the fact that we have no hard evidence linking Will Foster to any external entity trying to steal Vyrogen's formula, and the suspicious transfer of Foster to the Chiarek Norse in Prague, leads me to conclude that we have compelling reason to engage in a sampling operation. Opinions?"

K. Immel—*RS:Physical*: "You already know my opinion . . . definitely worth a look inside."

E. VanCleave—*RS:Technical*: "No surprise there."

A. Mesnil—*RS:Social*: "Excuse me, Doctor, was that a yes or a no from you?"

E. VanCleave—*RS:Technical*: "Yes. But let the record show, a reluctant yes."

A. Mesnil—*RS:Social*: "Fine. Bio?"

A. Archer—*RS:Bio*: "Yes. I'd like a peek inside."

A. Mesnil—*RS:Social*: "Good. Then, we're all in agreement. Time is our most precious commodity. Mr. Parish, contact Founder One and obtain authorization for a sampling operation at Chiarek Norse, commencing at the earliest opportunity."

A. Archer—*RS:Bio*: "Hold on a minute. We're going to break into the facility in broad daylight? Shouldn't we wait until night?"

E. VanCleave—*RS:Technical*: "A common misconception popularized by television crime dramas. The reality is, at least for the Tank, that daytime ops have a statistically significant higher rate of success than nighttime efforts."

A. Archer—*RS:Bio*: "What? I don't see how that can be possible."

K. Immel—*RS:Physical*: "Think of us not as thieves, but as illusionists. It's a matter of redirecting your target's attention. Like when I lifted your wallet in the Public Garden . . . while you were gawking at Albane's tits. Or, a minute ago, when I lifted your phone while I was arguing with VanCleave."

A. Archer—*RS:Bio*: "How do you do that?"

K. Immel—*RS:Physical*: "It's called practice. With time, your talents will blossom too."

A. Mesnil—*RS:Social*: "Kalen, how long do you need to prep?"

K. Immel—*RS:Physical:* "For which scenario?"

A. Mesnil—*RS:Social*: "I was thinking Bravo Eight Delta."

K. Immel—*RS:Physical:* "Not bad. But I was thinking more along the lines of Bravo Fourteen Echo."

A. Mesnil—*RS:Social*: "Interesting. I like it. VanCleave?"

E. VanCleave—*RS:Technical*: "Too dangerous. Archer has no training for an Echo scenario. I recommend Bravo Fourteen Delta."

A. Mesnil—*RS:Social*: "Mr. Parish, your thoughts on executing Sampling Scenario Bravo Fourteen Delta?"

R. Parish—*RS:Coordinator*: "I concur with Bravo Fourteen Delta."

A. Mesnil—*RS:Social*: "Kalen, how long do you need to prep?"

K. Immel—*RS:Physical:* "Ninety minutes to wheels up, assuming VanCleave can be ready in time."

E. VanCleave—*RS:Technical*: "Of course I'll be ready."

A. Mesnil—*RS:Social*: "We'll need paperwork."

V. Viskaya—*EMBED: Czech Ministry of Health*: "I'll take care of that."

A. Mesnil—*RS:Social*: "And an Electrician."

R. Parish—*Coordinator*: "We have two in Prague. I'll make the calls."

A. Mesnil—*RS:Social*: "We'll probably need an ambulance too."

K. Immel—*RS:Physical*: "We'll definitely need an ambulance."

R. Parish—*Coordinator*: "Understood."

A. Mesnil—*RS:Social*: "Okay, then it's decided, we prep and wait for the green light from Nicolora. Any questions?"

A. Archer—*RS:Bio*: "Um guys, could somebody please explain to me what a Bravo Fourteen Delta is?"

Chapter Twenty-One

Vienna, Austria

WILL WOKE IN Julie's bed, alone. He checked the clock on the bedside table. It read 10:47 AM. He did not hear Julie leave and had no idea what time to expect her return. She had not left a note, but he assumed she had gone to her lab to analyze his blood sample as they had agreed. He swung his legs off the side of the bed, stretched, and cracked his back. He took a hot shower and dressed grudgingly back in the same tired, dirty clothes he had worn since Miss Sophie's.

He wandered into the kitchen and poured himself a small glass of orange juice. He sat down at the tiny kitchen table and considered his predicament. Even with Julie's help, he still had plenty to worry about. His biggest problem was that he did not have any leverage over his adversaries. Nothing to level the playing field. He needed a bargaining chip. Something to trade besides just his body.

He retrieved the glass vial of synthesized product from his pocket and held it between his thumb and index finger. *This*, he thought staring at it, could be the last of its kind. He had destroyed the rest of the inventory the night he escaped. However, for the sample to be effective leverage, he needed to find a safe place to hide it. That way, if he were captured, the sample would still be at large. The hiding place needed to be secure and yet easily accessible. He brainstormed, trying to imagine where such an oxymoronic place might exist:

Bank safety deposit box?

Banks had security cameras, restrictive hours, and would demand him to provide ID and paperwork. Strike one.

Post office box?

P.O. boxes aren't like mailboxes; they're unidirectional. He could place the vial in a self-addressed envelope and leave it inside. No one would take it out but him. Unfortunately, the postal service was a federal entity, and he was certain they would require ID and paperwork just like a bank. Strike two.

Julie's apartment?

Easily accessible yes, but not particularly secure. Eventually his enemies would make the connection, and Julie's apartment would be the first place they would look for him. Strike three.

Dread washed over him. He'd put Julie and her roommate at terrible risk by staying in the apartment, and it was tying his stomach in knots. He needed fresh air and decided to go for a walk. Although it galled him to do it, he left the apartment door unlocked so that he could get back in if he returned before Julie.

As he walked the streets of the embassy district, he scanned the landscape, hoping a survey of the surroundings would coax an idea. Rising skyward from behind a nearby building, he noticed twin spires and a green-tarnished copper cupola topped with a gold cross. He smiled. A church. A church met both of his criteria: freely accessible, yet ironically secure. He would find a dark inconspicuous place to hide the vial. Perhaps inside a confessional, or simply taped underneath a pew. With renewed spirit in his stride, he set off toward the nearby church.

•   •   •

"I WAS GETTING worried, you've been gone awhile," Will said to Julie as she stepped across the threshold into the apartment. He glanced at a nearby wall clock. It was twelve thirty; she had been gone the entire morning. "How did it go?"

She shut the apartment door, leaned back against it, and exhaled deeply.

"Will, there is some really weird shit going on inside that body of yours."

"Tell me something I don't know," he said. "What did you find? Were you able to figure out what they injected me with? Am I infected? Am I contagious?"

"The tests show that your blood is packed with antibodies."

"What does that mean?"

"It means that you've been exposed to many different pathogens." Julie handed him a printout.

He scanned the list, aghast.

"Anthrax, smallpox, tularemia . . . I'll be damned."

"I know," she said and then, echoing Jon Henning's words added, "Your blood panel looks like a sample from either a special forces operative or a test monkey in a BSL-4 lab."

Will spied an entry on the list that made him blanch. *Yersinia pestis.* That was the name written on the vial that Rutgers broke at Miss Sophie's. He had forgotten the Latin name until now.

"What is this one?" he asked, pointing at the list.

She craned her neck to read the entry by his index finger. "*Yersinia pestis,* that's bubonic plague."

"Bubonic plague?"

She nodded.

"Everything on this list is something that I'm infected with?"

She smiled. "No Will, I wouldn't be sitting at this table with you if you were infected with all of these horrible diseases."

He cocked his head at her. "I thought you said all these pathogens were in my blood?"

"No. What I said was that you have antibodies in your blood for these pathogens."

"So, I'm not infected or contagious right now?"

"No. In fact, if this analysis is correct, you are probably the least contagious person on Earth, because your immune system is primed to eradicate every disease on this list. But there's more." She spread out the SEM images on the table.

"What are those?"

"Scanning Electron Microscope images taken of lymphocytes in your blood."

"Cool."

"Cool does not even begin to describe this," she exclaimed putting her arm around his shoulder as they stood hunched over the table. "We found a cell that we've never seen before . . . Oh my God, I'm such an idiot."

"I'm confused," he said.

She pulled away and started pacing. "I can't believe I didn't realize it until now. This . . ." she said tapping the picture repeatedly with her index finger, "is why they took you. I need more information. Is there anything else you haven't told me? Anything at all?"

Her question caught him off guard, and so he did not answer her.

"Come with me," she said, tugging him by the arm. She led him into her bedroom and sat down at her desk. She booted up her notebook computer, logged into her Wi-Fi network, and opened a browser window. She typed in the words Leighton-Harris Pharmaceuticals and ran a search. Instantly, she found the company homepage and clicked on the "About" button on the menu bar. A new page loaded and she scanned the text until she confirmed her suspicion.

". . . *Leighton-Harris is a wholly-owned subsidiary of Vyrogen Pharmaceuticals.*"

Chapter Twenty-Two

Prague, Czech Repubic

"**N**ERVOUS?"

"Yes."

"Don't be. You have the easy job. No acting, no speaking, just walking around looking for the servers," Kalen said to AJ.

"You can't be serious! I'm the one who has to sneak around the facility, break into secure rooms, and risk being shot by armed guards. Oh, and how can I forget, hold my breath the entire time so I don't contract the plague."

"You don't have to hold your breath the *entire* time. Only when you run into patients with purple pulsating pustules."

AJ shuddered.

"Any last minute questions before we go?" Albane asked the group.

"Yeah, just one. What percentage of Victoria's Secret's annual push-up bra sales do you generate anyway?" Kalen said staring at her liberal cleavage, strategically framed by the low-cut gray blouse that she wore.

"Any serious questions before we go?"

"Actually, I'm still a little foggy on my role," AJ said.

"That's because it's open ended. Sometimes ops are fluid, sometimes dynamic, sometimes chaotic. The truth is these things don't go down in the real world like they do in the movies. We never have all the answers before we go in. Once Veronika, Kalen, and I have

151

obtained the facility floor plans, the Coordinator will tell you what to do. To use a military term, think of yourself as being in 'Hot Standby.' You'll be waiting outside in case we need you. If VanCleave is able to hack into their servers remotely, then your entry will be aborted. If not, you'll be going in," she explained.

"All I have to do is plug this device into the server rack, and Van-Cleave's program will do the rest?" AJ said, holding up a memory stick with an Ethernet connection on one end, and a USB fitting on the other.

"Yes," VanCleave replied, "Unless, of course, the server room is locked."

"And if the server room is locked?"

"Hold out your hand," VanCleave said.

AJ extended his hand, and VanCleave dropped in his open palm three, slightly flattened, oval-shaped objects. Each device was about the size of a grape and was constructed of black plastic and polished metal. A groove ran axially along the flattened side, and four smaller equally spaced lines radiated transversely outward from it. Upon further scrutiny, he noticed seams, as thin as hairs, scribing the entire surface in a complex geometric pattern.

"They look like mechanical origami. Whatever they are, they're all folded up." AJ said, inspecting the ovoids.

"Mechanical origami . . . I like that one," VanCleave replied, "I'll have to add that to the list."

"What are these things?"

"They have lots of names: spiders, crawlers, Abbey's ants, robo-bugs."

"What do they do?"

"They crawl into wire ducts, server racks, computer terminals. They can plug themselves into ports, bite into data cables, and stream data wirelessly. They were my idea," VanCleave sniffed. "The good old days when you could hack into anybody's mainframe are gone. No organization concerned with file security would network their data centers to the Internet when their files contain ultra-sensitive information. Even the best firewall can be hacked. But the best hacker in the world can't remotely access a physically segregated network."

"You're telling me these things are remote control bugs that hack computer networks?"

"Autonomous mechanical infiltrators . . . yes."

"Next you're going to tell me that the Coordinators aren't actual people but Artificial Intelligence programs," AJ said.

"Don't be ridiculous. We're at least five years away from having virtual Coordinators," VanCleave replied stone-faced.

"All right boys, I'm sure this is all very interesting, but we have a timetable to meet. Our ride is waiting," Albane said. "VanCleave, we'll be live in twenty minutes."

"I'll be ready."

"YES, I UNDERSTAND, Madame Viskaya, but we were not made aware of this inspection, so I have no authorization to let you into the facility," the sturdy woman at the reception desk insisted.

A small crowd had gathered in the lobby of the Chiarek Norse research hospital. The day manager had been called down from her office, and despite her bulldogged stance, was beginning to sweat. Two security guards had also joined the mix. The senior guard, a heavyset middle-aged man with dark circles under his eyes, and the door guard, a tall, muscular boy of about nineteen, had taken post on opposing corners of the desk. Like a pair of unmatched bookends they stood at attention, gargoyle and knight. Standing opposite the day manager was Veronika Viskaya with her hands planted firmly on the desk leaning forward over a stack of official Ministry of Health inspection documents she had ramrodded through the proper channels an hour earlier. To her left stood Albane Mesnil, and to her right Kalen Immel. They were dressed in fine dark-colored suits tailored in the physique-accentuating European fashion. Veronika had taken the lead and assumed a direct and assertive posturing. Kalen feigned boredom, frequently yawning and checking his watch. Albane had remained silent, but was passively garnering the attention of the male security guards.

Think Tank Scenario Bravo Fourteen Delta was proceeding precisely according to plan.

"Of course you do not have pre-authorization. This is a *surprise* inspection. If the Ministry were to inform your management in advance, it would no longer be a surprise, now would it?" Veronika barked in Czech.

"This is a secure building, and I simply cannot let someone walk in from the street and grant access for a tour," the day manager retorted.

"I don't think you understand. I have official government paperwork here that says that you must make your facility available for a health and safety inspection. We have received information that a biological contamination breach occurred at this very facility within the past seventy-two hours. An inspection is mandatory. We are not asking for your permission, we are informing you that we *will* be conducting the inspection and demand your cooperation."

"I am sorry, Madame Inspector, but we are under strict instructions that no unauthorized personnel may enter these premises at any time for any reason," the woman replied with conviction. "I am authorized to order the guards to use force to protect this mandate."

Veronika looked at Albane.

Albane removed her eyeglasses, carefully folded them, and placed them inside her breast pocket. She then stared directly into the reception attendant's eyes, holding the gaze in silence until the other woman looked away. Then she removed her mobile phone from its belt holster and began to dial.

The woman fidgeted. "What are you doing? Who are you calling?"

"This facility is hereby closed, until further notice by the Ministry of Health. I am calling the state police," Albane replied stoically in Czech.

"What? You can't do that!"

"I can, and I am." Albane leaned forward, pretending to strain to read the name tag on the woman's shirt. "Not to worry, Ms. Provst, in my report I will be sure to document that you were steadfast in your truculence and hindrance of official Ministry business. I'm certain that your management will take your loyalty into consideration when they are rehiring security positions six months from now when the facility reopens."

"What? You can't close this facility for six months! How am I supposed to provide for my family?"

"It is funny that you keep telling me what I can and cannot do. The Ministry does not care about your opinion. Now, either you give me your full cooperation this instant, or you and your coworkers will all be arrested by the state police. *Do I make myself clear?*" Albane slammed the bottom of her clenched fist on the reception desk with such force that Ms. Provst, the security guards, and even Veronika, were startled.

"Okay. Please, please do not call the state police. You will have our cooperation. I have never had one of these inspections before. What do we need to do?"

Albane put her mobile phone back into its holster. "It's quite simple really. Madame Viskaya will stay here and interview you. Once your interview is complete, then you can begin filling out the official paperwork, while she interviews the guards. My colleague and I will tour the facility and then conduct a record review."

"How long will the inspection last?"

"That depends on what we find, now doesn't it?"

"We have a shift change soon."

"That's okay, we don't mind. You will need to make sure that someone is available during the next shift to answer our questions should we have any. If the hour grows late and the record audit is not complete, we'll return in the morning to finish."

"But, I'm not sure that—"

Albane interrupted, "But, nothing. We are wasting time." She then retrieved her eyeglasses with hidden nano-camera technology from her suit pocket, and put them on. "The first thing we'll need to look at are the blueprints of this building."

C. Remy—*RS:Coordinator*: "Technical online?"

E. VanCleave—*RS:Technical*: "Technical online."

C. Remy—*RS:Coordinator*: "Technical, report status of acquiring network access."

E. VanCleave—*RS:Technical*: "Negative access. Bio is a go for entry."

C. Remy—*RS:Coordinator*: "Bio, online?"

A. Archer—*RS:Bio*: "This is Bio, I copy you."

C. Remy—*RS:Coordinator*: "You are a go for entry. Social has scanned the building plans. I am uploading the data now."

A. Archer—*RS:Bio*: "Is my route inside the building mapped yet?"

C. Remy—*RS:Coordinator*: "Standby. I'll advise you when it is . . . Electrician online?"

Local Embed—*Electrician*: "This is the Electrician, online and in position at the underground electrical distribution box. Standing by to cut power on your mark."

C. Remy—*RS:Coordinator*: "Roger. What about the backup generator?"

Local Embed—*Electrician*: "Disabled."

C. Remy—*RS:Coordinator*: "Roger . . . Physical, this is the Co-ordinator. All Resources are in position, you're a go for blocking the door."

THE MIDDLE-AGED SECURITY guard flashed Albane a furtive grin; she pretended not to notice. After twenty-three years working security, smiling was as foreign to the muscles of his face as performing a cartwheel is to a nursing home patient. Even after the tongue lashing Albane had given Ms. Provst, Officer Clive Moderkiek had eagerly volunteered to escort the inspectors during their tour of the facility. It was not for fear of losing his job; he wasn't worried about that. It was simply to be near her. He had never encountered a woman as beautiful and confident as this Inspector woman before, and now he was captured by her gravity.

"Officer Moderkiek, please show us where the contamination breach occurred," Albane directed in Czech.

"Do you mean the emergency exit where the patient escaped?"

"Yes. We can start there and work backward. I want to see the exact path that he took. I want to know how he escaped from his room and got outside this building."

"Okay, no problem. All compromised areas have been thoroughly decontaminated. Follow me," Moderkiek said. Leaving his colleagues behind in the lobby with Veronika, Moderkiek led Albane and Kalen past the elevator bank and through a closed door with an exit sign overhead.

"This is an old building. The elevators were not installed until the 1980s. At one time, this stairwell was the main stairwell for traveling between all the floors of the building, but now it functions as the emergency exit. During the incident, the patient jumped from the fourth floor and landed here," Moderkiek explained.

Albane looked down at the concrete floor. "How did he accomplish such a feat without injury?"

"I wasn't on duty that night, but the story is that he tied bedsheets together into a rope and used it to repel down to the ground."

Kalen snorted.

"Interesting. What did he do next?" Albane asked.

"He went through this door to Corridor E. At the end of the corridor is the emergency exit door which leads to the street."

"Show us."

"There is nothing to show. It is a typical emergency exit door."

"I want you to show us anyway."

The guard nodded obediently and led the pair down the long empty corridor until they arrived at the red metal door. "See, just a door."

"Does this door have a magnetic lock?"

"No," the guard replied quizzically.

"So my colleague can just push it open?"

"Of course, it's an emergency exit . . . Hey, what are you doing? Don't open that. The alarm will sound!"

A shrill pulsating alarm reverberated in Corridor E, and white strobes on the emergency exit sign above the door flashed. Kalen had opened the red door and was pretending to peer outside onto the street. With his hip depressing the horizontal rocker bar, he used his body to block the guard's view of the lock mechanism. In his left hand, he held a small cylinder—the size of a tube of lipstick—which contained a quick-dry epoxy adhesive mixed with propellant. He sprayed the adhesive liberally over the door latch mechanism while it was retracted. The epoxy film hardened on contact, instantly seizing the latch. Behind him, he could hear the security guard yelling, arguing with Albane. He released the rocker arm, looking down to make sure the latch did not spring back into position. It did not. He then let the door swing shut and turned to face the others, while slipping the epoxy back into his pocket with the fluidity of a magician.

"What the hell did you do that for? That is a security violation. I have to file a report on all security violations," Moderkiek complained.

"Officer Moderkiek," Albane said, "This emergency exit door was the point of a major contamination breach. We are here to evaluate the level of biosecurity for this facility. I see absolutely no controls in place at this boundary for biosecurity. This door can be opened by anyone."

"With all due respect, Madame Inspector, this door is an emergency exit. It is supposed to be free to open without any interference. If this door were locked, then during a fire anyone trapped inside corridor would die! Fire escapes are not biosecurity boundaries. Biosecurity is established via access checkpoints on each floor of the building, according to the classification of the work being conducted on the floor. The convention we use here is that Building Level Four, in other words the fourth floor, has BioSafety Level Four controls. The third floor has BioSafety Level Three controls. That way it is not confusing. You can only imagine the mess we'd have if the third floor had Level Four controls and the fourth floor had Level Three controls," Moderkiek explained, chuckling as did.

"Yes, well, that is one way of doing it, I suppose. We can talk about that later with our supervisors. Now, take us to the biosecurity access point on Level Four. We want to see the controls you have in place there."

• • •

C. Remy—*RS:Coordinator*: "Bio, this is the Coordinator. Take station at the emergency exit door."

A. Archer—*RS:Bio*: "This is Bio, roger that. Moving into position."

C. Remy—*RS:Coordinator*: "Electrician, standby to cut power."

Local Embed—*RS:Electrician*: "Standing by."

A. Archer—*RS:Bio*: "Coordinator, this is Bio. How is the video feed from my glasses?"

C. Remy—*RS:Coordinator*: "Receiving your feed on two-second time delay. It looks good."

A. Archer—*RS:Bio*: "I'm in position now."

C. Remy—*RS:Coordinator*: "Electrician, cut the power."

Local Embed—*RS:Electrician*: "The power is off. Standing by to restore power on your mark."

C. Remy—*RS:Coordinator*: "Bio, you are a go for entry."

A. Archer—*RS:Bio*: "Roger, I'm going in."

AJ PRESSED THE flat bottom of the star-shaped knob against the metal surface of the emergency exit door and turned it ninety degrees clockwise, just like Kalen had instructed him to do. From the street, the emergency exit door had no handle, so AJ needed to make one. Kalen had called the device a vacuum clamp; it worked like a suction cup, except it was orders of magnitude stronger and could adhere to virtually any solid surface. Turn it ninety degrees clockwise to engage, ninety degrees counterclockwise to disengage. Presto, instant doorknob.

AJ took a deep breath and pulled. The emergency exit door swung open with ease, the latch mechanism still frozen in the retracted position by Kalen's epoxy. AJ removed the vacuum clamp, slipped it back into his pocket, and stepped across the threshold. Corridor E was pitch dark, save the shrinking triangle of daylight that disappeared quickly as the door swung shut behind him. He had only eight minutes of darkness to complete the mission and no time to waste second-guessing. He needed to move. He extended his arms and walked at forty-five degree angle to his right, until his hand bumped into the wall. He turned his hand to the thumb down position so that his right palm laid flat against the wall. With a surface to guide him and aid his balance, AJ shuffled down the corridor.

C. Remy—*RS:Coordinator.* "Bio, report?"

The sound of C. Remy's voice suddenly in his ear startled AJ, almost causing him to trip.

A. Archer—*RS:Bio.* "I'm inside, moving down Corridor E, but it's pitch black."

C. Remy—*RS:Coordinator.* "Why aren't you using your light?"

A. Archer—*RS:Bio.* "Because . . . because I forgot I had a light."

AJ reached into the left pocket of his navy blue maintenance worker coveralls and retrieved the LED minilight. The beam from the flashlight illuminated a fifteen-foot cone in front of him. He jogged to the end of the corridor and then pressed his ear up against the door. He heard nothing. With the building power off and the elevators inoperable, traversing the stairs would be his biggest risk of counterdetection.

He turned off his light, opened the door, and crept into the bottom of the stairwell. Overhead, he heard another door swing open, followed by the sound of footsteps, then the door slammed shut with a reverberating echo. On a metal landing somewhere above him, two men began arguing heatedly in Czech; their individual flashlight beams zigzagged wildly over the concrete walls as they gestured.

He hesitated.

He had two choices: Slink up the stairs to the second floor now using their argument as a distraction, or wait for them to leave. With option one he risked an ill-fated mid-stair encounter; with option two he risked being pinned down too long to complete his mission.

His heart pounded.

He wanted someone to tell him what to do, but this time, he was on his own.

• • •

A BEAD OF sweat rolled down Albane's forehead. It was hot, uncomfortable, and rank inside the yellow biosafety suit, but she was smiling. Smiling in the dark. Scenario Bravo Fourteen Delta was going swimmingly. As soon as the power had gone out Officer Moderkiek had begun to panic. He had instructed his two charges to stay put at the security checkpoint at Corridor C, while he went back through the double doors to talk with another guard about checking on the emergency diesel generator. But staying put was the last thing she and Kalen intended to do. Nicolora had unexpectedly changed the Op Plan to include accessing the Level Four laboratory. No further explanation had been given. The instructions were simple, search for and retrieve any samples related to Vyrogen's secret formula. Entering the Chiarek Norse facility had gone smoothly. Exiting with the samples in hand and without blowing their cover was another matter altogether. Their success going forward hinged solely on Kalen's talents.

Albane nudged Kalen.

"Ready?"

"Yes."

"Let's go. Before Moderkiek comes back."

IN ALL THE years Moderkiek had worked in the building, he could recall losing power only once, and that time the emergency diesel generator on the roof had kicked on automatically. He was angry. The timing of this power outage could not have been worse for the Chiarek Norse security detail. First, the infected American escaped, and now this. With government inspectors present no less! He wanted to scream, and so he did, at the Corridor B security guard. Arguing with his colleague didn't solve anything, but it did make him feel better. It was imperative that someone check the diesel generator, but he did not want that someone to be him. He had assigned himself the responsibility of escorting the beautiful inspector woman, a responsibility he had no intention of delegating. Unfortunately, the Corridor

B security guard was steadfast in defending his obligation to remain at his post at the BioSecurity Level Four boundary door. As much as Moderkiek wanted to overrule the junior guard, he could not. As the senior guard on duty, if he could not find another guard to check on the diesel generator, he would have to do it himself.

From the corner of his eye, Moderkeik caught a glimpse of a flashlight moving in the stairwell below. He abruptly stopped yelling at the Level Four guard and peered down into the darkness. Someone had just entered the stairwell on the ground floor. Good. Whoever it was, Moderkeik would order him to check the diesel generator, so he could quickly return to his official escort duties.

AJ's LEGS SEEMED to make the decision for him, because he felt his body moving while his brain was still engaged in debate. He powered on the LED flashlight and aimed the beam downward toward the stairs. He could not afford an untimely tumble. Besides, all facility employees would be using flashlights—to do otherwise would be conspicuous.

To his dismay, the stairwell fell silent. A deep, angry voice bellowed in Czech above him. He knew the utterance was directed at him, but since he didn't speak Czech, he was unable to translate.

He kept moving.

The voice called out again.

He did not look up. Only a few meters left to go. As he reached for the door handle to access Level Two, he heard footsteps echoing above. He yanked and the door opened freely. He was in.

C. Remy—*RS:Coordinator.* "Good job, Bio. Proceed ten meters down the corridor. Turn right at the first intersection."

This time, the sound of the Coordinator's voice did not startle him. The opposite was true. Like an invisible wingman, C. Remy was with him. Guiding and emboldening him.

If the men in the stairwell were in chase, then he needed to be clear of their line of sight before they reached Level Two. He needed to make that right turn. He sprinted down the corridor to the first intersection, rounded the bend, and slammed into someone walking the opposite direction. He heard a woman yelp, followed by the sound of a body hitting the floor.

His heart pounded. Like a hyperventilating scuba diver, fighting the fatal urge to tear the regulator from his mouth, AJ resisted addressing the woman in English. He stood over her, legs straddled, looking down in silence.

R. Nicolora—*Founder One*: "AJ, this is Founder One, listen to my voice and repeat exactly what I say."

The voice in AJ's ear was calm and steady, and he recognized it immediately. Nicolora pronounced a short phrase in Czech, carefully enunciating each word. He repeated the phrase in a normal speaking cadence, and then again a third time.

AJ repeated the phrase verbatim, mimicking Nicolora's intonation as best he could.

The woman collected herself and put on a good face, seemingly satisfied with AJ's simple apology. She spoke to him in Czech as she extended her hand for him to help her to her feet.

R. Nicolora—*Founder One*: "She just chastised you for running in the dark. Now repeat exactly what I say and then laugh in a self-deprecating way."

AJ mimicked Nicolora's Czech words as he pulled the woman to her feet. She laughed, brushing her clothes with her hands as if to straighten out any wrinkles from the tumble, a pointless exercise in the dark.

AJ smiled and began to walk away. The woman called out after him.

AJ could hear Nicolora laugh on the line. AJ laughed, mimicking Nicolora.

R. Nicolora—*Founder One*: "Good. Now say good-bye in Czech. Keep moving. Don't look back at her."

AJ did exactly as Nicolora instructed and to his relief, the woman did not follow him. With the corridor now empty, he picked up the pace.

A. Archer—*RS:Bio*: "I've got to know. What did I say to her?"

R. Nicolora—*Founder One*: "You told her you were very sorry, but you are not especially skilled with women in the dark. To which she replied that was too bad and she hoped you fared better with women in the light."

A. Archer—*RS:Bio*: "Nice."

R. Nicolora—*Founder One*: "Humor is a powerful diffuser of tension. A well-timed joke can save your ass in our line of work."

A. Archer—*RS:Bio*: "Yes, Sir. I'll be sure to remember that."

C. Remy—*RS:Coordinator*: "Bio, this is the Coordinator. According to the building plans the server room is the third door on your right."

A. Archer—*RS:Bio*: "Third door on my right . . . got it. I'm there."

He peered through the small glass window on the door and saw something he did not expect—rows and rows of modular computer towers—a city of blinking LED lights in an otherwise dark room.

A. Archer—*RS:Bio*: "Uh guys, I've never actually seen one in person, but from the hardware they're packing in here, I'd wager our friends have got themselves a supercomputer."

E. VanCleave—*RS:Technical*: "Are you certain? Describe what you see."

A. Archer—*RS:Bio*: "Four rows of black cabinets six and a half feet tall, four feet wide. The enclosures look like parallelograms. Everything is humming, so they definitely have UPS. I'm going to try the door . . . Negative, it's locked."

E. VanCleave—*RS:Technical*: "What you described sounds like IBM Blue Gene Towers. Supercomputers. Coordinator, access the registered and unregistered IBM client list. See if Vyrogen has purchased a Blue Gene supercomputer."

C. Remy—*RS:Coordinator*: "Copy. Assigning the task."

E. VanCleave—*RS:Technical*: "Bio, check if there's a gap between the bottom of the door and the floor."

A. Archer—*RS:Bio*: "There's a gap. Approximately one half inch."

E.VanCleave—*RS:Technical*: "That will do nicely. Deploy the spiders."

AJ reached into his pocket and withdrew three ovoids VanCleave had given him earlier.

A. Archer—*RS:Bio*: "Um, how do I turn them on?"

E. VanCleave—*RS:Technical*: "Squeeze each one three times between your forefinger and thumb. Then, set it down on the floor, smooth side up."

AJ did as instructed. After the third squeeze, a blue LED on the belly of the spider turned on, and the tiny object came to life. He took a step backward and shined his light on the trio to watch the transformation. Silently, eight tiny legs unfolded, extended and elevated the body off the floor. The micro-bots shuddered in unison, like ducks shaking water from their feathers after a swim, and then began to rotate in place. One full revolution clockwise, then one counterclockwise.

A. Archer—*RS:Bio*: "What are they doing?"

E. VanCleave—*RS:Technical*: "Calibration sequence."

A. Archer—*RS:Bio*: "It's creepy."

E. VanCleave—*RS:Technical*: "Any second they should finish calibrating and attempt to log into our network, using your phone as a modem."

AJ watched the robot spiders complete their calibration sequence, blink twice, and then scurry under the gap of the door. He stepped toward the door and peered in the window, looking down at the floor. He could see three faint blue lights moving across the floor straight toward the server rack.

A. Archer—*RS:Bio*: "My God, they're fast little buggers. So that's it? They'll do the rest by themselves?"

E. VanCleave—*RS:Technical*: "Yes."

A. Archer—*RS:Bio*: "Good. Then get me out of here."

C. Remy—*RS:Coordinator*: "Negative. Founder One has changed your tasking. Standby for routing to the record room."

A. Archer—*RS:Bio*: "What? Why?"

C. Remy—*RS:Coordinator*: "Founder One wants to see Foster's paper files. Your new tasking is to find his medical charts."

E. VanCleave—*RS:Technical*: "Coordinator, this is Technical. I strongly recommend against this course of action. All the information we need is on the servers. Re-tasking Bio increases the probability of detection forty-one percent. It increases the probability of mission failure thirty-three percent."

R. Nicolora—*Founder One*: "Objection noted, but the potential payoff justifies the risk. Even in this day and age of electronic records, one thing I can tell you for certain is that doctors take notes. Doctors who are research scientists, I surmise, take copious notes. I want Bio to look at Foster's handwritten records. Meredith didn't give us copies of his paper charts. Maybe we need to ask ourselves why. Coordinator, where is the record room?"

C. Remy—*RS:Coordinator*: "Central records is on Level One, but the building plans also show a record room on each floor."

R. Nicolora—*Founder One*: "What floor was Foster kept on?"

C. Remy—*RS:Coordinator*: "According to Social, Foster was kept on Level Four."

R. Nicolora—*Founder One*: "Where are Social and Physical now?"

C. Remy—*RS:Coordinator*: "On Level Four, en route to the lab."

R. Nicolora—*Founder One*: "Resources listen up. Op change as follows: Bio, proceed to Central Records on Level One. Objective: find and film Foster's medical charts. Social, deviate to the record room on Level Four. Objective: find and film Foster's medical charts. Physical, proceed to Level Four lab and retrieve samples as planned. Social, regroup with Physical upon completion of new tasking. Mission extension granted. You have eleven minutes until lights on. Coordinator, remap the timeline, and get these Resources moving."

C. Remy—*RS:Coordinator*: "All resources, this is the Coordinator—request status report?"

A. Mesnil—*RS:Social*: "Coordinator, Social. I'm in the Level Four Record Room. It's been cleaned out. There's nothing here."

K. Immel—*RS:Physical*: "Coordinator, Physical. Ditto for me in the Level Four Laboratory. The sample fridge is empty. All the drawers and cabinets are empty, and the instruments and lab equipment are wrapped in plastic. Looks like our friends are skipping town."

A. Archer—*RS:Bio*: "Coordinator, Bio. I'm inside the Level One Record Room. I've hit the jackpot. All the files are here, packed into boxes.

A. Mesnil—*RS:Social*: "Physical, this is Social. Meet me back at the Decontamination station. As soon as that diesel is back on line, Moderkiek will be back looking for us. The priority now is to clear Corridor E on Level One for Bio's egress."

K. Immel—*RS:Physical*: "Roger."

C. Remy—*RS:Coordinator*: "Bio, Coordinator. Have you found Foster's files yet?"

A. Archer—*RS:Bio*: "Negative. Still looking. The boxes complicate things. I was expecting nice, organized file drawers. But nooo . . . that would have been too easy."

K. Immel—*RS:Physical*: "Look for the box with a big 'F' on it."

A. Archer—*RS:Bio*: "Thanks, I never would have thought of that. The boxes aren't labeled. I have to open each one . . . Shit, there are a ton of boxes."

C. Remy—*RS:Coordinator*: "How are they organized?"

A. Archer—*RS:Bio*: "Each box has a sealed manila envelope and approximately thirty file folders. The folder tabs are labeled using an alphanumeric code. I don't see names anywhere. This is bad. Very, very bad. It could take me hours to figure out which records are Foster's."

C. Remy—*RS:Coordinator*: "You have seven minutes."

A. Archer—*RS:Bio*: "Technical, this is Bio. I need your help."

E. VanCleave—*RS:Technical*: "Technical online, go ahead Bio."

A. Archer—*RS:Bio*: "I'm trying to locate Foster's records, but the files are organized using an alphanumeric scheme. We have two minutes to decipher."

E. VanCleave—*RS:Technical*: "Read the folder tabs to me in order, one by one. Front to back, back to front, it doesn't matter. Just don't skip folders. Go in sequence."

A. Archer—*RS:Bio*: "Got it. P-17.F.01.11.11 . . . P-37.F.02.22.12 . . . P-37.F.03.05.12. . . ."

E. VanCleave—*RS:Technical*: "Okay, that's enough. Go to the next box."

A. Archer—*RS:Bio*: "All right, hold . . . P-21.M.17.12.11 . . . P-21.M.16.01.12 . . . P-21.M.15.09.11."

E. VanCleave—*RS:Technical*: "Stop. Check three more boxes. Tell me if you see any other alphanumeric scheme besides 'P,' two digits, 'M' or 'F', two digits, two digits, two digits."

A. Archer—*RS:Bio*: "Copy, hold . . . No. The other boxes use the same system."

E. VanCleave—*RS:Technical*: "With ninety-five percent confidence, the scheme is 'P' for Patient, followed by ID number, 'M' male or 'F' female, followed by day, month, year, which is the European date convention. You need to find Foster by his patient number."

A. Archer—*RS:Bio*: "Which is?"

E. VanCleave—*RS:Technical*: "Standby. Searching the files Meredith Morley gave us on Foster . . . multiple hits on P-65."

A. Archer—*RS:Bio*: "Copy P-65."

C.Remy—*RS:Coordinator*: "Bio, Coordinator. You have four minutes."

THE FILE ROOM was windowless and pitch black, except for the reddish glow from AJ's flashlight. He clenched the light between his teeth, freeing both hands for shuffling through boxes. His heart was pounding, and he was beginning to feel frantic. Nicolora was counting on him, and time was running out. What he needed now was a little luck.

The boxes were stacked six high. He had already been through three stacks and he counted at least five more. His search method was to lift the top box off the stack, set it on the ground, open the lid and check folders. He then repeated the process placing the next highest box from the stack on top of the previous one he just moved. He was reversing the stacking order, but he didn't have time to worry about that. Hopefully it wouldn't be noticed as long as when he left the room the boxes were in stacks of six.

He was rushing, and the stiff edges of the new cardboard boxes were giving him paper cuts as he worked. The most recent slice felt slippery. He held his hand under the light beam; his right index finger was bleeding. Stacking order was one thing, but blood smears on the boxes would certainly not go unnoticed.

A. Archer—*RS:Bio*: "Shit! I cut my finger. I'm going to get blood on everything."

C. Remy—*RS:Coordinator*: "Do you have a tube of spray epoxy with you?"

A. Archer—*RS:Bio*: "Yes."

C. Remy—*RS:Coordinator*: "Good. Wipe the fresh blood off on your socks. Spray the epoxy right into the cut. One quick pulse. Don't touch anything for fifteen seconds with that hand."

A. Archer—*RS:Bio*: "Into the cut?"

C. Remy—*RS:Coordinator*: "Yes. A small cut is nothing. Resources have used this technique for life-threatening wounds."

A. Archer—*RS:Bio*: "Okay . . . it's done. It seems to be working."

C. Remy—*RS:Coordinator*: "*Bio*, you have two minutes."

AJ revised his search pattern, tossing the lids off the remaining boxes so he could quickly glimpse inside. On the fourth box he found it—P-65! He lifted the box down, set it on the floor, and crouched next to it.

A. Archer—*RS:Bio*: "I've found it. I'm starting with the envelope."

E. VanCleave—*RS:Technical*: "No, start with the folders. You need to scan as many pages as possible."

A. Archer—*RS:Bio*: "I see tons of folders, but only one envelope. I'm starting with the envelope."

AJ unwound the string clasp holding the envelope flap closed. The envelope was heavier than he expected. He tilted it and shook it gently over a cupped hand, but the contents slid out en masse, like an avalanche, spilling onto the floor. He cursed under his breath.

C. Remy—*RS:Coordinator*: "Bio, switch your light from red to white. The image quality from your camera-glasses is poor in the red spectrum. We want to record as much detail as possible."

A. Archer—*RS:Bio*: "Roger, switching to white light. I've emptied the contents of the envelope. It contains Foster's personal effects. I'm checking his wallet now. Credit cards, driver's license, insurance card, cash, couple of pictures . . . who is this? Brunette, pretty. Must be his girlfriend. What else . . . his mobile phone. Note, the battery has been removed. Car keys. Sunglasses."

R. Nicolora—*Founder One*: "Bio, this is Founder One. Take his phone, forget the rest, and start scanning the damn files."

A. Archer—*RS:Bio*: "Yes, sir."

AJ quickly shoved Foster's belongings back into the envelope and secured the string tie. Then he shifted his flashlight beam to the box of files and pulled the file with the oldest date. He opened the folder and smiled. The folder contained Foster's daily medical chart, full of hand scribbled notes, just as Nicolora had predicted. He flipped the pages of the file under the glow of his light.

A. Archer—*RS:Bio*: "Coordinator, Bio. Are you getting this?"

C. Remy—*RS:Coordinator*: "Yes. The feed is good. Keep it coming."

A. Archer—*RS:Bio*: "How am I on time?"

C. Remy—*RS:Coordinator*: "You're over. Founder One is extending you. You have until my mark."

A. Archer—*RS:Bio*: "Roger. Scanning until you mark . . . that file was first in line . . . I'm assuming it was Foster's day one chart. We don't have time to scan all of these. Any requests for other dates?"

E. VanCleave—*RS:Technical*: "Bio, this is Technical. Like any good story, we need a beginning, middle and end."

A. Archer—*RS:Bio*: "Roger . . . day two file scanned. Moving forward in time . . . this box has only one month's worth of charts . . . I'm closing it up and moving to the next box . . . okay, good, this box is P-65 too . . . grabbing two folders . . . the dates would be about two months in, not exactly the middle but close enough . . . scanning . . . okay, looking for the last P-65 box . . . no . . . no . . . no, damn it, where is it? . . . Bingo, I've got it . . . pulling the last file . . . this was five days ago . . . scanning. . . . Oh shit! . . . the lights just went on. They've restored power!"

C. Remy—*RS:Coordinator*: "Electrician, Coordinator. Report?"

Local Embed—*RS:Electrician*: "Clear at my location. Main power is still off. They've started the diesel generator. We are plus fifteen minutes on the timeline. What did you expect?"

R. Nicolora—*Founder One*: "All Resources, this is Founder One. Bio will be egressing with Social and Physical. Execute Exit Scenario Delta on Social's mark—Location: the Level One Record Room."

A. Archer—*RS:Bio*: "Roger."

A. Mesnil—*RS:Social*: "Roger."

K. Immel—*RS:Physical*: "Roger."

E. VanCleave—*RS:Technical*: "Roger."

Local Embed—*RS:Electrician*: "Roger, restoring primary power and exiting."

Admist the stack of boxes in the Level One Record Room, AJ stripped off his coveralls, revealing a paramedic uniform. The door to the record room was shut, but he heard the faint sound of footsteps approaching. It was time.

"WE DON'T WANT to hear your excuses. The fact remains that it took your detail almost twenty minutes to restore power to the facility with the emergency generator, when it should have started automatically and immediately on the loss of primary power," Albane yelled.

Officer Moderkiek cowered. "Yes, Madame Inspector, you're right. The response time was unacceptable, but I can show you the inspection records on the emergency generator. It passed the annual certification test just last month."

Kalen turned his head to the side, hiding an insuppressible grin. Even though he did not speak a word of Czech, he had seen Albane in full dominatrix mode enough times to know exactly what was happening. The systematic humiliation of Officer Moderkiek was at a crescendo, and Kalen relished watching it. In thirty seconds, however, the spotlight would shift. All eyes would be on him.

Kalen slowed his pace to a half step behind the others, clearing his throat as he did. Albane looked at him and nodded. It was time. Out of Moderkiek's peripheral vision, he slipped a clear dissolvable strip onto his tongue.

"I WANT TO see *all* the maintenance records for the emergency diesel generator," Albane said to Moderkiek.

"Yes, Madame Inspector," Moderkiek said as he reached to open the door to the Level One Records Room. "We maintain hard copies of all maintenance records in addition to the annual certifications."

Albane screamed.

Moderkiek spun around.

Kalen was collapsed on the tile floor at her feet, writhing like a serpent. His legs and arms flailed in rhythmic violent contractions. A puddle of urine pooled on the floor underneath his midsection. Beneath his rapidly fluttering eyelids, his pupils were rolled back, leaving only the white of his sclera visible.

"This man is having an epileptic seizure," Moderkiek yelled. He knelt and began to reach for Kalen's arm.

"No, don't touch him," she ordered. "He told me what to do if this ever happened. Do not restrain him." She pulled her mobile phone from her pocket. "I'm calling an ambulance."

Moderkiek raised his two-way radio to his lips and called in the medical emergency to the front desk. Within minutes a small crowd of Chiarek Norse personnel had gathered around Kalen, who continued to have clonic seizures.

Nearly a minute passed before Kalen's body went still and then fell limp. His head flopped lifelessly to the side, and the gathering crowd of onlookers gasped.

Albane knelt, checked his pulse, and looking up at the circle of concerned faces said, "He is unconscious, but alive. The paramedics should be here momentarily."

Albane remained at Kalen's side until the squeal of stretcher wheels and pounding footsteps announced the arrival of the medical team. Two men in paramedic uniforms pushed their way through the circle of people and converged on Kalen.

As Albane stood, extracting herself from EMT duties, she whispered, "Mark."

C. Remy—*RS:Coordinator*: "Bio, that's your cue. Move toward the door. When the paramedics address the crowd, you slip in and take position on the stretcher. Two paramedics came in, three go out."

A. Archer—*RS:Bio*: "Roger. I'm ready."

"OKAY, EVERYONE, THE show is over. Please make some room. We need to load this man onto the stretcher," one of the paramedics said to the crowd in Czech.

"You heard him. Move back people. The paramedics need room to work," Moderkiek said, taking charge of his gathered coworkers.

The other paramedic began pushing the onlookers away—creating confusion and commotion—and no one noticed a third paramedic take position at the foot of the stretcher. This man wheeled the stretcher into position as the other two paramedics readied Kalen for lifting.

"On the count of three, we lift him . . . One, two, three, LIFT," the paramedic in charge directed, and they lifted Kalen onto the stretcher bed.

"Officer Moderkiek, please get these people out of here," Albane ordered.

"Yes, Madame Inspector. I'm very sorry." Moderkick raised his arms and barked at the crowd. "Back to work. The inspector is in good hands. Everyone, back to your stations."

"Thank you, Officer Moderkiek." She extended her hand, which he gladly took within his. "Given this event, the inspection is over. However, your diligent cooperation will be noted in my report and will reflect positively on you as an individual regardless of how the facility fares overall."

"Thank you, Madame Inspector," Moderkiek said with a smile, clutching her hand in both of his until at last she pulled it free from his sweaty palms. "If you have any future questions, you know you can count on me."

He watched the inspectors hurry toward the ambulance. He was proud of himself. He had shown initiative today. And leadership. Maybe instead of being fired, he would be promoted, from Section Leader to Chief of Security. "Chief Moderkiek"—he liked the sound of that.

•   •   •

WITH SIRENS BLARING and lights flashing, an ambulance sped away from Chiarek Norse through the streets of Prague at 100 kilometers per hour. In the cramped rear compartment, AJ sat in silence, his knees wedged against the metal frame of Kalen's stretcher. With every jarring pothole, his kneecaps suffered a new bruise.

He peered down at the motionless Kalen, resting on the stretcher. Kalen's eyes were closed and his face was drenched with beads of sweat.

"This sort of thing is hard on a body, even for someone as fit as Kalen. Maybe you better check his breathing," said Albane, from her position next to him on the narrow bench seat.

A lump formed in his throat. No one had warned him that Kalen's health would be put in jeopardy by the stunt. Damn, The Tank was hardcore. He leaned over the stretcher and put his cheek close to Kalen's mouth and nose. He felt a warm moist breath against skin, but it seemed faint and labored. He was about to suggest that they take Kalen to a real hospital when without warning, Kalen's hands shot up and clutched him by the shoulders.

"BOO!"

He jerked free from Kalen's grasp, knocking his head on the ceiling of the ambulance.

Kalen howled with glee. Veronika wiped tears from her cheeks, she was laughing so hard. Even Albane could not help but chuckle at the scene.

His initial confusion gave way to laughter as he joined in his colleagues' revelry at his expense.

"Nice one, Archer," Kalen said, slapping AJ on the upper arm. "Very nice."

Chapter Twenty-Three

Boston, Massachusetts

MEREDITH RUBBED HER eyes. Instead of rousing from her nightmares, lately it seemed she was waking into them.

"These inspectors, were they Americans?" she seethed, her iPhone pressed hard against her right ear. She had not bothered to get out of bed nor had she turned on the lights in her Boston hotel suite.

"No, Ms. Morley. They were Czech," the nervous voice on the phone replied in heavily accented English. "They were from the Ministry of Health."

"Did they have official Ministry paperwork?"

"Yes, of course."

"Email me a scanned copy of every document they issued. Do you understand?"

"Yes, Ms. Morley."

If she had a detonator linked to that sorry-ass excuse for a covert facility, she would have pressed the button. She had once seen a bumper sticker that read, "You Can't Fix Stupid," and by God her people were validating that aphorism on a daily basis. "Is anything missing? Did they confiscate materials? Samples, records, hard disks? Anything?"

"No, Madame. Nothing appears to be missing. But, we are still conducting an inventory of the facility. All patients and research were already transferred to the Bucharest facility. So there was nothing for them to see, other than the facility itself. And with the power outage, most of their inspection was conducted in the dark."

"Power outage! I was not made aware of any power outage."

"I'm sorry, I thought you were already informed of the incident. We suffered a power outage at the facility today. About fifteen minutes after the inspectors arrived we lost primary power and the backup generator failed to start. It's good the transfer was complete, because ventilation and refrigeration were down for twenty minutes," the head of Chiarek Norse security explained.

"How is it possible that the backup generator failed to start?"

"We are still investigating, but apparently the fuel transfer line on the diesel generator was clogged, so the diesel was starved of fuel even though the fuel tank was full."

"What was the line clogged with?"

"The mechanic says it was sludge."

"Don't you find that a bit suspicious?"

"No. The mechanic says this can happen if the fuel tanks are old, if the fuel is contaminated in some way, or if the maintenance is not proper on the machine."

An awkward silence persisted before Meredith finally said, "Is Dr. Pope with you now?"

"Yes, he is standing next to me."

"Put him on the phone."

"Hello, Meredith."

Xavier Pope's dulcet voice was a lullaby. With all the stress of recent events, she found herself suddenly yearning for his company. She missed their late-night sessions in Prague. She missed the euphoria they had shared during the early days of the project. The start of a new project was what she lived for. So much hope. So much anticipation. It was the same feeling she had as a girl, just after opening the first present on Christmas morning. Holding a new treasure in hand, but knowing that many other gifts, each possibly more grand and exciting, still awaited unwrapping.

Now, that feeling was gone. Anticipation replaced by anxiety, fervor supplanted by frustration.

She was cleaning up other people's messes.

She hated messes.

"Have you positively identified the people who paid us the visit today?"

"No. I've not seen a decent image of any of the inspectors' faces. We lost all camera footage during the blackout, and the video feed from the lobby wide angle camera was corrupted before the power loss."

"How convenient," she mumbled.

"Indeed."

"And where the hell were you when this all went down, Xavier?"

"I was en route to the airport. You told me to personally oversee the final preparations in Bucharest."

"Unfortunate timing . . . What about the server room?"

"No forced entry as far as we can tell. The servers have a thirty minute UPS, so they stayed online for the duration of the black out. Most of the doors in the facility have magnetic locks that fail when power is lost, but the server room has a key lock for double security. But it doesn't matter anyway. All project data was exported off the servers before they arrived, and the clean files you provided were imported in their place, as instructed." Pope assured her.

"Excellent," Meredith said. "And the record room?"

"I pulled Foster's charts yesterday myself and replaced them with the ones you sent by FedEx."

"Well done, Xavier. It's good to know I have at least one person in this organization I can count on."

"Is there anything else I can do, Meredith?"

"Find Will Foster before someone else does," she laughed.

The line fell silent.

"Call me when the identity of the inspectors can be corroborated," she said.

"Do you still want me to go to Bucharest, or should I remain in Prague in case the inspectors come back?"

"They won't be back. Leave on the next available flight. We've lost three days of research time. I can't afford to lose any more."

"You realize it will be difficult, if not impossible, to proceed without Foster."

"We have his entire genome mapped, Xavier, and months of research data. You should be able to continue the work without Foster now."

"It's not that simple, Meredith. There are over twenty thousand genes scattered among three *billion* base pairs in the human genome. And just because you've identified a gene, doesn't mean you know what protein it encodes. It also doesn't tell you what function that protein performs, or how it interacts with other proteins. The Foster mutation is something we've never seen before. It could be expressed by a single gene, or by multiple genes—we're still evaluating."

"I never said this would be easy, Xavier. And you still haven't answered my question," she said, her ire rising. She heard him exhale loudly on the other end of the line and it annoyed her.

"Identifying the genes that express the Foster mutation is not the same thing as understanding *how* the mutation works. Before I can devise a gene therapy that confers Foster's unique mechanism of immunity, I have to understand exactly how his immune system operates. For that, I need more time."

Her tone soured. "Enough. He'll be back in your custody by week's end," she said and ended the call without salutation.

She looked down at her iPhone. She wanted to throw it across the room, but she resisted the urge and set it gently down on the bedside table. She exhaled slowly and told herself that she was proud of herself for showing restraint. Then, she picked up the iPhone and hurled it across the room. It hit the facing wall with a thud and dropped to the carpet. She was tired. So very, very tired. When she was in college, pulling one or two all-nighters a week was no problem. Now, her thirty-nine-year-old body was not as forgiving, and the events of the last several days had left her haggard. Mentally and physically. She was functioning more on instinct than intellect at the moment, and her usual vicelike control over her emotions was slipping.

Foster was proving to be vexingly more allusive than she had anticipated. She was not surprised that Raimond Zurn and his half-wit brother Udo had still not located Foster. Hiring the Zurns had been a mistake, but Nicolora's team's impotence thus far was as appalling as it was astonishing. No sooner had she finished damning Nicolora's team than she began to second-guess herself. If her relationship with Nicolora had taught her anything, it was that his competence was overshadowed only by his cunning. If the Tank did not have Foster yet, then she had reason to worry. With Nicolora, the straight line was never the shortest distance between two objectives.

"Surprise Ministry of Health inspection," she scoffed in the dark, "I know it was you Robért, you devil."

Her iPhone rang.

She turned on the bedside lamp, got out of bed, and walked over to where she had thrown it. She picked it up off the carpet and looked at the caller ID. Fantastic, more bad news.

"What?" she barked.

"Ms. Morley, this is Bart Bennett at Wien BioScience . . . We need to talk."

Chapter Twenty-Four

Prague, Czech Republic

"WHAT'S A BLUE GENE?" Kalen asked.

"It's a supercomputer made by IBM," VanCleave said, without looking up from his laptop screen.

"Why would they have a supercomputer at Chiarek Norse?"

"That's what I'm trying to figure out, but I'm having trouble concentrating because someone keeps interrupting me," VanCleave snapped.

"You must have a couple of guesses what they're using it for."

"I have a theory."

"But you're not saying?"

With a sigh, VanCleave looked at Kalen. "It appears they are using it for DNA sequencing."

"DNA sequencing of what in particular?" AJ interjected.

"Again, I am still assessing the data the spiders were able to transmit before they went dark. I've found some inconsistencies. The data on their mirror drives does not match the data on the primary drives."

"What does that mean?"

"It means that someone scrubbed their primary drives and uploaded new data, but they forgot to scrub the mirror drives," VanCleave sniffed. "Amateurs."

"What was on the primary drives?" Albane asked.

"The same information Vyrogen gave us in Boston."

"And on the mirror drives?"

"I'm not a microbiologist, but if I had to guess, I'd say we're looking at the entire genome of Patient-65 . . . aka Foster."

AJ looked at Albane.

She nodded.

Kalen cleared his throat. "Okay, I'll ask the stupid question. What does sequencing Foster's DNA have to do with drug testing?"

"I don't think Vyrogen is studying a particular drug. I think they're studying William Foster," AJ mumbled. "Did you find anything else on the mirror drives?"

"Yes, but I haven't had time to pour through it," said VanCleave.

"Can you give me access? I'd like to take a look at the data."

"Of course, grab your laptop and pull up a chair."

•   •   •

"THIS CAN'T BE coincidence," AJ said pointing to the computer screen.

Albane walked over and stood behind him so she could see over his shoulder. "What did you find?"

"Somehow, Vyrogen must have gotten access to my research data, because they copied my AAV vector protocol exactly. What I was testing on mice, they've been testing on real freaking people in a gene therapy preclinical trial for the past three months at Chiarek Norse."

When Albane didn't respond, he spun around in his chair to face her.

She met his gaze.

"You're not surprised by this?"

She said nothing.

"Because . . . you already knew. Didn't you?"

"We had our suspicions."

"Of course. That's why Briggs recruited me in the first place. You knew they stole my fucking research! I'm such an idiot."

"There are no accidents in our line of work, AJ."

"How did you find out?"

"The editor of the science journal *Immunology* tipped off your advisor, McNamara, that Meredith had gotten her hands on a pre-publication draft of your paper. McNamara was concerned, so he contacted us. He and Briggs have history."

"And when were you planning on telling me this?"

"Does it make a difference?"

"Hell yes, it does."

"Breathe, AJ," Albane said, resting her hand on his shoulder.

He shrugged her off, stood up, and starting pacing. He ran his fingers through his hair and let out an exasperated sigh. "Why wouldn't you tell me? That's a better question. We wouldn't have wasted all this fucking time."

"That's not true. Everything we've done, we would do again, regardless of whether you knew Vyrogen had commandeered your research or not. We needed proof. And now, I need you to help us understand the connection. To what end does Vyrogen intend to use your research? Why do they need it? It's your turn to do the heavy lifting, AJ. So stop whining, and do what we hired you to do."

The prideful, defiant side of him wanted to challenge her, but the scientist in him knew she was right. More importantly, she was in charge. The conversation was over.

Having witnessed the entire drama, Kalen swept in with perfect timing.

"Hey guys, you should come take a look at this," he said. "You won't believe what VanCleave found."

VanCleave cleared his throat. "Do you remember the data anomaly that Veronika briefed us on when we first arrived in Prague?"

"Yes, the spike in homeless deaths and the coroner's reporting of toxic shock as the cause of death," Albane replied.

"I think I've figured out why. Chiarek Norse was a participating hospital in the free vaccination program this winter in Prague. That's how they found their test and control groups of human subjects," said VanCleave.

"Let me guess, they used homeless people to form the test group," AJ said, aghast.

"Twenty-five homeless persons were involuntarily enrolled in a project code-named the Calypso Directive and received treatments which ultimately culminated in twenty-one of their deaths," said VanCleave.

"Wait a minute, isn't that unorthodox for a drug company?" Kalen interrupted.

"Unorthodox, unethical, unfathomable . . . not to mention entirely illegal," said AJ.

"Why would they do something like that?" Kalen pressed.

"Expediency. Greed. Complete madness, who knows," AJ sighed.

"Not true. You do know why," Albane said.

"I do?"

"We all do. Project BioShield. Vyrogen needs to show BARDA proof of concept before the money dries up. They're under pressure, racing against the clock, and so they're rushing."

"During her briefing in Boston, Meredith implied that her wonder drug was in the final stages of testing," said Kalen.

"The evidence we've uncovered contradicts that," VanCleave said.

AJ nodded. "I agree. Vyrogen is still early in the development phase. The data I looked at indicates at least four different AAV DNA prime-boosted vaccine formulations were evaluated over the past three months."

"Say again, in English this time," Kalen said.

AJ sat down and faced the group. "Is anybody interested in a five-minute Immunology 101 course?"

The group nodded.

"Like an army, the human immune system also uses scouts to identify and tag foreign invaders that enter the body. These scouts are called lymphocytes. The invading pathogens have proteins, called antigens, on their surface that the scouts use to identify the pathogen as *self* or *not-self*. When a lymphocyte finds a pathogen, it tries to connect to the invader's antigens. If it recognizes the antigen, in other words if the immune system has a memory of the pathogen, then it activates other lymphocytes to rapidly produce millions of antibodies specific to that particular invader. The antibodies spread throughout the body, latching onto the antigens of the invading pathogens. Sometimes, by binding to the pathogen, the antibodies are able to neutralize it. In other cases, the antibodies simply mark pathogens for destruction by macrophages.

"But, if the immune system has no memory of a pathogen, the body doesn't know which antibodies to produce. In these cases, the immune response takes longer. The scouts take the antigen back to the lymph nodes, aka central command, and recruit lymphocytes to manufacture antibodies that will work against the new threat. Once the antibodies are released, the rest of the immune system is alerted, and the macrophages and lymphocytes go to battle. The problem is that while the central command is gearing up for its retaliation, the invader is multiplying unfettered."

"That's the reason for vaccines," Kalen said, "to give a small dose of the bad stuff so the body can fight back if it ever sees the germ again."

"You get an A+," AJ said.

"But that's not what Vyrogen is after, is it?" Albane said.

"No. They're investigating an entirely new path in medicine. They are trying to use gene therapy to prime or program a subject's immune system to respond quickly to an infection, even in cases when the subject has no 'memory' of the invading pathogen."

"How can they accomplish that with gene therapy?" Kalen asked.

"By copying my dissertation," AJ said, laughing at the irony. "At BU, I was investigating the possibility of using gene therapy to program existing lymphocytes to recognize antigens they had never seen before and produce antibodies they had never produced before; thus, conferring immunity to the subject even after first contact with a new pathogen. I used a specific type of virus called an Adeno-associated vector virus, or AAV, to insert DNA into existing Memory B cells in mice. The new DNA contained instructions for making antigen-specific receptors and antibodies that the Memory B cells of the mice were not previously programmed to make. Then we injected the mice with a target pathogen to see if they would mount a robust immune response. To everyone's utter disbelief, including mine, it worked."

"Why is the gene therapy approach any different or better than using a vaccine?" VanCleave pressed.

"Aaahh. The billion dollar question. There are three main problems with vaccines. First, many vaccines require dosing regimens of multiple shots, spread out over many months, with periodic boosters to confer immunity. Vaccines must be administered prior to infection to be effective. Once a person is sick, administering a vaccine is like handing a bulletproof vest to someone who has already been shot. Second, vaccines are not without side effects. In addition to introducing DNA from the target pathogen, vaccines also contain toxic adjuvants and unintentional viral or bacterial DNA that can cause systematic and lasting side effects in patients. Third and finally, many pathogens exist—Lyme disease, Ebola, HIV/AIDS, to name a few—that we don't have vaccines for."

"Immune boosting through gene therapy appears to confer immunity much faster than vaccines do. Recent research on prime boosting for anthrax shows that subjects could have full immunity in as little as three weeks, as compared to eighteen months when relying on the existing anthrax vaccine. Even more exciting than that is the idea of using gene therapy as a therapeutic for patients that are already infected. In my experiment, I was able to elicit full-scale antibody production against a new pathogen in infected mice within seventy-two hours of treatment. Ideally, we'd like that surge to occur within half the time—"

"This is all fascinating, but what does gene therapy have to do with Foster? And more importantly, why the hell is Vyrogen decoding his genome?" Kalen asked.

AJ nodded. "Kalen is right, it doesn't make sense. Back in Boston, Meredith Morley told us that Foster was infected with a mutated strain of H1N1, but I can't see how sequencing Foster's genome relates to that. As we collect more pieces of this puzzle, the less Foster seems like a mole and the more he looks like a test subject."

"How can we confirm that?" Kalen asked.

"Maybe it's time to ask him," Albane said, with a straight face.

Kalen laughed. "I think you're forgetting something, my dear. We still don't know where Foster is."

Albane smiled. "VanCleave, will you please show the others the probability matrix you've been working on?"

VanCleave grabbed his tablet computer. "Using the data the Coordinators compiled investigating Foster's background, I built a probability matrix to analyze his social network. I wanted to identify and rank the people he is most likely to contact for help. The top ranked prospect is this woman, Julie Ponte," he said, turning the screen so the others could see her picture. "Ponte is thirty-two, unmarried. Graduated from Tulane University, Foster's alma mater, one year after he did. According to her work visa, she lives in Vienna and is employed by an Austrian contract research company called Wein BioScience which, I might add, was purchased eighteen months ago by Vyrogen Pharmaceuticals."

"That can't be a coincidence," AJ said.

VanCleave sniffed. "I don't deal in coincidences, only in probabilities."

AJ laughed. "Okay, then I think the probability is high that we will be taking a road trip to Vienna in the very near future."

Kalen jiggled the keys to his Ducati. "Race you there."

Chapter Twenty-Five

Boston, Massachusetts

"HOW DID YOU get this number?" Meredith said into her iPhone. "From Xavier Pope. I've been trying to reach him for the past two hours, but he hasn't been picking up. He gave me very specific instructions: in case of an emergency where he cannot be reached, I am to contact you directly . . . I think this qualifies as an emergency," said Bart Bennett with a hint of trepidation in his voice.

"You have my attention, Dr. Bennett. So please, start at the beginning." She listened without interruption as he related the morning's events. He went on to explain that Pope had sent him hundreds of samples for analysis over the previous two months, and how he believed the connection between today's sample and the others was indisputable. When at last he fell silent, she said, "You did the right thing calling me. Loyalty and discretion are prized and rewarded in our organization. Since Vyrogen acquired Wien Bioscience eighteen months ago, your name has crossed my desk more than once as someone who is a rising star. It looks like that director position might have just opened up. Now, tell me, does anyone else know about this?"

"Yes, the woman who brought me the sample, Julie Ponte, and my lab assistant, Jon Henning."

"I want you to listen very carefully. All computer files and records associated with this event need to be deleted. All hard copies and prints need to be destroyed. Any slides or sample volumes need to be packaged and locked in the secure refrigeration unit for pick up by one of my couriers."

"Okay, I understand. What do you want me to tell my assistant, Jon?"

"Don't worry about Mr. Henning. He's going to be reassigned."

"Reassigned? Nothing bad is going to happen to him, right? I mean, it's not his fault he found out. He was just doing his job," Bart protested feebly.

"What would ever make you think such a terrible thing? Of course nothing is going to happen to him. We just need to occupy his mind with other things right now. A transatlantic reassignment will give Mr. Henning other things to think about besides antibodies and lymphocytes."

"He's been a great lab technician. I'd hate to lose him."

"The world is full of great lab technicians. Besides, *Director* Bennett will have much more pressing responsibilities to fret over than the job satisfaction of lab technicians. Am I making things clear?"

"Yes, crystal clear."

"Good. Now, tell me about the woman who brought you this sample, Julie Ponte. I want to know everything."

•　　•　　•

MEREDITH COLLAPSED ONTO the king-sized bed in her hotel suite at the Copley Plaza and stared at the ceiling. Her morning had begun with a slap in the face, but thanks to Julie Ponte, she was officially back in the game. To say she was in control of the situation would be an overstatement, but at least she was equipped with knowledge she could use to influence each of the players' next moves. As she lay there, still dressed in the frayed Princeton University T-shirt she wore as nightshirt, she weighed her options.

The report from Pope needled her. Yes, the surprise Health Ministry inspection could have been legitimate, but she harbored doubts. If Nicolora had directed his minions to infiltrate her Chiarek Norse facility, then it was because he didn't trust her. She wondered if he truly trusted anyone. When they were together, he was always probing, testing her loyalty. It had driven her crazy. One day, when she'd finally had enough, she blasted him in a fiery, accusatory assault. Instead of denying her allegations, he had argued vehemently that she adopt a similar philosophy, stating that trust is a luxury that people in power cannot afford. Surveillance is the cornerstone of prescience, he stated; intelligence collection the cornerstone of insight. She asked him to teach her to think as he did—like a field general in battle—and he had granted her request.

In the years since their split, she had honed her skills.

She had contemplated a variety of security breach scenarios concerning Chiarek Norse, and prepared for them. Tracks had been covered. Electronic files, paper documents, and official statements for multiple contingencies had been readied in advance. If the inspectors had been Nicolora's team, she was confident they hadn't discovered anything of consequence. Still, she couldn't stand *not* knowing. Her lips curled into a coy little smile. It was time for her to spend some private time with her old teacher; collect some intelligence of her own. She had reserved her hotel room for an extra day for this very exigency. In her experience, a man's mind was surprisingly unfettered after a fierce orgasm. She decided she would not tell Nicolora about Julie Ponte—at least not before she knew his true agenda.

Her hunting dogs, the Zurns, were another matter. When she had last spoken to Raimond, he was still in Prague, trying to pick up Foster's trail at the infamous cybercafé. His pride was bruised after the events in Prague; she was confident he would not underestimate Foster again. Still, he had threatened to blackmail her, could she rely on his discretion? She had already tried firing him, but that had only enraged him. She exhaled slowly. Realistically, she was stuck with the Zurns to the bitter end. With a single phone call, the brothers could be standing in Ponte's apartment in less than four hours. Better to send them to Vienna now, while the window of opportunity was still open. There was no telling how long Foster would linger in one place before running again.

Next, her mind drifted to Julie Ponte, and how she could best use this new chess piece that had appeared on the board. Was Ponte a knight or a pawn? Could she intimidate Ponte into cooperating with her? From talking with Bennett, it was obvious that she was clever. Had Bennett not already been read into CALYPSO, Ponte would have succeeded in using his laboratory to uncover Foster's secret—and possibly Meredith's agenda—without anyone the wiser. If she had not yet pieced together the connection between Vyrogen, Leighton-Harris, and Chiarek Norse, she undoubtedly would in short order. Meredith inspected her fingernails. French-manicured, polished, elegant . . . nothing like the razor sharp claws she deployed in battle. If she were in Ponte's position, she would size up her enemy, quickly realize it was a fight she couldn't win, and ditch Foster. Actually, if *she* were Julie, she would negotiate a lucrative payoff and turn him in herself. This begged the question, what type of woman was Julie Ponte? How deeply did she care for Foster? Would she be willing to sacrifice her career to help him escape, or would she cave under pressure?

Meredith picked up her iPhone. It was time to find out.

Chapter Twenty-Six

Prague, Czech Republic

"I'M SORRY, BUT the hard disk from the computer at the cybercafé is a dead end," announced Stefan Zurn to his brothers Raimond and Udo, as they walked into the hotel room carrying sandwiches. "Public computers in cybercafés are notorious for being infected with keystroke-logging spyware—a phenomenon I had hoped to exploit. But in this case, the computer had an updated security suite installed. Also, cookies were disabled in the browser, and there was nothing useful cached in virtual memory. I found no clues to help lead us to Foster."

"It's okay. I know where he is," Raimond replied, clapping his hand on his younger brother's shoulder.

"How?"

"It appears the American made a fatal mistake—he trusted a woman," Raimond said. Udo laughed loudly at the comment, too loudly, and it annoyed him. "As I was saying, Foster contacted a woman who lives in Wien and asked her for help. She's also an American; her name is Julie Ponte."

"And your source is?"

"Our employer, Frau Morley, she phoned me personally with the good news five minutes ago."

"Even the coldest of bitches eventually warm to your charms, brother. How do you do it?"

Raimond laughed. "After you hacked her VoIP account, I called her directly in her office and blackmailed her. She's been most co-operative ever since. The hack was a nice piece of work, by the way."

"Danke. It was nothing. A child could have done it," Stefan said and then added, "Blackmail is terribly underrated in my opinion; it has been working so well for us all these years."

Raimond tapped the top of Stefan's laptop computer screen and said, "Let's find out where Julie Ponte lives, shall we? Ponte is spelled "P-O-N-T-E."

Stefan opened a browser window and performed an Internet search. "Hmm," he mumbled as his eyes scanned the list. "I find only one woman in Wien named Julie Ponte. I'll SMS the address to your phone."

Raimond's phone chimed and the text message with Julie's address appeared on the screen. Their job had become so much simpler with the advent of the Internet and mobile phones. Finding people had once been a tedious and painstaking endeavor, now it was as simple as a click of button.

"What now?" asked Udo.

"We pack the van and drive to Wien. It's time to collect our fee."

"Tell me something, Raimond. Why is this American, Will Foster, so important?" Stefan asked.

"They don't tell me why, and I don't ask. Remember, we are like garbage men; we get paid to clean up other people's messes. They don't want to see us. They don't want to talk to us. And most of all, they don't want to know what we do with the trash."

Chapter Twenty-Seven

Vienna, Austria

"OH, MY GOD," Julie uttered. Will looked at the screen and then at Julie, perplexed, "Is it significant that Vyrogen owns Leighton-Harris?"

She stole a glance at the maroon-colored mouse pad on her desk. Printed beneath the company logo in bright white letters were the words:

Wien Bioscience
a Vyrogen Company

She repositioned the mouse so that it covered the text. Dodging his question, she redirected, "What was the name of the facility in Prague where you were held in quarantine?"

"I don't know. It was total information blackout at that place from the day I arrived. The facility was part research hospital, part laboratory. All I know is that my pants had the words 'CN Hospital' stenciled across the butt."

Julie opened a new browser tab. She entered "Prague + CN Hospital" as a new search string in Google and pressed the search button. The page refreshed with the search results. She scanned the list and clicked on a link she thought looked promising. The site was written entirely in Czech and had no English language option. As she scrolled, she quickly ruled out the site, as it was full of pictures of dogs, cats, and smiling veterinarians. She clicked back to Google and entered a new search string: "Vyrogen + Prague + CN Hospital." The screen populated with a new list of links, and she read through them until one caught her eye. She clicked on the link and it took her to a BBC World News article reporting:

". . . US-based multinational drug giant, Vyrogen Pharmaceuticals, has announced today that it has acquired Chiarek Norse, the fifth largest research hospital in the Czech Republic . . ."

"Holy shit! That's it!" Will said, reading over her shoulder.

Julie looked up at him. "So it seems. I have one more hunch I want to check."

She opened a third browser tab, and repeated the drill. This time she searched for "Vyrogen + CDC + Xavier Pope." The first hit was a link to a *Wall Street Journal* article. She clicked on it and found an announcement listing:

"New Jersey-based Vyrogen Pharmaceuticals has announced today that Dr. Xavier Pope, formerly of the Centers for Disease Control and Prevention, has been hired as the director of the company's Immunological Therapeutics Division."

"When did you enroll in the vaccine trial?"

"About five months ago."

"Look at the date of this press announcement," Julie said.

"Four months ago." Will grimaced. "So, Vyrogen recruited Pope away from the CDC because of me."

"Do you know how huge this is, Will?"

"That's what I've been trying to tell you."

Julie rubbed her temples. She didn't dare tell him that, technically, she worked for Vyrogen too. When she had accepted the position at Wien Bioscience five years ago, it had been an independent and privately held Austrian company. Eighteen months ago, Wien Bioscience had been acquired by Vyrogen. As was the Vyrogen strategic policy, any acquisition that had strong brand equity retained its name and was permitted to function with tolerable autonomy. Julie had never really considered herself as working for "Vyrogen," but she knew who wrote her paychecks. She could only imagine how Will would react, if she told him. He would immediately reclassify her as the enemy and distance himself from her, if not physically, definitely emotionally. His trust in her would be obliterated.

Her mobile phone chimed. She retrieved it from her purse and checked the caller ID.

BLOCKED.

"Hmm," she said, and then warily pressed the TALK button. "Hello?"

"Julie Ponte, my name is Meredith Morley," said the voice on the line, "You have something that belongs to me, and you're going to help me get it back . . ."

• • •

ASHEN-FACED, JULIE HUNG up her phone and turned to Will.

"What was that all about?"

"I'll explain later. Right now, we need to get the hell out of here." She darted to her closet, grabbed a backpack, and began stuffing it with essentials.

"Talk to me, Julie. Who was that on the phone?"

"Vyrogen. They know you're with me. It's only a matter of time before they come here."

The look in her eyes was all the motivation he needed. He swiped her mobile phone from her hand and powered it off. "They can track us with this," he said, handing it back to her. "Keep it turned off." Then, he grabbed the computer printouts off the desk and began stuffing them into the bag.

"Shhhh—quiet," she whispered.

Will froze. In the stillness, they heard the deadbolt click open on the apartment door.

"Shit, they've found us!"

Chapter Twenty-Eight

WILL DUCKED BEHIND the half-closed door to Julie's bedroom. She handed him a pair of scissors from her desk, which he turned point downward and gripped like a knife. Her Viennese city apartment was small and bereft of hiding places. Their only hope was for Julie to distract the intruder momentarily so that he would have the element of surprise for an attack.

"Ask who's there," he whispered to her.

"Hello? Who is there?" Julie yelled out in German, still standing inside her bedroom behind the threshold.

Silence.

Her legs begin to quiver. Maybe they had been mistaken and it was not her front door that they had heard, but the tenant arriving home in the apartment above. If an intruder had entered, he would have had to break down the door. Unless, the intruder had picked the lock. Or, what if he had killed the building superintendent and taken her key. She could hear footsteps in the hall. She felt her courage wane, and her feet began to backpedal. She looked at Will, who put his index finger to his lips, and raised his hand holding the scissors in a striking position next to his temple.

A woman screamed.

Julie's roommate, Isabella, stood in the doorway, her hand pressed against her chest. She exhaled with pursed lips and pulled a pair of white ear buds from her ears.

"Oh my God, you scared the hell out of me, Julie! I didn't think anyone was home. I was walking by your room, on the way to mine, and out of the corner of my eye I saw someone standing in the doorway," Isabella stammered in English flavored with an Italian accent.

"You scared me too! I thought someone had broken into the apartment. Did you not hear me call out?" Julie asked.

Isabella pointed to her iPod, peaking out of her front right jeans pocket. Will silently lowered the scissors from the ready position and set them down on the carpet. He shook his head to signal to Julie not to reveal his presence, but she was not looking at him.

"I thought you and Peter weren't returning from Greece until tomorrow night?"

"Peter's boss called him and said that he needed him to come in because the head chef had taken ill, so we had to fly back early," Isabella explained. "Speaking of being home early, shouldn't you be at the lab?"

"Yes, but an old friend called me unexpectedly. He is in Vienna on business, so I agreed to meet with him."

"Have I met him before? Is it that hot guy from Milano?"

Julie blushed, embarrassed and glanced back at Will. "Well, no, but . . ." She extended her hand toward the half-closed bedroom door. "Isabella, meet . . . Bob. Bob, meet my roommate, Isabella."

Will stepped out from behind the door and raised his hand in an awkward half-wave. "Hello, I'm Bob . . . not from Milano. Sorry to disappoint."

"Um . . . very nice to meet you, Bob," Isabella stammered.

An awkward silence filled the bedroom as they all stood looking at one another.

"We had better get going, Bob, if we want to make our appointment," Julie said, grabbing Will's sleeve and tugging.

"I agree. Look at the time. It was nice to meet you, Isabella."

Isabella shook Will's hand. "Very nice to meet you too. Maybe we'll see each other again."

Julie quickly gathered her computer, her wallet, sunglasses, and the remainder of the printouts from the lab and stuffed them into the backpack; she gave Will a gentle push toward the door. He walked past Isabella and smiled at her.

Isabella raised her eyebrows at Julie and silently mouthed, "What is going on?"

Julie shrugged and gave her friend a devilish grin.

"Will you be back before dinner? Maybe the three of us can go out tonight, for dinner and dancing?" Isabella called after her.

"I wouldn't count on it tonight. Let's plan on dinner tomorrow night instead. Okay?"

"Great, then Peter can join us," Isabella added. "Where are you headed off to now?"

"Just going to grab a coffee," Julie replied. She then took a step backward and whispered into Isabella's ear.

"If anyone comes by the flat looking for me, tell them you haven't seen me or talked to me recently okay?"

"Ummm, okay?"

"And don't say anything about Bob."

"Julie, what's going on?"

"Nothing. Bob and I just need some alone time."

Isabella eyed Will suspiciously and then grabbed Julie by the shoulders. "Are you sure you're okay? You know I'm here for you if you need me. You can tell me anything."

"I know. Really, everything is fine. But we need to go."

"Okay, then. Ciao," Isabella said as she gave her friend a hug.

"Ciao."

Chapter Twenty-Nine

"SHE SAID HER name was Meredith Morley and that she worked for Vyrogen. She knew you were with me," Julie said, as she whipped her Opel Astra around a corner so fast that the tires squealed. Her eyes darted right and left, combing the avenue ahead for an open parking spot. An instant later, she slammed on the brakes and jerked steering wheel to the right, bringing the little sedan to an abrupt halt in an open, angled slip. She turned the car off and immediately dropped her face into her hands.

"That name is not familiar. What else did she say?" Will asked.

"She said I needed to make a choice, between you and my career."

"What? I don't understand. How did she find us?"

"Isn't it obvious? Bart Bennett at my lab must have contacted her. He was acting really strange after Jon brought me the test results. Never in a million years would I have thought he was connected to all this."

"Awfully convenient to be a coincidence," Will said, eyeing her.

She looked up at him. "What's that supposed to mean?"

"I'm just saying, what are the odds that you're helping me *and* your buddy Bart happens to be collaborating with Vyrogen."

"I didn't rat you out Will," she said with heat. "I'm offended you'd even go there."

They sat in silence for several minutes, before Julie confessed in a quiet voice, "There's something I need to tell you . . . Vyrogen owns Wien Bioscience."

Will choked on his own saliva. Coughing, he said, "Excuse me?"

"I didn't know that Leighton-Harris was owned by Vyrogen—not until I ran the Internet search back at the apartment. I swear. I didn't tell you then because I didn't want to plant a seed of doubt in your mind that would grow and fester the longer we were together. Things were going so smooth between us, I didn't want to poison the well with something that is outside our control. You've been through so much, Will. Emotionally, physically, psychologically. I made the unilateral decision at that moment that I would carry this burden for both of us, and that I would tell you when the time was right, and so I'm telling you now."

He flashed with anger. Was there no one he could trust? How far would he have to run to escape Vyrogen's reach? He looked at Julie. Unflinching, she met his gaze. Vyrogen had given her an ultimatum, and she had made her choice. She'd picked him. His anger ebbed and was replaced by something else: respect, gratitude . . . adoration?

He took a deep breath and grabbed her hand. "What next?"

"We need a safe, local hideaway with Internet access, where we can regroup."

"How about the Vienna Public Library?"

"After what happened in Prague, I'd prefer to stay away from obvious hotspots like libraries and Internet cafés. I have different place in mind called the Four Bells—it's a neighborhood Irish pub." She glanced at her watch: 2:14 PM. "It should be completely deserted at this time of day, and I've known the owners and the waitstaff for years. We can trust them."

Julie led Will inside the pub and after exchanging pleasantries with the lone waiter/bartender, they slid into a semicircular booth against the wall in the otherwise unoccupied pub.

She opened a browser window on her laptop and logged into the Four Bells free Wi-Fi. Then she turned to Will. "We know *who* is responsible, but we still don't know the *why*. Is there anything else you haven't told me yet? Anything at all?"

"Yes," he said in a low, solemn voice. "The night of my escape, I stole a glass vial filled with a substance they had injected me with during the most recent round of experiments."

"Do you know what that substance was?"

"Can I see that list of disease antibodies you showed me back in the apartment?"

She retrieved the printouts from the backpack and handed them to him. He leafed through the pages until he found it.

"This is it," he said, pointing to the name on the list.

"*Yersinia pestis*? You think Vyrogen intentionally injected you with live plague cultures?"

"I know that they did."

Julie's mind started spinning. She had joked about the antibody test results, because she had made the logical assumption that Will had been inoculated with vaccines for each of the bugs on the list. Never in a million years would she have imagined the antibodies were from exposure to the live organisms.

"What you're saying defies logic. You would be dead if you were injected with every pathogen on that list."

"You said if I had the antibody for the bug, then that meant I had been exposed to the bug."

"Exposed, as in vaccinated. That's what vaccines do—they safely expose your immune system to a specific pathogen so that your immune system can develop antibodies against it. But the pathogen is weakened, dead, or altered in such a way that it is rendered benign. I didn't mean to suggest that you were exposed to the actual live pathogens on this list."

"But I was."

"Are you sure that the vial you stole wasn't a *Yersinia pestis* vaccine? The label you read was probably the vaccine label."

"I know it wasn't a vaccine because the vial accidentally broke when I was in Prague. I told you that during our IM chat. Remember the two college kids from the youth hostel that I said were sick?"

"Honestly, no I don't, Will. I'm working off of only two hours sleep and my mind is mush right now. Besides, at the time, I thought you were delusional."

"I don't want to go into the whole story, but the vial of *Yersinia pestis* smashed on the floor and contaminated two kids who were staying in the same room as me. Twelve hours later, they looked like they were on their deathbeds. I don't know what happened to them though because I had to run when some guys showed up at the hostel looking for me."

Julie entered a new Google search: "Plague + Prague + youth hostel." The search list populated, and to her astonishment, she saw several relevant hits. She clicked on one with English subtext.

"Two American tourists died in a Prague area hospital after contracting a virulent strain of bubonic plague. A local woman, who was also exposed, is in critical but stable condition and expected to survive. Czech Health Administration officials released a statement that the infection resulted from exposure to improperly disposed medical waste and that this isolated incident in no way threatens public safety . . ."

She looked at him, dumbfounded.

"Oh Jesus." His lower lip began to tremble, and he fought back tears. He had been worried about Rutgers and Frankie, and the news that they had died uncorked a geyser of guilt and pain. "It's my fault they died."

She took his hands in hers. "It was an accident, Will. You didn't know what was in the vial."

"I should have been more careful."

"It's not like you intentionally infected those boys."

He stood in silence and did not answer her.

"Will, I know you're upset about those boys, but it doesn't change the situation we're in right now. I need you to focus. I need you to help me understand why Vyrogen would inject you with live *Yersinia pestis* cultures unless they were trying to kill you?"

"Because that's exactly what they were trying to do."

"Kill you?"

"No, *trying* to kill me. I was their experiment. They injected me with pathogens and watched to see what happened."

"How did you survive? Did they give you antibiotics after they infected you?"

"No."

"Then why didn't the plague kill you?"

"Because my body was somehow able to overcome the infection." He closed his eyes and reminded himself that she had proven her allegiance. It was time to tell her his secret. "Julie, in the time we were together, do you ever remember me getting sick?"

"Sure, don't you remember the time you puked your brains out the morning after your twenty-first birthday?"

"I'm not talking about that sort of thing. Do you ever remember me getting a stomach bug or a cold or food poisoning or athlete's foot or anything like that?"

"Actually, now that you mention it, no, I don't. Even the time that nasty flu had me laid up for days, you didn't catch it."

"I know. It was the same when I was a kid too. I won the attendance award every year in school. It was the running joke with all my friends that Will Foster's mom would never give him a sick day. In fact, when I think back on my childhood, I can't remember ever being sick. There's something inside me that's different. Something unique about my immune system. It's the reason I have immunity to all the bugs on your list. It's the *why* you've been looking for."

"I don't know what to say," she said.

"Do you believe me?"

"Of course, it finally all makes sense. The question is . . . what do we do now?"

"You need to tell me what these are?" he said, pointing to the SEM images of his mysterious lymphocyte.

"I'm an oncology researcher, Will. Not an immunologist."

"So?"

"This is out of my league. We need someone with subject matter expertise to look at these."

"Okay, then let's go see an immunologist. Vienna is a major city. There has to be somebody local we can talk to. Do you know anybody who fits the bill?"

Yeah, Bart Bennett, Julie thought, but did not say. "No, unfortunately, I don't."

"All right, then Google it. You're the search engine guru."

She sighed as she turned back to her computer. She entered numerous search criteria, but the one that finally yielded results was "Plague + immunity + Vienna + research."

He leaned in for a closer look at the laptop screen.

"Dr. Roger Johansen, head professor at the Institute of Micro-biology and Genetics, has real potential. His specialty is apparently using genealogy to trace patterns of immunity that develop in populations exposed to pandemics."

"I don't see what that has to do with me. How can he help us?"

"I don't know if he can, but this is the best option I could find who is local. We need an immunologist and I found one. Plus, I can't imagine that a guy who studies pandemics and genealogies in Vienna doesn't know volumes about plague. Vienna was practically the Black Death capital of Europe in the Middle Ages."

"Okay, let's go see Johansen. I like the fact that he works for a university. At least we don't have to worry about him being a Vyrogen spy!"

"Yeah," Julie said, as she wrote down the professor's office address, phone number, and email address. "You never know who might be on Vyrogen's payroll."

•   •   •

"HELLO, WE'RE HERE to see Doctor Johansen," Julie said to the middle-aged woman sitting behind an old wooden desk covered with piles of journals, books, and papers.

"You are?" the woman replied, peering over her reading spectacles.

"My name is Julie, and this is my colleague, Will. We have some microscope images we think the professor will be very interested in seeing."

"Doctor Johansen never mentioned this to me. Do you have an appointment?"

"No, but I assure you this will only take a few minutes of his time."

"Doctor Johansen does not see anyone without an appointment. You can leave the images here with me, and if he is interested, he will contact you."

Julie looked at Will. He shook his head, no.

"I'm afraid we can't do that."

The woman sighed with annoyance. "Show me your pictures."

Julie retrieved two prints of Will's lymphocytes from her backpack and set them down on the least cluttered area of the desk. The assistant looked carefully over the images.

She stood abruptly, carrying one print in each hand.

"Wait here."

Julie nodded and looked at Will. She tried to appear serious, but she could not suppress a smile. She looked back at Johansen's assistant to give her authorization, but the Austrian woman had already disappeared.

After what seemed like an eternity, Johansen's assistant returned with a lanky, balding, handsome gentleman of sixty in tow. The assistant handed the images back to Julie.

The man greeted them in English, flavored with a Scandinavian accent. "Hello. My name is Dr. Roger Johansen. Please, follow me."

They followed him down a hallway and into his immense office.

"Have a seat," said Professor Johansen, motioning to a group of vacant chairs set haphazardly around a large round table in the middle of his immense office. The remainder of the room was more reminiscent of an architect's model city than a microbiologist's office, with books and journals rising from the floor in stacks like skyscrapers. Several paths wove between the towers like city streets, the widest of which led to his partially occluded desk.

Main Street.

"This round table is where I hold all of our staff meetings. It is an excellent place for discerning discourse and heated discussion."

"Very Arthurian," Julie said.

"Indeed, except instead of Excalibur, in my laboratory I have one of the world's most powerful bright field microscopes."

Julie and Will chuckled, politely.

"Your names again, I'm sorry?"

"I'm Julie, and this is my colleague, Will."

"Julie and Will. Good. You are Americans, no?"

"Yes, we are."

"Good, I like Americans. Now, let us talk about why you are here, shall we?"

"We're here to discuss possibilities," Will began.

Johansen laughed, grinning ear to ear. "Possibilities. Marvelous! Did you rehearse that opening?"

Will smiled, uncertain how to respond.

"Forgive my sense of humor," said Johansen, settling down. "Let's take a look at the images together."

"Of course," Julie said. She retrieved all the pages from her backpack and spread them out across the table.

Johansen retrieved a pair of eyeglasses from his shirt breast pocket, put them on, and leaned forward to take a closer look.

"These are lymphocytes, yes?"

"Yes, except . . ."

"Except, this one is not a classical lymphocyte," Johansen interrupted pointing with the tail end of his pen at the image. "What is this cell here?"

"We don't know. Which is exactly why we've come to see you."

Johansen scrutinized the pictures in silence, while they waited patiently. Then he took off his eyeglasses, folded them, and looked up.

"What else can you tell me? This is interesting, that's for certain, but I can teach you nothing by looking at naked images. When were they taken? Do you have the blood panel that accompanies these? What was the medical condition of the subject? I can think of a thousand questions to ask you. So please, tell me, what other information can you provide?"

"These images were obtained using a scanning electron microscope on blood samples taken from a patient who demonstrates an unnatural resistance to infection. In this particular case, the patient had been exposed to live *Yersinia pestis* bacilli. The sample was drawn seven days after exposure to the pathogen."

"Excuse me?" Johansen replied, practically falling out of his chair. "By patient are you referring to a nonhuman primate?"

"No."

"Do you work with UNICEF?"

"No."

"This patient was encountered during fieldwork of yours?"

"No. Laboratory trial."

Johansen's face hardened. "Young woman, are you playing games with me?"

"Absolutely not."

"If what you are telling me is true, I should be reporting you to the police, not trying to help you with some sick experiment."

"This is not my work. This is not my patient. I'm an oncologist, not an immunologist. I came to you because this is way out of my league. When I found your biography on the university website, I thought you might have the expertise necessary to help us."

Johansen took a deep breath. "What you are telling me is that these images were derived from samples drawn from someone who is not your patient, enrolled in an experiment in a laboratory where you do not work, and in a field of study which you have no expertise?"

"Yes."

Johansen smiled and looked at Will. "What is your role in all of this? Let me guess, you operated the microscope?"

"No," Will said, "I'm the patient."

The professor looked at Will, then at Julie, and finally back at Will. He slowly and deliberately unfolded his eyeglasses, and put them back on. "Okay. I think I see what is happening here."

"What is that?" asked Julie.

"Either, you are both lying to me with this fantastic story—for what end I do not know—or, you are telling me the truth, and we have a bona fide mystery on our hands. From the look on your faces, I am inclined to believe the latter."

"Professor Johansen, we come to you now at considerable risk," Will began. "We have no one else to turn to. Nowhere else to go. There is something inside of me. Something that makes me different. I want to understand what that something is. We were hoping that with your help, I might finally be able to get some answers."

"If you want my help, then you must agree to my conditions."

"Which are?" asked Julie.

"First, we agree to be completely honest with each other at all times, even if the truth is unpleasant. Second, you must agree that I can include the findings in my immunology research."

"We will agree to your conditions if you agree to one of ours," Will said.

"Which is?"

"You agree to maintain complete and absolute secrecy about our identities and the nature of this finding."

"Without question. I will maintain complete confidentiality at all times. You have my word."

"Then you have mine," Will said. He turned to Julie.

"And mine," she added.

"Good. Where shall we begin?" asked Will.

"With a history lesson," Johansen said with a smile. "I came to Vienna almost twenty years ago. It was the logical place for me to locate my laboratory."

"Why is that?" asked Will.

"Vienna has a rich and fascinating plague history—a dubious distinction in most people's minds—but for my type of work, it's perfect. Geographically, Vienna is centrally located in Europe. The Danube River flows east through the center of the city and stretches 2,800 kilometers from Germany to the Black Sea. Through most of its history, Vienna has been a crossroads in Europe."

"A crossroads of what?"

"Trade, migration, war—the inevitable mixing and mashing of different peoples from different lands. All converging here, all carrying germs, making Vienna a crossroads for disease as well."

"Resulting in epidemics . . . you study epidemics, right?" Julie asked.

"Very good. It's true, Vienna suffered many epidemics over the centuries, the most famous of which was the Great Plague of Vienna in 1679. Death estimates from this massive epidemic range from 75,000 to over 100,000—literally half the population of the city was infected with bubonic plague. What is so fascinating about the 1679 scourge was that it was the result of two converging epidemics—one sweeping east from England and France, and one traveling west from the Ottoman Empire in Turkey. Taken as a whole, the bubonic plague was more than epidemic—it was pandemic—meaning it spread throughout most of the known civilizations of Europe and Asia."

"Why is that of interest to your research?" Will asked.

"Because I am keenly interested in immunity factors associated with disease epidemics. Bubonic plague is the ideal research candidate because it was common practice for afflicted cities to institute quarantines. In some cases, townships quarantined themselves, in entirety, to prevent the spread of the disease to neighboring towns. The death tolls in quarantined sectors were horrific."

"I don't get it. Why do you care about the death tolls in quarantine areas?" asked Julie.

"Good question. The death toll is only useful in the sense that it gives me an indication of the virulence of the particular strain of plague bacterium. What I really care about are the plague survivors, or more specifically, the survivors' progeny. For fifteen years I've been building a genealogical database tracing bloodlines of plague survivors all across Europe. Five hundred years worth of birth and death records, from over sixty towns, spread across twelve countries."

"What do you hope to find?"

"The descendants of plague survivors, of course," Johansen quipped. "Not just any descendants. No, I'm looking for descendants who might carry in their DNA specific immunity factors or mutations that allowed their ancestors to survive the plague. Mutations that the living descendants would still carry to this day."

"What do you do when you find descendants?" Will asked.

"We take DNA and blood samples from them . . . with their permission of course. Then we analyze the sample for immunity factors, and we enter the individual's DNA profile into my genealogical database."

"Like a family tree?"

"Yes, absolutely. Except this is a family tree for DNA. I am proud to say that our lab maintains the world's largest DNA-derived genealogical database focused on epidemiology. We have over half a million entries and counting. Would you like to become a member?"

"When you were talking about adding my results to your research, this is what you were referring to?" Will asked.

"Yes. Except, based on the images you've shown me, I think we'll be doing much more than just plugging your genome into the database. Are you ready to get started?"

"Yes, I guess so."

"Very good. Let's start with you telling me about your family history and anything you know about your condition."

"I am of European descent. English, I think. I am thirty-four years old and an only child. Both my parents have passed away, so I am the only surviving male heir on my father's side of the family. For as long as I can remember, I have never been sick—that is until I started receiving the injections."

"Explain what you mean when you say you've 'never been sick'?"

"Just that. From the time I was a kid, I don't remember being sick. My mother used to joke that I repelled germs. My father said that I had my grandpa's famous Foster constitution."

"Foster? Is that your surname?"

"Yes. Why?"

"That name is familiar to me."

"Did you know my grandfather?"

"No, I don't think so. I need to check my notes. I have interviewed hundreds of people over the years and made thousands of data entries. You're both young; your minds are still quick. When you get to be my age, you'll find it all begins to blur together. That's why I keep detailed handwritten notes. Then I make the grad students type them into the computer," Johansen said with a mischievous chuckle.

Julie laughed. "Grad students love grunt work. Don't let their bellyaching fool you." The professor picked up his office phone and rang his assistant. "Can you please pull any files we have on the surname 'Foster' from the United Kingdom and bring them to my office please?" He then turned his attention back to Will. "While we wait to see what she finds, let's talk some more about your experience never getting ill."

"When I was a kid, I never got sick. The other kids caught chicken pox, strep throat, the flu, but not me."

"Just so I understand, you are saying you have never been ill in your entire life?"

"Not that I can remember, no. Not until they put me in quarantine and started the injections."

"I don't understand. Who put you in quarantine? What injections?"

"It's a long story. You might want to grab a cup of coffee."

Johansen leaned back in his chair and clasped his hands behind his head. "I have nothing but time. Please, tell me everything."

Chapter Thirty

"THIS IS IT, the Ponte woman's apartment," Raimond Zurn said to Udo.

"Do you want me to kick the door in, brother?" Udo asked, eyes glimmering.

"Battering rams are for barbarians. I am not a barbarian. I'm an artist. Artists are refined, skilled with instruments of their trade," Raimond quipped, retrieving a lock picking kit from his bag with gloved hands. Thirty seconds later the door was unlocked. "Quiet, elegant, refined."

Udo snorted with feigned irritation. The truth was that over the years he had come to enjoy his brother's theatrics. Raimond made him laugh. Udo was not a clever man, but being around Raimond made him feel clever by proximity. Besides, Udo knew from experience that the time for barbarism would come soon enough; then he would have his fun.

Raimond pushed the door open to Julie's apartment and stepped across the threshold. He stood erect and perfectly still, like a wolf surveying a stretch of tundra just before a caribou hunt. The clamorous sound of a television commercial emanated from the kitchen. Raimond turned to Udo, motioning him to enter the apartment. Udo followed and then quietly shut and locked the apartment door. Raimond nodded approvingly at his brother, and then turned toward the sound. With a quick, deliberate stride he moved toward the kitchen, withdrawing a white handkerchief laced with chloroform from his pocket en route.

A tall slender woman with dark hair stood at the sink counter, her back turned, humming a tune and slicing mushrooms on a cutting board.

Raimond wrapped his left arm around her torso, pinning her arms against her sides. With his right hand, he held the handkerchief over her mouth and nose. She gasped, sucking in air through the chemical-laden cloth. Her body tensed and then fell limp in his arms. The paring knife hit to the floor with a thud. His strike was so efficient she never uttered a sound.

• • •

THE WORLD WAS blurry and bright. Time seemed to be passing in slow motion for Isabella as she struggled to regain consciousness. Her eyelids were heavy, and she very much wanted to go back to sleep, but a voice deep in her mind told her she needed to wake up. She was in danger. From what, or from whom, she could not recall, but the last thing she remembered was being deathly afraid.

"She's waking up," Udo announced. He walked over to Raimond who had fallen asleep in a chair and gave him a shake.

Adrenaline coursed through Isabella's arteries counteracting the waning effects of the anesthesia. She tried to move her legs; she could not. She struggled to free her arms; the effort was futile. She was securely bound to a chair by duct tape. Her pulse quickened, and she was surprised to hear herself panting as she writhed in the chair.

"You should save your energy," Raimond said to Isabella, now standing in front of her. "You're going to need it."

"Who are you? What do you want?" Isabella demanded, trying to sound tough.

"It doesn't work that way. I ask you the questions—not the other way around," he replied, shaking his index finger at her.

"Ja, we ask the questions, fräulein," Udo added.

"In my experience, everything progresses much more smoothly if I explain all the rules to you before we begin. I don't want any confusion or misunderstanding between us." Raimond walked around behind Isabella and put his hands on her shoulders. "Quite simply, this is an interrogation. I am the interrogator, and you are the inter-rogatee. You have information that I need. If you answer all of my questions truthfully, then you will live and this will all be over quite swiftly and painlessly. If you do not, then the interrogation will be quite long and painful. Do you understand the rules?"

Isabella began to tremble. "I don't understand why you are doing this. I own a little wine bistro downstairs." She began to stammer, "I, I, I, don't understand what you could possibly want from me!"

"I don't think you were listening. It is *very* important that you listen to me. I ask the questions. You answer truthfully. Do you un-derstand? These are the rules."

"Yes, yes, but, I have a question."

"Okay," Raimond replied, exasperated. "One question."

"How do I know that you won't kill me even if I answer your questions?"

"Because, number one, I am a man of my word. Number two, because I am not here to kill you—I am here to gather information. Let us return to the rules one final time. I ask you questions. You answer them truthfully, and you live. If you choose not to answer my questions, or you lie to me, then you will be tortured until your slow and painful death," Raimond expounded. "What is your name?"

"Isabella."

"That was very good Isabella, you answered the first question truthfully. You are a very nice young woman, Isabella, with a long happy future ahead of you. If you cooperate, you can return to your wine bistro and you will never see me or my colleague again. If you do not cooperate, then I can make no such guarantee."

Isabella began to sob. She could taste fear in her mouth. Her throat was tight. Her heart pounded. She could not believe this was happening to her.

Raimond maintained his station behind her. It was a technique he had developed by accident during an interrogation many years ago; it proved so effective, that he had used it ever since. First, he found it much easier to be brutal without having to look into the victim's eyes. Second, the victim could not see his face. Pain sears powerful memories in the brain, and he did not want his face to be recalled. But most importantly, standing behind the victim seemed to magnify the terror of the experience more than any other technique he had experimented with. Over the years, he had learned that interrogation was like baking; it worked best when one followed a recipe. His recipe was two parts fear to one part pain.

"Okay, let's move on," he announced casually. "Tell me, where can I find your roommate, Julie Ponte?"

"Um, Julie?"

"Yes, Julie Ponte. Where can I find her?"

"I don't know. Why? What do you want with Julie?"

"Isabella, you have broken the rules. Now I am forced to have my colleague demonstrate what happens every time you break the rules," Raimond reprimanded. Still standing behind her, Raimond grabbed her forehead and her chin and pulled her jaw open. Udo swiftly stuffed a balled up kitchen rag deep into her mouth. Isabella tried to scream, but the sound was almost completely muffled by the wad of fabric pressing against her tongue, checks, and soft palette. Udo then walked around to her left side. With his massive hands, he effortlessly peeled her clenched left fingers free from the end of the armrest. Before she knew what was happening, he gripped her left pinkie finger and snapped it like a fresh carrot at the knuckle joint. He released her broken finger at the angle he broke it—protruding ninety degrees to the side—for her to see.

Isabella shrieked in agony, but the gag in her mouth deadened the volume and pitch of her wail to a level undetectable outside the apartment. Tears streamed down her cheeks.

"Isabella, I want you to listen very carefully. This is the best that you will feel during the rest of this experience. From now on, it only gets worse. Now, I am going to ask you some questions with the gag in your mouth. You are going to nod your head up-and-down for 'yes' and shake your head side-to-side for 'no.' Nod your head if you understand," said Raimond.

Isabella nodded her head, trembling. She stared off into space, averting her gaze away from her left hand.

"Good girl. I am going to remove the gag from your mouth. If you scream, I will reinsert the gag, and break another finger. Do you understand?"

Nod.

"Are you ready to cooperate?"

Nod.

"Good. Let's try again. Where can I find Julie Ponte?" asked Raimond. He then motioned to his brother to remove the gag.

"I don't know where she is."

Raimond was silent for several seconds, and then suddenly grabbed her forehead and chin. Udo stuffed the gag back into her mouth. Isabella shook the chair and screamed a muffled scream. He nodded at Udo.

Udo gripped her left ring finger in his hand and twisted, snapping the bone between the second and third knuckles. Isabella shook the chair violently as tears gushed down her cheeks. Mucus was beginning to fill her nose and clog her throat.

Raimond tenderly stroked her forehead and dark brown hair, like a lover would do. "Isabella, I am very disappointed in you. You've broken the rules again. This time you lied to me. Look at your fingers."

Isabella continued to sob and looked up at the ceiling, resisting the urge to see her mangled left hand. Raimond grabbed her face between both hands and jerked her head down.

"LOOK AT IT!" he shouted.

The power of his voice dominated her will, and she looked at her left hand, two of her fingers protruding at unnatural, oblique angles. She began to hyperventilate. The rag stuffed in her mouth exacerbated the problem, causing her to panic. The veins in her neck and forehead bulged. Her face flushed red.

Raimond sighed. He pulled the rag out of her mouth and waited while she panted in terror, trying to catch her breath, sweat now pouring from her brow.

"Isabella. Isabella, listen to me. This is not going very well. I'm going to ask you the same question again. This time, I want you

216

to tell me the truth," Raimond said to her. "Where can I find your roommate, Julie Ponte?"

Isabella struggled to answer him in between sobs and gasps for air. "I told you . . . I don't know . . . she left the apartment this morning . . . and she didn't tell me . . . where she was going."

Raimond stood silently behind her. Udo watched Raimond, like a guard dog stares at his master, awaiting the order to attack.

"I swear! I don't know where she was going . . . she didn't tell me . . . and I didn't ask."

"Okay. I believe you. Was she alone or was she with someone? An American man perhaps?"

Isabella paused. She had not betrayed Julie. Not yet. Now, he was forcing her to make a choice: self-preservation or self-sacrifice to protect a friend. She liked Julie, but she was not family. They had known each other not even two years. These crazy Germans would break all her fingers if she did not cooperate; she was certain of that. She had no choice; she had to look out for herself.

"She was alone," she said and could not believe the words as they came out of her mouth.

Raimond nodded at Udo, who moved to stuff the rag back into her mouth.

"Wait! No. You're right. There was an American. He went with her," Isabella blurted.

Raimond nodded again, and Udo pressed the gag back into her mouth anyway. "Break another finger. She lied to me."

She wailed as Udo grabbed her middle finger on her left hand and broke it as he did the others.

"Isabella, you are beginning to make me very angry. This is not a game. Do you understand? DO YOU UNDERSTAND THIS IS NOT A GAME?" Raimond shouted in her ear.

After giving her a few moments recovery, Raimond removed the gag.

"I told you the truth," she stammered.

"But you lied to me first," he said. "That is not a good strategy, Isabella. We are going to run out of fingers soon, and then I have to start breaking bigger bones."

Udo snorted happily; he quite enjoyed the middle portion of interrogations, and this one was no exception.

The pain in her left hand was unbearable. It was impossible to concentrate on anything else beside the pain. Fear of pain consumed her now. Her will was broken. There was no chance she could persevere against these devils.

"This American—what was his name?"

"Bob. Julie said his name was Bob," Isabella answered nervously, watching Udo to see if punishment was forthcoming.

"I believe you are telling the truth, but I believe Julie lied to you. Was he tall?"

"Yes."

"Was he ill with fever or cough?"

"No, he was not ill," she panted. "Not that I could see."

"How much time did you spend with them?"

"I only returned to Vienna this morning. I arrived at the apartment as they were leaving. I only spent a few minutes with them."

"What did they say to you before they left?"

"Julie introduced him to me as her American friend who was in Wien on business. She said they were going out for a coffee. That's all."

"What else can you tell me?"

"What else can I say? I just met this man for the first time in my life. They left, and I unpacked my luggage."

"You're hiding something. Tell me now, or my colleague breaks another finger."

"Sir, there is nothing else to tell!" Isabella begged.

Raimond nodded at Udo who gagged Isabella and snapped her left index finger. This time he broke it to the right, opposite the others—a little variety to amuse himself.

The intensity of the pain radiating from her broken index finger was more severe than the others and caused her to hyperventilate. Mucus flooded her nose and throat, blocking her airway. Her eyes bulged with panic; black curtains eclipsed her field of vision. She tried to cough and blow the mucus clear, but it didn't work. The movement of her tongue only made her predicament worse, drawing the rag deeper into her throat. She was suffocating and powerless to stop it. Raimond let her writhe—to the brink of unconsciousness—before pulling the gag from her mouth.

In between lurching gasps for air, she coughed and spat a thick and frothy mucous all over herself. It took several minutes, but eventually she gained control of her breathing and felt her wits returning to her. Her left hand was swelling and port wine-colored bruises flourished under the skin. Inadvertently, she looked at the mangled hand. The irregular angles of her fingers were grotesque. Nauseating.

She vomited.

A splatter of gastric juices and partially digested food painted Udo's right shoe as he tried to jump out of the way. Angered, he slapped her across the mouth with an open hand. Blood trickled from her lower lip, and coated her white teeth with red.

"You are evil, terrible men. Both of you. Devils," she sobbed.

Raimond smoothly caressed her hair again, which was now saturated with sweat.

"Isabella? You are a very brave, very strong woman. But it's time you stop this foolishness. What did Julie say to you when she left? What are you hiding from me?"

Isabella sobbed and did not answer.

Raimond waited for a moment and repeated the question.

In between sobs, she said, "She told if anyone came by the flat looking for her . . . to tell them . . . that I had not seen her recently."

"Good. Very good, Isabella. What else did she say?"

"Only that she needed some time alone with him."

"Did she say where she was going?"

"No."

"Did they take luggage with them? Like they were going on a trip?"

"No . . . only a backpack."

Raimond rubbed his chin thoughtfully. "I believe you are telling me the truth at last. I have only one more question before we go. Where can I find a picture of Julie?"

Isabella trembled. "You know the answer to that question."

"I suppose I do, but I want you to tell me anyway. So you remember betraying your friend."

"Look in her bedroom, you'll find pictures of her there," she mumbled, her head down.

Raimond wandered out of the kitchen and found Julie's bedroom. He walked over and stood by the window. He checked the signal strength on his mobile phone and dialed Stefan.

"We're at Ponte's apartment, but she's not here. Do you have any ideas how we can locate her?"

"Give me a little time and I'll find Ponte for you. I'll have my contact at Orange Telecom look up Ponte's mobile number and ping her phone. With three towers pinging, we can easily narrow her position within a fifty-meter radius. But remember Raimond, we pay five hundred euros *per* ping, so I hope we're making a big fee on this job," Stefan replied.

Raimond smirked. "Don't worry about the fee. I've got that covered. You just worry about finding Ponte. Text me when you get the first triangulation."

"Ja, okay."

Raimond ended the call and walked over to Julie's dresser. Neatly arranged in three rows, stood a variety of pictures, each mounted in a unique frame that complemented the mood and color palette of the photograph. His eyes darted from one image to the next as he methodically dissected her features, burning her face into his memory. A serendipitous encounter on the sidewalk, a backward glance in a crowd, or a glimpse in a passing car window . . . no matter how fleeting the opportunity, he would be ready. After several minutes, he chose a picture for the taking. Careful not to knock over any of the others, he selected a picture of Julie and Isabella hugging each other, laughing, and wearing silly cone-shaped birthday hats. He walked back into the kitchen and showed the picture to Isabella.

"Remember this moment, because you may never see your friend again," Raimond taunted, showing her the picture.

Isabella began to sob. "Are you going to kill me now?"

"I told you, we are not killers. And I am a man of my word. You cooperated—eventually. So you will live," Raimond said. He then looked at Udo. "Let's go."

Disappointed that the interrogation session was over, Udo let out an angry grunt, and then turned and shuffled toward the door. Raimond followed behind in silence, waiving good-bye to Isabella casually over his shoulder.

"Aren't you going to untie me?" she called out after him.

Raimond laughed. "Brother, please go untie our little fräulein."

Udo turned and walked back into the kitchen. With the flick of his thumb he opened a stainless steel pocketknife, and cut free the duct tape that bound Isabella's mangled left hand to the chair, leaving her other limbs held fast.

"There, you are free," Udo said to her. "Now, we really must be going. We have a date with Fräulein Ponte, and we don't want to be late."

Chapter Thirty-One

PROFESSOR JOHANSEN SHOOK his head in disbelief. "What Vyrogen did to you violates the Hippocratic oath. It makes me ill. It is like a war crime, only you were not a soldier of any war."

"I think we may dealing with a different kind of war, Professor, but a war nonetheless. A war between powerful multinational corporations, fighting to bring the next blockbuster drug to market first. Will is an early civilian casualty of this war," Julie said.

"If what you are telling me is true, then I would agree. Please, Will, if you don't mind, tell me what happened after the injections."

"After the first several rounds of injections, nothing happened. Then six weeks became twelve weeks, and the injections became much stronger. I started to become sick. I think they were ramping up the virulence factor on what they were giving me, you know, trying to find my body's limit. They probably started with the common cold and ended with *Yersinia pestis*, but no matter how hard those bastards tried, they couldn't break me. I always recovered."

Johansen was dumbfounded. The irony of the situation was profound. He had dedicated his entire career to researching the role of immunity mutations in bubonic plague pandemics. And now, seated in front of him was a man who appeared to possess the very genetic mutation he had theorized to exist. To discover and decode such a mutation could mean a universal cure for all disease. Except where he would offer the panacea to the world for free, Vyrogen wanted to pirate it. Control it. Make it exclusively their own. They would chop it up and sell a hundred variants to remedy a hundred different afflictions to maximize their profits. But Will Foster had abandoned Vyrogen, and in doing so, stumbled upon him. Fate, it seemed, did have a sense of humor.

"Professor, I have the Foster files you requested," Johansen's assistant said, standing in the doorway to his office.

"Thank you. You can set the box on the table."

She did as he requested, looked at Will and Julie curiously, and then left the office without another word. Johansen picked up the Foster records and paged through them for a minute in silence.

"Ah yes, now I remember," Johansen said with a fine nostalgic tone to his voice. "This case dates back almost twenty years ago. It was one of my earlier investigations, only a few years after I decided to keep a genealogical database of epidemic survivors. As you can see, I used to store information in cardboard boxes!" The professor gently parsed through the contents of the tattered box with a smile on his face. He retrieved a small leather bound book and smiled broadly as he set it on the table. "I was looking for germs and I found a love story instead."

"What do you mean, Professor?" Julie asked.

"This is a diary. It chronicles the hopes, dreams and fears of a young woman who lived in Eyam, England during the infamous plague epidemic of 1665. I went to England specifically to research Eyam. It's quite a famous little town in epidemiological circles, because it has such a unique plague saga."

Johansen stroked the closed cover of the diary and leaned back in his chair, getting comfortable. Julie looked at Will and smiled. The atmosphere in the office had softened considerably; Johansen's story was something they all could use.

"The story goes that in 1665, the town's tailor ordered some fine fabrics from London. Unbeknownst to him, and to the rest of the town's residents, the fabric that was delivered was infested with fleas, and the fleas were carrying the plague bacteria, *Yersinia pestis*. You see, at that time, London was suffering from recurring plague outbreaks. When the tailor opened his package, he released the infected fleas, and he was bitten. The tailor became infected and so did many others as the disease quickly spread through the town.

Recognizing the severity of the outbreak, the town rector convinced the elders to do a most unprecedented thing; they enacted a mandatory quarantine of all the town's residents."

"Why did they do that? Sounds like suicide to me," Will said.

"In one sense, you're right. For the people of Eyam it was a death sentence. But in another sense, the town leaders demonstrated both wisdom and compassion. By instituting the quarantine in Eyam, they prevented the plague from spreading to all the surrounding villages. The sacrifice of the few saved the lives of the many."

"Utilitarianism," Will mumbled.

"Yes, I suppose that's one view. You could also call it altruism."

"I think it would be altruism if everyone in the town had been given a choice, and they all came to the same conclusion as the elders. A mandate like that is a different story in my book. Don't get me wrong, I think what they did was noble, but at the end of the day, who really has the power to decide when some people's lives should be sacrificed for the greater good, and when they should not?"

"Philosophers have debated the question for a thousand years, and here we are still discussing it today."

"It hits pretty close to home for me, because some rich executive decided to put me in quarantine under the auspice of serving the greater good, and I didn't have any choice in the matter. I definitely can relate to the people who lived in Eyam."

Johansen chuckled. "Maybe more than you know." The professor slid the leather bound diary across the table to Will. "Be gentle with that. It's almost four hundred years old."

"Where did you get this?"

"In a souvenir shop in Eyam. It was one of the most expensive items in the shop. I paid two hundred pounds for that over twenty years ago. Imagine what it would fetch today."

Will opened the cover and gingerly began turning the pages. "Whose diary was this?"

"It belonged to the tailor's daughter, Kathryn Vicars, who married and became Kathryn Foster. She lived in Eyam when the plague hit."

Will eyed the Professor with curiosity. "What happened to her?"

"She became infected, and she died."

"And her family? Did they all die too?"

"No, not all. Kathryn's father, the tailor, was the first to die; but Kathryn eloped with her young lover, Paul Foster. Together, they avoided infection during the first outbreak in the fall of 1665. Months later, the couple returned to Eyam, only to find the town infested with plague. They decided to live at the Foster family farm. Kathryn became pregnant and birthed a son, George. Sadly, there was a resurgence of the plague that lasted almost all of 1666. Kathryn fell ill and died in August of that year. When the plague had finally run its course, only 20 percent of Eyam's population remained. The story is all inside. The pages of the diary are laden with emotion. Pain, sorrow, suffering. Love, joy, new beginnings. I read it cover to cover. It could be made into a movie."

"And Paul Foster, he lived because he was immune?"

"Yes, and so did the son, George Foster," Johansen said. He grinned at Will. "Now, I suspect the answer to my quest may be sitting at this table. I tried to trace the Foster lineage to the present, but the line went cold in the mid-seventeen hundreds. Maybe that is because one of your ancestors sneaked across the pond and became a Yank without telling anyone."

"That would be incredible if it were true."

"I can propose one surefire way to find out," Johansen said with a raised eyebrow.

"Take a sample of my DNA?"

"Yes."

Will looked at Julie, who was beaming. "Absolutely, do it, Will. This is what you were hoping for. Answers to what makes you special."

Will rubbed his chin and then said, "First let me ask you one more question. If you had to come up with a theory about why my immune system is impervious to disease, what would you say?"

Johansen laughed, and then replied. "I can't answer that question without conducting years of research. It's the very question I've dedicated my professional career to. If I knew the answer, I would retire tomorrow."

"But if you had to guess? Let's say the Nobel committee told you to forward your hypothesis today, or they would never listen to you again," Will pressed.

"That sounds like the Nobel committee all right," Johansen laughed. "Since you are being very persistent, I will tell you my theory. Understand, however, I have no conclusive evidence to support this idea; it is only a theory."

"No problem."

"I speculate that you have a genetic mutation—passed down from Paul Foster via your paternal lineage—which is responsible for the unusual lymphocyte in your pictures. I have postulated for several years now that, theoretically, a *skeleton key* lymphocyte could exist."

"Skeleton key lymphocyte?" Julie questioned.

"Let me explain: T cells and B cells are specific, meaning a single lymphocyte has receptors that can bind only to a particular antigen. Think of this as a lock and key system—a single key fits a single lock. Now, imagine a mutation where a lymphocyte could bind to a variety of antigens expressed by a variety of pathogens. Instead of being effective against only one specific type of pathogen, a skeleton key lymphocyte could mount a defense against many different pathogens—just as a skeleton key can work on many different locks. Such a mutation would bestow upon its owner an extremely efficient immune response."

"How can we determine if Will has this skeleton key mutation?"

"I know only one way to do that my dear, and it's the hard way. Research. Lots and lots of research," Johansen laughed. "But let's start with the DNA test to confirm Will's ancestry first, shall we?"

"How long will that take?"

"I can draw the blood sample in the lab now, but the analysis will take some time. I should have a preliminary answer within a couple of days. I would also like to draw additional vials of blood to begin an analysis on that mystery lymphocyte of yours. Are you opposed to that?" Johansen asked.

Will looked at Julie.

"Were going to need some assurances from you and the university before we tread down that path," she said.

"Of course," Professor Johansen replied. Then he took Will's hand between both of his and squeezed, while looking Will in the eyes. "Please understand, I might be a man of science, but I am also a man of conscience. I'm morally opposed to the patenting of genes. I maintain the belief that your genome is your property. I have no more right to patent it for my own personal gain than I do the right to pilfer the contents of your wallet. Vyrogen tried to exploit you, make you the Henrietta Lacks of our time, but I assure you that will never happen here. I sign a written contract with every research subject in my genealogy study, waiving any and all patent rights to genes discovered while conducting my research. The university doesn't always like it, but I've made it a condition of my employment."

Gene patents? Henrietta Lacks? He turned to Julie again. "What is he talking about, Julie?"

"Medical practitioners and medical researchers have always been joined at the hip, but with the advent of modern genetics, we've become strange bedfellows," Julie said. "It all started in early 1950s with an American woman named Henrietta Lacks. She was diagnosed with an aggressive form of cervical cancer. She was treated at Johns Hopkins. For diagnostic purposes, her doctor ordered a tissue biopsy of her cervix. A scientist in the culture lab by the name of George Gey noticed that Lacks' cancer cells did not die off in the culture dish like normal cells did. Instead, they survived and multiplied unfettered. He dubbed these resilient cells HeLa cells, borrowing the first two letters from Henrietta and Lacks. As a scientist, Gey realized that these *immortal* cells would be invaluable to the field of medical research, so he cultured a HeLa cell line for this express purpose. This did nothing of course to help cure poor Henrietta of her cancer, but it did lay the foundation for sixty years of groundbreaking research based on her cells."

"How do you know all this?" Will asked.

"I'm an oncology researcher, Will. I've been using HeLa cells my entire career. Every man, woman and child on this planet owes Henrietta Lacks a debt of gratitude. Without HeLa cells, modern medicine would not be where it is today. Vaccine creation, cancer research, pharmaceutical drug development, our understanding of infectious diseases like HIV and influenza . . . all these things rely on the use of HeLa cells," she said. Then, exhaling slowly, she added, "But there's more to it than that. In recent years, Henrietta Lacks has become the poster child for biomedical exploitation."

"Why?"

"Because the HeLa cell line was cultured, patented, and commercialized without her knowledge or consent. Moreover, her family was kept in the dark and never financially compensated or paid a royalty from the subsequent profits. I think the point Professor Johansen was making is that if your mutation turns out to be the miraculous discovery we all think it is, then you and Henrietta Lacks would be kindred spirits—genetically exceptional and thus exploited for both patent and profit."

Will narrowed his eyes. "Are you saying that Vyrogen could patent my genes and make millions of dollars from my immunity mutation simply because they happened to stumble across it first?"

"Billions of dollars," Johansen said, beating Julie to the punch. "And yes, the US Patent and Trademark Office has been granting patents on genes since the Supreme Court case of Diamond v. Chakrabarty in 1980. A recent study estimated that approximately 20 percent of the human genome has already been patented. It is disgusting. Patent holders are granted a virtual monopoly on applications associated with their patented genes, a practice that not only undermines scientific freedom and the collegial exchange of information, but also jeopardizes each and every person's right to have free access to and use of the information encoded in their own DNA."

"So Vyrogen has already won," Will said, his eyes cast down. "Once they patent my mutation, they control everything."

"Not necessarily," Johansen replied. Then with a sly grin he added, "I would never presume to tell you what to do in a scenario as extraordinary as yours. I can, however, tell you what I would do if our stations were reversed."

"And what would you do?"

"I would publish my genome on the Internet, for the entire world to see. It would be my gift to humanity," said Johansen.

"And, it would make life hell for Vyrogen," Julie added. "If Dr. Johansen can identify the genes responsible for your mutation and make a public disclosure before Vyrogen, then you win and Vyrogen loses."

Johansen nodded. "The irony of trying to sell something which is priceless is that one should never try to sell it to begin with."

Will nodded, contemplating his words. "Thank you, Professor, for everything."

"Don't thank me yet. Were just starting this race," said Johansen, shaking Will's hand.

"You've done plenty already. You've given me hope."

Johansen smiled and looked down, almost embarrassed. He liked Will Foster. It took great courage to do what he was doing, especially considering the ordeal he had been through with Vyrogen, and great courage was hard to find in people these days.

"This," Johansen said, taking the diary off the table and handing it to Will, "should belong to you. I think you will find the story to be inspirational."

"I couldn't," Will stammered.

"Don't be ridiculous. The words on these pages are no more mine to possess than the information encoded in your DNA. I'm just along for the ride. Please, take it. Meet Kathryn Foster. Meet her husband, Paul, and their son, George. Know what it was like to be a Foster in 1665."

Will nodded and took the diary in his hands. He gently opened the worn leather cover and paged to where a black silk ribbon page divider rested and read a short entry.

May 27, 1666

Dearest Diary,

At length the day has come on which I am a mother. My tears flow as I write at the idea, for I am both full of joy and wrought with fear at the prospect. My dearest Paul and Mother Alice have been steadfast at my bedside since the labour, and they chasten me for talking nonsense whenever I speak of my fears.

Little George is so fair, but Alice says he is of nice colour. To my eyes, his likeness is that of Paul, but Paul of course says the opposite, that he is wholly a reflection of me. It is no matter, because all in the family agree that nary have they seen a child so handsome, pleasant, and hungry as George. I have placed a cutting of his hair inside the crease of this page so that I might never forget how soft and fair he was on this, the day of his birth.

As I look upon my son, asleep at my bosom, I think that there is nary a child in the world—perhaps one in one hundred generations—as perfect as he. I pray that the plague never finds him, and that God grants me the good fortune to be able to love him for a thousand thousand to-morrows.

Chapter Thirty-Two

Boston, Massachusetts

H E GAZED UPON the length of her long, arched naked back. Her skin was the color of crème and smelled of lavender and honey. Caramel freckles accented her shoulders, and together with her rich auburn locks, dutifully honored her Irish lineage. Starting at the nape of her neck, like a running bead of water, he ran his fingertip over her trapezius muscle, and then along the arc of her protruding, angular shoulder blade. Inward next, his touch danced across the plane of her latissimus dorsi, toward the middle of her back. Then downward, he surfed along her spine, and through a herringbone stream of delicate white-blonde peach fuzz that covered the small of her back. She purred, almost inaudibly, with delight. His caress terminated, finally, at a tiny indentation at the junction of her tailbone and bare, exposed buttocks. In this spot, he deposited a single, gentle kiss, before retracing the same path upward, to its origin, with more kisses.

"You paint me with your touch. This must be how the stones of the Sistine Chapel felt beneath Michelangelo's brush," Meredith mused.

"Michelangelo considered himself a sculptor, first and foremost. Painting was conscription labor, for the Pope. Forget about the brush. If you were made of stone, which we can debate later, you would be my David. But hewn as Michelangelo should have hewn it. As a woman," Nicolora replied, his voice baritone and seductive.

Meredith rolled to her side, and inched toward him. He drifted onto his back, propping himself up slightly, and then extended his arm outward to cradle her. She nuzzled close, pressing her right breast softly against his bare chest, and depositing her cheek in the comfortable depression between his shoulder and pectoral muscle.

"You've been a naughty boy, Robért," she whispered. "Very naughty."

"And you've been a naughty girl, Meredith. Especially about thirty minutes ago."

"Don't be cheeky, you know *what* I'm talking about," she mewed.

After a pause he said, "If you're referring to Countess Carlysle, then you should consider the discussion tabled, because I have nothing to say on the matter."

"I'm not talking about another woman, you stupid lout; I'm talking about you sending your minions to spy on me." Then, punctuating each word with a bite she moved her mouth across the span of his chest, and said, "*I . . . don't . . . appreciate . . . that.*"

"I'm sure . . ." he said, devoting considerable effort not to flinch with each new and painful nibble, "that I have no idea what you're talking about."

Meredith sat up abruptly, facing him. Chest puffing, face flushed, nipples erect.

"Don't play coy with me, Robért Nicolora! I know it was you."

He did not answer, nor did he look her in the eyes, but rather let his gaze linger on her nakedness.

"Oh, you men are so pathetic," she huffed, as she turned abruptly to exit the bed.

He caught her by her trailing arm before she was completely off the mattress and pulled her forcefully on top of him. "Now wait a minute, Meredith. Don't do that," he implored. "I did not mean to offend."

"Let go of me, you wretch. I never should have come to you." She squirmed to free herself from his iron grip. "And I never should have trusted you."

He held her tight. After a halfhearted struggle, she collapsed onto him.

"The team is making steady progress on locating Foster. But this is not an ordinary assignment. You've handed me a hornet's nest, Meredith, and I'm trying to manage it without getting stung," he said, his eastern European accent emerging, charged by the emotion she had ignited in him.

"I know. It's just that I'm anxious, Robért. We have to find Foster soon, before more innocent people get hurt by him," she mumbled, her face pressed tight against his chest.

"I know we do." They laid together in silence for several minutes and then he said. "I have concerns, Meredith."

"Like what?"

"First, why did you keep Foster in-house? Why didn't you hand him over to the CDC or a proper hospital for quarantine and treatment? It seems a tremendous liability for you, and for your company, to accept for the sake of one man in a vaccine trial."

Meredith grinned unfettered, knowing her face was hidden, buried against his chest. It had required one of her best theatrical performances, but she had finally managed to win the upper hand.

"Do you think I'm heartless, Robért? *Those* bureaucrats would have argued over treatment protocols, insurance coverage, public safety, and God knows what other red tape for weeks. Meanwhile, poor Will would have been dying inside a giant inflatable Ziploc bag. Someone had to act. Someone had to do the responsible thing. I felt I had a duty to try to help him, using any and all means at my disposal."

"What about Vyrogen's miracle product? Why would you offer something so experimental to him?"

"If you were in his shoes, staring death in the face, wouldn't you take it? Even if it's a long shot, it's better than doing nothing at all," she said, avoiding the heart of his question.

"Yes, I suppose you're right." He paused, and then added. "Something else I don't understand is what makes you suspect that Foster is the mastermind behind the espionage? We've performed a thorough investigation and background assessment on Foster, and to be perfectly blunt, the piece does not fit the puzzle. He was an advertising exec. Not even a very good one, I might add. Yes, he was down on his luck, but we found nothing in his profile to suggest that he's capable of contemplating something of this magnitude, let alone capable of orchestrating it. Seriously, Meredith. We are perplexed. Foster has a bachelor's degree in economics. A nontechnical background, with no experience in microbiology. He has no criminal record. No apparent ties to the pharmaceutical industry whatsoever. Your logic of implicating him escapes us."

Her mind raced. He had brought up several points she had not considered before she briefed the team. She needed time to think of a proper rebuttal. He was horsing her into a corner. She decided to snarl at him and see if he backed down.

"He *did* steal the formula and sabotage the lab. That much is fact, Robért. Whether Foster is the mastermind of the plot is a separate matter. Let me remind you that I've never claimed to have the answers to this case. In fact, I've made it quite clear that my theories were only conjecture based on my extremely limited experience in such matters, and that I am relying on your expertise to unravel the case. That's why I hired you. I should have never opened my mouth about Foster's role in the espionage, because I set your team looking down a path that may not be the true path."

"I know, I know. I'm sorry I'm pressing you, but it's only because you are the person closest to the heart of the case." He squeezed her affectionately. "One more question?"

Her stomach churned. "Of course."

"If we pursue the line of reasoning that Foster is *not* the mastermind behind the espionage, then we must assign a different role to him. Our hypothesis is that Foster was simply a mule to steal and deliver your intellectual property to a buyer."

"Okay, but where is the question, Robért?" She laughed, awkwardly.

"Yes, yes. I'm getting there," he said. "Now, assuming Foster is a mule, we can say with confidence that no mule works alone. So, this begs the question—who is Foster in collusion with?"

"One of our competitors, no doubt."

"Yes, that was our initial inclination as well. However, shaking this tree has yielded no fruit. We can find no external connection, relationship, or even record of communication between Foster and persons of interest in the pharmaceutical industry."

"Really, that's surprising. Maybe your team needs to broaden their search," she said.

He shook his head. "No, no. Certainly not. Our investigative capability is unrivaled. If a connection existed, my people would have sniffed it out. This leaves us only one place left to look. We have turned our investigation inward."

"Inward?"

"Yes, inward. The logical hypothesis is that Foster is colluding with someone inside Vyrogen. Only an insider would know about the experimental product. Only an insider would know about the H1N1 vaccine trial. Only an insider would have access to Foster while he was in quarantine."

He hugged her again. Tight.

Her heart pounded. Gooseflesh stood up on her arms. Her mouth went dry. He was squeezing her, literally and figuratively. Her mind stumbled over itself. She grasped for something to say. Anything. No words would come. Her mouth was a black hole, agape and devoid of all sound, and all potential for sound.

"Robért, I," she stuttered, "I can't imagine that someone on my staff would . . ." She stopped abruptly. The taught corners of her mouth curled into a wicked grin. He had opened a door for her. Not the exit she had expected, but an exit nonetheless, from her burning house of cards. "Actually, there *is* one person who is capable of such a thing."

"Yes?"

"Yes. His name is Xavier Pope."

•   •   •

"STOP LOOKING AT me that way," Nicolora said to Briggs from across the white tablecloth and over the art deco stemware.

"What way?"

"You know exactly what way. Now wipe that smug look off your face and eat your damn soup."

Briggs lowered his spoon and raised the napkin from his lap to wipe his mouth. "It's not smugness; it's lobster bisque," he said. "You look flushed, Robért. Did you have to run to lunch? Is that why you were late?"

"I was working," Nicolora said, suppressing a smile. "Gathering intelligence."

"Is that what we're calling it these days . . . I'll have to remember that for my expense reports." Briggs dropped his hands into his lap. "They still haven't found Foster, have they?"

"No."

"Do you know where he is?"

"No."

"Does Meredith?"

"No."

Briggs grunted and turned back to his soup. He was about to press Nicolora about his one-time flame, but he had danced that dance enough times to know better. Best to keep quiet and let his friend talk.

"Don't ask," Nicolora said.

"I didn't say anything."

"You were thinking it. I can see it in your beady little eyes."

"I've never asked you about it before, and I see no reason this meal has to be any different."

"Underneath that cover-girl facade and flowing mane of auburn hair is a deeply competitive and focused woman. I find her to be, in a word, irresistible."

"I know."

"You weren't there, Jack."

Briggs laughed, "I know, but I dined with the two of you in Boston several times."

"Twice."

"Fine, twice. But even then, she had you by the—" Briggs cupped his hands explicitly, finishing the sentence.

"I have things under control."

"Do you trust her?"

"Absolutely not," Nicolora said without pause.

"Do you think this is her deal, or is someone else pulling the strings?"

"That is *the* question, isn't it? On the one hand, Meredith is certainly capable of something like this on her own. On the other, I can't shake the feeling that this goes higher up. It just has the stink of Client One all over it. She's implicated Xavier Pope as the mastermind. With CDC involvement, we can't rule it out. What do you think Uncle Sam would be willing to pay for soldiers with absolute immunity to biological warfare agents?"

Briggs nodded as he stuffed half a dinner roll, slathered in white cream butter, into his mouth. "If you're right," Briggs mumbled over the food in his mouth, "It won't be long until agency boys start showing up."

"I know, I know. I'm surprised she's had this long to clean up her mess. Patience has never been one of their defining characteristics."

"It's going to be the devil's circus if that happens. We need to have a contingency plan in place."

"I'm working on it. By the way, take it easy on the butter there, Chief. We don't want to have to Roto-Root your arteries again any time soon."

"Peck, peck, Mother Hen," Briggs quipped. Then, rubbing his chin, he asked. "When we finally do locate Foster, you're not really going to turn him over to her?"

"I haven't decided. But one thing is certain, Foster is too valuable for us to let him slip away into the night."

Chapter Thirty-Three

THE OBSIDIAN-COLORED, V12-POWERED, BMW 760Li sedan glided across the Austrian countryside effortlessly at 130 kilometers per hour. Somewhere, many kilometers ahead, Kalen was rocketing past Porsches and BMWs on his Ducati Diavel. AJ had never ridden a real motorcycle, only his scooter. He had asked Kalen what the allure of the Ducati was, fully expecting to hear a soliloquy on the exhilaration of wrangling raw power, or the rush of adrenaline from catapulting oneself from a standstill to a ludicrous velocity in a heartbeat. Instead, what he got was a nasal snort. "If you have to ask, then you'll never get it, kid."

Wearily, AJ glanced at his watch. "What is our ETA in Vienna?" he asked the driver.

"Approximately forty-five minutes, sir."

He reclined his head against the headrest. He had not slept since they had arrived in Prague, and he was losing the battle against unconsciousness. In the rear passenger's seat to his left, sat Albane. She looked at him, studying him in profile.

"Tired?" she asked.

"Tired would be an understatement," he mumbled.

"Here, take this," she said handing him a white pill.

The surface of the caplet was etched with the words: PROVIGIL—200 MG. "What's Provigil?"

"In our line of work, that's salvation in a pill. We all do it. It's not a stimulant, rather a class of drug called a wakefulness agent. The military has been using it with soldiers and pilots for years."

"I was wondering why I was the only one who seemed to be dragging like a jet-lagged zombie."

He popped the pill in his mouth and washed it down with a swallow of luke warm bottled water. Albane smiled at him, but her eyes showed a hint of melancholy, as if to say, "Another chemical convert, and I'm his maker."

She pressed "0" on her phone and summoned a Coordinator. After several minutes of rapid-fire dialogue with C. Remy, she ended the call and grabbed her tablet computer. The screen sprang to life; images and files downloaded on command from the Think Tank servers.

"What's going on?" AJ asked her.

She turned the tablet screen to show him.

"Okay, I'll bite. Who is he?" he asked, staring at the picture of a handsome gentleman in his midthirties on the screen.

"His name is Xavier Pope."

"Meredith mentioned him in her brief. He's the heavy hitter from the CDC, right?"

"Yes, but she didn't tell us the whole story. Pope *was* at CDC, but then four months ago he suddenly left and went to work for . . ."

"Vyrogen Pharmaceuticals," VanCleave said from the front seat.

"Precisely. Here is Pope photographed at a black-tie benefit dinner with Meredith Morley standing to his left, and the CEO of Vyrogen to his right, along with some other VIPs. This picture was published with an article from the *New York Times* and was taken ten days before Vyrogen announced Pope as their new Director of the Immunological Therapeutics Division. But, that's not all. Are you ready for the bomb?"

"Hit me."

"According to Founder One, Meredith has just implicated Xavier Pope as a possible mole trying to steal Vyrogen's breakthrough research," she said.

"Unlikely in my opinion," AJ said. "Unless . . ."

"Go on."

"It's a stupid idea, a total conspiracy red herring."

"In my experience, even suppositions we second-guess are still worthy of consideration. Tell me."

"I was going to say, that seems highly unlikely unless Pope never *really* stopped working for the government. Maybe the military wants to get his hands on Vyrogen's research, and Pope's connection with the CDC made him the perfect mole. If Meredith is telling the truth, that's one plausible explanation."

"Interesting theory, but we know Meredith has been hiding things from us. Implicating Pope could also be a ruse. Especially if she suspects we were behind the Chiarek Norse surprise inspection. If I were in her position, I'd be getting nervous."

"We could question him," AJ said.

"Not a bad idea," she said, pondering for a moment. Then she shook her head. "Right now, pursuing the Julie Ponte lead is our number one priority. We'll keep Pope on the back burner."

"If we don't find Foster with Ponte, then what?"

Albane pulled up a map of Vienna on her tablet. AJ saw two dots—one static, one moving. She selected the two dots. Then, using a swiping motion with her finger, she connected them with a line. A pop-up window appeared with data.

"Kalen is only ten kilometers from Ponte's apartment now. Keep your fingers crossed, and hopefully we won't have to worry about a plan B."

Chapter Thirty-Four

K. Immel—*RS:Physical*: "Social, this is Physical. I'm standing outside Ponte's apartment, and we've got a problem."

A. Mesnil—*RS:Social*: "I'm listening."

K. Immel—*RS:Physical*: "Ponte wasn't here, but her roommate, Isabella, was. Unfortunately for Isabella, a goon squad got here before I did, and they broke every finger on her left hand."

A. Mesnil—*RS:Social*: "Interrogation?"

K. Immel—*RS:Physical*: "Roger that."

A. Mesnil—*RS:Social*: "Will she talk to you?"

K. Immel—*RS:Physical*: "Yes. She's been very helpful."

A. Mesnil—*RS:Social*: "What alias did you use?"

K. Immel—*RS:Physical*: "Special Agent Nelson. I told her I was with Justice. She bought it."

A. Mesnil—*RS:Social*: "Good. Was she able to ID her torturers for you?"

K. Immel—*RS:Physical*: "No. Just physical descriptions. Two men, one with a shaved head, thirties or forties, of Austrian or German nationality."

A. Mesnil—*RS:Social*: "Okay. Make a report to Founder One and have a Coordinator open a file. This changes things."

K. Immel—*RS:Physical*: "I know. We've got another player. Someone local, from the sound of it."

A. Mesnil—*RS:Social*: "Did you call an ambulance for the roommate?"

K. Immel—*RS:Physical*: "No. Her injuries were painful, but not life threatening. I paid for a taxi and sent her to the ER. I'll meet you in the nest in fifteen, and we can finish debriefing then."

A. Mesnil—*RS:Social*: "Roger. Social out."

•   •   •

"SO THE ROOMMATE confirmed that Foster is with Ponte?" Albane asked Kalen as he walked in the door of their Vienna hotel suite.

"Yes, they were in the apartment when she arrived midday, but then left in a rush. She had no idea where they were going, but said that Ponte seemed very nervous," Kalen said.

"What about the thugs that tortured her? What's their story?"

"They showed up several hours later. Picked the lock and chloroformed her. When she woke up she was strapped in a chair. They broke all the fingers on her left hand questioning her about Ponte and Foster. She said she told them everything she told me. They left her bound to a chair in the kitchen. If I hadn't shown up, she might have been trapped for days. It would have been real ugly."

Albane pursed her lips. "Not exactly the scenario we were hoping for, but it's progress. We've confirmed Foster is with Ponte. Now, it's a matter of chasing them."

Kalen smiled.

"What's so funny?" Albane asked.

"Do you know what the problem is with chasing chickens?" Kalen said.

VanCleave, who was sitting at the table between Albane and AJ, looked up. "Excuse me?" he said, cocking an eyebrow at Kalen.

"The problem with chasing chickens is that they're damn near impossible to catch. Have you ever tried to catch a chicken, VanCleave?"

"Are you speaking allegorically, Kalen, or are you talking about the actual bird? I don't recall you ever using a metaphor before."

Kalen winked at VanCleave and continued. "When I was a kid, I spent one summer working on my grandfather's farm. One of my chores was to replace some rotting wooden slats in the fence around the chicken coop. I made so many trips in and out of the chicken coop that one time I forgot to latch the door, and a hen got out."

"This story is relevant because?" VanCleave moaned.

"I chased that damn hen around for hours. I tried sprinting after her, sneaking up on her, dive-bombing her. Hell, I even tried to chase her into a shed. I never could catch her. Chickens are just too fast. They always stay three paces ahead of you."

"What did you do?" AJ asked.

"I stopped chasing it."

"You gave up?"

"No. I just realized that I was never going to catch that chicken by chasing it all over the farm. To catch it, I had to outwit it. To do that, I had to figure out: 'What is important to a chicken? What motivates a hen?'"

"Not getting plucked is what matters to a chicken," VanCleave said. "I could have told you that."

"Very insightful, Eugene, but I don't think chickens possess that kind of foresight," Albane quipped.

AJ looked at Albane and mouthed "EUGENE?" silently, with a schoolboy grin across his face.

She smiled impishly.

"Anyway, as I was saying," Kalen continued, "I realized that the only thing that motivates a chicken is chicken food. So, I laid a trail of kernels along the ground leading to a pile of feed under an old milk bottle crate that I propped up on one side with a stick. I tied a ten-foot length of string to the stick and hid around the corner. Then I waited. The hen pecked its way along the ground, following the feed trail all the way into the crate and then, WHAM, I pulled the stick out. That was that. Captive chicken, game over. The point I'm trying to make here is, I'm tired of chasing chickens."

"Interesting analogy," said Albane. "What sort of trap are you suggesting for Foster?"

"That's for you guys to figure out. You're the brains of this operation; I'm the biceps," Kalen said, propping his feet up on an ottoman and clasping his hands behind his neck. "I know chickens want chicken feed, but I have no idea what Foster wants."

Albane closed her eyes. "If a man is drowning?" she said to the ether.

"Then throw him a rope," AJ answered.

"Exactly," she said with a smile. "We're going to offer Foster the one thing that nobody has offered him yet."

"Which is?" asked VanCleave.

"A way out."

"Why would Foster deal with us? He doesn't know us. He'll presume it's a trap," VanCleave argued.

"Yes, but why does a rabbit leave the safety of its burrow even when it knows the fox is nearby? Because sometimes it has to. Because the allure of a carrot can overwhelm the fear of the fox." She grabbed a piece of paper, jotted four short sentences down, and handed it to VanCleave.

"That's what we're going to tell Foster?"

"Yes," she replied.

Kalen swiped the paper from VanCleave's hand and read it. "This could be more fun than Chiarek Norse," he beamed.

"Time to play SMS poker," she said. "VanCleave, do we have Julie Ponte's mobile number?"

"Of course."

"Can you please text her that message?"

Kalen handed the paper back to VanCleave, who then composed the text message on his phone. After double-checking his work, he pressed the SEND button, and transmitted Albane's carefully crafted words to Julie Ponte's mobile.

To Will Foster:
We know about Vyrogen,
We're here to help.
We can get you home and clear your name.
Special Agent Nelson - FBI

"It's done," he reported to the group. "Now what?" With eyes narrowed, Albane replied. "Now, we wait."

Chapter Thirty-Five

––––––––

"WHAT NOW? WE can't go back to your apartment." Will said to Julie as they walked down the stone steps outside Johansen's office.

"We need to keep moving, but I'm so exhausted I can't think clearly. We need to go somewhere where we can rest," Julie said, taking hold of Will's hand. "Just for a little while."

"What did you have in mind? A hotel won't work. Too many security cameras, and don't they require ID to check into hotels in Europe?"

She gave his hand a squeeze. "I have another idea. I know somewhere private, safe, and off the grid."

He squeezed her hand back and said, "Okay. Lead the way."

•   •   •

WILL SURVEYED THE small modest bedroom with a measure of skepticism. Sunlight filtered through the room's only window onto a white and blue flowered duvet, covering a double bed. A simple five-drawer dresser, stained the color of honey, occupied the wall to his right. To his left, a door fitted with an ivory and brass antique knob was partially open, revealing a tidy bathroom. It was tiled entirely in white, with accenting blue tiles interspersed in a diamond pattern on the floor and shower walls. He set Julie's backpack on the hardwood floor, and then took a seat at the foot of the bed.

"How do you know this place?" he asked. "Are you sure we can trust that woman?"

Julie chuckled. "Auntie Heigel? Of course we can trust her. I've known her for years, since I came to Vienna."

"Auntie Heigel, huh? Is she really your aunt?"

She lowered an eyebrow at him playfully. "No, that's just her nickname. One day she started referring to herself as my Tantchen Heigel. So, I honor the convention. She'll always be my auntie."

"How did you meet her?"

"I rented this room when I first moved to Vienna. I stayed here for eight months; it took me a while to find an apartment I liked that I could afford. She's a good, honest woman. Mother of two. A recent widower. She's been like a second mom to me."

He nodded.

"Relax, Will, we're safe here. Vyrogen can look up my apartment address, but nobody knows about this place."

"If you say so."

She walked over and sat down next to him on the bed, her thigh pressed against his. She looked at him, but said nothing.

"Vyrogen is never going to stop hunting me," he said, his voice solemn.

She nodded.

"I don't want to be on the run forever. I don't want to live like a fugitive."

"I know."

"I wish I didn't have the immunity mutation. I wish I could go back to the way things were before. Living in ignorance . . . blissful ignorance."

She put her head on his shoulder. "We can't control the cards we're dealt. All we can do is find the courage to play the hand we've been given. Most people wouldn't have had the cunning and courage to escape from Chiarek Norse. Most people would have folded their cards and quit the game. You didn't do that, Will, because you're a fighter. You *are* still fighting . . . right?"

He nodded.

They sat together in silence for a long while before he spoke.

"Johansen said if he was the one whose DNA was encoded with a skeleton key mutation, then he would publish his genome for all the world to see."

"Yeah, I remember."

"He's looking at the situation like open source software—applying the same principle to my DNA."

"Give your genetic code away for free and see what people can build with it. Like Wikipedia," she said.

"It would save millions of lives."

"Yes, *you* would," she said and laid her hand on his thigh.

"Morally, it's the right decision."

"I agree."

"Once everyone has access to my genetic code, Vyrogen will have lost their competitive advantage," he said, with hope in his voice.

"That sounds logical," she said. "But going public exposes you. And, if Johansen beats Vyrogen to the punch and kills their patent efforts, it might incite them to seek retribution. Are you prepared to face those consequences?"

"Yes."

She gazed at him.

"What?" A wave of lustful, nervous expectation rippled through his body.

"I'm proud of you."

He blushed. "It's what anybody would do."

"No, it's not. Your journey has led you to a crossroads today. On the left is the path of self-preservation: keep running, keep hiding, forever looking out for yourself above all else. On the right is the path of self-sacrifice: exposing yourself, giving away your genome, standing in defiance of your enemy. You've chosen the harder path, the noble path. That takes courage."

"I couldn't have made it this far without you. I was trapped in a deep dark hole, and when I called for help, you came and pulled me out. You're my angel."

"I'm happy you found me again." She paused a moment before she continued in a softer voice. "I'm just beginning to realize how much I've missed you."

"I've missed you too."

Before he could move to kiss her, her lips were on him. Wet, flush, and warm. He gently cradled the back of her neck with his hand, his fingers becoming entwined in the fine strands of her hair. His tongue found hers—circled, caressed, and tasted.

She pulled away from him, gasping, grinning. He leaned in for another kiss, but missed. She moved in front of him, straddling his knees. She touched his lips with her finger. Staring into his eyes, she began to unbutton her blouse, slowly, one button at a time.

•   •   •

"HOW LONG HAVE I been asleep?" Julie asked.

"An hour, maybe," Will replied, turning to face her. He set Kathryn Foster's diary down on the mattress next to him, reached over, and stroked her forehead, tenderly along the hairline.

"Mmmm. That's nice . . . Did you sleep?"

"Couldn't. My mind was racing."

"What have you been doing?"

"Reading this," he said, holding up the diary for her to see. "I'm drawn to it. I feel like one of them."

She propped herself up to a reclined sitting position against the headboard of the bed, next to him. The bedsheet slid to her waist, exposing her breasts, but she made no attempt to cover herself.

"Tell me about it," she said.

He picked up the diary and opened it to the page where he had placed the black silk ribbon bookmark. Instead of trying to recount the individual diary entries, he wove the events and details into a coherent narrative. She listened, enraptured, to a tale of love, self-sacrifice, courage, and tragedy. He concluded by reading Kathryn Foster's dying words, and it left them both in tears.

"It's a remarkable story," Julie said at last, wiping her cheeks. "Paul Foster reminds me of you."

He smiled at her. A long, but comfortable silence lingered in the room, as they both drifted off into private musing, until Julie's stomach interrupted their daydreams with a loud, rolling growl. They both burst into laughter.

"Sounds like I've got a monster in there," she said. "I'm starving."

"Me too. What time is it anyway?"

She reached across his body to grab her mobile phone from the bedside table. She pressed the power button, turning it on, and was greeted with a notification that she had a voicemail waiting. As she listened to the recorded message, Will saw her go pale.

"That was my roommate Isabella. She's in a taxi on the way to the hospital. Two brutes showed up at the apartment looking for us. They broke every finger on her left hand. She called to warn me," Julie said, her voice shaky. "She said if they find us, she's certain they'll kill us."

"I'm sure it was the same guys who jumped me in Prague. Bastards . . . I'm sorry about Isabella."

"I want to go see her in the hospital," she said and began to hurriedly get dressed.

"You can't. That's exactly what they want. They'll be waiting for us."

Her phone chimed again, signaling that a text message had been received. "Will, you'd better look at this," she said and tossed him her phone.

To Will Foster:
We know about Vyrogen,
We're here to help.
We can get you home and clear your name.
Special Agent Nelson - FBI

Will stared at the lines of text on the phone's color LCD display.

"I don't buy it. How would the FBI know I'm with you? It's a setup, orchestrated by Vyrogen."

"What do we do?" Julie said.

"Nothing. Ignore it. Turn your phone off so they can't trace us here," he barked, grabbing the phone.

"Will, we need to consider all the possibilities here. The FBI could protect you." She started rubbing her left hand. "What happened to Isabella changes things. These bastards are out for blood. Maybe we need to rethink our plan."

"C'mon, Julie. It's obviously a trap."

"Not if the FBI really is investigating Vyrogen."

Will's brow furrowed. "You're too trusting. I've been burned once by putting my faith in 'The Establishment,' I don't mean to be burned again."

"Okay, then let's test whoever sent this message. If they fail the test, then we know it's a trap. But if they pass, then we consider talking with them."

"What exactly do you have in mind?"

•   •   •

"WE'VE GOT SOMETHING," said VanCleave, picking up his phone.

"Kalen, get a Coordinator on the line and ping Ponte's phone. If we're quick enough we can triangulate their location," Albane ordered.

"I'm on it," Kalen replied.

VanCleave turned the screen toward his colleagues who had gathered around his phone.

Need proof to trust u.

"Excellent. He's still with Ponte, and we've got his attention," Albane said. She scrawled a note on a sheet of paper and handed it to VanCleave. "Send this."

VanCleave nodded and thumb-typed:

**Investigation of Vyrogen's Chiarek Norse facility
uncovered illegal research on human test subjects.
There have been suspicious deaths, but you survived.
Went to Ponte's apartment, found roommate tortured.
You and Julie are in terrible danger. Call me at 1-555-724-2341!**

• • •

JULIE'S PHONE CHIMED with receipt of the text message. She read it aloud.

"He knows about Chiarke Norse, and Isabella, but that's not definitive proof. It could be the bounty hunters pretending to be FBI," Will said.

"Those mercenaries wouldn't have access to Vyrogen's research records," Julie said.

Will rubbed his chin. "True, but why wait to contact me until now? Where were they when I was locked up in that hellhole?"

She shrugged. "Good point. Let's ask them." She thumbed a message back:

Why wait until now to contact me?
Where were you when I was locked up
inside that hellhole being tortured?

"Will, I'm calling Isabella now. I need to make sure she's safe," Julie said, with eyes that screamed, *"and don't even try to stop me."*

• • •

VANCLEAVE READ JULIE'S reply for the group.

"So now we know," Albane said, pacing. "Foster is a victim, not a mule for an industrial espionage plot. I need to inform Nicolora." With her mobile in her hand, Albane left the room and walked into the adjoining suite.

"Do we have a fix on their location yet?" Kalen asked.

"Yes. They're here, in this building near Stephansplatz," Van-Cleave replied. He pointed to a red dot on a digital map on his tablet computer.

After several minutes, Albane returned. "Nicolora wants us to arrange a meeting. If Foster cooperates and confirms our preliminary findings of Vyrogen foul play, then we have instructions to protect him until we can turn him safely over to the real FBI. If not, then we're still on the case for Vyrogen."

"I'll send a message requesting a meeting." VanCleave said.

Albane nodded. "Let Foster pick the location. We want him to feel in control."

•　　•　　•

"HE WANTS TO meet," Julie said, looking at the incoming text message. "What do you think?"

"I don't know. It doesn't feel right."

The strain in his voice made her want to wrap her arms around him and tell him it would be okay. That she would protect him and that together they could take on any foe. But after what happened to Isabella, she knew she couldn't protect Will. She wasn't rich or powerful or well connected. Yes, they could keep running, but eventually the money would run out. Eventually, they'd be caught or maybe even killed to ensure their silence. The FBI was Will's best chance to get his life back.

"Isabella confirmed that an American calling himself Agent Nelson rescued her after the thugs left her for dead. I think we should meet him—somewhere public that he can't grab you and stuff you in the back of an unmarked van. I know a good place; it's called the Hotel Sacher. It's a popular tourist attraction, well lit, and crowded. Most importantly, the hotel has security."

"How far away is it?"

"Walking distance. It's near the Vienna State Opera House."

"Julie, I don't think it's a good idea for us to meet him together."

"Why not?"

"If it's a trap, they can grab both of us. We need to split up. If something happens to me, you can call the Austrian police. I need you as my backup."

"All right. I'll watch you from across the street at the State Opera. It sits on the corner of Kärntner Strasse and Philharmoniker Strasse."

"Where should we meet if I'm forced to ditch?"

"Stephansdom Cathedral. It's the most famous and crowded church in Vienna; we'll be safe there." She powered on her computer and using Google Maps, showed him a bird's eye view of the streets around Hotel Sacher and Stephansdom.

"Okay. Sounds like a reasonable plan," Will said, feigning confidence. His mind drifted back to the taser match in the middle of Wenceslas Square in Prague. Nobody in the crowd had intervened to help him there. Why would this be any different if things went south?

Although he acquiesced, she could see he was riddled with doubt. "I have an idea. Why don't I meet Agent Nelson instead of you?" she suggested. "It keeps you safe and your location secret. I'll go to the meeting alone, ask questions, and report back to you here."

"Absolutely not. No way."

"Why not? Give me one good reason?"

"First, it puts you in danger. And second, this is my fight, not yours," Will barked.

Julie's faced turned red. "Oh really! So all this time, everything that's happened since I picked you up in Prague hasn't put me in danger? Really. Interesting, because I seem to recall you telling me repeatedly that I'm in danger as long as I'm with you. And since when did this become your fight? I thought we were in this together?"

"You're twisting things. That's not what I meant."

"Oh? That's what it sounded like to me. Why don't you tell me, Will. What did you mean?" She crossed her arms and stared at him.

He gently set his hands on her shoulders.

"Julie, listen to me. I'm sorry. That came out completely wrong. What I meant to say was that I appreciate your offer. It is very brave of you to want to protect me and to risk yourself for me, but this is something that I need to do."

She glared at him. He pulled her to his chest until he felt her relax in his arms. "Okay. What time do you want me to tell him?" she mumbled, her face buried in his shirt.

•   •   •

Café Sacher.
7:30 pm

VanCleave's phone buzzed. "He agreed to meet," he announced. "1930 at the Café Sacher."

"Game on," Kalen said and started moving toward the door. "I need to scout the location. C'mon VanCleave, I need your help, and we don't have much time."

"Give me ten seconds; I'm just sending him an acknowledgement," VanCleave replied. Then, chasing after Kalen, he added, "I'm taking the BMW, Immel. You're insane if you think I'm riding bitch on the back of your damn motorcycle."

Chapter Thirty-Six

"I STILL DON'T see why I have to play Agent Nelson," AJ protested. "Because VanCleave will be providing tactical direction from the bird's eye position, I'll be providing emergency egress, and Foster knows Agent Nelson is a dude because I was the one who rescued the roommate at Ponte's apartment," Kalen said.

"I'm not trained for this shit like you guys are. I'm a lab geek. Not a field operative. You're crazy if you think I'll be able to pull this off."

"That didn't seem to stop you at Chiarek Norse. You were a pro."

"Beginner's luck," AJ whined.

"Enough. You can and you will do this. End of discussion," Kalen said, sternly.

AJ looked at Albane, protesting, but she shook her head. The decision was final.

Kalen made a "gather round" gesture to the group with his hands and outlined the plan. "In all likelihood, Foster won't approach until he sees our agent first. AJ, you should be seated with your back to the exterior hotel wall so you have good visibility and Foster can see you. We'll text Foster that you'll be wearing a black sport jacket with a blue pocket square. Make sure, AJ, that you maintain a clear line of sight with me at all times. I'll be idling with the Ducati a half block away, ready to jump in, if the situation warrants."

"What do I do if Ponte is with him?"

"Unless she crashes the party with a police escort, I don't see her being a factor."

"What if the goons from Ponte's apartment show up?"

"If anything goes awry, anything at all, I can extract you within seconds. I'll be on the Ducati, twenty-five yards away from your position with a clear line of sight. My visor will be up, and I'll be pretending to flirt with Albane and showing off my bike like the testosterone-charged egomaniac that I am. You can signal me covertly by standing and saying 'This meeting is over' emphatically, or by saying the code words 'Echo November.'

C. Remy will be the Coordinator for the op. We'll be on open mikes. If we split up, rendezvous back here. The most important thing to remember is that if you can't convince Foster to come with you willingly, then it is imperative that you mark him so we can track him. I will consider this meeting is a success even if the only thing you accomplish is tagging Foster," Kalen said.

"The primary method for tagging Foster is to get him to accept this bug that looks like a USB memory stick. The bug is equipped with a thirty-day battery, microphone, and GPS transponder. I've loaded it with a subset of Foster's medical files from Chiarek Norse. If he checks them, he'll know we're telling him the truth," VanCleave explained. "As long as Foster has the USB key in his possession, we can track his movements."

"What if he plugs it into a computer, but ditches it after he downloads the files?"

"The USB key is also equipped with a virus. If Foster plugs it into any computer with Internet access, I will be notified instantly, and bingo, we have his location."

"What's the backup tagging method?" AJ asked.

"The back up tagging method is for you to touch Foster's shoe or pant leg with the tip of your shoe. I've applied a radioisotope marker to the toe of your right shoe. If you graze him, it will rub off and I can track him," VanCleave said.

"What if I actually convince Foster to come with me? What then?" asked AJ.

"That's the goal, AJ. The driver will pick you up in the Seven series and bring you both back to the nest."

"Okay, so what do we do once we get this guy?"

"Silly boy . . . we interrogate him," Kalen laughed.

Chapter Thirty-Seven

K. Immel—*RS:Physical:* "They're here. Standing behind the corner arch support of the State Opera. Technical, can you see them from your position in the hotel room?"

Kalen had taken station strategically at the northeast corner of Kärntner and Philharmoniker, in front of a Starbucks coffee shop, and catty-corner to where Julie and Will were standing at the Wiener Staatsoper, the Vienna State Opera House. From his location, he would be able to observe the meeting between AJ and Will at the Café Sacher and intervene within seconds if necessary.

VanCleave had rented a room at the Hotel Sacher facing south and positioned almost directly above the hotel's outdoor café. From his bird's eye vantage point, he could see all the players, monitor foot and vehicle traffic in and out of the T-shaped intersection, and use a directional microphone listen to conversations within a seventy-five meter radius.

E. VanCleave—*RS:Technical:* "Got 'em. Calibrating the directional mike . . . I have good audio . . . Ponte is wishing Foster good luck. She just kissed him."

K. Immel—*RS:Physical:* "Foster is moving. He's crossing the street. Bio, get ready."

A. Archer—*RS:Bio:* "Roger."

THE SECOND AND third stories of the State Opera overhung the first story, creating a covered walkway and allowing more space for pedestrian traffic along Kärntner. The portico was supported by stone columns that formed a series of arches. Occupying the southwest corner of Kärntner and Philharmoniker, the portico was two arches deep by five arches long. Will and Julie had taken position under the portico and behind one of the many columns.

"I think I see him," Julie said to Will, peering around a cream-colored stone column toward the Hotel Sacher. "There, in the black jacket with the blue pocket square. He's looking around. . . . He just sat down facing the street."

"Wish me luck," Will replied.

Julie leaned in and gave him a quick kiss. "Good luck. I'll be right here watching."

He crossed Philharmoniker Strasse and walked toward three maroon awnings, each adorned with a printed golden 'S' encircled by a wreath—the logo of the Sacher hotel and café. Seven small round bistro tables, each with two chairs, formed a modest row along the window front. The brisk evening air made the café's indoor seating a more welcome choice for most diners, so only five people sat outside. Only one sat alone facing the street.

Will paused ten paces from the tables and surveyed the landscape. He scanned the crowd, looking for men in black with curlicue wires dangling from their ears and government-issue overcoats. He found none. Only automobile traffic, wandering tourists, and a man showing off his sport bike to a raven-haired girl in front of a Starbucks down the sidewalk. Will took a deep breath and walked up to the table where the agent was seated.

A. Mesnil—*RS:Social*: "Talk to him, Bio. Engage him, or we'll lose him."

"Mr. Foster, my name is Special Agent Nelson. Thank you for coming."

Will stood motionless, considering. "You look a little young for a federal agent."

"Would you believe I'm five years out of the academy? My nickname in the Bureau is Babyface. I hate it, but watcha gonna do," AJ improvised.

A. Mesnil—*RS:Social*: "That's good, Bio. Keep it up."

"Please, Mr. Foster. Have a seat. We're just going to talk. That's all," AJ said.

Will stared into the young man's hazel eyes. AJ met Will's gaze and held the eye contact. After several seconds, satisfied, he pulled back the empty chair and sat down. "You called this meeting. Talk."

"You asked for proof, so I brought it. This USB key contains data and documentation we've obtained from the Chiarek Norse facility—the very facility where you were detained. Vyrogen Pharmaceuticals took extreme measures to keep these files secret, and now we know why. We're here to help you Mr. Foster, but we need your cooperation." AJ said and placed the USB key on the table in front of Will.

A. Mesnil—*RS:Social*: "Don't say things like that. You sound like you're setting him up. Tell him your goal is to protect him *and* Julie. Help him get his life back. Empathy, Bio, empathy."

"Cooperation?" Will said. "So you want me to testify against Vyrogen? Is that the only reason you're here?"

"We're here to protect you *and* Ms. Ponte. I want to help you get your life back. That's our number one priority. From the files we've commandeered, we have a pretty good picture what Vyrogen has been up to. But I'm not going to lie to you, we could definitely use your help to fill in some of the blanks . . ."

A. Mesnil—*RS:Social*: "Good. Now appeal to his sense of duty. We need to protect other innocents like him."

AJ continued, "We can protect you against Vyrogen, but we also need to know if there are others. Others like you, research subjects who survived and need our help. My job is to make sure that Vyrogen is stopped, and to help the innocent people who they've hurt."

A. Mesnil—*RS:Social*: "Beautiful, Bio."

"Assuming I believe you, what are you proposing?" Will asked, still making no move to pick up the USB key.

E. VanCleave—*RS:Technical*: "Bio, he's not going take the USB. Go to secondary marking protocol. Gently swipe your right toe on Foster's leg. Do it now."

"I'm proposing that you come with me. Ms. Ponte can come too, if she chooses. We'll debrief in a safe location here in Vienna. Then, when you're ready, we'll take you home under protective custody." As he spoke, AJ slid his right foot forward six inches and hit the table leg, awkwardly. He missed.

"Before I consider going with you, I need to see your credentials," Will said.

AJ nodded. Below the table, he made another sweep with his right foot, this time successfully brushing Will's left pant leg.

"HAVE YOUR CONTACT at Orange Telecom ping Ponte's phone again," Raimond Zurn barked. "I still don't see them."

"The accuracy is only plus or minus fifty meters, brother. The last triangulation puts their position at these GPS coordinates. We need to be patient. Remember, they could be inside a building. The ping works anywhere that the phone has a signal," Stefan said.

"There," Udo said, pointing out the right passenger window of the van. "The girl is there, standing against that stone column."

"Good eyes, Udo," Raimond said, pressing the brake pedal and slowing the van to a crawl. "She's alone. Look for Foster."

"He is there," Udo said. "At that café on the other side."

Raimond smirked and brought the van to a stop along the curb. He shifted the automatic transmission into park, flipped on the hazard flashers, and turned to face Udo and Stefan. "Stick to the plan and everything will be fine. In twelve hours, my brothers, we'll be counting our money and drunk on Augustiner."

K. Immel—*RS:Physical:* "Bio, we have a bogie, incoming, your three o'clock. Grey jacket, blue jeans, black boots."

AJ turned his head to the right, looking east toward Kärntner Strasse. A man in a grey jacket was walking straight toward them, quickly and deliberately. His face was expressionless and cold.

Will scooted his chair back away from the table. He turned to his left to see what AJ was looking at.

Raimond Zurn crossed the threshold of the Café Sacher outdoor dining area. He stepped around two empty tables and was upon them.

"You," Will said with disdain to the bounty hunter he had tussled with on the streets of Prague. His stomach tightened. How could he have been so stupid as to agree to meet this guy Nelson? It had been a double-cross from the beginning, and he had fallen for it.

"I believe we have unfinished business," Raimond Zurn said with a malevolence that made Will's skin crawl.

"Funny, as I recall, our business was concluded when I left you clutching your balls at the cybercafé in Prague," Will said, trying to mask his fear.

"Who is your friend? Don't tell me you've hired a bodyguard." Raimond turned to AJ. "You're not going to be any trouble, are you, little boy?"

Perplexed, Will looked at AJ and then back at Zurn. Was this charade part of the double-cross?

E. VanCleave—*RS:Technical:* "White van traveling east on Philharmoniker Strasse. It just stopped in front of the Ponte woman. We've got trouble!"

A white cargo van with black tinted windows stopped on Philharmoniker Strasse, directly in front of Julie, blocking her line of sight.

"Oh, you've got to be kidding me," she said, exasperated. "Move, stupid van."

The van did not move.

The passenger door opened and a muscular man with a shaved head stepped out and onto the sidewalk. Julie tensed. It was just a coincidence, she told herself. He turned around to face the van. The passenger window had been rolled down, and he was talking to the driver. He then stepped away from the window, waved good-bye to driver, and began walking south, down Kärntner Strasse. She watched him for several seconds, just to be certain, until he was halfway down the block. Never once did he look at her. Satisfied, she turned back to watch Will, but the white van was still there, idling at the curb, blocking her view.

"Damn it!" She surveyed the area, looking for another vantage point with cover. She noticed another stone column, three meters to her left, where she might gain a clear line of sight around the van.

It was time to relocate.

"I'M SORRY I didn't catch your name," AJ said, turning his chair forty-five degrees toward Zurn.

"That's because I didn't tell you my name," Raimond replied. "I think it's time for you to leave. Mr. Foster and I have some unfinished business we need to discuss in private." Raimond pulled the flap of his leather jacket open, revealing a Sig Sauer pistol, with suppressor, suspended in an underarm shoulder holster.

AJ looked at the weapon, then up at Zurn's face. He had never met a killer—until now. The eyes confirmed it; eyes full of malice and pompous impunity. This man would gun him down where he sat without a second thought. AJ glanced to his right, surveying the van that VanCleave had just reported. The van was idling at the curb. The driver window was tinted, so he could not make out a face inside. His stomach went sour, and his mouth turned to parchment.

Udo Zurn walked a half block south on Kärntner Strasse before he glanced back at Julie. To his surprise, she was no longer there. He immediately turned right, toward the State Opera building. She had been standing behind the corner column on the perimeter of the portico, nearest to the street. He darted between two columns, entering the portico to the south, behind her. He looked north. From his new vantage point he could see that she had shifted one column to her left; she was now peeking out from behind the middle column instead. He smiled. Perfect. From his left jacket pocket, Udo retrieved and donned a pair of black leather driving gloves. From his right jacket pocket, he pulled a Ziploc plastic bag. Sealed inside was a chloroform-laden handkerchief, which he withdrew and wadded up in the palm of his gloved right hand.

He moved quickly, covering the distance separating them in mere seconds. By the time Julie became aware of the footsteps closing in behind her, it was too late. Udo's grip was all encompassing. Suffocating. She stiffened as she felt folds of silky fabric against her lips. Her nostrils tingled and she felt queasy, then light-headed. Darkness swept into her field of vision, gobbling up the light like a shade pulled down over a sun-filled picture window. She threw an elbow into the wall of flesh behind her. It was futile. He was iron, and she was . . . unconscious.

Her body was limp as Udo lifted her. He carried her 125-pound frame, as effortlessly as he would a sleeping toddler, back to the white van. Stefan Zurn had opened the side cargo door from the inside, and he was peering out the opening toward them. Udo trotted over to the van, ducked his head, and stepped inside with Julie in his arms. Stefan closed the door behind him. The rear compartment of the cargo van had no seats. Udo's motorcycle stood inside, held upright by nylon straps lashed to four metal tie-down rings bolted to the bare sheet metal floor. The motorbike took up the majority of the cargo hold, so Udo laid Julie down parallel to the bike, up against the sidewall of the van. He looked at Stefan for approval.

"Perfect," Stefan said. "Now we wait for Raimond."

E. VanCleave—*RS:Technical*: "They're making their move. A male, Caucasian, just grabbed Ponte. He's dragging her into the van. Damn it! They're here for Foster. Change of plans, extract Foster."

K. Immel—*RS:Physical*: "Roger."

AJ STOOD ABRUPTLY. "This meeting is over! We're leaving," he commanded.

The high-revving whir of the Ducati engine pierced the nighttime air. Kalen popped the clutch and the motorcycle launched forward like a missile. He jumped the curb and sped across the pedestrian-only section of Kärntner Strasse. In less than two seconds time, Kalen and his motorcycle had covered the distance between the café and his starting point.

All three men, Zurn, Archer, and Foster, turned toward the direction of the motorcycle engine. Pandemonium erupted on the sidewalk, as pedestrians screamed and jumped clear of the speeding motorbike's path.

Zurn drew his pistol from the concealed holster and took aim at the rider.

At the same time, Kalen shifted his center of gravity, turned to the left, and powered on the throttle—dipping and spinning the Ducati into a controlled slide. His head and torso dropped below the line of fire as three bullets whisked through the air above him. At the last second, he hoisted his left foot up onto the fuel tank so that his leg would not be pinned and abraded across the concrete. Bike and rider surfed along the ground at sixty kilometers per hour toward Raimond. Empty bistro tables and chairs flew into the air like popping corn off a hot stove, as the undercarriage of the bike clipped the legs of everything its path. The rear wheel of the bike crashed into Raimond's shins, just above the ankles, precisely on target. Raimond spun like a pinwheel—his legs catapulting up, his torso arcing down. The force of the impact with the concrete jolted the Sig Sauer loose from his grip; the weapon tumbled through the air and landed with a thud on the ground a meter away. Raimond grunted and rolled onto his side. He scanned the ground, looking for his pistol. Both AJ and Raimond located the handgun simultaneously and then glanced knowingly at each other. AJ dove over a fallen bistro table at the same time Zurn lurched for the gun from his fallen position.

Kalen popped the Ducati back up to the riding position, revved the throttle in neutral, and turned to Foster. He flipped the black visor up on his helmet and looked at Will.

"If you want to live, come with me," Kalen said.

Will looked at Kalen and then glanced around him at the van parked across the street, blocking his view of Julie.

"Julie!" he exclaimed, taking a step toward the street.

"It's time to go," Kalen ordered, seizing Will's arm and pulling him toward the bike. "They've already taken her. Get on the bike!"

AMONGST A PILE of toppled tables and chairs, AJ and Raimond tussled over the Sig Sauer on the ground. AJ locked one hand around the barrel and with his other gripped the suppressor of the pistol, controlling the direction of the muzzle. Raimond clutched the pistol grip with his right hand, repeatedly jerked the weapon, trying to pull it free from AJ's grasp. With his free left hand, Zurn rabbit punched AJ in the face. Once. Twice. As Raimond cocked his fist back for a third blow, AJ tucked his knees and swung his lower body around 180 degrees so that the soles of his feet were now toward Raimond. He pulled with both hands on the Sig Sauer, drawing it close to his chest, straightening and lengthening Raimond's right arm. The maneuver had repositioned AJ's head out of fist striking distance and gave him additional leverage. But, in doing so, the muzzle angle had changed. Raimond grinned. He squeezed the trigger, sending a round whizzing centimeters past AJ's face. The errant bullet struck a metal table behind AJ with a clang.

WILL JERKED AT the strident sound of the bullet ricocheting off the metal table. He looked down at AJ and Raimond wrestling on the ground over the gun, then at the Ducati, and then back at the van. His expressionless eyes belied the turmoil he felt inside. How could he abandon Julie now?

Will stared at Kalen, motionless.

"We'll get her back," Kalen said. "I promise."

Will reluctantly climbed on to the motorcycle behind Kalen. He locked his arms around Kalen's waist and placed his feet on the passenger stirrups.

"Keep your forehead pressed in the middle of my back. Close your eyes, and no matter what happens—DON'T LET GO," Kalen instructed, yelling over his shoulder. He flipped his helmet visor down with a thud, engaged the clutch, and twisted the throttle. Kalen's black Ducati streaked away from the Café Sacher in a blur.

"RAIMOND IS IN trouble," Stefan said, looking out the driver's side window of the van at the commotion across the street.

"What do we do?" Udo asked, leaning forward from the cargo compartment of the van so that his head was even between the driver and passenger seat headrests.

"We're behind on the timeline. If someone saw you take the Ponte girl, then the police will be coming soon," Stefan answered, panicked. "We need to go."

"We can't leave Raimond behind! I'll crush those bastards."

"There's no time, Udo. Raimond can take care of himself. Foster is getting away. Take the Kawasaki and follow that bike. Do not lose Foster. We're switching to the backup plan. Remember, no matter what happens, we rendezvous at the warehouse at 2200."

"Okay, ja, I'll get him back."

AJ'S EYES BULGED as he looked down and saw the open muzzle pointing at his face. He twisted the barrel violently, reorienting the line of fire away from his head and up toward the sky. As he did, Raimond squeezed off another round—this time piercing one of the maroon colored Hotel Sacher awnings. AJ pulled Raimond's arm straight between his legs and drew his knees up to his chest.

With all his might, AJ kicked with both feet at the same time. The sole of one shoe impacted the top of Raimond's head, and the other foot glanced off Raimond's left shoulder. The force of the blow had its desired effect, popping the handgun free from Zurn's grip. AJ scooted backward, crablike, pushing with his feet to distance himself from his foe. Raimond grunted and grabbed the top of his head in pain, before rolling over onto his hands and knees into a crawling position. Raimond lifted his head up to look at AJ, who had backed himself up against the stone facade of the building. AJ sat with his back upright, legs extended in "V," and both arms fully extended as he aimed the Sig at his rival.

"Fuck you," said Raimond with disdain, staring at AJ. He then stood up, and dusted himself off.

AJ said nothing, but elevated the barrel of the gun to maintain his aim at Raimond's chest.

In the background, the scream of a second motorcycle engine echoed in the night. Raimond turned in the direction of the sound. A red Kawasaki Ninja launched out of the open rear cargo doors of the van parked across the street. Both motorcycle tires chirped when they hit the pavement—the bike skidded and wobbled momentarily—before the rider skillfully recovered his balance. The rider sped west on Philharmoniker Strasse in pursuit of Kalen and Will. Raimond turned back to look at AJ, and then limped toward the van idling across the street. He hauled himself into the rear cargo compartment and pulled the two doors shut behind him, as the vehicle raced away down Kärntner Strasse.

AJ looked for the safety on the Sig Sauer, finding none, he stuffed it inside the waistline of his pants at the small of his back. He looked up. Two shapely female legs in high heels and black stockings filled his frame of view.

"Let's go. We don't have much time," Albane said to AJ, extending her hand to help him up. He grabbed her wrist and rose to his feet. Her grip was firm, and the pull she exerted on his arm both impressed and surprised him. Albane had some muscles packed on her lithe frame.

In the background, the sound of police sirens blaring grew louder with each passing second. The Tank's armored BMW 760Li was waiting at the curb for them with the rear passenger door open. AJ and Albane ran to the sedan and jumped inside. The driver wasted no time, pressing the accelerator to the floor before AJ had shut the door. The V12 engine roared and the svelte sedan raced away into the Viennese night.

•   •   •

AS INSTRUCTED, WILL pressed his forehead against the middle of Kalen's back. His fingers clenched the folds of Kalen's leather jacket, like a madman holding the reigns of a demon stallion galloping toward the gates of hell. Will was not an experienced motorcycle rider, but he knew that any attempt by him to balance the bike, or anticipate an evasive maneuver by the driver would have a deleterious effect. As long as he was deadweight, the driver's reflexes would naturally compensate for his presence. A backpack. That was what he aimed to be, a 170-pound human backpack.

The speed was ludicrous. Will knew this because the loose fabric of his chinos stung his thighs as it flapped violently in the wind. He kept his eyes shut, pretending like a small child that what he couldn't see wasn't really happening. A terrible jolt, followed by a skid caused Will to instinctively open his eyes. Bright red taillights swept by in a blur. Tires squealed as drivers in passing cars slammed on their brakes. Will squeezed his eyes closed, for fear panic would cause him to fall off the bike. Behind, he could hear the whine of another street motorcycle. But no sirens. He assumed the worst— one of the thugs from Prague was in pursuit. He cringed. For one motorcycle, the chase was certain to end badly.

Kalen panted inside his helmet. Evasive driving was exhausting. Exhilarating. Hot pain shot through his right knee. He grunted, but his concentration did not waver. He had clipped something— a fender, a bumper, a small dog. It didn't matter, the pain was a reminder. With Foster on the bike, he was severely hampered. Like a gymnast trying to compete with a lead weight strapped to one foot, maneuvers he could normally perform with ease were impossible with a passenger. His pursuer had no such handicap. Time to level the playing field.

K. Immel—*RS:Physical*: "This jerkoff on my ass is starting to piss me off. Give me the count."

C. Remy—*RS:Coordinator*: "Three minutes forty seconds—seventy seconds past the evacuation timeline. Physical, you need to escalate your evasion tactics."

K. Immel—*RS:Physical*: "No shit, really. The problem is I've got a two hundred pound gorilla on my back. I can't cut for shit. I'm shredding my tires."

C. Remy—*RS:Coordinator*: "Be advised, the police have just issued a pursuit call on the police band to units in your vicinity."

K. Immel—*RS:Physical*: "That's just fucking great. I need real time routing."

C. Remy—*RS:Coordinator*: "Standby for routing. . . . In four hundred meters execute a U-turn. Three hundred. Two hundred. Standby for the turn. Mark the turn."

K. Immel—*RS:Physical*: "Turn executed. I think I . . . ooooh, that's a four, no five-car pile-up in my wake."

C. Remy—*RS:Coordinator*: "And your bogie?"

K. Immel—*RS:Physical*: "Checking . . . he made it through. Still on my ass."

C. Remy—*RS:Coordinator*: "In five hundred meters execute a left turn. Three hundred. Two hundred. Standby for the turn. Mark the turn."

K. Immel—*RS:Physical*: "The light is red, do you have traffic cameras? Can I burn it?"

C. Remy—*RS:Coordinator*: "Negative, take the sidewalk."

Kalen braked the bike hard and turned left onto a sidewalk just before the cross street of the busy intersection. A twist of the throttle and he catapulted the bike forward on the new vector, blowing past 100 kilometers per hour in three seconds. Kalen bobbed and weaved between potted trees and shrieking pedestrians on the sidewalk like an alpine skier negotiating the flags on a downhill run.

Udo braked late, wrestled his bike through a skidding turn, and scraped along the side of a parked Audi as he recovered his balance. He accelerated in pursuit of his quarry, electing to drive against the flow of traffic in a narrow gap between a row of parked cars and on-coming vehicles in the right lane. Horns blared and tires squealed as drivers reacted to the reckless motorcycle racing past.

Kalen jumped the curb back onto the street; the rear tire squealed as it grabbed asphalt. Udo shot through a gap across two lanes of ongoing traffic, a red blur, and merged into the southbound flow behind Kalen and Foster. Three police cars were now in pursuit, dodging and weaving clumsily behind the more agile racing bikes. Kalen took up a position precariously piloting the divider line, over-taking two lanes of moving traffic between the cars. Udo followed two hundred meters behind, steadily closing the gap. The light at the upcoming intersection was green.

K. Immel—*RS:Physical*: "Shit, I still have my bogie. . . . I need a blocking fullback. Where the hell is Bavarian One?"

C. Remy—*RS:Coordinator*: "Bavarian One is in egress with Bio and Social. Do you want me to reroute?"

K. Immel—*RS:Physical*: "Shit . . . umm, hold on.

Kalen glanced to his right, looking down the cross street, checking the flow of traffic. The front cars were crossing, but the lagging cars were slowing.

The light ahead changed to yellow.

K. Immel—*RS:Physical*: Never mind, Coordinator, I have a crazy idea."

This was his chance—the transition—the two-second period when the intersection was vacant between the switching of traffic flows. He would need to time the maneuver perfectly. If it worked, he would trap the police cruisers behind the blockade of stopped cars at the light and peel his bogie off into the grill of a crossing vehicle moving into the intersection. If his timing was off, or if some bastard ran the light, then it would be him and his precious cargo that the EMTs would be scraping up off the pavement.

Kalen twisted the throttle, accelerating toward the column of cars ahead slowing at the intersection. The space between the doors of adjacent cars was just wide enough to permit the clear passage of a motorcycle and rider, provided, he maintained a perfectly straight trajectory . . . and nobody opened a car door.

One hundred meters to the intersection.

The light changed red.

Braking was not an option.

Kalen clenched his teeth.

Headlights flashed.

Someone was about to die.

Chapter Thirty-Eight

"CHECK HER," RAIMOND ZURN ordered Stefan.

Stefan walked over to the chair where Julie was bound. Her body sagged, like a wet paper doll. Only the duct tape they'd bound her with kept her from sliding off the seat onto the floor in a heap. Stefan leaned over at the waist and put his right cheek next to her nose and mouth. Her faint warm breath caressed his smooth, boyish skin.

"She's alive, and still unconscious," Stefan said.

"Wake her."

"How do you suggest I do that? The chloroform is still in her system."

"Slap her, yell at her, use the smelling salts, I don't care. Just wake her!" Raimond yelled.

Stefan tensed. He was not accustomed to seeing his brother Raimond in such a manic state. Then again, fieldwork was rare for Stefan, so it was possible that Raimond was always this way in the field. Stefan preferred to stay behind in Munich, functioning as a one-man computer command center for the brothers' assignments. He left the wet work for his two older brothers; they seemed to enjoy it immensely. Stefan did not have the stomach for it. Tooth and nail were not his weapons of choice; the pain Stefan inflicted on his victims was in the form of ones and zeros. The anonymity of his firewall was his shield, the software hack his blade.

Stefan stared at the American woman. She was completely vulnerable, oblivious. He had never held a position of power over a woman like this before. Stefan Zurn had been dominated by women his entire life, starting with his mother and then followed by every woman he had encountered ever since. Women were an enigma— enchanting and enraging—and Stefan was a boy of a man. Even at age twenty-four, he had yet to know a woman. Now, at this moment, he had the sudden urge to strip this woman of her clothes. Make her naked, while he stood over her, clothed. Dominant. Erect. Powerful.

"Stefan!" Raimond yelled, startling his brother out of his trance. "Wake her up. I'm not waiting for Udo any longer. I want answers."

"Yes, I'm sorry. I was just . . ." Stefan stammered.

He pulled a tiny sealed container of pungent smelling salts from his pocket. He unscrewed the black cap, held his breath, and wafted the open container beneath Julie's nose.

Her head jerked once, but her eyelids did not open.

He repeated the process, this time letting the open vial linger beneath her nostrils several seconds longer. Stefan was not sure if smelling salts could wake a person from drug-induced unconsciousness, but he had no intention of arguing with Raimond about the point. She would wake up as soon as her body metabolized the sedative compound in her bloodstream, and not one second before. Until that time, he would appease his brother by trying his damnedest to wake her.

After several attempts, she made a gurgling noise and pulled her face away from the source of the piquant odor. Her eyelids opened a crack, and then quickly shut again.

"Julie Ponte. Julie Ponte, wake up," Stefan said in her ear, shaking her by the shoulder.

"Sleeping," Julie moaned. "I want to sleep."

Stefan put the salts under her nose again. This time her eyes popped open.

The warehouse where they had taken Julie was empty. Once a storage facility for a plastics company, all that remained inside were rows and rows of barren metal shelving. Each storage rack was ten feet tall and stretched off into the darkness. Julie sat, duct-taped to a decrepit metal chair. The only light in the warehouse emanated from the headlamps of the van, parked ten feet away and facing

Julie. Raimond had cut a rusty padlock from one of the loading dock doors, and Stefan had pulled the van completely inside so they could not be seen.

"Hey!" Raimond snapped at Julie, annoyed at his brother's ineffectiveness at such a simple task. "Wake up!"

Her head bobbed; she was still in a fog.

Raimond slapped her across her cheek. "Wake up, bitch!"

The slap sent adrenaline pumping through her veins, and she regained consciousness. The shadow in front of her moved, letting the headlights from the van blind her. She tried to raise her hand to shield her eyes, but it was securely lashed to the frame of the chair. Panic set in.

"This is an interrogation, Ms. Ponte. Before we begin, I am going to explain the rules. Listen very carefully. I ask you questions. You answer them truthfully. If you answer truthfully, you will live. If you try to deceive me, I will torture you until your death," said a voice from behind her. "Do you understand the rules?"

The last thing she remembered was watching Will across the street at the Café Sacher meeting with Agent Nelson. Something went wrong. Someone had grabbed her from behind. She had no memory of the events that transpired afterward. She had no knowledge of her captors, their motives, or where they had taken her. One thing she did know was that her life was in grave danger. She looked left and then right, trying to catch a glimpse of her interrogator.

"I said, do you understand the rules?" Raimond repeated, growing more and more agitated by the second.

"I understand the rules," she mumbled.

"Good," he replied.

"What is your name?"

She paused. He already knew her name; he had said it earlier. This was a test, she told herself.

"My name is Julie Ponte."

"What were you doing at the Wiener Staatsoper?"

He was setting her up. Baiting her to lie so he could punish her and begin the process of breaking her. She had never been interrogated before, but her instincts told her this was no time to be coy. Every answer was a high-wire crossing. One misstep, and she would pay.

"I was watching a meeting take place across the street."

"Where was the meeting?"

"At the Café Sacher."

"Who was at the meeting?"

"You already know the answer to all these questions," she said.

"Don't test me. I *will* hurt you if you break the rules again. This is my promise to you," he said quietly.

"It was a meeting between a man named Will Foster and a man calling himself Agent Nelson."

"Agent Nelson? What kind of agent?"

She took a deep breath. The easy part was over now. She was at the crossroads now. She had to make a choice: tell the truth and risk him not believing her, or lie, and risk him seeing right through her. She knew what she had to do.

"He's not a real agent. It was all part of the plan."

"What plan?"

"Meredith Morley's plan to get Foster back."

Raimond took a step backward. "What are you talking about? Who do you work for?"

"I work for a company called Vyrogen Pharmaceuticals. Mr. Foster was enrolled in a drug pilot program at my company involving highly infectious diseases. A few days ago, he broke out of our research facility in Prague. Mr. Foster is an extremely dangerous individual. I have been trying desperately to bring him back into quarantine. But at the moment . . ." she said, wiggling her bound hands at the wrist, "you are making my assignment extremely difficult."

Raimond locked eyes with his brother. Stefan motioned for Raimond to follow him, away from Julie, so they could talk in private.

"We fucked up, Raimond, She works for Vyrogen," Stefan whispered, with a hint of panic in his voice.

Raimond rubbed his chin. "It seems our employer has been withholding critical information from us. Frau Morley already had an asset in place with Foster, while she left us wasting time looking for him in Prague."

"Why would she do that, when we could have easily brought Foster in?"

"She was stalling. Probably because she doesn't want to pay. The last time we spoke, she tried to cancel our contract."

"I thought you changed her mind?"

"So did I." After a pause, Raimond added, "We *need* this fee, Stefan."

"I know, but what do we do with her? If we let her go, she'll call Morley."

"So we don't let her go."

"You're not suggesting that we kill her?"

"No. At least not yet. First, we find out everything Morley is doing. Then, we decide what to do with her. She could be valuable bargaining leverage if Morley chooses not to pay."

"Jah. Agreed."

Raimond and Stefan walked back toward Julie. Raimond stood behind her and began to caress her hair.

"You have been very cooperative so far, Ms. Ponte. You have followed the rules. This makes me very happy. Now, I want you to tell me everything."

"I'll try," Julie replied. Her skin crawled as he stroked her. She steeled herself so as not to shudder under his touch.

"Tell me about this ploy with the man you called Agent Nelson. I don't understand the purpose. If you are working for Vyrogen and Ms. Morley is working for Vyrogen, what are you doing in Vienna wasting time?"

She lowered her eyes.

"Ms. Ponte?"

"Foster doesn't know that I work for Vyrogen," she said. "Morley couldn't risk him running again, so we had to think of a different way to get him back. The stick wasn't working, so we decided to try the carrot. My assignment was to get close to Foster; get him to trust me. But it was taking too long. So, Morley came up with the idea of setting up a meeting with a confederate FBI agent. Nelson was going to offer Foster protection."

Her candor surprised Raimond. He expected to be breaking fingers by now. "This is a very clever plan, but there is still something that confuses me. Your plan seemed to be working. So why did Meredith call me today and direct me to your apartment?"

A volcano of fury and fear erupted inside her. This was the bastard who had tortured Isabella—broken every finger on her left hand. "You'll have to ask her that question," she said, through clenched teeth. "I didn't even know she'd hired you until now."

Raimond began to ask Julie another question, when he was interrupted by the ringing of his mobile phone. He answered the call in German. As he listened to the voice on the other end of receiver, he began to shake. Stefan walked over to his brother and tried to listen to what was being said. Something was very wrong.

Raimond finished the call. His fingers opened and the phone dropped to the ground with a clatter.

"What is it?" Stefan questioned in German.

"Udo is dead. Our brother is dead."

"What? How?"

"Traffic accident. He drove his motorcycle into a fucking trolley. He was killed instantly. They didn't even take him to the hospital."

Stefan stared at Raimond, but said nothing.

Raimond began pacing back and forth behind Julie's chair. Then, he stopped and unleashed a guttural, primeval scream full of rage and anguish. His throaty roar reverberated off the metal shelving and uninsulated ceiling structure. The hairs on the back of Julie's neck stood up.

Julie was fluent in German, although she had no intention of making this detail known to her captors. She had not met Udo Zurn, but she surmised that he was the thug who grabbed her from behind at the State Opera. Terror welled up inside her. The violent brother, the one pacing behind her, was infinitely more of a danger to her now than he was five minutes ago. Before, he had been agitated and cold. Now, he was burning with rage and hatred over the news of his brother's death. Julie knew that she would be the likely target of his fury. She would be bludgeoned, whether she cooperated or not.

She began to tremble.

"This is your fault, bitch!" Raimond screamed at Julie. He walked around in front of her, boldly facing her. "You and your American bitch boss, Meredith Morley. If it hadn't been for the two of you, Udo would still be alive."

Julie looked down at her knees in silence, saying nothing so as to avoid provoking him with her eye contact.

"Answer me!" Raimond screamed at her.

"What do you want me to say? I don't even know what you're talking about."

He struck the side of her head with his open palm. "Liar!"

"Raimond!" Stefan screamed in a high-pitched voice.

Raimond glared at his younger brother.

"This woman did not kill Udo!"

Raimond grabbed Julie's face with his left hand, gripping her from below the chin—his fingers and thumb squeezing her cheeks. He raised her chin angle so that she was looking up at him.

"Who was the man on the black motorcycle that took Foster?" he questioned, releasing her jaw at the end of the sentence.

"What man? I never saw a man on a motorcycle," she replied, trembling.

"You lie!" He struck her again, this time across the cheek. She yelped and her eyes began to fill with tears. "It was part of your plan. You arranged the meeting," he said.

"I have no idea what you're talking about. You parked your fucking van in front of me, blocking my view. Then, someone grabbed me from behind and drugged me," she said, brazenly.

Raimond drew his hand back to strike her again, but Stefan seized his wrist. "She's telling the truth, Brother. We grabbed her before the motorcycle chase. She was already unconscious by the time the black motorcycle appeared."

Raimond's face contorted with rage. He jerked his hand free from his younger brother's grip. He walked quickly over to the van, opened the rear cargo door, and disappeared inside. Seconds later, he reemerged, face expressionless, and clenching a pistol in his right hand. He marched over to Julie and pressed the muzzle of the pistol firmly into her temple.

"Tell me who killed Udo!"

"I don't know," she cried.

"Who is the black rider?" he screamed, spit flying from his lips, veins bulging in his neck and forehead.

"I don't know. I swear I don't know," she screamed back.

"TELL ME. . . . TELL ME NOW, OR I SWEAR I'LL BLOW YOUR FUCKING HEAD OFF!"

Chapter Thirty-Nine

"WHO THE HELL are you people?" Will asked, scanning the four stoic faces seated opposite him inside a luxury appointed suite at the Wien Intercontinental Hotel.

"My name is Special Agent Reed. You've already met Special Agent Nelson," Albane said, nodding at AJ. "Collectively, we are members of a special US government interagency task force assigned to investigate cases of multinational espionage and corruption. That is all I am at liberty to disclose to you at this time."

Will nodded, stood up, and started walking toward the door.

"Where are you going, Mr. Foster?"

"If you're not going to be straight with me, then I'm outta here."

"The minute you walk out that door, you can forget about rescuing Julie," she called after him. "You can't get her back on your own."

He stopped in his tracks, but he did not turn around. With his back to her, he said. "Will you help me rescue her if I stay?"

"We *will* rescue her if you stay. All we ask in return is that you answer our questions about Vyrogen."

He turned. "What would you like to know?"

• • •

ALBANE LOOKED OVER her shoulder into the adjoining room at Will. He was sitting on a sofa, lost in thought. She turned back to AJ. The look in AJ's eyes told her damage control was necessary. She could see that his mind was a whirlpool, spinning with questions and doubt. She had years of experience in the Tank to call upon, giving her perspective on the tangled, thorny events of the Vyrogen case as it had unfolded. With less than two days on the job, AJ did not.

"I know what you're thinking, and no AJ, it's not always like this," she said. Then, laying a hand on his shoulder, she added, "This case is an aberration."

He searched her eyes, hoping to find a glimmer of truth he could never glean from her perfectly anodyne speech. "Everything has gotten so twisted, I don't know what to think. Since we've left Boston, we've committed espionage against our client, impersonated Czech and US government agents, and kidnapped a man. I thought we were supposed to be the good guys."

"I know it might not feel like it, but we *are* the good guys. We don't wear uniforms or carry badges, but we do serve a higher calling. Meredith Morley put us into a horrible situation. Not only did she hire us under false pretenses, but she meant to use the Tank as an instrument of malfeasance. We don't work that way, no matter how much money the client is offering." She gave his shoulder a squeeze. "And for the record, we didn't kidnap Foster, we saved him from the real bad guys."

AJ saw the glimmer in her eyes he needed to see. "You're probably right, but that doesn't quell the indigestion I'm feeling right now. This is nasty business. I had no idea the world outside academia was like *this*."

"The real world is guns and roses; you'll get used to it." Then, with a smile she added, "Next thing you know, you'll be asking to borrow keys to Kalen's Ducati."

AJ laughed.

Her expression turned serious. "I need to debrief Nicolora. Please go in the other room and keep an eye on Foster. Don't let him do anything stupid."

He nodded and did as she instructed.

Albane pressed "0" on her phone.

C. Remy—*RS:Coordinator*. "Coordinator."

A. Mesnil—*RS:Social*: "Coordinator, Social, request conference call with Founder One."

C. Remy—*RS:Coordinator.* "Founder One is standing by; let me patch him in."

R. Nicolora—*Founder One.* "I listened to the entire broadcast of your Foster interview. Consider me up to speed."

A. Mesnil—*RS:Social.* "I believe him."

R. Nicolora—*Founder One.* "So do I."

A. Mesnil—*RS:Social.* "Now what? Foster is clearly the victim here: kidnapping, genetic piracy, human rights violations, torture . . . it's a long, dirty list. What Vyrogen did is unconscionable."

R. Nicolora—*Founder One.* "I know, but before we deal with that, we have the immediate problem of the bounty hunters and Julie Ponte. After Kalen's report from Ponte's apartment, I confronted Meredith about torturing the roommate. She admitted to hiring German bounty hunters to find Foster, but swears she never authorized torture. I have the Coordinator uploading the bounty hunters' bios to your computer as we speak."

A. Mesnil—*RS:Social.* "I'm receiving them now."

R. Nicolora—*Founder One.* "The men we're dealing with are brothers: Raimond, Udo, and Stefan Zurn. Raimond is the brain, Udo is the brute, and Stefan is the tech."

A. Mesnil—*RS:Social.* "I don't understand why they are still in the picture. When Meredith hired us, why didn't she have the Zurns stand down?"

R. Nicolora—*Founder One.* "According to Meredith, she tried, but Raimond Zurn refused and went rogue. The case became personal for him. Now, with Udo Zurn dead, we must consider Raimond to be unstable and likely to seek revenge for his brother's death."

A. Mesnil—*RS:Social.* "They have Ponte. What do you want us to do?"

R. Nicolora—*Founder One.* "What we always do in situations like this. Rescue her."

A. Mesnil—*RS:Social.* "Assuming we're successful, what do we do with Ponte and Foster when we're done?"

R. Nicolora—*Founder One.* "Fly them back to Boston on NIATROSS. From what I've learned tonight, Foster deserves to get his life back. I'll even help him out with a new identity."

A. Mesnil—*RS:Social*: "What about the client?"

R. Nicolora—*Founder One*: "Don't worry about that; you have more urgent matters to attend to. I'll handle Meredith. Founder One out."

Albane strode into the adjoining suite and with fire in her eyes, addressed her colleagues. "Gather round. . . . we've got a rescue mission to prep."

• • •

"HAVE YOU EVER participated in a hostage negotiation, Mr. Foster?"

"Call me, Will. And no, I haven't."

Albane crossed her legs and leaned forward in her chair. "Although some would disagree with me, I consider hostage negotiations to fall under the umbrella of Game Theory. Are you familiar with the logic problem commonly referred to as the Prisoner's Dilemma?"

Will nodded. "I studied it in college, but it's been awhile."

AJ shook his head. "I've heard the term, but to be honest, I can't say I'm well versed on the subject."

"Okay, let's walk through an example to refresh everyone's memories," Albane said reassuringly. "The Prisoner's Dilemma is a simple but powerful logic game with two players. In the classic scenario, two criminals are arrested for reckless driving after committing arson. However, the police don't have sufficient evidence to convict either criminal, that is, without defecting testimony from one criminal or the other. So they place the two criminals in separate rooms for interrogation and offer them deals for their testimony in court. Both criminals find themselves to be players in a game with four outcomes; each outcome is dictated by whether the players choose to defect or cooperate with the other player.

Case One: Both criminals cooperate with each other and remain silent. Each man is sentenced to one year in jail for reckless driving. Neither is implicated in the arson.

Case Two: Criminal A defects by incriminating Criminal B in the arson, while Criminal B remains silent. Criminal A goes free.

Criminal B is sentenced to ten years in jail for the reckless driving and the arson.

Case Three: Criminal A remains silent, and Criminal B defects by incriminating Criminal A in the arson. This time, Criminal B goes free and Criminal A is sentenced to ten years in jail.

Case Four: Both criminals defect and testify against the other in the arson case. Each criminal is sentenced to six years in jail."

AJ rubbed his temples, concentrating. "Okay, so if I heard you clearly, the best scenario is for both criminals to cooperate and remain silent so that they'll receive only one year jail terms."

"Yes, the best mutual outcome occurs when both players cooperate with each other. But remember, each player would do best for himself if he defects and his partner remains silent," Albane explained. "Game theory says that rational self-interested players will always defect in a single iteration prisoner's dilemma. In the effort to achieve their personal best-case scenario of zero jail time, both criminals will defect. In doing so, each will end up with six years. Another way to think about it is, when the participants in a prisoner's dilemma do not trust each other implicitly, then fear of being the sucker stuck with the ten-year jail sentence will drive both players to defect."

"What do you mean by a single iteration prisoner's dilemma?" AJ asked.

"What I mean is that cooperation only emerges as a strategy when the players both intend to participate in another round of the game. Keep in mind, prisoner's dilemmas can be redefined in an infinite number of scenarios: business, finance, military strategy, evolution . . . you get the picture. The outcomes don't have to be punishment; they can be tangible goods, currency, time, goodwill, etcetera. The point I'm trying to make, Will, is that screwing your opponent is a perfectly acceptable strategy if you plan on never seeing him again. But, if he is anyone you intend to have future interaction with— a business acquaintance or a friend, for example—then cooperation emerges as a leading strategy."

"How does any of that relate to hostage negotiation?" Will questioned.

VanCleave interjected, "Two-party hostage negotiation is just a prisoner's dilemma with window dressing. Both parties have two choices: cooperate or defect. In hostage negotiation, both sides feign cooperation while pursuing the strategy of defection. It is important that you realize this fact in our upcoming negotiation with the bounty hunter Raimond Zurn. The laws of game theory dictate that he will defect on any promise."

Will deflated. "Whatever Zurn promises, it will be a lie?"

"Yes."

"Then Julie will die . . . no matter what we do?"

Albane smirked. "No. Because our strategy is also to defect."

"May the shrewdest defector win," Kalen cheered.

"Then what is our plan?" Will asked.

"We negotiate a hostage exchange," Albane said, her voice velvet.

"We ask for Julie and they ask for . . ."

The four compatriots stared at him, but they said nothing.

His eyes darted from face to face to face until at last, quietly, he said, "Me."

Chapter Forty

JULIE TREMBLED UNCONTROLLABLY.

Raimond was pressing the cold, steel muzzle of his pistol against her temple so hard that her head was craned over to the limit, her ear nearly parallel to the floor. She did not know the identities of her interrogators, but she had learned that Meredith Morley had hired them. Bounty hunters, she surmised. The nature of Raimond's questions told her that they knew little about her, save her name and the fact that she was with Will. Clearly, Meredith had not told them anything substantive about her. They didn't know that she was fluent in German, because they had conducted their side conversations within earshot—a lucky break, and one that had saved her a great deal of pain.

But the phone call moments ago had changed everything.

The news of his brother's death had flipped a switch in the German boss man's head, and now he was like a rabid dog. She gave herself a 10 percent chance of survival. Since he couldn't kill the man on the black motorcycle who he blamed for his brother's death, odds were she would be an acceptable stand-in for his revenge. It didn't matter what she said. Talking only would infuriate him. For the first time in her life, she could feel Death's breath on the nape of her neck. This was not a nightmare; it was real.

She began to sob.

"WHO IS THE BLACK RIDER? WHO KILLED MY BROTHER?" Raimond screamed.

"I told you. I don't know. That wasn't part of the plan. My job was to stay close to Foster and keep him from running. Everything else was orchestrated by Meredith Morley; she didn't tell me the details. I was just supposed to get Foster to the meeting. She was in charge of transporting Foster back to Prague. I don't know anything else. I swear. I've told you everything I know."

Raimond yearned to pull the trigger and unleash on this American girl all the hatred and fury he felt against the black rider. Against Meredith Morley. Against William Foster, and against the whole fucking world. But his index finger was noncompliant.

He withdrew the pistol muzzle from Julie's temple. Her death would revenge nothing. Her murder would not quench the fire raging in his soul. Julie Ponte would serve his needs better as a bargaining chip. He threw the weapon onto the concrete floor of the warehouse, raised his fists toward the sky, and unleashed a bloodcurdling scream. When he was done, Raimond collapsed to his knees and buried his head in his hands.

Stefan looked down at Raimond. His older brother's reaction to Udo's death had been immediate and visceral. Raimond had spared Ponte, but he would unleash hell on whomever he ultimately deemed responsible for Udo's death. Stefan's mind had not yet internalized the news of his brother's death. He was in denial, but it was a denial that he was strangely conscious of. He would not start to mourn his dead brother for days, maybe even weeks. Pain would find him, but later. Grief would overwhelm him suddenly and completely. During a subway ride, or while he was having a beer at a pub. For now though, he felt nothing.

The sound of a mobile phone ringing pierced the silence.

Julie lifted her head instinctively. The ringing phone was hers. Raimond jumped to his feet.

"That's your phone, isn't it?" he asked her.

"Yes."

"Where is it?"

"My right jacket zipper pocket," she replied.

Raimond walked around her and retrieved the phone from her pocket. He looked at the LCD screen. The caller ID was "BLOCKED".

Raimond pressed the Talk button on the phone and raised it to Julie's ear. "Answer it."

"Hello," she said.

"Julie?"

"Will!"

Raimond pulled the phone from her ear and raised it to his own.

"You are causing a great deal of trouble for everyone."

"Funny, I was going to say the same thing about you and your mercenary brothers. You took someone I care about. I want her back."

"You're going to get her back in little pieces in a garbage bag unless you give me what I want."

"Then I propose a trade."

Raimond cackled. "A trade! What could you possibly trade that I want?"

"Me."

"Interesting. What are your terms?"

"Release Julie unharmed, and I will turn myself over to you. After that, you can do with me what you will."

"No deal."

Silence persisted on the line for several moments.

"What do you mean no deal?"

"I will only release the girl in exchange for you *and* the motorcycle rider who stole you away from the Café Sacher."

"That is going to be impossible."

"Then the girl dies."

"It's impossible because the motorcycle rider you are talking about is dead."

Raimond held the line in silence. His mind was racing. Maybe the police had made a mistake. Maybe his brother Udo was alive and it was the other motorcycle driver who was killed. Maybe this was a trick.

"There was an accident during the chase. Both motorcycle drivers were killed. I was thrown from the bike and managed to hobble away from the accident before the police arrived. I'm tired of running. I'm ready to end this."

Raimond rubbed his temples. He could not decide if the American was deceiving him. Foster spoke with confidence and without hesitation. His answers were logical, and they did not sound rehearsed. Unless he was an accomplished liar, odds were that he was telling the truth. Raimond decided that it didn't matter anyway. He occupied the position of advantage. As long as he had control of the American woman, he could manipulate Foster. After the trade, he could torture Foster for the truth about the black rider. Raimond smiled. He would enjoy torturing Will Foster.

"I agree to your terms."

"Meet me at the Karlskirche Catholic cathedral at ten o'clock. I want to make my peace with God first."

"At this hour? The church will be locked," Raimond said.

"I have never known a priest to turn away a man requesting his last rites."

"Leave the church when you're done. We'll make the trade outside."

"No deal. I don't trust you. If you want me, then this exchange is going to happen in front of God's witness. When I leave with you, Julie stays behind with the priest."

Raimond had not anticipated this little wrinkle. A man of faith he certainly was not, but the idea of killing a priest did not sit well with him. Then the voice in his head reminded him that his brother Udo was dead; unless he was a coward, nothing should stand in the way of his revenge. Raimond shrugged. He would see how it played out, and do what was necessary in the end. If a priest needed to die, then a priest would die. Karlskirche would serve his needs well. The surrounding area would be deserted so late at night. The thick marble walls would conceal the sound of any gunshots, should things get out of hand.

"Ten o'clock. Come alone or the girl dies." Raimond hung up the phone. He turned to Julie and studied her face a moment before speaking. "It seems your charms were quite effective. Will Foster just agreed to trade his life for yours. You must have quite a mouth on you to seduce a man so completely." He turned to Stefan. "What do you think, Stefan? Should I let her try to earn her freedom?" he said and unzipped the fly on his pants.

Stefan laughed. "Careful, women are unpredictable. And this one has teeth."

"I can solve that problem; teeth are removable. I just need a good set of pliers."

Julie looked up at him in terror, and he met her gaze. He took pleasure in her fear. He let her mind churn. Her skin was pale, and she looked nauscous. He smirked and then zipped up his fly.

"Come, Stefan. We haven't much time. We need to plan for this meeting," Raimond said as he turned and walked toward the van.

"What do you have in mind, Brother?" Stefan asked, speaking in German and trotting to catch up.

"I want you to take the sniper rifle and go to the Karlskirche in advance. Find a position in one of the balconies. Choose your location carefully. Pick a balcony where you have a clear line of fire to all locations in the congregation area below. If Foster brings help, then you know what to do."

Chapter Forty-One

WILL STARED AT the twin spires and ornate copper cupola of the Karlskirche from across the reflecting pool in the courtyard. Moonlight and the breeze danced a Viennese waltz across the surface of water—the reflection of the church was a grand mosaic—a thousand ripples moving in melody. Ironic that his journey would end here, at this church dedicated to pay homage to the hundreds of thousands of Austrians who had died of the plague centuries ago. It was no accident that he had insisted on this location for the final showdown with the Zurn brothers. Fifteen hours earlier he had entered the Karlskirche sanctuary and inconspicuously hidden the stolen glass vial under a wooden pew.

Special Agent Reed knew about the vials. Apparently, Meredith Morley had reported them stolen from Chiarek Norse. But in trying to extract details from Will about the location of the vials, Reed revealed that one of the vials contained a gene therapy, believed to derived from Will's DNA, Will had responded to Reed's questions with a lie, and said that both vials were lost when they shattered on the floor of the youth hostel. He had no choice but to lie, the remaining vial was the only bargaining leverage he possessed. Other than his life, that was. He doubted the FBI understood the true nature of his mutation; he had not told them about his meeting with Johansen. Will estimated the formula was worth tens of millions of dollars on the black market, and he was certain that even Raimond Zurn, despite all his fury, could be persuaded by that much money. If Reed and Nelson knew the vial's true worth, he doubted their government masters would let them hand it over to Zurn, even in exchange for Julie's life. All that mattered now was that the vial stay hidden until he could make the trade. He would do whatever was necessary to save Julie, just as she had done for him.

Albane patted Will's shoulder. "Are you ready?"

"As ready as I'll ever be."

"Nervous?"

"I'd be a liar if I said otherwise."

"Good, then you're not overconfident. Overconfidence, in my experience, is an omen of failure."

Will offered up an awkward smile, but said nothing.

"Raimond Zurn may be vicious, but I promise you, he has no idea what's about to hit him," she said. She reached into her pocket, retrieved a button with an adhesive backing and fixed it to the inside of his shirt collar.

"What's that?" he asked.

"A microphone transceiver, disguised as a button. When you talk, we'll be able to hear everything you say."

"Like a wire they use on cop shows on TV?"

"Exactly, just much smaller. Do you remember your handle?"

"Yes. It's Foxtrot."

"Coordinator, this is Social. How do you copy Foxtrot?"

R. Parish—*RS:Coordinator*: "Social, this is your Coordinator. I copy Foxtrot, Lima Charlie."

"Good. We can hear you perfectly."

"How will I hear you? Shouldn't I have an earpiece or something?" Will asked.

"I don't think that would be a good idea. There will be a lot of chatter on the circuit, and if you're not used to it, it makes it hard to think. Trust me, I'm speaking from experience. It's better if you're not distracted. You're going to have your hands full just talking to Zurn."

Will nodded. His eyes expressed all the emotions he felt without uttering a word to her. He pulled his jacket collar up and began walking toward the church.

The front entrance of the Karlskirche was situated behind six Corinthian stone pillars supporting a Doric portico mimicking the Parthenon in Athens, but these doors were kept closed and locked except for special occasions. Regular access to the church was via a set of tall wooden double doors on the west side. Viewing hours for tourists ended at five o'clock. Catholic evening mass began at six o'clock, and the church was closed to the public after the conclusion of mass. The west entrance was locked promptly after mass, and the church was closed until the next morning.

Kalen had arrived thirty minutes before the rest of the team, bypassed building security, and unlocked the doors from the inside. After a survey of the nave and transept, he exited the public area of the church through a set of doors beyond the altar that lead to the restricted areas of the church where he would complete his final preparations for the engagement.

Also already inside the church was Stefan Zurn, who had arrived before Will but after Kalen. To his delight, he had found the west entrance unlocked, which allowed him to sneak inside without having to fuss with breaking in. However, an unlocked entrance also meant that he was not alone. He took care not to make a sound as he crept along the dark west corridor. Before entering the nave, he stood motionless and surveyed the pews to ensure no one was praying in the church. Killing a man or woman of the cloth was not on his agenda.

Karlskirche was undergoing extensive interior renovations. A massive scaffold occupied the west side of the church, stretching from the ground level up, over one hundred feet in the air to the top of the cupola. The scaffold was so tall that an elevator had been installed within to facilitate travel to and from the dome. Marble structures everywhere were being polished to remove centuries' worth of candle smoke from their surfaces. Frescoes adorning the dome of the cupola were being meticulously freshened and retouched. The division between the old and the renovated portions of a structure was dramatic visual evidence of how the grandeur of the church had faded over the years.

For Stefan, the scaffolding had been an unexpected gift. A sniper's dream. The interlocking steel trusses were bathed in shadow.

Horizontal platforms with interconnecting ladder stairs formed staggered tiers all the way up to the ceiling and offered him a firing angle to every location inside the church except for directly beneath him. It was almost too easy, he thought to himself as he worked his way up to the fifth level platform. Once in position, he assembled his sniper rifle from memory in the dark and chambered a round. Then, he waited.

• • •

WILL PUSHED AGAINST the heavy wooden door of the west entrance. The hinges creaked as the massive door stubbornly gave way. The west corridor was dark, the only illumination coming from the end of the hall where it intersected the nave of the church. He stepped across the threshold and pulled the door closed behind him, erasing the triangle of moonlight on the floor at his feet. His stomach was uneasy. Fear and foreboding washed over him in waves. He was a soldier marching to battle; he was a condemned man shuffling to the gallows. He had agreed to the agents' plan to confront Zurn. It was a sound plan. Certainly a better strategy than he could have conceived. But in his heart, he did not expect it to work.

He walked slowly and deliberately into the nave. His eyes were now adjusted to the dark. Two candles flickered at the altar, which was located past the transept at the head of the church some thirty meters away. Moonlight shining through the glass windows of the cupola cast a bluish hue throughout the church. He moved down the center aisle. He extended his left hand and let his fingers brush lightly across the tops of the aged oak pews, one by one.

One, two, three . . . seven, eight, nine . . . thirteen, fourteen.

He stepped sideways into the fourteenth pew and sat down. He scooted along the bench until he was in the approximate middle. With his right hand, he reached down under the bench and swept back and forth, feeling for the vial. After a moment, he felt a lump and a texture he immediately recognized as the gauze tape. He peeled the tape free from the underside of the pew and retrieved the glass vial he had hidden—his insurance policy. He stripped the gauze tape off the vial and held it up into a beam of moonlight. The liquid inside shimmered as he tilted the glass tube side to side, watching the angle of the meniscus change.

Above, from his hiding place on the scaffold, Stefan watched Will's every move through his monocular night-vision scope. He zoomed in on the vial. He could see that the glass tube contained a liquid, but he did not know what the liquid was. Raimond had never mentioned a vial before. Maybe Raimond did not know about it. Maybe it was valuable. Maybe it was dangerous. He would have to inform his brother of this new development. Taking care not to make a sound, Stefan set the rifle down on the plywood decking. He retrieved his mobile phone from his pants pocket and began composing a text message to Raimond.

Will wrapped a piece of gauze tape around the top of the vial, to help secure the rubber cap. He then slid the tube into his right pants pocket. He lowered his head into his hands.

A creaking noise broke the silence and startled Will out of his fretful monologue. The sound came from behind him. He turned his head and looked toward the back of the nave where it intersected the west corridor. He heard footsteps.

He exited the pew and took position in the center aisle facing the back of the church.

"It's time," Will said into the microphone button pinned to his collar. "They're here."

E. VanCleave—*RS:Technical*: "I just detected an electronic transmission from inside the church. Not one of ours. I'm running a trace."

K. Immel—*RS:Physical*: "Who has eyes on Romeo Zulu?"

R. Parish—*RS:Coordinator*: "Social is trailing Romeo Zulu. Social, maintain radio silence: click once for yes, twice for no. Do you have eyes on Romeo Zulu?"

A. Mesnil—*RS:Social*: "*click*"

R. Parish—*RS:Coordinator*: "Is he talking on his phone?"

A. Mesnil—*RS:Social*: "*click, click*"

R. Parish—*RS:Coordinator*: "Is our Juliet with him?"

A. Mesnil—*RS:Social*: "*click*"

A. Archer—*RS:Bio*: "Shit. Who's transmitting then? Did we confirm Udo Zurn's death?"

R. Parish—*RS:Coordinator*: "Yes."

A. Archer—*RS:Bio*: "Then it's the other brother, Stefan. We need to locate him. According to their bios, the Zurn brothers like their guns."

K. Immel—*RS:Physical*: "If Bio is right, then we've got a shooter on our hands. Shit, that complicates things. The north end of the nave has a balcony that houses a pipe organ. Good sniper location. The staircase off the west corridor leads up to it. I swept it clear, but someone could have ducked in after me. There is also a tower of renovation scaffolding beneath the cupola that could be trouble."

A. Archer—*RS:Bio*: "Technical, can you pinpoint the location of the transmission?"

E. VanCleave—*RS:Technical*: "Standby . . . pinging the phone . . . the target is inside the church . . . initiating handshake. It's a mobile phone. Running a trace . . . the number is registered to one Mr. Stefan Zurn. Confirm Bio's hypothesis; the other brother is in the game."

K. Immel—*RS:Physical*: "Social, do you have your Kevlar on?"

A. Mesnil—*RS:Social*: "*click*"

K. Immel—*RS:Physical*: "Social, divert to the balcony. Eyes only. Do *not* engage Sierra Zulu. Bio, if you're in the car, I need you inside ASAP, to cover Social."

A. Mesnil—*RS:Social*: "*click*"

To HIS ASTONISHMENT, AJ found himself reaching into the duffel bag on the back seat of the BMW and grabbing the Sig Sauer pistol he had taken from Raimond Zurn. Instead of wishing he were back in the familiar safety of his lab at BU, all he could think about was protecting his colleagues. He had bumbled his way through the sampling op at Chiarek Norse, with the Coordinator and Nicolora telling him what to do every step of the way—but he had survived. He had improvised during his meeting with Foster at the Hotel Sachar, and gotten lucky scuffling with Zurn—but he had survived. This time would be no different, he told himself. As he reached for the door handle, a hand gripped his shoulder and pulled him back.

"Slow down," said VanCleave, his eyes fixed on AJ.

"They need me in there. You heard Kalen."

"AJ, we're not real special agents. We're not the Navy SEALs. As a rule, we don't run around toting guns. We don't kill people. This organization solves people's problems, but we don't fight their wars for them. This case has mutated into the worst type of assignment, the kind The Tank wants nothing to do with. We're magicians, not warriors."

The VanCleave before him was not the VanCleave AJ was accustomed to. The condescending pompous techno-god was gone, replaced by a concerned father figure.

AJ met his gaze and said. "VanCleave, I'm going."

VanCleave shook his head. "Then you'd better take EDGAR with you."

"Who's Edgar?"

AJ followed VanCleave out of the car and to the trunk. Inside the trunk were three, hard-sided, black suitcases. VanCleave opened the middle one and retrieved a device the size of a handheld camcorder.

"This is EDGAR. It's an acronym for Electromagnetic Detection, Geometry, And Ranging. This device uses modulated radar pulses to detect structures and movement through solid objects, a.k.a. walls. EDGAR will find your sniper for you, wherever he's hiding," VanCleave said. "Turn it on, point, and look at the LCD display. Moving things turn red."

"So it's a thermal imager, like firefighters use?"

"No. Thermal imagers measure irradiated heat. Imagers are passive. They can't see through walls or windows. EDGAR uses modulated EM signals to see through objects. Think Superman's X-ray vision."

"If the sniper is not moving, how will it find him?"

"EDGAR is sensitive enough to detect even the slightest movement. It will ID a stationary living target based on the expansion and contraction of the chest cavity during respiration."

"VanCleave, I *almost* feel liking hugging you right now."

VanCleave grimaced.

"Oh, one more thing," AJ said, nodding sheepishly at the Sig pistol in his hand. "Before I go, can you please show me where the hell the safety is on this thing?"

RAIMOND ZURN EMERGED from the shadows of the west corridor with Julie standing on his left side. Her posture was erect and awkward. Something was wrong. They shuffled together toward the center aisle, stepping into the moonlight and stopping shy of the first pew. Will could not make out exactly what it was, but Zurn had something wrapped around her neck. It was pulled taught underneath her jaw and disappeared beneath her blonde hair. The tension on her neck was causing her visible discomfort. Will could not see Raimond's left hand, but surmised it held a cord that he was using to choke her. In his other hand, Zurn gripped a pistol and pressed it against the side of her face.

"I'm surprised you came, Foster. I figured you for a coward the way you're always running away," said Raimond, his voice reverberating in the empty church.

"You mean like the time I kicked your ass in Prague," Will said. "Let her go, Zurn. I'm the one you want."

"Pretty arrogant for a man who's about to . . ." Raimond was interrupted by the sound of his mobile phone vibrating in its holster. He raised one eyebrow. He wanted to ignore the call, but if it was Stefan, the information could be critical. Raimond turned to Julie. He pressed the muzzle of the pistol firmly into the fleshy part of her cheek. "Reach down and grab my phone off of my belt. Show me the screen. Don't say a word. Don't press any buttons. Fuck with me and I'll blow a hole right through the middle of your pretty face."

Julie did as he instructed, retrieving and raising the phone so he could see the backlit LCD screen. The screen read:

FOSTER HAS A GLASS VIAL IN HIS POCKET

"Put the phone back in the holster on my belt." Raimond said.

She struggled to complete the task. The piano wire he had strung around her neck made it impossible for her to tilt her head to see what she was doing. Eventually, she felt the holster and slid the phone back inside.

"It seems that you've been holding out on me, Foster," Raimond said. "The glass vial in your pocket. Let me see it."

Will blanched. He thought he had been alone when he retrieved the sample. There was only one way that the bounty hunter could have learned about it. Someone else was in the church.

R. Parish—*RS:Coordinator*: "Physical, this is the Coordinator, standby for revised tasking from Founder One."

K. Immel—*RS:Physical*: "What? Foster is in trouble, I need to get in there."

R. Parish—*RS:Coordinator*: "Tasking sent. Check your handheld."

Kalen pulled his phone from his pocket. The screen flashed with a text message:

REVISED TASKING
FROM: *FOUNDER ONE*
TO: *RS:PHYSICAL*
PRI 1—OBTAIN SAMPLE VIAL FROM FOXTROT
PRI 2—EXECUTE HOSTAGE RETRIEVAL

Dressed in black pants, a black shirt, and a Catholic priest's white collar, Kalen emerged from a door on the west side of the altar. His dark hair was colored with streaks of gray, and he had applied make-up to accentuate the fine wrinkles around his eyes and fore-head, visibly aging him twenty years. He took three strained steps toward the altar, using a wooden cane in his left hand to assist him, and then stopped.

"What are you people doing in here? The church is closed!" he called out in German. "You must leave immediately or I'm going to call the police."

"You're not going to call the police, Father," Raimond replied from the other end of the church.

"Why not?" Kalen called back.

"Because if you do, I'll blow this nice young woman's brains all over your beautiful marble floor."

Kalen feigned dismay, raising his right hand to his heart. He hobbled forward, pretending to try to get a better view of the intruders in his church.

Will turned toward Kalen, verifying the priest he heard was the priest he expected to see.

"Father Heigel?" Will said.

"Yes, I'm Father Heigel," Kalen replied in English flavored with a thick Austrian accent.

"Just the person I was hoping to see."

"Excuse me? Do I know you?"

"No, we've never met. I'm the one who left the message on your answering machine to meet me here tonight. Thank you for coming. As you can see, things are not going very well for me and my lady-friend," Will said, gesturing to the captive Julie down the aisle.

Kalen shuffled down six steps from the altar into the nave. He hobbled slowly across the marble floor toward Will, leaning heavily on the cane. With his right hand raised in the air, palm facing forward he said, "Gentlemen, I'm not sure what is going on here, but you are in the Lord's house. This is no place for violence. Please, put down your guns. We can end this peacefully."

"I'm sorry, Father," scoffed Raimond, "but that is not going to happen. Why don't you just shut up and sit your holy ass down in one of those pews where I can see you."

"Listen Zurn, you've got what you want. Why don't you let Julie go, like we agreed? She can stay behind in the church with Father Heigel, and I will go with you."

A. Archer—*RS:Bio*: "Social, report status of balcony sweep."

A. Mesnil—*RS:Social*: "The balcony is clear."

A. Archer—*RS:Bio*: "Roger. I'm in the west corridor, but I can't see shit. Technical, I thought you told me that this EDGAR radar-scope could see through walls."

E. VanCleave—*RS:Technical*: "Try adjusting the penetrating depth. Use the dial on the left to set the focal range. You'll see the number change in the top left corner of the screen. That's the focal depth in feet. If you turn the knob all the way to the left, past the detent, EDGAR will sweep automatically across a range of depths. I suggest you use sweep mode."

A. Archer—*RS:Bio*: "Okay, I see it . . . going to sweep mode . . . It's working . . . I've got two bodies, our Romeo and Juliet I presume . . . and there's Foxtrot, and Physical . . . Bingo, I've got the shooter. EDGAR puts him directly above Foster and Immel. He's on some sort of truss structure.

A. Mesnil—*RS:Social*: "There's a scaffold in the middle of the church, on the West side of the nave. It goes all the way up to the top of the dome ceiling. That is the structure you're seeing."

A. Archer—*RS:Bio*: "This shooter has taken a bird's eye position. Physical, this is Bio, you've got a shooter hiding in the scaffolding on the fifth level almost directly above you."

E. VanCleave—*RS:Technical*: "Social, do you have a view of the shooter?"

A. Mesnil—*RS:Social*: "Negative. What's worse is that his position is 100 percent defensible. It's impossible for someone to approach the scaffold without traversing his line of fire."

E. VanCleave—*RS:Technical*: "I have an idea. Bio, egress to the main entrance, and wait for me there. I'll need your help."

JULIE GAGGED. RAIMOND was unconsciously ratcheting up the pressure on the piano wire around her neck, matching the rising tension in the air. A drop of warm blood trickled down her neck. The piano wire complicated the scenario. He had absolute control of her. She couldn't crack him in the balls and run away. If he were to be shot, her head would almost certainly be severed from her body by the force of his body crashing to the ground pulling the piano wire with it.

She was trapped in a human guillotine.

"You're choking me," she rasped.

Zurn ignored her.

"I said sit down, Father," Raimond repeated with vehemence.

Kalen had crept forward to the point that he was now standing beside Will in the center aisle.

"Okay, okay. But please put down your gun." Kalen made a lowering motion with his free hand.

Raimond cocked his head and lowered his eyebrows. A disapproving look for a disobedient child. He removed the pistol from Julie's cheek and took aim at the priest.

Kalen bowed his head subserviently, but did not move to take a seat.

Raimond tweaked his aim and fired a warning shot. The muzzle flare lit up the interior of the church like a flash of lightning, followed by the crash of thunder from the shot. The bullet whisked through the air and slammed into the back of a wooden pew with a splintering thud.

Will instinctively cowered.

Kalen collapsed on the ground at Foster's feet in a quaking heap, holding his right hand over his heart.

Will glowered at Raimond. He looked down at the fallen, crumpled Kalen at his feet, and then extended his arm to help the impostor priest to his feet.

Kalen clutched Will's right wrist with his right hand and pulled hard, yanking Will off balance. Will buckled at the waist and reflexively his left foot shot forward to catch his balance so he did not fall over. Kalen swung his body around, so his back faced Zurn. With his left hand, the priest pawed at Will's waist, finding a handhold on Will's right pants pocket. Will heaved Kalen up to his feet. Kalen feigned difficulty loading weight onto his supposedly bum left leg. He stumbled to the left, leaning heavily on Will.

"Help me to the pew, my son," Kalen said to Will, trembling and eyeing the bounty hunter in mock terror.

Will lugged the groaning priest toward the closest pew. He could feel Kalen's thick and sinewy muscles flexing with each movement beneath the black garments. A lamb carrying a lion. Kalen played his part with the dramatic flare of a seasoned stage actor. With great effort Will helped lower him onto the pew bench.

Raimond watched the proceedings with increasing agitation.

Will stepped back into the aisle and bent at the waist to retrieve the priest's wooden cane from the marble floor.

"Leave it!" yelled Raimond.

Will froze, and then stood back up, leaving the cane to lie where it fell.

"Enough of these games!" Raimond snarled. "You lied to me, Foster. You have lied to me from the beginning. In your pocket, you have a glass vial. It contains something important. Important enough that you would risk your life, and Fräulein Ponte's life, to retrieve it. I want to know what it is. Give it to me now!"

Will stood motionless. The vial was his insurance policy. Turning it over to Zurn would shift the balance of power. It was a move he could not afford to make.

"I will separate this woman's head from her body if you test me, Foster. You have three seconds to show me the vial."

Raimond increased the pressure on the piano wire around Julie's throat. The metal strand sliced into her soft skin like a cheese cutter. She whimpered. A dark stain grew across the front of her white blouse as dual trickles of blood snaked down either side of her throat, creating a Y-shaped crimson necklace.

"Julie," Will mumbled, pleadingly.

"One . . ."

"TWO . . ."

"All right! All right. You can have it. Please, just let her go," Will pleaded.

"Not until I see the vial."

"TAKE THIS," VANCLEAVE said, trying to catch his breath after sprinting from the BMW to the church.

AJ set EDGAR down on the marble floor and took a stainless steel case from VanCleave. The case looked familiar; he had seen it before. "What's going on?"

"Open it," VanCleave instructed, while he powered on a tiny notebook computer. "Inside you'll find a thermos-like cylinder with Abbey's spiders. Unscrew the lid and dump all the spiders on the floor. Count them."

AJ did as instructed.

"Seven."

"Good," said VanCleave, and he began typing furiously on his laptop. Three-dimensional models of different polyhedrons on x, y, and z coordinates appeared and then detonated on his computer screen. The sequence accelerated, flashing through permutation after permutation, and then suddenly stopped. The screen depicted an elongated hexagonal pyramid and flashed the text: OPTIMAL YIELD GEOMETRY.

"Activate all seven spiders; just like you did in Prague. Do you remember?"

"Yes, I remember." AJ moved quickly, methodically performing the activation procedure for each spider, and then setting it on the ground.

"They're activated. Now what?"

"Inside the case you will find six strips of plastic explosive. Three black. Three light green in color. Remove one of the green strips. Pinch off seven equal size portions. Roll them into a ball about the size of a gum ball," VanCleave ordered, never looking away from his computer screen. AJ glanced at VanCleave's screen and noticed that the exploding polyhedron graphics were gone, replaced by the spider interface control software.

"Are you crazy! I'm not touching plastic explosive!" AJ protested.

"This compound requires a detonator charge. It's very stable. Now shut up, and do as I say."

Reluctantly, AJ peeled a strip of green plastic explosive from a stowage slot in the briefcase. The feel and consistency of the material reminded him of modeling clay he played with as a kid. He pinched off seven blobs of the stuff, while trying to suppress gruesome mental images of his hands being blow off.

"Now what?" AJ asked, showing VanCleave his handiwork.

"I'll take it from here," VanCleave said. He pressed the blobs of plastic explosive firmly onto the backs of the robot spiders, taking care not to let any of the substance cover the head sensors or leg joints. Then cupping his hands together as if he was going to take a drink of water from a stream, he added, "Now, hold out your hands like this."

AJ extended his cupped hands, and VanCleave then gently placed the seven explosive laden micro-machines inside.

"Okay, let's go," VanCleave said.

WILL REACHED HIS right hand into his right pants pocket and felt for the vial. To his dismay, his fingers found nothing but pocket fabric. He began to panic. The vial was gone.

Raimond's expression morphed from smug satisfaction, to dismay, and then to rage, as the realization of what was happening began to register.

He had been set up.

"STEFAN, SHOOT THE PRIEST," Raimond yelled.

A hollow dissonant moan from the organ echoed throughout the church. The sound reverberated throughout the nave, reflecting off the marble walls and floor, filling the air with a baritone thrum— completely drowning Raimond's voice before Stefan could hear the end of his brother's order. Albane had been listening to the entire exchange from above, hiding in the shadows of the organ balcony. She had waited until the last instant to intervene and bravely played the organ, her back facing the nave. Stefan turned to the organ balcony. He trained the crosshairs of his night vision scope on the middle of her back and pulled the trigger.

The bullet struck her in between her shoulder blades. Her body fell forward onto the organ keys, adding new a new chorus of dissonant notes to the air for several seconds, before she collapsed onto the floor.

The organ fell silent.

Satisfied, Stefan chambered a second round in the sniper rifle and shifted his aim away from the balcony down to the center aisle below—zeroing in on the location where Will and the priest had been standing. He quickly found Will, but the priest was nowhere in sight. He scanned left, sweeping the viewing circle of his night-vision scope over to Raimond's position. To his astonishment, he watched as the priest head butted his brother and then freed the American girl. Stefan adjusted his torso and slid his index finger over the trigger in preparation for his next shot. But the firing geometry did not offer him a clear shot at the priest without risk of hitting his brother. He would have to wait for the scuffle to play itself out; eventually he *would* have a clean shot. Stefan exhaled. Patience.

THE ORGAN BLAST gave Kalen the opportunity he needed. During the few seconds Zurn turned his head to look at the organ balcony behind him, Kalen closed the distance between them. Eyes forward, arms and legs and churning, he sprinted down the center aisle like an Olympic athlete out of the blocks. He decelerated to a stop in front of the bounty hunter.

Kalen saw shock in Zurn's eyes when he returned his gaze to the front and found the priest's face mere inches from his own.

Kalen grunted and smashed his forehead into Zurn's right eye socket.

With his left hand, Kalen pushed Julie's face to the left, away from the gun barrel pressed into her cheek, until her jaw was parallel to the muzzle. He then slid his fingers down her throat and into the small triangular gap between the piano wire and the two outside ligaments on either side of her neck. He pulled the wire away from her throat with both hands. The razor sharp wire sliced into the fleshy pads on the underside of his fingers as he created a triangular opening slightly larger than her head. He wailed in pain—a guttural primal bellow—but it was drowned out by the thunderclap of two successive gunshots.

STUNNED BY THE priest's precision head butt, Raimond wobbled and blinked his eyes. Coming to, he squeezed the trigger of the Sig Sauer, twice.

JULIE YELPED AS the muzzle flares seared her left cheek, but the bullets sailed harmlessly by. The acrid smell of scorched hair and skin wafted through the air. She opened her eyes. The hot steel barrel of Zurn's weapon was resting next to her left ear and cheek. She became acutely aware of her lips, her tongue, and her teeth, all intact and unmolested. She had *not* been shot. Thanks to the foresight of the priest, her face had been clear of the line of fire.

She wasted no time. This was her chance, and she knew it. The priest was holding the wire several inches away from her face, and suffering greatly for it. Julie tucked her chin to her chest and squatted. She felt the wire scrape against her ear, nose and forehead as she ducked her head through the triangular opening, but she was free.

RAIMOND YANKED THE wire noose, a split second too late to foil Julie's escape, but before the priest could extricate both his hands.

The razor wire cinched tightly around the priest's left hand, compressing and cutting deeper into his fingers. Raimond grinned with sadistic pleasure as the priest dropped to a knee in front of him. With the butt of his gun, he struck a powerful blow across the priest's face.

"Good-bye, Father," Raimond sneered. Then, pressing the pistol against the priest's forehead, he added, "See you in Hell."

AJ AND VANCLEAVE crouched side-by-side, peering around the corner of the main entrance into the nave. VanCleave had his laptop open, balanced precariously on his thighs, while he wirelessly piloted the spiders toward the scaffold. Each spider was equipped with an internal self-destruct charge, designed to erase any trace of the device after the completion of a data-reconnaissance mission. VanCleave's plan was to use this self-destruct charge as the detonator for the payload of plastic explosive each spider carried on its back. In theory, his tactical improvisation should work, but it had never been tested.

A baritone organ blast caused him to bobble his computer, and he nearly dropped it onto the marble floor. AJ ducked by his side. Recovering their wits, both men turned and looked up at the organ balcony in time to see a female shape—bathed in moonlight—fall onto the organ keyboard and then collapse to the balcony floor.

A. Archer—*RS:Bio*: "Oh, God. Social must have used the organ to distract the sniper, but I think he just shot her!"

R. Parish—*Coordinator*: "Social, this is the Coordinator, over . . . Social, this is the Coordinator, do you copy?"

E. VanCleave—*RS:Technical*: "She's not responding. Bio, go help Social. But don't be stupid. Stay below the balcony railing, or the sniper will take a shot at you too."

A. Archer—*RS:Bio*: "What about the spiders?"

E. VanCleave—*RS:Technical*: "They're almost in position. I can handle this. GO."

VanCleave glanced to the center aisle, where a scuffle had just broken out. A bead of sweat rolled down his forehead and plopped onto the keypad. Every passing second could be Kalen's last. Were he a religious man, VanCleave thought to himself, he would be praying.

VanCleave's computer screen flashed a message.

POSITION GEOMETRY OBTAINED
PRESS "ENTER" TO INITIATE SELF-DESTRUCT SEQUENCE
COUNTDOWN TIMER: 0 SECONDS

Prayer answered.

He pressed the ENTER key.

THE EXPLOSION ROARED through the cavernous main hall of the Karlskirche like a twelve gun salute from a battleship. The power of VanCleave's shaped-charge blew out a two-meter section of steel in the southwest corner of the scaffold frame, causing the platform tiers at each level above to tip abruptly downward in the direction of the break. Stefan Zurn was jolted out of his prone shooting position into a sideways slide; his body skidded uncontrollably toward the dipping corner of the platform. Reflexively, he let go of his sniper rifle with both hands and flailed desperately for a handhold. The sniper rifle sailed off the platform edge and bounced on the marble floor below with a triple *clack*. Like a thousand burning needles, splinters from the plywood decking raked the pads of his fingertips and palms of his hands as he clawed wildly for his life. His right forearm contacted a metal strut. He tried desperately to grab the strut as he slid by, but the side of his head slammed into the corner post, knocking him senseless. His limp body rolled over the edge and started to fall, before abruptly jerking to a halt. Nearly five stories above the unforgiving marble floor of the Karlskirche, Stefan Zurn swung, upside down and unconscious. He was saved by the calf strap of his ankle holster, which snagged a protruding bolt on a scaffold clamp affixed to the corner post.

SEVEN DETONATIONS OF plastic explosive, erupting simultaneously, provided Kalen a stay of execution. Raimond, who was facing the scaffold when the charges blew, stumbled backward in shock.

"Stefan!" he cried, as he watched his younger brother fall off the scaffold platform into shadow.

Taking a page from Kalen's playbook, Will seized the moment.

He picked up Kalen's walking cane, closed the gap to where the others stood, and swung it at Zurn's head.

The blow connected squarely with Raimond's mouth; blood exploded from his lower lip like a bursting piñata. His head snapped back and then forward. Howling in pain, Raimond pulled the trigger on the Sig Sauer, but Kalen had already moved clear of the line of fire. Kalen performed a scissor kick, sweeping the bounty hunter's legs out from underneath him. Raimond landed flat on his back; the impact jarred the handgun loose from his grip, and sent it spinning across the marble floor, until it came to rest at Julie's feet. She bent and picked it up.

Julie looked at the pistol in her hand with a glassy, distant stare.

All three men fixated on her. She was standing in the middle of the center aisle, six feet from where they were clustered.

Her face flushed, and her eyes erupted with fire. Her neck and chest glistened with her own blood, and her disheveled hair glowed like a golden halo in the moonlight.

She pointed the gun at Raimond.

Will shivered.

"And behold, the angel of death came to pass judgment upon him," Kalen mumbled under his breath.

"You're a monster," she seethed, her eyes fixed on Raimond.

"And you're a traitorous bitch." He laughed and raised himself into a sitting position, his legs extended in "V" in front of him. "Should I tell your boyfriend how you betrayed him? That you've been working with Meredith Morley all along."

"That's a lie."

"We're on the same side, you and me. We're both working for the same goal—to put this lab rat back in his cage." Raimond turned to Will. "Don't look so surprised, Yankee. Never trust a beautiful woman. Just an hour before we came here, she was begging me to fuck her like a whore."

Will looked at Julie. Her lip was quivering; her hand was trembling. "Julie, don't do it. He's not worth it. This guy is a psychopath. His words are poison . . ."

The muzzle flashed, illuminating the church like a strobe. Raimond jerked and reflexively clutched his crotch as the bullet ricocheted off the marble tile in between his legs, inches from his groin.

Will walked to where she stood and peeled the pistol from her grip before she could fire another round. She turned and faced him, tears streaming down her cheeks. He put his arm around her and pulled her into his chest.

"It's over now," Will said softly.

AJ KNELT BESIDE Albane's fallen body at the base of the organ. She faced away from him, sprawled on her right side. He stroked her left cheek with his hand.

She stirred. "Oaagghh."

"Albane? Albane, can you hear me?" he whispered.

"It feels like someone ripped my spine out of my body," she moaned. "I think the round hit my upper back. How long have I been out?"

"I don't know. Not long. Do you have your vest on?"

"Yes. Kalen made me wear one with ceramic armor inserts."

"Good. Can you feel this?" AJ asked, squeezing her right hand.

"Yes."

"Can you feel this?"

"Yes, that's my foot."

"Very good. Next, we need to check if the bullet penetrated through your vest. To see if you're bleeding. Also, we need to determine if you have any broken vertebrae; if you do, moving you could damage your spinal cord."

"That would be bad. How do you know this stuff, AJ?"

"Before grad school, I was an EMT-in-training for two years."

"You're full of surprises today."

He smiled. "Here's what we're going to do. I want you to stay very still; I'm going to slide my hand underneath the vest to check for blood."

"You just want an excuse to get your hands up my shirt, don't you Bio?" Albane said feebly.

"You're right, I should probably check your chest first to see if the bullet passed clear through."

"Don't you dare!" Albane chuckled and then moaned in pain.

AJ slid his hand along the small of her back and felt for wetness under her vest. He gently pulled his hand out and rubbed his thumb and forefinger together. Dry, nothing slippery. He then held his fingers up into a beam of moonlight, to double check himself.

"No blood. I think the vest did its job. But that doesn't guarantee against a broken back. The force of a round at that velocity is like getting hit with a crowbar. We need to get you out of here."

"What about the shooter?"

"He's been neutralized. You have VanCleave to thank for that. And Abbey's spiders."

"Do you hear that?" Albane asked in a hush.

"Sirens."

"The police, no doubt."

"It sounds like they've brought a chopper too."

"Time to go."

"THE AUTHORITIES ARE coming. We should go. *Now,*" VanCleave yelled to Kalen.

"What about Zurn?" Will said, keeping Raimond on the ground and at bay with the Sig. "We can't just let him go."

Kalen glared at Raimond as he freed his bloody left hand from the piano wire noose. "Tie him up. Leave him for the police."

"And him?" Will asked, glancing up at Stefan Zurn, who was still hanging upside down precariously from the scaffold platform.

"Leave him. He's not going any—"

Before Kalen could finish his sentence, the calf strap on Stefan Zurn's ankle holster gave way, and the unconscious sniper plummeted head first to the ground.

"STEFAN!" Raimond screamed. He looked at the broken body of his fallen brother, splayed unnaturally across the marble tiles, surrounded by an expanding pool of dark red blood. Hatred welled up in his eyes. He had nothing left to lose. Nothing left to live for, nothing except for revenge. Zurn slipped his right hand inside the flap of his button down shirt. His fingers found the grip of a Glock 26 9mm pocket pistol concealed snugly in an underarm holster. He looked away from his fallen brother to Will, the man who had ruined his life.

"Weapon!" VanCleave yelled, but it was too late.

A single shot reverberated like a thunderclap inside the church.

Will buckled.

Julie screamed.

She looked from Will to Raimond, expecting him to fire another shot. Raimond's eyes twitched; he had a strange vapid smile on his face. Then, he collapsed prone onto the marble floor: his shooting arm extended, the barrel of the Glock still smoldering.

Kalen knelt and withdrew a small dagger from the base of the bounty hunter's skull. He could not bring himself to look at Julie; his were eyes lowered in shame. He had failed, delivering the death strike a split second after the impulse from Raimond's brain had traveled to his trigger finger. The 9mm round had found its target and pierced Will's chest.

Julie ran to Will and knelt at his side. His face was already going pale. She cradled his head in her hands, tears streaming from her eyes.

He reached up and touched her cheek.

"I never betrayed you," she said.

"I know," he whispered.

"Can you hear those sirens? Help is coming. You've just got to hang on until they get here," she pleaded, stroking his forehead.

He managed a fragile, tentative smile. "My legs are cold."

"Don't you leave me, William Foster. Do you hear me? Please, please don't leave me."

"I love you, Julie."

She held him tight against her chest as she wept. "I love you too."

Chapter Forty-Two

Boston, Massachusetts

"WHAT I'M SAYING is that I don't fucking believe you, Robért," Meredith hissed.

"Believe what you want, Meredith. It is what it is," Nicolora said.

She glowered at him from across the table.

"I'm not Jesus; I can't raise Foster from the dead," he added, and then casually stuffed a whole piece of spicy tuna roll, dripping in wasabi-infused soy sauce, into his mouth with a pair of chopsticks.

A waiter approached the couple and asked if they would like another bottle of sake for the table. She ignored him. He shook his head no, and the waiter skittered away with prudent haste.

"Failure is the last thing I expected from your organization on this assignment. I've seen your teams negotiate impossible situations, solve intractable problems, some beyond mortal comprehension. But this? This was easy. A simple search and rescue, and you couldn't pull it off. I don't understand," she ranted.

"Meredith, what you fail to recognize is that this outcome is entirely your fault. If you want to blame someone, then blame yourself."

"My fault! My fault? I hardly see how this is my—"

"You were lazy and cheap. You hired amateurs, when you should have hired professionals from the beginning," he interrupted.

He thrust a scolding finger at her and continued.

"Haven't you learned anything from me? The most efficient way to solve a problem is to eliminate as many variables from the

315

equation as possible—not introduce new ones, for God's sake. Especially independent variables over which you have limited or no control. The Zurn brothers were absolute wild cards. You set a brush fire to try to catch your rabbit, but ended up burning down the entire forest. If anyone should be disappointed, it should be me."

She bit her lower lip. Abruptly, her expression softened. She blinked coyly, flashing him her best bedroom eyes.

"No," he reprimanded.

"Tell me where he is," she begged.

"I said no."

"What did you do with him?"

"I didn't do anything with him. After he was shot by your man Zurn, the Austrians intervened. I had no choice; I pulled my team."

"You must know something."

He shrugged. "My sources tell me that Foster died and was discreetly laid to rest. That's all I know."

"Where? I'd like to pay my respects."

"No, you don't. You want to dig him up!"

"Robért! How could you think such a thing?"

Nicolora stuffed another piece of sushi into his mouth, a rainbow roll this time. "This place is brilliant. Best sushi in Boston."

"You're really not going to tell me, are you?" She pouted.

"No."

"I could still salvage things if you just—"

He cut her off. "Enough, Meredith! There's nothing left to salvage."

She looked down at her lap. "This will ruin me, you realize."

Nicolora wiped his mouth with the cloth napkin from his lap. His thoughts drifted to the sample vial Kalen had lifted from Foster's pocket in the Karlskirche that fateful night. Contrary to the charade he was now playing with his ex-client and ex-lover, all had not been lost. At this very moment, AJ was working late in his lab at The Tank trying to replicate Vyrogen's work. And while it had never been Nicolora's intent to pirate Meredith's research, circumstances had left him no choice. The real FBI had since fixed its spotlight squarely on Vyrogen and Meredith, and he would not permit the greatest medical discovery of the twenty-first century to be confiscated away into some government black hole. No. He would be the secret's custodian. Both the Nicolora Foundation and The Think Tank could reap great rewards from this golden seed. He would leverage philanthropic and commercial opportunities to bring his public and private faces esteem and wealth. He was confident his new RS:Bio would succeed where Meredith's team had failed. In his experience, any problem could be solved with enough time, resources, and money . . . all of which he possessed in abundance.

After a painfully long pause Nicolora finally said, "Let's leave this dirty business behind us for the rest of evening, shall we?" Then, staring brazenly across the table at her stark cleavage framed by the plunging "V" neckline of her emerald-colored dress, he added, "Let's talk about something more stimulating. You look ravishing. Is that a new dress?"

Chapter Forty-Three

Eyam, England
Four months later

JULIE WIPED A stream of tears from her cheeks. "I miss you, Will," she whispered.

Huddled under her umbrella, she watched raindrops stream down the hewn granite headstone. Today was the third time she had come to Eyam to visit Will's grave since his death. It was also the third time she had been unable to fight back the tears. Losing him had been harder on her than she ever imagined it would be. She was taking life one day at time.

She had moved to London and taken a new job with a small biotechnology consulting firm, hoping to make a fresh start. She had not tendered a written resignation to Wien Bioscience, nor did she receive a termination letter. Apparently, the terms of her departure were mutually implicit. Her final direct deposit payment was prorated to the date she had taken Will's blood sample to the lab and had it analyzed by Bart Bennett. She wondered whatever became of Bart.

She had not heard from Meredith Morley again, although sometimes she had nightmares of picking up the phone to make a call, but instead of a dial tone being greeted by Meredith's bone-chilling voice. Because of the dreams, she had changed her mobile number. Whether it was prudent or paranoid she didn't care; it made her feel safer.

The enigmatic crew who had orchestrated her rescue at the Karl-skirche had vanished from her life as suddenly and mysteriously as they had appeared. The events of that night were so surreal and disjointed; she still had trouble stitching her memories together into a cogent narrative. One minute she was cradling Will in her arms, surrounded by the American agents who had just risked their lives to save her. The next, she was alone, arguing with a cadre of Viennese police officers and paramedics. The officer in charge at the scene had refused to let her accompany Will on the life-flight helicopter that fateful night. Instead, he had ordered her taken to a nearby precinct for questioning. After twelve hours of intense inter-rogation at the hands of the Austrian police, she had been abruptly discharged, with no charges filed against her.

For the next three days, Julie had stormed the city, trying to learn what had become of Will. But no one could—or would—answer her questions. She had checked every hospital in a sixty kilometer radius from the Karlskirche, but found no record of a man matching Will's description being admitted with a gunshot wound to the chest. Most upsetting, however, was when she was told by a senior official that there was no record of a life-flight helicopter pickup at the Karl-skirche on the night Will was shot. At every turn, her crusade was stymied.

The final rebuke came four days later, when she returned to the police precinct where she had been interrogated, only to learn that the OIC from the scene had been transferred to another division in Strasbourg. When she asked to speak with the precinct chief, the reception attendant said the chief was "prohibited" from discussing the details of the case with anyone and that her request for an audi-ence was denied.

Fourteen days passed, with no news about Will. Then, on the fifteenth day, she received a most unexpected visitor at her apart-ment: Xavier Pope. Her initial reaction had been to slam the door in his face. Through the closed door, he'd politely and persistently pressed her—saying repeatedly that he refused to leave until she gave him a chance to "say his piece." But it was the urn he held that swayed her, not the begging. To her astonishment, they talked for over an hour. Pope freely corroborated certain elements of Will's story and adamantly denied others. She had scrutinized Pope's every word and asked him the tough questions, but he never balked. After they had dispensed with the past, she opened the door to the present. Where had the life-flight helicopter taken Will? Why could she find no record of his hospital admittance in all of Vienna? Why was nobody talking about the events of that night? Pope took all her questions in stride. He explained that because of the perceived biosafety risks associated with the case, the Austrian Armed Forces had been tasked with locating and securing Foster. From what he had learned, Will had not been loaded into a life-flight helicopter that night, but rather into an Austrian military helicopter. He had been transported to a military hospital for emergency medical care, but, regrettably, had died en route. Pope went on to say that the Austrian military unilaterally made the decision to cremate Will's body . . . for biosafety reasons.

The details and emotion in Pope's story seemed genuine, and this left her confounded. On the one hand, she wanted to hate Pope, hold him responsible for all the pain she was feeling, all the pain he had caused Will. But on the other hand, Pope was the only person from Vyrogen who had reached out to her, apologized, and offered her closure.

Before leaving that night, Pope made a last and final gesture of goodwill. He explained that even though he had resigned from Vyrogen, he felt personally accountable for Will's death. As such, he insisted that he pay for all of Will's funeral expenses. An act of contrition, he had called it. Catatonic with grief and shock, she had graciously accepted. She instructed that Will's ashes be buried in Eyam, in the same cemetery as his ancestors. Something told her he would have wanted it that way. What remained of Will's legacy she decided to leave in Professor Johansen's capable hands. She informed Johansen of Will's decision to publish his genome, and instructed him to post Will's immunity mutation on the Internet as "open source code" so all the world could benefit from his gift. During their last conversation, Johansen had told Julie that Will's dream was still very much alive, and that he had recently obtained grant money from the university to sequence Will's entire genome. Will's sacrifice would not be in vain, he had promised her.

Of this fact, she was certain.

Meandering out of her daydream, she became aware that she was gently running her hand along her stomach, feeling the bump beneath the fabric of her raincoat. She was showing now. She'd already completed her first trimester and had her first ultrasound. Everything was normal. The baby was perfect. Beautiful. Watching the monitor that day had been the saddest, happiest moment of her life.

When she asked about the gender, the doctor had said it was too soon to tell. No matter, she knew it was a boy. She would call him Will . . . just as she had his father.

Epilogue

United States Army Medical Research Institute
of Infectious Diseases (USAMRIID)
Fort Detrick, Maryland

"I S HE BRAIN-DEAD?"

"No. He's in a medically sustained coma, but that's technically not the same as brain-dead," Xavier Pope replied, staring down at the gray body lying on a lone hospital bed.

An orchestra of automated commotion set an unnerving cadence in the room. Machines whirred, and monitors beeped. IVs dripped, and fluids pumped. Pope frowned.

There would be no miraculous escape this time.

He looked apprehensively at the figure standing next to him. Given the cloak-and-dagger communication protocols the Curator had insisted on over the past several months, Pope had imagined a very different character. His preconceptions were of the "Men in Black" variety: hyper-masculine, dark glasses, dark suit, and a humorless face chiseled from stone. He had been wrong about everything, except for the face chiseled from stone bit. First of all, the Curator was not a he. The woman beside him bore no resemblance to the stereotypical agency spook. To the contrary, she looked like the poster child for a World War II Nazi Aryan eugenics program. Her mane of shoulder length hair was the color of the midday Nordic sun. The white business dress she wore was fitted and tailored just above the knee, showing off her tight, sinewy calf muscles. She stood perfectly erect, and her square shoulders and taut stomach added an aura of military bearing. What struck him most were her eyes, so pale and cold they seemed carved from a glacier, shimmering, and arctic blue.

"Have you resumed the work you were conducting for Vyrogen?" the woman asked.

"Yes."

"Good." She reached in to her handbag and retrieved a mobile phone. She pressed a button on the touch screen. "The Curator would like to speak with you," she said plainly, handing him the phone.

Pope raised an eyebrow. "I thought *you* were the Curator?"

She smirked, seemingly pleased by his misconception. "No. I am his right hand."

Pope took her mobile phone and raised it to his ear. "This is Xavier Pope."

A coarse and curious voice said, "Dr. Pope, I understand from Myrh that your transition into the new position at USAMRIID has been seamless?"

"Yes, it has. Thank you for asking. And thank you for rescuing my career. I know I left a trail of red tape in my wake . . . complicating things."

"Red tape is easy to cut, if you have a sharp pair of scissors," said the voice. "Now, I want to make sure that going forward, we are on the proverbial *same page*. Understood?"

Pope shifted his weight nervously from leg to leg.

"I'm listening, sir."

"Do you understand that the test subject is the property of the United States Army now?"

"Yes."

"And that even though you are a civilian, you work for the United States Army?"

"Yes, of course."

"And that you also work for me."

"Um, no, I was not aware of that."

"I was afraid that detail might not have been made clear to you. No matter, I will explain. Until your debt to me is paid, you serve two masters: the United States of America, and me. Is that clear, Dr. Pope?"

"Yes," Pope replied.

"Good. These are my instructions, so listen very carefully. You will finish your research on the mutation within eighteen months. You will turn over the findings to your USAMRIID department head at that time. However, you will deliver a viable product, your methods, and all of your research data to me within nine months time."

"I don't understand. How am I supposed to finish the work in eighteen months, but . . ."

The Curator interrupted him. "The room you presently occupy is under surveillance Doctor, so choose your words more carefully."

"I'm sorry. What you said doesn't make any sense."

"It makes perfect sense. My deadline is nine months. The USAMRIID deadline will be set at eighteen months. You answer to me, first and foremost. I gave you your life back, and I am the one keeping the wolves at bay, but I can just as easily take away that which I have given. Cross me, and the pain and humiliation you'll suffer will be terrible. Is that clear?"

Pope nodded and answered, "Yes."

"Good," the voice said, satisfied. "One last thing, Dr. Pope. A storm is coming. When it does, if you've paid your debt to me, I will give you shelter."

"Thank you," Pope replied, confused. Then he added, awkwardly, "I won't let you down."

The line was already dead. He glanced at the phone's LCD screen, hoping to catch a glimpse of the caller ID, but the text displayed read "BLOCKED." He handed the phone back to the woman the Curator had called Myrh. Her glacier eyes sent an unnerving chill down his spine. He took a step back, increasing the space between them.

She held her stare, overtly passing judgment, before returning her gaze to the subject of her visit.

"What is his name?" she asked, staring at the comatose patient.

Pope paused before answering. Certainly, she knew the answer to her question. That meant the question had to be a test, the first of many tests in his *new* life. He chose his words carefully.

"His name . . . is Patient-65."

Acknowledgments

FIRST, I WOULD like to recognize Morgan Soutter, whose assistance brainstorming and editing early chapters of *Calypso* was invaluable. Morgan is a great friend and gifted writer; I can't wait to see his novels on the shelf in the coming days. Second, I would like to thank friends and family who encouraged me and critiqued early drafts of the manuscript: Brandon, Chris, Colleen, Dana, John, Erika, Jennifer, Mom and Dad . . . your support and advice kept me writing. Third, I would like to thank my agent, Kristin, and my editor, Lilly, for believing in the story and patiently shepherding me through the harrowing process of selling and publishing my first novel. Last and most importantly, I would like to thank my wife to whom this book is dedicated. Not only did she read every sentence in this book a least a hundred times, but her attention to detail, keen editorial eye, and insightful advice made this story ten times the work it would have been had I been left to my own devices.

Ring of Flowers—
The Untold Prologue

The year is 1665, England.

In the Derbyshire village of Eyam, a tailor, George Vicars orders a bolt of fabric from London to make a wedding dress for his betrothed daughter, Kathryn. To escape her fate of marrying the town's wealthiest and most odious bachelor, she elopes with her true love, farmhand Paul Foster. Kathryn's departure is fortuitous, because when the fabric is delivered, the parcel is infested with fleas carrying bubonic plague. First bitten and first to die, George Vicars' misfortune becomes the community's death sentence when the town Rector boldly imposes a quarantine on all Eyam residents. Months later, expecting a child, the newlyweds return home to find their world turned upside down. Once inside the township, they are forbidden to leave and Kathryn is forced to give birth in quarantine. Under the shadow of plague, and against all odds, Will Foster's paternal ancestor is born . . . with a genetic mutation that will change the world 345 years later.